A Song of Thieves

THIEVES OF FELSHAN: BOOK 1

JACQLIN GUERNSEY

This is a work of fiction. All the characters and events portrayed in this novel are products of the author's imagination.

Edited by Arielle Hadfield

Cover by Melody Jeffries

ISBN: 979-8-9878838-0-8

Kindle edition ASIN: B0BX14WNN7

For my boys. *Let your dreams come true.*

PRONUNCIATION GUIDE:

Ari (AH-ree)

Roan (ROHN- rhymes with "stone")

Adalena (ah-dah-LEE-nuh)

Lena (LEE-nuh)

Evander (ee-VAN-dur)

Otto (AH-toh)

Aiden (AY-din)

Tess (TESS- rhymes with "dress")

Liam (LEE-uhm)

Reynauld (RAY-nawld)

Jaren (JAIR-en)

Tamen (TAH-muhn)

Shiren (SHEER-in)

Name: Prue (PROO)

Country: Felshan (FELL-shun)

City: Turin (TUR-in)

City: Fort Lowsan (FORT LOW-suhn – like the "o" in "ouch")

City: Fort Kotar (FORT KOH-tahr)

Country: Thenstra (THEN-struh)

River: Rashan (rah-SHAN)

Continent: Haythen (HAY-thuhn)

City: Port Riga (PORT REE-guh)

Country: Jadeya (juh-DAY-uh)

Country: Venes (VEN-ess)

PROLOGUE: ROAN

"**I** CAN'T BELIEVE YOU convinced the king to let us come," I whisper next to me.

The forest is dense, a canopy of trees blocking most of the morning sun's first rays. Conversation wafts through the air, the seasoned men exchanging news from home. I breathe in the warm air of oncoming summer, my horse staying in step with the prince's black mare.

"I made the *I'm going to be king one day* argument. I told him it was good practice to see him interacting with his men during the hunt, watching how a true king presents himself to his people. I may have even thrown in a bit of vanity— how I wanted to learn from his prowess with a bow. He fell for all of it." Evander smiles and winks in my direction.

I don't care how he did it. The joy I feel being amongst all the Lords on my first official hunt, and away from the stifling classrooms, beams from every inch of me.

The endless lessons on mathematics, writing, languages, history, economics, and leadership back at the palace is enough to make a boy of fifteen crawl out of his skin. The only saving grace comes from the few times a week we get to practice with the sword and bow, relieving our bottoms from the hard chairs we must occupy all day, and our faces from the stale breath of our ancient instructors.

The preparation for the First Hunt spurred an excitement in me, the idea of being away for three whole days. Of finally experiencing a First Hunt for myself. Every year Prince Evander and I begged, and every year we were told we were too young, it was too dangerous, and it was simply not a place for children.

But this year— this year was our winning year.

"I bet if you go talk to your father, man-to-man, he will let us go this year," I told him.

"I don't know, Roan. I want to go, truly. But... I don't think my father will say yes."

"He definitely won't say yes if you never ask him!" My words were laced with frustration. "Stop being so afraid of him. You will be king one day. You need to learn how to talk to people who make you nervous— to hold your ground with confidence."

Yes, his father was the king. But he was still his father. How scary could he be? We are almost men. We need to stop our boyish fears and move into the men we are supposed to be.

Once Evander was on board, we conspired for days on how we could get ourselves a ticket. Not only would we get to see his father, the most renowned hunter and King of Felshan, make the first kill to signal the opening of the summer season, but we would get out of our lessons during the entire hunt.

For these three days, I wouldn't have to do a single math problem, solve any economic disasters, or figure out who married whose daughter three hundred years ago and why I should care. The fresh air smells of freedom, and I can't help but let the feeling warm me on this already humid morning.

A breeze tousels my hair as I listen to the banter between the men around me, old enough to be my own father, who unfortunately, couldn't travel for this year's hunt. The men recount stories of seasons past— who killed the biggest deer, the biggest boar, who left with cuts and scars to add grit to their tale, who got lost and made fools of themselves.

I listen intently, soaking in the tales they've weaved, and probably greatly embellished.

"My son won most kills three years in a row," says one.

"My brother assisted the king himself last year, watching the first kill get taken down by His Majesty in the flesh," recounts another.

"If any of us were half as good as Cassus Chattan, we may only need to hunt every few years!"

"Aye-aye! Long live King Cassus!" the crowd cheers together.

I give a gentle kick to Red, weaving through the trees to come parallel to the prince once again. These woods remind me of home, of being a young boy running with my little brother and sisters, playing games, and hiding from our nanny and teachers. There are so few memories I have with them that reliving these moments feel special and dear to me.

A tug in my heart pulls me east to my home, to Port Riga.

I just returned to the palace a couple months ago after spending a short summer with my family. I've completed eight of my ten years at the palace, learning from the best tutors and instructors that Felshan has to offer. My parents wanted me to grow with the royal children, to strengthen our ties between the Chattans and Montgomerys, and solidify our family in the kingdom. In two short years I will return home, permanently.

An ache forms in my chest, realizing how much I will miss living in Felshan's capital city of Turin— conspiring with Evander and the hugs and gifts from Lena. I've even stopped adding *prince* and *princess* to their names, and nobody gets on me about it anymore.

But something deep inside knows where home is, and knows where I belong.

"It's time to split off!" I hear a voice yell somewhere ahead of us, pulling me from my daydream.

"Come get your placements!"

The prince and I ride to find his father, just a few strides to the front of the crowd.

"Rentons, Gothreys, Santanas, and Davenports— take the northeast meadows. Buchanans, Reynaulds, Cranes, and Hathsteads— the south forest. Chattans, Sinclairs, Ashcrofts, and Alders— the west bank of the river Rashan. Meet back here after the sun passes the middle arc of afternoon. Be smart. Be safe. And most importantly, bring back some meat!" the king's personal advisor announces, eliciting a chuckle from the lords and their men.

The men begin to scatter as we make our way toward the western group.

"Evander," a deep voice calls from behind us. My friend looks to me, rolling his eyes. A smile creeps across my lips, and I try my best to stifle it before his father, the king, pulls up beside us.

"I want you and Roan to stay in the back."

Evander's eyes go wide. "Father!"

My heart drops at the declaration. I knew it was too good to be true when they agreed to let us come.

"It's the safest place for both of you. I agreed to this little adventure for you two based solely on the fact that you'd be observing. And I expect you to follow your word." His father moves away from us to head up our western group. I turn back to my friend, arms raised and eyes blazoned.

"You just sat there, Evan. Why didn't you say anything?"

"You heard him, Roan. What did you want me to say? The king's word is law. I can't argue with him. It... it would be futile."

I scoff, not even trying to hold back my displeasure. "We talked about this. You will be king one day. How will your word ever be law if you aren't willing to be firm with your desires *now*?" My friend's shoulders sink.

Cassus Chattan is a good king and a good father. When my parents came to me and told me I would live at the palace for ten years, I was angry, and part of me felt betrayed. But from the first moments of my arrival, he has taken me in as his own, treated me like his own son. I should heed his words, follow his instructions to stay back. I should advise the prince to do the same.

But the rebel in me is shouting.

My stubbornness wants to prove to the king and all his lords that Evander and I belong here. I want to show the country that Roan Montgomery is a force to be watched, someone to look out for. A boy who will soon become a man of great skill, power, and authority.

And ultimately, I make the latter choice.

"We are going on this hunt," I continue. "And not as onlookers. We are going to find the biggest deer they've ever seen, and bring it down, *together*." At this the prince smiles.

"Pull up the hood of your cloak," I instruct him.

We slowly make our way from the back of the group to a place just behind the king—far enough that should he look we will blend in, but close enough to be part of the action and claim our stake with our own first kill.

After an uneventful hour, a flurry of excitement reaches out from the men around us.

"Sire! Movement spotted on the banks!" a servant yells.

The king turns around to face us all, holding up his hand to silence the enthusiastic murmurs from the Chattan, Ashcroft, Sinclair, and Alder men.

"Let the hunt begin!" the king shouts.

The prince and I share an unabashed grin, our minds uniting in the same gleeful mission. Let the hunt begin, indeed.

The sun hasn't quite reached the cold blue center of the sky as I hold my dearest friend, the Prince of Felshan, as he takes his last breath in this world.

Water laps around both of us. I hear screaming in the distance, and I soon realize it's coming from me.

"Come back. Come back! Evander, Evander!" I shake him, but his dimmed eyes stare at the sky, unmoving. The river roars in the distance, devouring my cries in its torrent. I hold him, his body suspended amongst the swirls of red now filling the water around us, his blood seeping from the arrow lodged firmly in his chest.

I shout louder and louder as if my voice will somehow tether his spirit back to his body— that somehow the noise will cause him to look at me, his smile beaming, as if this were all a dream. Because surely— surely it's a dream.

But he doesn't wake.

I don't wake. He doesn't stir in response to my screams. Evander, the Prince of Felshan, my best friend, is gone.

1

THE THIEF

I PURPOSEFULLY TWIST MY foot into the mud as I walk in order to feel the familiar weight at my ankle. A sword has never been my weapon of choice, too bulky for my smaller frame, even as I've gotten taller. It just doesn't maneuver like a dagger can.

There may have been a time when my presence elicited the leery stares of passersby. The half-clothed, dirt-smeared little girl with hunger in her eyes. But with some added height and a few clean clothes that actually fit my frame, I now blend in with everyone else. Although, a woman in pants that isn't part of the Royal Guard may garner a side-eye, no one would directly challenge me on it. Not if they wanted to walk away unbruised anyway.

I reach up to brush the string on my bow, but find only air in its place. The market is not a place for such an obvious weapon. If I thought a woman in pants might draw attention, a quiver of arrows definitely would. My body tenses, but with each step the weight of my favorite Turinian blade puts me at ease. *I'm not defenseless.*

Water sprays around me, rolling off my boots as I step out of a puddle. The mugginess of an unusually hot, spring afternoon soaks my shirt, the air noticeably swelling around me as beads of sweat gather on my brow. A soft breeze filled with the ocean cools my face as I breathe in its salty scent.

The street is filled with people for market today, buzzing around from tent to tent, buying their weekly fare. Fresh crab and fish line a few tables, while fruit in every color line another. It's a flourish of greens, reds, blues, purples and oranges. Vendors from Jadeya and Venes, their exotic furs and spices, oils and beaded jewelry intersperse throughout our normal Felshanian goods.

Turinian steel is what keeps this city alive, boasting some of the best sword and metal work in all the kingdom of Felshan— and from what I hear, throughout the Four Kingdoms on our continent of Haythen. Three out of those four kingdoms, all but Thenstra, are represented in our diverse market square.

The vitality of the scene charges through me as I move deeper into the square and the intensifying thrum of voices. The longer I stay in Turin, the kingdom's capital city, the harder it becomes to forget what lies outside this central shape of patrons enjoying foreign and local ingenuity. The kingdom of Felshan doesn't offer much for its citizens anymore, delight and jubilance becoming more of a precious jewel— only available to those who can afford it.

The sun has reached the peak of its arch in the sky, signaling the last few minutes of today's market. This evening will be the yearly commemoration of the death of the prince, now seven years ago. I've heard the palace courtyard is quite the breathtaking scene as they honor their only son, once the crown prince of Felshan, with this venerable celebration.

The king and queen, along with their daughter, Princess Adalena, light the lanterns on the north balcony, followed by thousands lit by the congregation who wish to pay their respects. Most I suspect don't care much about the prince's death, wanting only to spend a night away from their destitution. A single night to forget where they really stand in this world.

These last seven years have truly been cruel to those born without wealth or a royal crown.

I considered going tonight, if just to see the one moment a year where the country doesn't feel so divided, so contrary to what I remember as a child. I never met the prince and hardly heard his name before he died. But perhaps I could light a candle for my mother instead.

The memory of her face brings a quick warmth, followed by a sharp and resounding cold. As rapidly as it came, I push the thought of her away, sliding it back into its tiny cell in the corner of my heart. The more days that separate me from my last memory of her, the less I remember the sound of her voice, and the feel of her arms wrapped around me.

I turn the corner, my feet stopping before I can even make conscious note of the scene laid out before me. The pinching, dark form of a man stands only a few strides in front of me, a sandy-haired boy, maybe ten years old, in his grasp. The man is clad in finery— a perfectly tailored velvet jacket, its trim embroidered with golden thread, custom made boots made from full-grain leather, garnished with a gold-hilted Turinian sword hanging by his side.

"You stole this," the man says, holding a large coin in front of the frightened boy's face. The rancid man towers over the boy in both stature and title, standing at least twice his height— the shadow of fortune disputing any chance of innocence.

"No, sir. No I didn't. My sister and I been saving up all year, sir. Saving up to buy a cart for market." The boy's tunic is so threadbare, it's hard to maintain a hold on his shirt without ripping it right off of him.

"You lie," the man spits. The boy's eyes are so wide I can see the whites from where I stand— his body paralyzed in such a way that he doesn't even move to wipe the spittle from his face.

I bare my gritting teeth, willing myself to stay put until necessary. The hum of anger beats through my heart, drowning out the murmurs from around me. A crowd has now formed to my right and left, unable to look away from the gap of fortune that plagues our city. The man breaks his gaze away from the boy, instead eyeing the gathering people and audience to his power. He releases his grip on the child's shirt, his other hand swinging across the young boy's face.

The sting echoes through the air, quieting any noise from the crowd. The boy lands hard in the dirt, the momentum of the hit twisting him around until he loses his balance and falls to the ground. Blood drips from his nose, accompanied by a large red mark on his cheek that I already know will badly bruise.

The quiet around me is deafening. No one will say anything. No one will step up for this boy. No one will risk themselves and what little they have, and I can't even fault them for it.

My hands and feet silently twinge, my body willing me to drive forward from mere spectator, to participant. I stay still, mind and body warring against each other as tension builds inside of me.

The man, Sir Reynauld as I've come to know him, owns the most lucrative trading business in our city, *Turin Costal Company*, which also happens to include many of our infamous steel blacksmiths. These people know the price of getting in his way. Their fathers, brothers, and sons will lose their only income, or they will quickly find themselves in the same position as the bleeding child sprawled out in front of them.

Many are already turning to leave, a few lingering on the outskirts to make sure the boy is well enough to stand. But no one will move in until Reynauld has made his exit. The sight isn't unfamiliar to them, just another day in their miserable lives as those in power take whatever they want.

A pang of indignation trills through me. I take a step back as the vile man scans the crowd once more, moving so I blend seamlessly into the line of people. This far in my employment for Marg, Reynauld has yet to know my face, and I won't give him that satisfaction today.

"Thenstra is looking better and better, eh?" I hear a woman whisper somewhere behind me.

"Only if you want to trade in their black market. I doubt the country is any better off than we are," a man replies. It's odd to hear talk of Thenstra among this crowd. I've never heard of a black market in that questionable country, but when you're desperate, anything makes sense.

Chatter of Thenstra shrivels in the dirt below me, stomped into lifelessness as Sir Reynauld once again catches my attention.

If it's possible for a man to scowl and smile at the same time, this one has mastered it. His back turns to me before he walks toward the market, yelling over his shoulder, "May the good people of Turin prosper today." His mockery fills the air.

His dark velvet coat writhes in tandem to his movements, weaving through a generous parting of the crowd. Even though I no longer see his face, I can't help but feel his smile as people make way for him to pass. His rich authority knows no bounds. The people's fear and desperation have given him more power than all the wealth in his coffers could ever hope to buy.

A few are brave enough to offer the boy rags to seep up the blood and help cool the angry welt on his cheek. He takes a few deep breaths, tears threatening to spill over at any moment. There's relief and anger underneath those tears, and I recognize it well— the echo of fear, that for a time his life was in the hands of another, while knowing the injustice he was just served.

I don't go to comfort him.

I have a different plan— one that buries my fury for something deeper. One last look at the boy drives in the nail, his red-rimmed eyes trying with all his might to keep his tears at bay.

I turn to follow Reynauld's path.

As I move closer into the heart of the market I skirt from table to table, listening to the haggling of buyers and sellers finding the right price. The top of my face is warmed by the sun as I fold through the crowd, knowing my renewed purpose is no longer to watch the people and relish the day. I have a new mission, and this time it's personal.

My eyes scan the masses as I walk, grabbing a neatly folded cloak from off a nearby table. The owner is busy loading up his cart, the end of market and hot day bringing little sales.

I promise I will bring it back, my friend.

A salty breeze rustles through my hair, kicking the flow of my borrowed cloak behind me. Sweat makes its way down my back, but I tuck the cloak in tighter. I keep my arms crossed as I walk, both to show I'm out of commission to the sellers and to keep a hand on my own purse. I'm not here to buy today, nor am I in the market to fund the thriving pick-pocket population. It may have been my way once, but I have much larger fish in my sights these days.

An involuntary shudder runs through me, and I pause to clamp my eyes shut until it passes. My empty stomach is a thing of yesterday. My need to steal is moot now as my toes are warm in my boots and my hollowed cheeks are full.

But mother is not here.

I shake my head forcefully, willing my eyes to open once again, demanding they search each tent for that familiar face. My focus slowly returns to the shouts of sellers and squeals of children in front of me, and I lift onto the tips of my toes to get a different vantage of the marketplace.

"Fresh fish! Off the boat just this mornin'! Cod, tuna, and sole!" one man yells.

"Pretty jewelry for your beautiful women!" another woman says.

"Get outta here, ya little thief!" A small child runs off, a swift kick in his direction from a hefty man selling what appeared to be all varieties of spring vegetables.

"I hope you got something," I mumble to myself in the direction of the running child, a softness to my gaze as I watch.

A few Royal Guards are interspersed among the crowd, attempting to keep things *honest* and *secured*. I glower in their direction. Marg tells me we are on the same side in our round-about way, but I refuse to see them as my equal. How many of them actually care about these people, or just want a few coins for the tavern after their shift ends? I spit on the ground, muttering a few curses in their honor before returning to the hunt.

My feet shift back and forth to avoid running into a table when I bump into a tall, trim man, the grays of his hair mixing into the dark locks of his youth. Sour breath hits my face, and my head involuntarily jerks to the side to avoid it. The familiar, cold eyes of Reynauld fix on me, unable to fully take me in as the stifling hood of my borrowed cloak covers most of my face. His scowl prompts me to take a step back, raising both of my hands in resignation.

"My apologies," I blurt through a side smile, ignoring the pit in my stomach as his dark eyes bore into mine. I give a small nod in both acknowledgement and adieu before I turn to slip away. The weight of a small pouch lies familiar in my palm.

Before I make my retreat, a hand snatches at my arm— cruel fingers digging into my skin, sinking further and further with every breath that passes. A throb begins its painful pulse in my forearm below. He looks as if he will strike me with his free hand, just as he did the boy. Instead he yanks me toward him, my feet fumbling off balance.

"Watch where you're going, girl," Reynauld says through gritted teeth, his face so close to mine I can see the purple, web-like veins threading around his sagging eyelids.

In just a single motion, I could grab the knife at my boot and shove it through his kidney, killing him painfully in mere moments. The satisfying thought pulls at my rigid muscles, flexing in preparation for the life-taking blow.

I can't kill him. Not yet at least. Instead, I will each part of me to surrender malicious desire, for composed reason.

I hide my disdain through feigned fear, even willing a palpable shudder to roll through me. He smiles in response, but I will be the only one amused when our exchange ends.

"So sorry, sir. I meant no disrespect. Just excited by the day, not watching where I was going." The lie flows out of me as easily as water down an eroded cliff. No resistance. No deterrents. No sudden change of trajectory. Just years of polished precision.

He hesitates, unsure if he should make a display out of me too. He must decide against it because he abruptly shoves me away, landing me against the multitude of people walking around us. I get my bearings, apologizing to the poor man who caught my fall, walking away as if no harm was done.

I make my way from the market-square, hurtling through patrons until the crowd begins to thin. Instinctually, I stop, looking behind me to make sure I can no longer see Reynauld.

Nothing.

My muscles relax limb by limb, but my hardened face remains. I slip off my cloak, folding it smoothly and laying the finished product over one arm. Another breeze blows through my freed torso, and I sigh as the air hits my now sweat dampened clothes.

Despite the exhilaration I feel, the deep, reverberating thump within my chest and my shaking hands tells another tale. *You're safe, Ari. You're safe,* I try and remind myself.

There's purpose behind my actions now. A reason bigger than just myself. Stealing from Reynauld just now was a small revenge on behalf of an exhausted and hungry people, but it lives inside the larger vision. Maybe it's justification for a less than legal life. But when a royal lady is backing my actions, it's easier to feel in the right. And when my gut is pushing me forward, I can't help but listen.

"Excuse me," I continue to mutter over and over as I pass.

Just ahead I see the table with a vacant corner. I set down the cloak in one swift motion not turning to see who, if anyone, witnessed my return as I continue on my way.

I grab the hidden purse out from my pocket, opening it to examine the prize. Coins jingle back and forth as I inspect the contents. More than enough to replace what was taken. *Good.* I close the sack, give it a good toss in the air for celebration and place it back into my pocket.

I walk faster, following the sodden road to the forest edge. Continuing past the trees I spot Prue, right where I left her. The corners of my mouth instantly turn up as I spot my buckskin beauty.

My wide smile evokes a whinny from her as I pull an apple from my satchel. I didn't even have to steal this one. The chinking of coins in my own purse reminds me just how far I've come from only a few years ago. If only Mother could see me now— no more bones sticking out from my skin or eating maggot infested fruit.

"Good girl," I whisper to my horse as I approach, one hand raised in deference. "Did you miss me?"

She meets me as far as her tied rope will allow. I raise the apple to her mouth as my forehead rests against her neck, my shoulders dropping as we touch. I press into her for another moment, breathing in her natural smell of earthiness and meadow grass. Nuzzling into Prue's mane is the closest feeling to home I may ever experience again in this life, and I don't take a second of it for granted.

I feel whole again as I pull away from her, reaching out toward a nearby tree to pick up my bow and string it around my back, hooking my quiver of arrows to the side of my saddle. I swing my leg up and over Prue.

A few rays of sunlight poke through stray clouds as we leave the cover of the trees, the sun continuing its arc across the sky signaling late afternoon. Marg will be expecting me soon, before the tribute service for the prince. Will I have enough time to stop beforehand?

I move Prue into a trot to pick up the pace, adjusting my direction toward the East Village, although eastern slums might be more appropriate. Call it a hunch, but I know the boy will be there.

A few city guards are posted at the mouth of the road. If anyone was looking too closely, they'd notice my attempt at an innocent smile being more of a grimace. I keep my eyes down as to not evoke attention and hopefully pass off my *smile* as genuine.

My fists clench when one of them looks my way. He seems to be admiring my horse, but slowly his gaze moves up my frame until it rests on my lowered face. Perhaps I shook the cloak loose a little too soon.

The guard stays focused on me, following the movements of Prue as we make our way past their check-point. I match my eyes to his, unwilling to cower under his stare and unwilling to bow to his station.

The guard's face is somewhat handsome— a troll hiding beneath a well-built guise. His blue eyes are so bold I can see their color from where I sit. I imagine what it would feel like to lock him into a cell, watching that blue slowly fade away as the months and years move on.

Another guard catches his attention, keeping me in my saddle and my hidden blade out of my hands. I sneer as the red and gold of their uniforms comes into focus. The color of blood and greed, perfectly fitting for royalty and their supporters. *Sorry Marg.*

I forget that I'm now supporting royalty, but it just doesn't feel the same. Marg may be royal in name, but she's a different breed. She is more like an obscure shade of royalty— someone who fell into it out of necessity instead of actual desire. It's hard to loathe someone, maybe the only someone, who is trying to piece this country back together.

I pass by the guards, no one stopping me or asking questions. Not even the handsome one who seemed to study me a bit more closely. I wish I could say I was relieved, but part of me itches for one of them to pick a fight before they disappear behind me.

I turn a corner into one of the poorest parts of the capital. Even after the rainstorm last night, the unmistakable smell of urine and rot fills the air. I cover my nose with my hand as I rummage in my saddle bag for a small cloth to wrap around my nose and mouth.

Further down in the village I spot the boy, blood still crusted around his nose. His eyes are clear, but two dry streams mark against the contrast of his dirty cheeks, the one already developing the purple and blue bruise I knew would blossom. I pull out the cloth purse from my hidden pocket as I approach him.

"Hello," I say, prompting him to look up at me. "I think this belongs to you." I toss him the sack, and the jingle of coins is evident as it lands on his lap.

His eyes look through clumped lashes, lines forming between his brow. The boy picks up the bag, the contents clinking together as he pours it out onto his hand.

"This... this isn't mine," he tells me, clearing his throat as his eyes dart around us before returning to me. His response feels heavy in my stomach. This boy knows better than to trust me— kind strangers no longer exist in these parts of Turin.

I bend down so I'm eye-level with the lad. "Can I tell you a secret?"

He nods, bobbing one knee up and down as I talk. "I have a magical ability to find lost things. And my senses tell me that whatever is in there belongs to you."

Magic is such an entrancing idea, encompassing so many different views in my mind. I've never believed in some other-worldly power. I view this fascinating concept more like a gift one has been born with. A natural talent that has been stoked and weeded and given the light it needs to grow. One look at this child and I decide a little white lie, one that gives hope and awe to someone in need, can't hurt.

"And when the beloved trinket is near," I continue, "my body hums in response, like the wings of a hummingbird as she goes in search of nectar from spring's first blooms. Getting louder and deeper the closer I get." The boy's eyes are so wide I can see the whites all around them.

"But lady, I didn't lose this. At least... not all of it," he says through his furrowed brow, his attention back to the coins in the purse.

"Think of it as payment—for that man's ill treatment of you." Hope wants to glimmer at my words, but his hesitation isn't unexpected. He's probably never had this much money in his possession, and it must feel both exciting and dangerous at the same time.

"But if he comes looking for me, comes looking for this," he holds up the money, and I can see him visibly shaking at the thought.

"Keep it hidden in your pocket until you find a safe place. Only take out a coin at a time as you use it. And if he comes again, so will I." I know I can't be everywhere at once, making sure he's safe while also attending to my duties for Marg. But if anything happens to this boy, I will personally make sure Reynauld lives to regret it.

"Thank you, miss." He still looks unsure as Prue and I walk away. But after a few moments he runs past us, elation finally brimming across his face. I can't hide my smile as he takes off down the road, I imagine to find his sister and share their good fortune. Perhaps the only good fortune they've seen their whole life.

Another wave of urine reaches my nose, my face crinkling in response.

As I turn around to mount my horse, a woman walks close by. She has light brown hair, the same shade as mine and the same length as my mother's when she walked these streets. The similarities stop there, but it brings an ache to my gut to be reminded of her and the silhouette of her presence in my life.

It's moments like these I dread, but also constantly search for. I want to forget, but I want to remember. Freedom of my pain also means freedom from my perfect memories of her. I'm just not willing to let go.

I soak up the image of her hair as the woman continues her path around me. On the outside my body feels relaxed, my face wholly content as I watch her retreating form.

But on the inside, around the healed edges of my wound, the deepened cracks and fissures of loss rip open once again.

2

THE CAPTAIN

MORNINGS ARE USUALLY MY sanctuary.

But not today.

The smell of the evening storm still wafts through the air as the birds begin adding their song to the wind. But their music turns to ash as it reaches my ears. I move my face toward the sun and let it warm my skin while my arms hang limply at my sides. My stomach clenches as if I'm being wrung from the inside out. The shame that I'm here enjoying the bright heat makes my head swim.

A long day lies ahead of me.

My chest methodically rises and falls as I stare out into the training grounds. Repeated use of this stretch of land has given way to large patches of dirt and mud within the scattered greenery. Last night's downpour left the ground softer than I prefer, but you never know what conditions you'll be in when fighting for your life, or for the life of another.

"Come on, put some pressure on him!" I shout toward the barrage of stick hitting stick.

Otto, our sword trainer in the Guard, is circling the other side of our recruits. His brow stays furrowed as he oversees their meager sparring abilities. He continues adjusting stances and holds of the men, getting better angles for attack while also showing them how to protect their face and vital organs.

"Raise your arm, lad. Up here. And your foot. This foot. Move it here. Now, try again." Otto steps back, massaging his neck, tilting it off the side as he watches. An audible pop of his joints murmurs underneath the clap of wood in the distance.

Otto was born and raised in Felshan, just as his parents before him. The loyalty in his blood runs through him like the river Rashan— the only river in the Four Kingdoms to pass solely though Felshan.

The mighty Rashan— a shiver runs through me.

I set my focus back to what is in front of me. Today I will hold my head high, pretending to be as strong as everyone thinks I am.

The crack of pounding wood rings through the air. "Go again," I say, staring intently. The boys look at me as I methodically circle their group, searching over to Otto, and then back to each other.

"You heard the captain! Again!" Otto shouts.

I don't bother learning the names of first years until I know they are here to stay.

Many may dream of being a guardsman, protecting Turin and Felshan's other surrounding cities. But few are willing to put forth the effort and grit it takes to actually get there. The early mornings and midnight trainings. Seeing first-hand the scum that prey on the weak and innocent. Making the hard decisions. Taking orders even when you don't always know why or agree. The blood splotching every piece of clothing you own.

Sticks clash over and over as the boys spar around the yard. If you can even call it sparring. More like two reluctant dance partners who are afraid they'll break a toe if they move too quickly. Ten seconds in real combat and both of them would be dead.

A plan forms in my mind, my lips turning upward in a sly grin. If I plan to survive this day, I need a distraction. Or, at the very least, I need to create a mask to the pain underneath.

"Line up!" I yell, eyeing Otto and nodding in the direction of the sword at his waist. His face is blank as I walk to the edge of the yard, retrieving my own sword. My eyes close as the swishing sound of metal releasing from its sheath reaches me, my lungs breathing in the gentle whoosh of air it creates.

Otto meets me off to the side. "Do you think this is wise today, my friend?" he mutters so only I can hear.

"Just raise your sword and meet me in the clearing." A smile crinkles his face, but I can see the unease in his eyes. He nods before turning away.

Otto is almost twenty years my senior. As the Master of Weapons for the Royal Guard for over twelve years, he trained me after I joined the Guard myself at fifteen years old.

The last seven years have passed in such a blur, particularly those four years of recruit training. The only way I could convince my parents to let me join the Guard at such a young age, and also receive the blessing of the king and queen, was if I was also willing to continue my education. For two years I trained all morning with the recruits, spent my afternoons sitting in a classroom, then headed back for round two of training in the evening.

If it weren't for Otto, I'm not sure determination alone would have been enough. Since the Guard trained all day, he personally trained me in the evenings to make up my hours. I'm also fairly certain there were a couple nights Otto had to carry me to bed, as I woke up on my cot within the barracks but couldn't figure out how I got there from the armory.

I head to the center of the battle arena. It's hard to miss an opportunity to spar with the one and only Otto. The only practice I get nowadays is sparring with him. And it's just what I need to burn away the flourishing ache weaving itself through my stomach and dissolve the anvil on my chest.

The prince should have been the one who entered the Guard, not me. As next in line for the throne he would have started as a recruit after his own educational tenure was completed. At seventeen years old he would have spent the next four years learning extended training on the sword and bow, as well as military strategy with his father. It is tradition within the country of Felshan for the prince to have spent time among his people, to train alongside them, earning their love and respect while also diving into war and battle strategies to prepare him for life and duty as the king.

But instead they got me. Roan Montgomery, *the prince-slayer*. My selfishness got the prince killed. Time may have helped the sting of truth bite softer, but the painful reality is always waiting for me.

I dig my feet into the ground, finding my steadiness and raising my sword. Our feet move slowly as we begin. Otto and I look each other up and down, sizing up our opponent as we anticipate their first move.

The clang of metal against metal reverberates through the air. Our swords meet again. Again. Again. The boys take a step back from where they have gathered around us, realizing these aren't the sticks that will simply leave a bruise. Many have ended up in the infirmary during training exercises. Mostly those who can't leave their ego at the door, or are trying to show off unhoned skills. I'm not stupid enough to think my talent alone is enough to beat the old man. But if I play it right I might just have a chance.

Someone steps in a puddle close by. The gurgling plop of water reaches my ears. Blood swirls around me as my fingers brush through dull wet hair while cold lifeless eyes look past me, a scream curdling the air. My legs buckle beneath me, but the strength of my sword gives me the leverage I need to stop myself before my knees hit the ground.

A cool sweat breaks out above my lip as I try to shake away the memory. My heart thunders as I attempt to catch my breath and reorient myself back to the training yard and my match with Otto. I wipe away the dripping perspiration, turning to face my opponent and charge forward once again.

I hold back nothing. Our weapons twist through the air, and I success-fully land the tip of Otto's weapon in the dirt, giving me time to grab my sword with my left hand and swing my fist to meet his jaw with my right. He glances back, leaving the majority of my blow gliding through air. He successfully dislodges his sword just as I get both hands back around my own to bring it up in front of me, catching his oncoming barrage.

I've never met someone as quick on his feet and just as quick with his blows. I block one, two, three. He catches me off balance, and I duck and roll off to the side, giving me time and room to get back on my feet. There's no rest with him, which is why I prefer our matches. As close to the real thing as you'll ever get without getting your throat slit or losing an arm. *And the best diversion in the entire city.*

Even when taking a much needed breath, the smile hasn't left Otto's face. He enjoys this as much as I do, even knowing my ulterior motives. "You can give up whenever you're done," he mumbles to me. My brows knit together in mock surprise.

He's taunting me. Of course I'm used to it from this cocky old man. And it's to be expected, obviously. It's important to get inside the opponent's head, messing with their thoughts and creating enough disbelief that they begin making small mistakes— landing me the win.

Otto knows what today is. I could tell from the way he approached me earlier, as if I would shatter at any moment like a glass tipped off the table. A tiny ray of gratitude simmers underneath the physical exertion. My friend, my mentor, is helping me escape.

Sensing my understanding, he opens his mouth, whispering so only I can hear, "You're not a child anymore, Roan. You will be king consort soon, ruling alongside Princess Adalena. It's time I treat you as such." I know he means no disrespect, but his words trigger something deep inside me. I am to be married to Lena in only a few short months, and it still doesn't seem real.

I bare my teeth. "I never asked for, nor need, your coddling old man." For the briefest moment his eyes go wide, and he shifts his feet on the soft ground. I'm not a child, and I won't apologize for my remark. Instead, I layer the bricks in my mental shield.

His arm flexes before he closes a fist to strike. I raise my arm to block, turning my sword so his blow lands on the hilt instead of my face. Distracted by his words, I miss his other arm going in for my side. I double over to the left, ducking and barely missing another swing of his sword. I shimmy my feet away, catching myself with one hand on the ground as I hit uneven terrain.

The sun is getting higher in the sky, and I wipe a layer of sweat from my brow, staring toward my opponent. My emotions have made me sloppy. I need to use them as I have in the past— harnessing the intensity to propel me into victory.

In the corner of my consciousness, chanting has erupted from the onlookers.

"Otto! Otto! Otto!"

"Captain! Captain! Captain!"

One side cheering the master in front of me, the other for their leader. I almost don't even register that they are referring to me. Maybe one day I'll finally get used to it.

A rush from my opponent has me throwing up my sword to protect my face and neck from his full force. The leathers wrapped around my arm and down to my wrist help me use both arms to keep my sword from falling back on me, the top of my weapon digging in to the thick material, but not breaking through. His strength has always astounded me, and the sheer weight of him has me dropping to one knee.

Otto holds his weight in his front leg, keeping him steady as he pushes down against my sword with all his strength. My arms and legs burn in response, and my mouth goes dry. He's going to win. A bead of sweat drips down the side of my face as I strain against him. I can count the times I've bested him on one hand, while he could notch out a large stick with the times the match was called in his favor.

No. Not this time. *Not today.*

I push up with the hilt of my sword, while ever-so-slightly lowering the arm with my blade resting on the leather. Otto ticks his face to the side before I kick my leg out against his, knocking away his steadiness just enough to use the last of my strength to push him off me and onto the ground. He lands with a hard *thud*.

I drop my sword, jumping to where he lies on his back. One leg lands across his torso, and I pull my other leg to pin his arm. I reach for the knife tucked underneath the side of my belt, pulling it up to his throat.

"I win," I say through heaving breaths.

Otto winks at me. "Aye. You got me, boy," he whispers, more from lack of breath than trying to be quiet. Cheers erupt all around. A rare win against their master has the recruits in an uproar. I may be captain, but the respect they all have for Otto trumps any deference for me.

Perhaps he let me win to help gain esteem in the eyes of the recruits. Haythen knows I've had my work cut out for me in that regard.

It was not what I had planned for at only nineteen years old, the king appointing me Captain of the Guard. It was not the future I had intended. But as I've learned the hard way, nothing goes as planned.

I was to study at the palace alongside the prince and princess, building those ties between my family, House Montgomery, and those of the king and queen, House Chattan, and House Sinclair. It's an honored position— a tradition saved for one or two lucky children in Felshan. Although I've come to learn luck has nothing to do with it. The family with the strongest wealth, military advantage, agricultural, or economic dominance within the country with children of age are all put in the hat of choosing. My family is certainly wealthy, and Port Riga could, in theory, be its own country.

My ancestral home of Port Riga produces many of the kingdom's seasonal crops, vast orchards line the hills on the western border, strong fishing waters to the eastern shoreline, and strong trade with Jadeya who borders less than fifty miles north of the port. And from what I've heard, my father has started several dozen pens of livestock. It's expected the herds will triple by next year. Port Riga is almost completely self-sustaining, and growing by the day. People flock to our prosperous shores, especially now.

It's still habit to say *we* and *our*, one I have yet to break. Even after learning three years ago that I'll never be returning home, at least not to stay. It still seems second nature to refer to my fate as the future of Port Riga. My shoulders stiffen as I bring myself back to the reality of what my future now holds.

No one knows more than me that I am an imposter. Training as a recruit. Becoming Captain. Being betrothed to Lena. None of this was in the future I had planned. That anybody had planned.

I tense as the recruits clap me on the back, the crowd surging forward to where I still hold Otto pinned to the ground. But I don't revel in their congratulations. I press my lips firmly together, my vacant eyes moving to the gathering crowd. "Enough for the morning! Go get some water. Be back here after lunch," I yell.

I wipe away a bead of sweat from my brow as I enter the palace. I'm later than I expected, stopping to inspect some of the guard checkpoints around the market square. I got distracted, and time slipped away from me.

My stride remains fixed as I spot the throne room door.

As a child, Evander, Lena, and I would concoct ways to get through these doors. Elaborate ventures that would distract the guards while we tried to sneak through. Of course we were always caught, promptly scolded, and sent on our way. The ever elusive throne room that we could never enter. Now, I've passed through these doors so many times any magic I once thought they held has almost completely vanished.

It's rare for me to be summoned to the palace outside my weekly dinners with Lena. Once I started my training with the Guard, I opted to stay in the barrack dormitories. And once I was made Captain, I stayed to be closer to my men. But these walls are as familiar to me as my home.

Two guards stand on either side of the entrance in their red and gold, swords sheathed but hands at the ready, eyeing me as I pass. I nod to the two on the right. "Buchanan, Ashcroft." I nod to the two on the left. "Aldren, Crane."

"Captain," they all say in turn.

I haven't seen these men regularly for a couple of years, as they left the recruit barracks in favor of the king's sister's instruction. Lady Margaret, preferring the title of *Lady* to that of *Princess*, prefers to keep and train her own set of Palace Guards, separate from the city barracks and the captain's instruction. I never put up much of a fight in that regard. She keeps out of my way, and I keep out of hers.

Lady Margaret and I have never warmed to each other, but her curious background has always left a bit of question in my mind. When she came of age she began her Royal duties as Ambassador of the Crown of Felshan, often traveling and spending long stretches of time within two of the three countries that border the kingdom: Jadeya to the northeast and Venes to the south.

Lady Margaret now holds the title of Grand Emissary of National and Foreign Affairs, whatever that is. All I know is she has a royal ticket to question anything I do as Captain of the Royal Guard. I don't even think her current position existed until she created it. But as the king's favored sister, it seems she can do whatever she wants.

As predicted, Queen Amelia is not alone as I enter. I hear small bouts of laughter echoing from the small tea room— Princess Adalena, Lady Margaret, and another I don't recognize.

I continue making my way down the hallway lined with a deep red carpet, marking the entry of a columned corridor leading into the throne room. High ceilings and tall windows create an air of grandeur, doing their job well. Each brick and each window reminding me how important every piece is in the grand scheme of the space. Much like the people making up our country.

The magic that left me at the doors returns for just a moment as I stop and take in the room and the intention the creators designed this space to hold.

The throne stands high on a dais, an honored and extraordinary piece in and of itself. A massive stone, rough and rudimentary around the edges, bridges into an immaculately polished yet simply carved out seat in its center. Flecks of light catch off the many cutlets made throughout the grand structure as if stars themselves reside deep inside. My eyes get lost for a moment as I stare at it, imagining the many promises this one object contains.

Red and gold accents show through in the large tapestries lining the walls, depicting Felshan's history. Portraits of the current and previous royal families lay throughout the room as well. I spot Prince Evander in the portrait nearest the throne, and my stomach constricts. I try and swallow to dislodge the lump forming in my throat so I can breathe again, giving myself an extra few seconds before I turn and move directly into the presence of Queen Amelia and her guests.

Lady Margaret and Princess Adalena sit to the left of the queen. A woman, around the same age as the queen and two others who appear to be this lady's daughters, sit to her right.

As I get closer, it's hard to miss the darkened shadows beneath the queen's eyes. Are her cheeks a little more hollow than they were yesterday? A swift bout of nausea roils through me. The only thing keeping me upright is my duty and responsibility to this family who has lost so much at my hands—the reckless boy who consistently convinced the prince to color outside the lines.

"Hello, Roan!" the queen says, trying to animate her somber voice. I turn to face her as she waves me over with a slight flick of her hand. Her smile doesn't quite reach her eyes.

My shoes beat against the hard tile as I continue my way to her side, surveying the guests and scanning the space around me. "My Queen," I say, giving a slight bow of my head.

"Roan, how good of you to join us today. I was just telling Princess Adalena, Lady Margaret, and Lady Davenport what a hard-working and loyal captain you've been these last few years," says the queen.

"It's because I have a king, queen, and princess worth being loyal to," I tell her. Lena purses her lips, and I realize too late that I left Prince Evander out of that line-up. The smile falters from the queen's face. I inwardly kick myself for not using the all encompassing *royalty* or *monarchy* to name them all. It's not that I've forgotten him. Obviously I will never forget.

I've far from made peace with his passing, but I've learned to acknowledge that he isn't coming back. On occasion that acknowledgment allows me to see past my grief to the people who are right in front of me. But most of the time it still feels like a punch to the stomach leaving me gasping for air.

The queen is still attempting a smile, but now it seems plastered, like that of a sculpture or painting. I know the only reason that smile is still in place is from years of training and habit, of the practicing and pretending to be happy, when inside she felt as if she were slowly dying. I mastered that smile many years ago.

"You look like it's been quite the day, Captain," Lady Margaret interjects.

"A morning of training our recruits and checking our checkpoints at the market, Lady Margaret," I state, my gaze firmly meeting her own. I try to recover the conversation as I look over at the other women. "Princess Adalena— you are looking radiant, as always." The other mystery women, the presumable mother and daughters, shift in their chairs as they attempt to sit up a little straighter.

"Thank you, Roan. I mean, Captain Montgomery. Mother just had this dress made, and I couldn't wait to try it out." Her eyes are wide as she tries to help me with the quick change of conversation.

She doesn't care much about dresses. I know this more than most. But the lavender does bring out the color of her eyes. Her hair is done up on top of her head, two braids wrap around each other with small frills of hair framing her face. I wish she would leave it down more. I know that's what she prefers, but she always lets her maids convince her to keep it in *style*.

"How rude of me, Captain. Let me introduce you to our guests," the queen begins. "This is Lady Rebecca Davenport and her two lovely daughters, Marya and Eloise Davenport." I nod to each of them respectably.

"Lady Davenport is here visiting her cousin, who has something terrible to report, indeed. He had his purse stolen this morning at market. A young lady he believes is the culprit. Lady Davenport so kindly asked if you would mind assisting this cousin in bringing the thief to justice," Queen Amelia says.

"Of course. Anything I can do to assist my queen, and the wonderful people of Felshan. If you would be so kind, Lady Davenport, to give me your cousin's name and where I can find him. I will go straight away."

"He is loyal, Amelia. Thank you for suggesting I seek his help." Lady Davenport beams up at me, and an odd discomfort fills me at her smile. "His name is Sir Reynauld, and his estate resides over in Thene Valley."

It seems I've taken a few pointers from the queen. My face is a mask of respect, but inside annoyance flutters freely. The mere mention of Reynauld brings a growl up my throat, halted only by sheer willpower. Many times I've wished I could run my sword through Sir Reynauld simply to be rid of his cocky and obstructive presence in our city. But it seems a young lady did the next best thing. It takes great effort to keep my lips from ticking upward in a satisfied smile. If only I could've been there to witness the scene, to see his face when he realized what had happened.

"Roan? Roan, are you okay?" Lena's voice interrupts my thoughts.

"Yes," I respond, blinking away my musings. "I know Sir Reynauld. I would be more than happy to help him track down this thief." Lena smiles up at me, but more to cover her concern than any joy for my commission to help Reynauld.

"So devoted to whatever our queen needs," Lady Margaret says. When I look at her, my smile fades. "Like a dog," she finishes. I take a deep breath, unwilling to be baited today of all days.

"Aunt." Lena says firmly, wide-eyed as she stares at Lady Margaret.

Lady Davenport's smile raises the hair on my nape. "Don't discount dogs, Lady Margaret. I've never met anything as obedient and steadfast as my hounds. If only more of our subordinates would take their lead, and Captain Montgomery's."

My fists ball at my sides. *A dog.* This is what my presence and service to the Crown have become? I narrow my eyes at Lady Margaret, attempting to hide the pointed stare from the other women. The light is evident in her eyes as she watches me squirm underneath her and Lady Davenport's words.

Good thing I'm here to keep her entertained. A solid retort plays on my lips. If they want to compare me to an animal then they will learn just how beastly I can be. But Lena stares at me, pleading through her eyes to let it go.

Another look at our fragile queen gives me the strength to swallow my words. "Well, it's a good thing I smell better than a dog." I let my renewed smile reach my eyes as I say it.

"On occasion, I suppose," chimes Lady Margaret.

Lena turns fully in her chair to face her Aunt, eyes wide. "Would you like more tea, *Aunt*?" She accentuates Lady Margaret's familial title.

"Thank you, niece," She responds, breaking her precarious gaze from me as she holds out her cup for Lena to fill.

Part of me admires Lady Margaret. A deep, deep part of me. I've heard rumors that she runs an underground effort to protect the city of Turin. Our beloved king and queen have never fully recovered from Prince Evander's death, but Lena isn't old enough to take the throne until her birthday this Autumn, now only a few months away. In the absence of an attentive leader of our country, Lady Margaret has tried to fill the role. So I'm told. I don't know the details of her efforts, or if there's any truth to them. But witnessing her forceful demeanor and fierce protection of Lena, I wouldn't pull the idea from off the table.

I'm distracted by the princess as she finishes pouring Lady Margaret's tea. I still find it hard to believe that soon we will be married. All I see when I look at her is the little sister of my best friend, tagging along as we snuck out of the palace to the pond to catch tadpoles and whatever slimy creatures we could find, ruining her dresses in the water and mud.

"Yes, well. I'll expect a full report in a few days about Sir Reynauld," says Queen Amelia.

"Of course, my queen." I bow to her directly, before bowing to the other ladies to signal my exit. *Let the dog take his leave.*

3

THE PRINCESS

I WATCH ROAN LEAVE the tea room. He turns in my direction just as he crosses the threshold, a hint of a smile crossing his face as our eyes meet. The room feels instantly colder after he's gone.

My mother is talking to Lady Davenport, but I don't register her words. I dress my face as a good princess should— smiling, nodding, laughing when everyone else does. But all I hear are the waves crashing down on the beach, and the sound of my own breathing.

This room is one of my favorites, I realize. There are so many memories here from my childhood. Roan and Evander crashing afternoon tea with my mother and whatever guests she was entertaining that day. All while I sat in my chair watching in absolute delight, doing everything I could to keep a straight face. It was impossible not to laugh when those two were together. Their energy and zest for life were palpable.

Tears begin to fill my eyes at the remembrance, but also a hint of a smile tugs at my face. This is my life now. To be burdened with both joy and sadness at the memories of my brother.

The windows are opened just a crack, enough for a breeze to hit my clammy face. "Excuse me," I say, scooting back my chair and standing slowly.

"I'm feeling a little tired. I think I'll go lie down for a bit. Rest up for tonight." I smile at my mother and our guests.

Lady Davenport's daughters look like eccentric porcelain dolls in their bold colored gowns— sitting across from me, hardly moving, talking, or doing much of anything the entire lunch. They barely twitch in response to me getting up to leave.

I want to ask if they're part of the traveling festivals, but stop myself. Come see the human dolls! Complete with unflinching precision, unblinking tenacity, and a spirit of halting dullness.

A princess is always polite. My aunt's words ring through me. If ever there was a time I wish I could speak my mind it's now, just to see the look of confusion on their faces when I ask.

"Oh dear, are you feeling alright?" My mother stands and puts her cold hand against my forehead. My own fingers lace through hers, pulling her hand from my face. I cradle that hand between mine, only allowing a brief moment of concern to reach my eyes.

I catch her gaze with my own, which is fairly easy now that we are almost the same height. "I'm ok, Mother. Truly." I look straight in her eyes and their emptiness, void of everything but a single spark as she stares back. "I'm just going to take a nap, and maybe a quick walk around the gardens before tonight. I promise I will be there right on time for you and Father."

Her eyes glaze over at the mention of tonight. The fact that my mother can't openly grieve in her own home is infuriating. Who cares if there are people around we barely know. I might even be excited to be queen, in a small way, if I didn't feel like everything was one big secret hiding behind fake smiles.

Mother finally snaps back to our present company. "Yes, yes. Well. Go rest, my little dove."

I turn to leave, giving a brief curtsy to the frozen puppets, and a peck on the cheek to my aunt.

"See you tonight, sweet girl," Lady Margaret whispers to me.

"Maybe you could wear the green dress tonight. You know how much Roan loves green," my mother calls to me as I make my exit. My lips purse at the comment. Thankfully, my back is to the room and no one can see.

It's not that I don't like Roan. In fact, he might be the only person not walking around in a shell of skin and bone, at least since he's become Captain.

I know today will be hard for him. It will be hard for all of us. But the thought of dressing in order to please or be desired by him— it's strange. Actually, it's completely bizarre. He was like another brother to me when we were children. And after my own died, he became even more so. I don't know why my parents betrothed us, other than their weak attempt at keeping my brother's memory alive.

Before Roan, I had been betrothed to Lady Davenport's son, the lively yet severe woman that was just sitting across from me. I'm surprised she has kept such great relations with my parents after what I assume was a great slight to her family. It must have taken great lengths to break that promise with the Davenport's. And my parents motives, as far as I know, were only born from grief.

Everyone says Roan and I will grow to love one another in time, but I already love him. I love him like you do your favorite blanket, or a treasured spot in the garden. The excitement to see him is my excitement for normalcy, for a real conversation, for someone who won't look at me like I'm made of glass. But love? I suppose I've never really been in love in a romantic way, so I don't know what that would feel like. Perhaps I *love* love him, and I don't even realize. Or maybe I'll be doomed to see him as a second brother for the rest of my life.

There are worse things, I suppose. At least we will like each other. At least we enjoy each other's company. Probably more so than I ever would have the Davenport's son. And who knows— maybe everyone is right, and there will come a time where we romantically care for one another.

I make my way down the white columned corridor of the throne room and out to the connected hallways, pausing when I exit through the doors. If I turn left, I will end up at the ballrooms, both upper and lower. They are beautiful and over-the-top extravagant.

The Isolde Ballroom, named after my great-grandmother Queen Isolde, is my favorite. It's on the second floor and always has fresh flowers adorning each table, even when there's no imminent party. The smell of roses, lilies, peonies, and hydrangea connect me to this woman I never had the privilege of meeting. My aunt has told me stories of her goodness— of how kind and funny she was, always smelling of mint and whatever flower was in bloom. I long to have known such a woman, to be part of the legacy of the great women in our family.

"Princess Adalena," a low voice says behind me. One of the four guards stationed outside the throne room takes a step forward, bowing at the hip as I turn to face him. "Is everything ok?"

His long dark hair is pulled back, tied low behind his neck, his equally dark eyes meeting my own. He's actually quite handsome, his knit brows and pursed lips accentuating his perfect jawline and strong face.

"Yes, yes. I'm fine. Just thinking," I say, trying not to sound too breathy in response to his smoldering concern. I do my best at a kind smile and wave a flimsy hand through the air to dismiss my odd behavior.

"Would you like me to escort you somewhere? I would feel better knowing you've arrived safely," the guard says.

Rarely has a guard in the palace spoken to me, let alone offered to escort me when he has no assignment to do so. And such a handsome one to boot. I'm taken back by the thoughtful suggestion, internally at war with this outspoken guard in front of me and the usual stoic behavior of these men, who so clearly aren't just statued soldiers, only coming to life when called upon. And because it feels strange for him to have proposed he leave his commissioned post to walk me. If I had asked, they would be required to be my convoy until I said otherwise, the only orders trumping my own being those of my mother, father, and aunt Margaret.

You're being weird to the handsome guard, Lena.

"I appreciate it, sir..." I pause, waiting for him to fill in the sentence with his name.

"Aldren. Parker Aldren." He gives me another bow.

"Well, thank you, Parker Aldren. I feel optimistic that I'll make it to my destination in one piece."

"Of course, Princess." Another bow from the dapper guard. How tiring it must be, bowing three hundred times to the same person each day.

I turn the corner, away from the Palace Guards, only to bump straight into Roan.

"Princess," he says, bowing slightly.

"Don't you know better than to hide around corners and scare unsuspecting women?" I look up at his grinning face.

"I do. But it doesn't make it any less fun," he says. I swat playfully at his shoulder. "So, who's the handsome guard?" His chin juts out to point behind me.

My limbs freeze. He saw that interaction? I rub at my ear before crossing my arms and ironing out my flustered face. "You know who he is. Don't tease me."

"Parker Aldren. He's a nice enough fellow, from what I know of him. Do you talk often?"

I'm trying to read him, to see if there's any jealousy there. But I find none. He is genuinely curious about my relationship with that guard. Seeing me talking to another man hasn't fazed him in the slightest.

I should care that he doesn't seem to care. My betrothed joking with me about the dashing guard. But I can't seem to find even a flicker of dismay in the act.

"No, we don't talk often. In fact, you eavesdropped on our very first conversation." Roan only raises an eyebrow as I accuse him. He reminds me so much of Evander sometimes, both to his detriment and favor.

"Let me walk you," he says, holding out an arm. My stomach feels heavy as I take it, and side-by-side we walk down the hall.

Roan drops me at my room. Once he's disappeared down the corridor, I escape and run for the ballrooms. Truthfully, I just need space today. Space to feel, to think, to prepare. So much will happen in this coming year. I will finally reach eighteen and be crowned Queen of the Realm—to take my place among the other three monarchs of the Four Kingdoms of our continent of Haythen.

My head swims as I think of all that will need to be done. Of all that has been left alone. Of all that has broken these last seven years. I don't blame my parents and the grief that took them away from me and from Felshan. Some days even taking their desire to just live. But I do know the steep path ahead of me. One that, at only seventeen, feels like something only magic and dreams could begin to mend.

I arrive at the Isolde ballroom door, peering in as the heavy weight on my shoulders lifts almost immediately. The floor and walls are white like the rest of the palace, but it's one of the only rooms not decorated in the traditional red and gold. Six floor to ceiling glass windows wrap around the south of the room, each one flanked by deep violet drapes. Purple was my great-grandmother's favorite color, and our family has always kept this room in her tradition.

Tulips of all colors and peonies in every shade of white and pink are bunched on every table and corner. Yellows, reds, purples, and pinks mix effortlessly with the violet accents of the room, threading together the makings of the beautiful life of my grandmother, reminding me of sunset and the night sky. If only I could stay here all afternoon, and spend this miserable day wrapped in the comfort of a grandmother I never knew.

I allow myself a moment for each of my senses to come alive. The intense hue of each flower. The scent of a warm spring day. The delicacy of every petal's softness between my fingers. The taste of sunshine raining through the windows. The quiet calmness of evening as it approaches. *Just one more minute.* Another minute of basking in the life this room possesses.

"Your Highness!" squeaks a small woman standing in the doorway, her arms once full of flowers that are now strewn across the floor. "I'm so sorry. You startled me."

"Don't be sorry, Marta. Here, let me help you." I drop to help her pick up more tulips from the floor. "I should be getting ready for tonight anyway."

"I thought you were in the Tea Room with your mother and Lady Margaret. Isn't there some high-to-do ambassador of Fort Kotar in residence?"

"Yes. Although I wonder if the higher elevation and subsequent lack of oxygen robbed her daughters of a personality."

Marta's eyes go wide, blinking a few times before her mouth breaks into a smile, a few giggles escaping her. The sound briefly dispels my worry, it's tinkling melody like a rush of fresh air after I've been stuffed inside all day. She curtsies to me as I start to exit the room, dread for the next few hours filling me from top to bottom.

"Well, I must go start preparing for tonight," I tell her. Our small bubble of bliss pops at the statement. Marta's brows fold together, her eyes drooping at the edges.

"I will ring down for the cook to bring you a plate of freshly baked bread and a drizzle of honey to eat while you dress."

My chest warms. All the staff know of my infatuation with bread and honey. If it weren't for the growing ache in my gut, my mouth would already be watering with anticipation.

"Thank you, Marta," I reach to give her a hug, her body rigid and tense, still not used to the outward display of affection by a princess. But I've almost worn her down with my unorthodox approach to the servants. She softens into the embrace, even patting my back a few times before unwinding herself from my arms and smoothing out her rumpled skirt.

I leave Marta and the respite of the ballroom. The fatigue that prompted my early departure from afternoon tea has waned now that I've had a few minutes away from Lady Davenport's useless chatter. Perhaps I'll go to the kitchens myself, saving a trip from one of the servants and taking my mind away from the day.

I make my way down the stairs, shoes clicking on the white tiled floor with each step down before they turn into the muted stomp of wood underneath. The white abruptly switches to the browns that mark the definitive line of the staff's section of the palace.

The smell of cooking meat and bread fills the air as I reach the bottom of the staircase and turn the corner into the kitchen. It's a flurry of activity as they frantically put together tonight's event.

Shouting fills the space.

"I need eight eggs, Aretha!"

"Don't let that burn!"

"Coming in behind you!"

I dodge a couple elbows vigorously kneading their soon-to-be bread concoctions, moving back and forth as I walk around the massive center counter. Five women call the kitchen their home throughout the day, not to mention the countless scullery maids, butlers, and maids coming to fetch their query at their host's whims. Today they are one mind, working together to get everything completed.

The earthiness of wooden browns and the grays of a large stone oven contrast each other beautifully, making the kitchen one of my favorite places to visit, not to mention the fresh cookies made after breakfast each morning. A flurry of flour has settled in the air, its bitterness prompting me to keep my mouth closed as I walk through.

No sooner did I begin my search for the bowl of honey when I see Aunt Margaret standing in the back pantry. Her head is bent down, whether reading or praying I'm not sure. What would my aunt be doing down in the kitchens? Slowly, I move around the corner, trying my best to emanate the stealthy, human-sized cats I learned reside in Jadeya, moving just out of her line of sight.

"Did you miss me after I left today," I say, jumping out of a shadow.

She gasps, eyes wide and mouth agape. When Aunt Margaret sees me, she takes another deep inhale, smoothing her skirts, standing a little straighter than before as she turns to fully face me. Her widened eyes diminish to their normal size, and her stiffened body loosens again.

She takes her free hand to rub at her eyes. "I don't know why that brings you so much pleasure." Her eyes narrow at me, followed by a smile that matches my own. "Yes, yes. I missed you today. You left me with Lady-never-stops-talking and her tedious daughters, who seem to be having a competition on who can move the slowest."

"A lady rises above gossip and unnecessary, scandalous conversation," I reply, in the best impression I can do to mimic my aunt.

"Your sarcasm isn't earning you any favors. And I promise you, it was necessary to say." A long exhale escapes her.

My aunt has become one of my greatest confidants over the last few years. If it weren't for her, I'm not sure I would have any clue how to be a queen. Once she heard of Evander's passing, she cancelled all her planned visits as Ambassador of Felshan, and came to me almost straight away.

"With Evander gone the kingdom needs you, Lena. We need you to be strong. We need you to be brave. We need you to be more than you ever thought you could be until now," she told me, a hysterical ten-year-old little girl whose entire world was flipped upside down.

It would take another two years for her to convince my mother that I needed proper training as the newly appointed Crown Princess of Felshan. Of course, that didn't stop her from giving me lessons on the side, underneath the watchful gaze of my mother and father. Their anguish induced fragility just couldn't take seeing their young daughter fill the role of their lost son. If it weren't for the woman in front of me, the overwhelming burden of rising to rule a country would have been too great to bear. I shudder to think of where I would be without her.

Lady Margaret smiles at me. There's nothing I love more than seeing her break her own rules, poking fun at the boring trio my mother decided to invite as honored guests for tonight's events.

"It was unkind of you to call Roan a dog." My eyes are firm, but soft around the edges. I've never understood why she disliked him, and I wish they would find a way to make peace with one another.

"Yes. I suppose that was underhanded."

"Perhaps an apology when you see him next would be appropriate," I say, eyebrows raised.

"An apology? Please, Lena. Let's not be dramatic."

"It's not dramatic. It's right."

She takes a deep breath, one eyebrow raised while her lips press tightly together. "I'll think about it." I know that's the best I'll get from her, so I change the conversation.

"Tell me, Aunt Margaret. What brings the king's sister down to the dark hole of the kitchen pantries?" It is strange for her to be down here. She's not one to nab a newly baked pastry, nor is she in charge of the menu this evening.

She narrows her eyes at me as she decides what to say next. "Do I need a reason to be down here?" My aunt turns toward the door, peeking her head out and scanning from side to side before popping back in.

She's waiting for someone. I feel a bolt of delight at the idea. A lover, perhaps? I'm no fool to her beauty and strength, or the desires usually saved for marriage. It would be natural for her to have a love interest— even a secret one since she has never married.

It's strange to think of her this way. When my brother died, she turned into my shoulder to cry on, the kind words whispered for reassurance as I passed by, the one who went riding with me when I couldn't take any more of the constant crying of my mother, or the ghost that my father had become. The one who came and added the finishing touches to my outfits before dinner. All the things Evander and mother used to do.

Grief had turned everything backward, and Aunt Margaret did her best to right it again. She may not be the most affectionate woman, but there are wells within a woman's heart that run deep, often unseen by anyone except *the one*.

She senses my distraction, using it to her advantage. "It's getting late, and you need to go get ready. I can walk you back up and help you get dressed if you'd like."

I'm mentally preparing to ask about her mystery man when suddenly, a girl enters the room. I'm not sure I've seen her here before, but it's hard to tell without full light. There's a familiarity with her that I can't quite pinpoint.

Her light brown hair is tied neatly back into a braid that reaches midway down her back. She's wearing a dark blue maid's dress, but it doesn't fit her quite right. I don't know that she's the most beautiful woman I've ever seen, but she is certainly attractive. My brother would have definitely approved. Roan would approve. I tick my head to side, remembering how he'd teased me earlier about the handsome guard, Parker Aldren.

Suddenly the girl bends down, grabbing the hem of the dress and flinging it up over her head. I jump back, turning my face to shield my eyes at the scene before me. I stifle a gasp so as not to draw attention to our little pantry corner.

"Oh Ari, for heaven's sake. It's not that bad," my aunt whispers sharply, raising her hands in the air and shaking her head.

"I don't know how women wear these things all day!" the girl exclaims.

My eyes open when I hear her speak, spotting the blue dress crumpled on the floor. I expect to find her standing in her underclothes, but she's fully clad in an entirely different outfit.

As I stare at her more attentively, I realize *girl* isn't a great assessment of her. She can't be more than a couple years older than me, but definitely older as the sharp lines of her face boast the noticeable absence of the pudginess of youth. The way she holds herself brings an air of confidence and awe to the room. She is most definitely someone who's won her fair share of poker games, or fights, or both. Maybe brute strength isn't everything someone needs to take care of themselves on the streets of Turin.

Her green eyes remind me of summer dusk just before a storm, and I don't think I've ever seen a woman's figure so perfectly accentuated by dark, slim pants— a light colored shirt thickly belted at her waist. The room is quiet as I look up, her questioning eyes fixed on me.

"Marg, who is this?" the brown-haired girl— or woman— says pointing in my direction with a jut of her chin. Did she just call her Marg? Lady Margaret, sister of the king, reduced to the simplistic tag of *Marg*. My eyes widen, waiting for the trenchant response from this stern high lady. But nothing comes.

"She was just leaving." My Aunt gives me a nudge toward the door. "I will be up in a bit, Lena."

"But—" I try and resist before the door closes in my face. I stand there a moment longer trying to make sense of what just happened.

Perhaps more goes on in this palace than any of us truly know.

4

THE THIEF

EVERYONE HAS A TELL. When they lie, I know it.

Could be lack of eye contact. Moving too much or fidgeting. A tilting of the face. A fluttering of the eyes.

"Who was that?" I ask Marg, a short silence following my question.

"One of my lady's maids. No one of importance."

For Lady Margaret of House Chattan, it's the most minuscule pause before she speaks the falsehood. She always commands authority in her words, having an answer for everything. That brief pause before she spoke, the split-second war with herself to come up with an answer, is all I need.

The girl isn't her lady's maid. I'm not sure why she doesn't want to tell me the truth, but I'm used to only hearing what I need to know. I can't imagine a random girl having much importance in my future, so I let it go.

"Alright then," I say, more to myself than anyone else. "You have something for me today?"

Marg wastes no time. "Yes. Have you seen this man before?" She holds up a drawing of an older, somewhat haggard gentleman in what I decide is a black velvet jacket, his eyes and hair similarly dark. Recognition slams into me, a snarl rising up my throat. Sir Reynauld. The sound of the reverberating slap and smell of his rancid breath on my face takes the stage once again as I relive those moments from earlier this afternoon.

Of course I've seen him many times before today and have wished for the time he'd show up on Marg's list. I am her eyes and ears within the capital of Turin, following the whispers of the people and investigating anything that feels questionable— anything that makes the hum in my chest stir.

Sometimes Marg gives me something to fish around for, other times I use my instincts to take me where I need to be. And I've been drawn to Reynauld many times over.

She can see the flicker of familiarity on my face as I stare at his picture. "Good," Marg replies before I even have the chance to speak.

I look up from the drawing to meet her gaze. "If the job is to end this guy, I'll have it done before morning," I say flatly, trying to hide my pernicious excitement. I've already proven I can get a leg up on Reynauld, the ghost of his purse weighing down my pocket. But I keep today's success to myself.

Paid thugs and petty thieves do most of his dirty work. His crimes can't be overtly traced back to him, keeping him clean and untouchable. Until now it seems.

"Oh, no. No, no. There will be none of that. Good gracious. He's a cousin of Lady Davenport," she states, as if I know who that is. Marg looks a little annoyed as she continues. "With relations completely cut with Thenstra, we get almost all of our ore, coal, and precious stones from the Kotar Mountains. Killing off a beloved cousin of Lady Davenport wouldn't be in the best interest of Felshan," she says.

Damn Lady Davenport and her precious commodities.

"I mean, as satisfying as that would be for pretty much everyone in this country," Marg continues, her eyes open but focused somewhere else. She nods her head, probably imagining the good that would come from killing such a man. "We can't hurt him. Not yet anyway. I need more proof of what he's doing." She rubs the back of her exposed neck, her hair weaved perfectly together high upon her head, before bringing her hands together in front of her.

"I've been following him for some time, and the reports of his unscrupulous nature could fill the thickest book in the library. Things he, or his lap dogs, have done, but nothing concrete. Mostly rumors. And upon questioning, nobody ever pins it back on him. They claim they acted alone or were paid from some mysterious stranger. Desperate people taking desperate jobs to survive. I need something that sticks to him. *Directly*."

I know even before she stops speaking that this will be the easiest job on my conscience, and one I will take great delight in carrying out. Whatever Marg says to do, I do. But not because I only have half a brain and don't know how to think for myself. Not even because she pulled me from the streets after my mother died, saving me from the hell that awaits most destitute children alone with nowhere to go. It's not like my mother and I weren't already suffering before Marg. One day the sun stopped shining and winter came to everyone in Turin.

I say yes because I want these people, the ones who closed their doors to us, to know the pain of an empty stomach. To never quite be warm enough. To know what it's like watching everyone and everything you love get dragged away— all because you simply wanted to live.

"I will give you food, a warm bed, and place to stay. I will teach you everything I know," Marg told me. "You will become the hand of justice this country needs. And in return, you will work for me until your debt is paid. You will give me your life, and with that, you will save the lives of the people of Turin, maybe even all of Felshan."

Marg also gave me Prue, the most beautiful horse I'd ever seen, which made my *yes* almost imminent. Except for one thing.

"Will I have to work with the Guard?" I asked.

"The Guard?" she questioned, confused. "No, I can't say that you will." She looked at me like she wanted more, but I gave her no other context. That information was for me alone.

"Then, I'm in," I said. My motivations at the time may not have been Turin's survival, but I came around once I saw men like Reynauld all but running this city.

Marg probably thought a half-starved, half-frozen young girl with nowhere to go was an easy yes. And it was, except that *yes* wasn't because of her promise of food and shelter. What she promised me was to become the hand of justice— a hand I had once desperately needed, and didn't get. I would be able to hurt the people that hurt me.

And I have. I didn't become a monster, killing all those who wronged me in a streak of vengeance. But I became something better. Something more. I became the shadows. The darkness that once hid corruption became the shining blaze of truth under my hand. Marg knew Felshan needed more, someone who could work outside the lines of integrity and law. She found me, and together the country has gone from failing miserably after the death of their prince, to decently surviving.

Anytime I bring up the apathetic king and queen, Marg just glares at me and tells me to mind my own business. It feels like the country has been trapped in amber, awaiting a princess we hardly know to take the throne and, hopefully, fix the broken pieces of this land— permanently.

Princess Adalena is to marry some wealthy lord's son I never bothered to learn the name of, and together change the depressing trajectory of Felshan.

"Ari, do you understand?" Marg says, pulling me from my thoughts.

"Reconnaissance only. Got it." I nod to her, slightly annoyed that I won't get to extend some payback tonight on behalf of the people. Reynauld may not have directly hurt me and my mother, but his web of exploitation is a large part of why Turin can't seem to recover, and why the people are still suffering.

"Ari..." Marg eyes me, waiting for my compliance.

"I promise. I won't touch him until you give me the word," I say, the annoyance hard to keep out of my voice.

"It could be problematic if he comes crawling to the palace tomorrow, demanding an audience to say I sent someone to harass him. Or worse— he shows up dead, and it somehow links back to you, and therefore, me."

I stare back at her. "If he shows up dead you'll at least know he deserved it," I quip back.

"No, Ari. He isn't some random guard that comes up missing and nobody cares. Or some low-life bully you just don't like so you make him disappear. His business employs half the city. He has people who will know he's gone and will make us pay for it. Unless we have proof of illicit behavior. This one has to be taken through the proper channels. It will end badly for Felshan if you don't do this one right." She stares me down until I take a step back with both arms raised in subjugation.

"You win," I say, disappointment eating away at my earlier excitement. "I'll stick to the orders, and I won't harm Reynauld until you tell me to."

"*If* I tell you to."

"If... If you tell me to." I wink at her, her hard eyes not softening to the sarcastic gesture.

"Let's go, before anyone else sees you," she says.

"Oh Marg, haven't you paid the kitchen off already?"

"No need to take chances that aren't necessary." Her eyes dart toward the door before she reaches her hand toward me, gripping a small cloth sack. I take it and weigh it in my hands, instantly knowing what it contains. Yes, I want the country to thrive once again. But I'm no saint. I still need to eat.

She gave me one more *I'm serious* look before walking out the door.

I follow suit, not bothering to pick up the too-tight dress of my previous disguise.

I turn left out of the pantry, swiping a berry tart from the counter on my way down the back stairs and out the side door. It is warm against my lips as I take a bite, savoring the sweet sensation of ripe spring berries popping against my teeth.

If only all of life could be so sweet.

5

THE CAPTAIN

"**A**H, SIR REYNAULD," I say, walking up to him with my hand out-stretched. A wagon passes behind him, a few crates stamped with *Turin Coastal Company* stacked in the bed.

His estate isn't the most grand I've ever witnessed, but I know this is only one of several residences in his name. The home rests on a few acres of land, with a good size stable, a small warehouse for his many businesses, and a bunkhouse for traveling employees.

"Captain," he returns, eyes beginning to narrow as he reaches out to shake my hand. "So good of you to join us today. May I ask what the occasion is?"

I've been here mere moments and already I feel like I've just stepped onto an ant hill, but I'm not allowed to brush the tiny insects off of me. I can only stand here while they slowly crawl up my leg.

"I was able to meet your cousin, Lady Davenport." Reynauld nods his head as I speak. "She requested I aid you in a search for a thief."

"Oh yes, yes, yes. My little thief problem." He turns his head, gesturing a hand as if calling someone forward. "Jaren, that will be all for today."

A man with slicked back hair, a pinching nose, and dark eyes steps from behind Reynauld, irritation at my interruption evident on his face. At least that makes two of us. I don't want to be here any more than he wants me to be.

Reynauld turns to face the man now at his side, but the man doesn't move. A few long seconds pass, and I can't help but look between the two. From what I know of Reynauld I doubt this man's obstinance will be well tolerated.

A final, silent glare from Reynauld spurs the man forward. "Of course, Sir. I will see you later this evening." His superior makes no note of farewell as Jaren turns to leave. The man glowers at me, even daring to bump a shoulder into mine as he passes. A chortling sigh escapes me. I've met enough unfriendly pettiness in this city that it hardly fazes me anymore.

Reynauld turns, moving toward his stables. I assume I am to follow, although he says nothing nor gives me any kind of gesture to do so. I'm next to him in only a few large strides.

"Some of us struggle with authority more than others. I apologize for his rude behavior. It will be dealt with, I assure you," Reynauld tells me. "Now, as I was saying. I was in the market earlier today, and my purse was stolen right out from under me. It's difficult times indeed when you aren't quite sure if you'll return with everything you left with."

I eye him warily as he talks, his words dripping with counterfeit innocence. He sounds ridiculous, playing the victim. He's one of the wealthiest people in all of Turin. So many of our renowned blacksmith's are owned by Reynauld, and our famous steel has all but been monopolized by his power. A few missing coins mean nothing to him.

"It's definitely something the Guard is aware of—ensuring safety of person and property for *all* the citizens of Felshan is our highest priority." I give him a pointed look.

"You definitely have your work cut out for you. Since the king and queen took their *temporary* hiatus from country affairs." His sarcasm doesn't go unnoticed. "It seems everyone has become a victim of theft nowadays. I'm sure the monarchs want to remedy this as soon as possible."

It takes all my energy not to laugh in response to the hypocrisy he's peddling, or punch him square in the face for openly insulting Cassus and Amelia. Probably just testing my loyalty, picking at it each time we cross paths. If even one crack forms in a dam, it can be prodded and dug through until eventually the entire thing crumbles down. He will never get that satisfaction from me. This dam of loyalty will never crack.

It would be nice for him to have the Guard Captain on his side, doing business out in the open instead of jumping through time-consuming hoops to keep it hidden. If he weren't personally upholding the economy of Turin, bringing in more trade from his ties in the Kotar than any other citizen, and employing half the Turinian steel blacksmiths, the Guard would have raided his properties years ago.

Nobody ever knows exactly what he's been up to, never able to pinpoint his crimes in a way that our laws will uphold were he to be arrested. He's smart. He knows how to hide. And he has everybody so afraid of economic collapse that not even King Cassus will move against him.

"Well, that's why I'm here." I bow slightly, arms stretched out on either side. Reynauld purses his lips as he stares at me, clearly understanding my sarcastic gesture before he begins.

"I was at the market. There was a sack of coins in my satchel I was using to purchase a gift for my wife." His wife? I steel my face at the lie, stopping a loud scoff from rising to the surface. "I'm fairly certain it was a young girl bumping into me that did it. She was maybe eighteen or nineteen years old. Hit me just below my chin. Brown hair, the color of wet sand. Wearing a dark cloak and trousers."

"A cloak? And trousers?" I question.

"I thought it odd as well in heat such as this. Perhaps a guard, playing undercover tactics."

I laugh out loud this time. "A guard, stealing your money at the market-place?"

"Crazier things have happened," he says, straight-faced.

All seriousness has left my body, and the smile doesn't leave my face. "The only women currently under my command are stationed at Fort Frennin or Port Riga, at least a two days' journey from here if they rode all night on the fastest horse in Felshan. It was not one of mine."

"I'm not as convinced as you are. But if you say it wasn't one of yours, then it wasn't one of yours." A smirk crosses his face as he finishes speaking, his beady eyes like that of a rodent as he looks at me.

"I promise you. If the Royal Guard wanted to steal from you, it would be much less obvious than a young girl in trousers at the market."

"It sounds as if you've thought about it, Captain Montgomery."

"Never," I say, a grin giving away my real answer. "I do wonder though," I continue, "why you care so much about a single sack of coins. You seem to be doing quite well for yourself." I gesture with my hand around his home and estate. "I wonder why you'd put up such a fuss for a tiny bit of money."

In a rare moment, his facade drops. "It's the principle of it, *Captain*. That someone would steal from *me*." He speaks so forcefully I almost want to take a step back. But he straightens quickly and wipes at his jacket and sleeves, his mask returning with a single laugh. He reaches out and claps my shoulder. "I thought you of all people would understand that, as you deal with thieves all the time." I glance at his hand on my shoulder before angling myself back until his arm falls back to his side.

"How sure are you this girl is the one who took your money?" I ask, unable to hide my disdain.

He quickly closes the space yet again. "Very certain," he says sternly.

I eye him up and down. "Ok, so we're looking for a young woman, not tall and not short, brown hair. Trousers. Maybe wearing a cloak. Anything else?" I reply with a smile that doesn't reach my eyes, holding my ground this time.

"She's a malicious little witch who took enough to cover a week's worth of supplies. I want it all returned plus fifty percent. Or I want her prosecuted and thrown into prison." He turns away from me, giving me time to drop the act as dutiful captain and mimic my silent disgust in his direction.

"You know the law is ten percent," I respond.

"I want fifty."

"I don't control the amount owed in recompense, *Sir* Reynauld." I wait to finish until he turns to face me. "But I can find this girl. And if she took your money, it will be returned plus ten percent and a few nights lockup depending on how much she stole. As per the law," I state.

"Good enough I supposed," Reynauld concedes. I turn to leave, but he keeps talking. "I want to know as soon as the girl is found."

I chuckle quietly, but loud enough he catches the action. "Maybe you forgot Reynauld, but I'm not your employee." Just when I'm sure he will explode again I add, "I'll do my best to keep you informed, but promise nothing."

I dip my head in his direction, unable to keep the smirk from my face as I turn away. But my haughtiness fades once my back is turned.

As if having been underwater for too long, I take a deep breath once I'm out of eyeshot from his property, my body needing to clear out any remnants of the acrid air surrounding Sir Reynauld.

Now off to find some random girl with nothing to go on except she's wearing pants. As much as I don't care if Sir Reynauld's money is returned, the distraction is most welcome— something to keep my mind occupied, even if it will be utter misery.

I suppose I deserve all the misery this day will bring.

6

THE THIEF

MY BODY HUMS AS the sun disappears on the horizon.

I circle around the property, staying in the shadows of the trees until dark. Evening finishes its final transition to night as yellow and orange clouds streak into darker blues and purples. *Perfect*.

I saw Reynauld leave with his entourage over an hour ago, and no one has come or gone since. Like most of the city, they're probably headed to Prince Evander's commemoration, which means he won't be back for a few more hours at least.

I make my way from the cover of the tree line and down to the stables. I'm about to duck over to the house when I see something on the back of the property— a small, box-like structure from what I can make out. Could it be a second stable? A warehouse of sorts? On a hunch, I abandoned my original trail and make a dash for the outlying building. Even though the sun has set, warmth rushes to my cheeks. The thrill of the chase never seems to dim.

I slow my steps as I come up to the last thirty paces or so. A small barn, left to be swallowed by the limbs of the forest, stands in front of me. A couple windows scatter across the side, and after a few attempts to open them, I discover they are all locked.

A quick look around shows I'm alone, at least on the side that sits exposed against the back of the property. I move around the building until I make a complete circle of the plot, showing nothing but empty space and abandoned greenery.

My cheeks warm again, the hum of a racing heart filling my ears. The hair stands up on the back of my neck as I move to check the door handle. Everything is screaming at me to turn and run, to abandon my impulsive curiosity. But like a boulder rolling down the mountainside, once I'm set in motion nothing can stop me. My need to know what lies within is too compelling.

My hand moves of its own volition, twisting the handle until I hear the satisfying *click* of the now open door.

"Now, what do we have here?" a deep voice booms behind me. I turn quickly, bending in one fell swoop as I pull the knife from my boot and raise it in front of me, crouching to attack if necessary.

"Oh, come now. There's no need for that," the strange man says, holding up both hands as he walks toward me. It's not Reynauld. My stiffened body releases some of the tension as I make the realization. My cover isn't blown. *Yet.*

We make eye contact briefly as I assess the man. He's a decent size. Tall, but not like the men of Venes. Strong jaw, clean shaven. Dark hair from what I can see, but it could just be darker from the night. His muscular build is defined in the moonlight as he moves out of the screen of the bushy tree-line. His thick arms and legs don't escape my notice. I suppose this ruffian could hold his own in a fight if one presented itself to him.

But I only smile. While strength may be, well, his strength, strong men usually don't run or move quickly. Hence why a girl with my frame doesn't have to count herself out from a win with a man like this.

He still moves with both hands raised before deciding to plop himself on a large rock, finishing his monologue. "So what brings a girl," I glower at him, "excuse me, woman, to this stretch of Sir Reynauld's property?"

I say nothing, listening for anyone else in the bushes or trees, watching for any sudden moves to charge at me. He looks at my pants, down to my boots, then moves his gaze up to my face. A pair of piercing blue eyes stare back at me. I've seen those blue eyes before— the guard, or troll, from earlier today.

"Pants tend to be an unusual choice for a woman," he says. "Not that I have anything against pants, you see. I love my pants. Don't go anywhere without them." He pats both hands on his legs, effectively drawing my attention. Who is this man? Is he really talking about pants when I have a weapon aimed straight for his heart?

My breathing is shallow as my gaze takes in my surroundings once more, searching for something— anything. To my left is wide open space, out to the stables and to the estate further down. I can hear and see nothing from that direction. I dare a glance to my right and into the trees.

"Don't worry. No one is in there," he says, gesturing toward the surrounding forest. "I do have a fellow further back, but he won't come unless signaled. I'm not even sure he can see me to be honest. So really, it's just you and me here, talking and getting to know each other." A smile lights up his face.

I falter for just a moment as I take in that smile before hurriedly masking my face back into disdain. No one is this friendly to someone they just saw breaking into someone else's property.

I make a few slow movements. My mind is drawn in the direction of the stables and further away from this man, but my feet don't want to leave. Prue is grazing on a small patch of grass just a few strides into the forest behind the stables. If I could just get to her...

"Oh, let's not do anything irrational." He stands from his rock and takes a step in my direction, both hands raised once again as if he's trying not to spook a large bear. I suppose he's not wrong— my bite is just as lethal. "We're just talking. Let's start with something simple— I don't even know your name."

Still I say nothing. "Ok let me start. I'm Roan. I'm a guard in the capital, and I've been sent to help the man who owns this property uncover a thief." A guard. He *is* the one from earlier today. A snarl rises up my throat.

"Thieves are tricky to find. Especially ones who don't want to be found." My eyes narrow before I continue. "Especially wealthy ones, like the man who owns this property."

He nods as if considering my words before clasping his hands behind his back and taking another step toward me. I reply in kind with a step further away. His smile fades to a thin line as he sees me moving back, our eyes still locked. "Why don't you sit down and let me ask you a couple questions before you go? I simply want to know if you've seen anyone else around here. Any other women, perhaps, wearing pants?" There's a gleam in his eye. Is he willing me to run? I could stay and fight my way out of this, and Turin would be short one more guard. *Good riddance.*

But I hesitate. I've never met this man, this guard, before today. But it feels like I know him somehow. Not the kind of knowing that comes with a direct introduction. But the kind of knowing that comes when I find the perfect spot to watch the sunset, and I don't want to leave. Or when the first green of spring makes its debut, and the cold finally melts away to the warming seasons.

In my curious daze, I miss the couple steps he takes in my direction, closing the space between us.

Just before he reaches me, I dig both feet into the ground and run.

7

THE CAPTAIN

T HE GIRL IS DISTRACTED. I want to think she's as distracted by me as I am of her.

Is this really the thief Sir Reynauld is looking for? This girl, or woman, can't be much younger than me. She isn't delicate by any means. I can tell by her stance and quick draw of her blade that she's had training. Her instincts, from what I can see, are honed like the sharp end of a sword. But something about her, something I can't quite point to, doesn't fit the spiteful person who Reynauld described.

It's hard not to look at her with admiration. She hurt Reynauld in a way I've never had the ability to do. I can't help but wonder what would drive a young woman such as her to risk herself against one of the most powerful men in the city.

Pieces of hair have come loose from her braid. They frame her face like a repoussoir guiding me to take in her full intensity, her focus resting solely on me, and her features made even more fierce within the shades of night. For just a moment all words, all judgment, all reason have become frozen inside of me.

Never have I had to keep to my training so intently before. I've battled men twice my size without hesitation, without acquiring so much as a scratch— but here I am. Roan Montgomery, Captain of the Guard. Bested by a woman half his size without her even having to lift a finger.

I blink away my stupor, attempting to remember my purpose once again. I need to keep her talking so I can get closer to her, but I can't tell if I'm getting closer to soak up more of her or try and capture her for questioning. Either way, my feet are moving.

I keep my eyes focused straight ahead, not giving away my second in command this evening, Aiden Gothery, who I left behind as lookout after we spotted someone running across the property. This girl.

She looks me up and down, not returning the conversation. How desperately I want to hear her voice...

Pull yourself together, Roan. This is a mark just as any other— most likely the thief I've been searching for. And she needs to be held accountable for her actions, even if it's on behalf of a man like Sir Reynauld. I've seen pretty women before. Just keep talking, keep her distracted, move forward, and everything will be fine.

I see my window when her gaze turns distant, and I lunge. But her focus snaps back before I can reach her. She maneuvers out of my grasp, her form fading into the darkness as swiftly as an arrow glides to its target.

I loathe to run, dread already filling me. But I spur myself into action nonetheless. I signal Aiden to follow, hoping he can see me through the dark. Maybe he can intercept her from the other direction. Because I don't know how she's doing it, but she's beating me— badly. I was one of the fastest recruits in my year, yet she's making me look like a child. I don't know whether to be impressed or upset that my pride has taken such a hit. My legs move as fast they can go, but she still hits the tree line a few paces ahead of me. Did Reynauld ever stand a chance once she set her sights on him?

As I finally duck into the foliage, I can't see anything. The illumination from the moon is swallowed up in the leaves and branches overhead. I keep moving though, following the sound of crunching leaves and panting breaths.

A whinny sounds in the distance. A horse nearby. Her horse. *Must move faster.*

I drive for one last burst of speed before pushing through to nothingness. A small clearing lies before me.

Her horse is tied up on the edge, the silver hue of moonlight accentuating the girl's movements as she pulls the reins free of a nearby tree and grabs the saddle to swing herself up. I run, reaching both arms out to stop her, crashing headfirst into the girl.

We fall together, an entanglement of limbs under the open night sky.

8

THE THIEF

MY BODY HITS THE ground hard, the breath completely knocked out of me. The panic of not being able to breathe grips me tightly. Somehow I pick myself up from the forest floor before I can mindfully make the decision, ready for whatever comes next.

The guard is up before my lungs can recover enough to take a full breath. I search him up and down for close range weapons. No sword. Maybe a knife hidden in his belt or boot. I keep my eyes forward, my dagger still clutched in my own hands.

I find my ground, my feet steady, even though my breathing is still hot and heavy. The words from Marg's training hit me: *You won't win without structure. Quiet the panic. Quiet the chatter. Calm your heart. Calm your breath. Trust yourself, and you will win them all.*

My focus returns as I take my first full breath since this man, easily a head taller than me and at least fifty percent more bulk to his form, plowed straight into me. He stands unmoving, chest heaving, his eyes locked on a single target— me.

He breaks the silence. "I'm sorry, but I need to ask you some questions. And since you don't seem to want to talk out here," he gestures to the woods around us, "I'm going to have to bring you with me."

I smile at his statement. I'm not going anywhere, nor do I have any plans on answering his questions. He glances around the clearing, his eyes searching. What is he looking for? My smile falters as his words come back to me. *I do have a fellow further back, but he won't come unless signaled.*

My focus darts to the trees, searching for a sound, a movement, anything. But only silent stillness greets me. If he's telling the truth, the *fellow* clearly can't find where we are after our chase through the woods. Otherwise I would have a rope tied around me by now.

If the guard was telling the truth.

There are only moments left to shake this man, grab Prue, and get the hell out of here. I spring in his direction before I can finish another thought, my mind and heart steady. His confusion melts into unblunted discipline, his instinct and training meeting my own.

I jab left, then right. He ducks, and both shots miss. He brings a fist to my side as I circle back and out of the way of the blow. My leg swings high as I twist around, but not high enough to meet his head. It's a direct kick to his shoulder and arm, but from what I can see, he doesn't even wince.

Trust yourself, and you will win them all.

We go again. A quick block deflects his swinging fist, but he pulls back effortlessly, his form still unwavering. He's pulling his punches, not aiming to hurt me. Is he afraid I can't take it? Do I look that fragile?

I falter for a moment. He can fight, I'm certain of that. The way he moves— he's not just some dumb guard. There's practice here. Skill even.

We circle each other for a few breaths, both of us unsure, maybe even slightly perplexed by the other. But I lock my curiosity away. Whatever his motives are, I'm not sticking around to find out. I swing another kick from the left side, high enough this time to connect with his jaw. He pivots, opening up his right side just enough for me to swing my elbow around. He grunts as it sinks into his side.

As I turn to face him an arm reaches around me, grabbing and gripping me tightly. "I just want to talk," he says through ragged breaths.

I curse under my breath. He purposefully opened himself up to be hit, and I hate that I fell for it. I bring my knee up to connect between his legs— just enough to break his concentration so I can get away. He lets go of my waist to catch my incoming knee, seeing its path and intention. In that single motion of deflection he grabs underneath my leg, pulling hard and landing me on my back.

I roll as he tries to land on top of me, threatening to pin me down with his weight. My leg hooks behind his neck. His size is definitely his advantage on the ground. He rolls to the side before I can swing my other leg to push him away, instead pinning me to the ground. If he makes it all the way over, I will be vulnerable for a severe beating. Or worse, tied up and taken to wherever he will question me.

I'm not afraid of this man, or Reynauld for that matter. But freedom is definitely superior to a black eye and broken ribs, or a quiet room with prodding eyes. I release my leg from his neck, kicking him hard in the chest with the heel of my foot. I smile as he grunts hard and falls back.

"Your size has always been your advantage," I whisper down to him as I move to my knees, a trickle of sweat beading down my back.

He's clutching his chest like I actually made a dent. *Good.* I have only a few breaths to stand up, jump on Prue and ride out of here before he comes to, or before his hidden man follows the grunts and bursts through the trees and joins our little soirée.

But I'm frozen. For whatever reason, I can't leave just yet. Maybe it's pride or sheer hatred, or something else entirely, but I kneel down, one leg straddling his waist as my other burrows into the dirt preparing to spring.

My hand digs into his shirt, grabbing a fistful before I open my mouth to speak.

"But not when you fight someone who has spent her entire life learning how to pave her way against strength and power." His eyes bore into mine. A sliver of moonlight reflects their urgency, a question lurking there. I stare, getting lost as I search for the answer, missing when his gaze snaps into a determined focus.

Before I know it, I'm thrown on my back again. Both arms are bound at my stomach in his grip, and his legs are firmly hooking mine.

"You think you're the only one who's spent their life learning how to use other people's strengths against them." He looks down at me. "If it wasn't for my mesmerizing face, you may have actually won this one," he quips, looking a little too smug with himself.

I roll my eyes, making sure the dramatics show my disdain. "Your face is as mesmerizing as the bottom of my horse," I choke out, trying to get my arms free from his grip, but failing miserably. He's trying to tire me through my struggle. But my anger at losing to someone so obviously winnable is giving him exactly what he wants.

His hands are warm against the cooling night air, a prickling sensation moving across my entire body. He's staring at me now, and I cease my struggle. There are no words and no movement between us. His dark hair falls into his face, swaying in the light breeze weaving through the air. If my hatred of the guard didn't run so deep, I may even take this time to admire his handsome face.

Instead I close both eyes, saving my energy as I lie still under his weight.

9

THE CAPTAIN

HER GAZE IS SWIRLING as I look at her, my weight the only thing keeping her small frame in place. A stray strain of violet rests in the color of her eyes, the shade of night reflecting what must normally be a vibrant whorl of greens. She struggles against me before going still, her eyes closing. The longer I touch her, the more it feels an invisible string is knitting my hands to her skin.

The crunching of leaves in the distance signals that Aiden has finally found us. He walks into the clearing, panting and wide-eyed at the scene laid before him. "I'm sorry. It took me a moment to figure out where you ran."

"Aiden. Impeccable timing," I say, nodding in gratitude and acknowledgement toward my subordinate before looking back to the girl underneath me.

Her face is now devoid of emotion— once as curious and lit up as my own, it now seems passive and indifferent. Our eyes meet again briefly. Her impassivity reaches everywhere but those eyes. I don't know what I see there, but suddenly I wish Aiden was anywhere but here. A part of me feels drawn to follow this thief to the end of the world if she asked it, and the ridiculousness of it nearly causes me to double over with laughter.

"Do you have any rope on you?" I ask, purposefully breaking away from our unspoken tether.

"I have enough to tie her hands," he responds, grabbing a piece of rope he had knotted from his shoulder, across his chest, and down to his waist.

Seeing the rope breaks through the strange hold on me, bringing my senses back on board. "I'm not sure that will be enough. But perhaps between the two of us, we can get this young lady back to the grounds."

Aiden walks over to me, bending down to bind the woman. I hold both her hands together while he ties the rope around and in between her wrists. She continues to stare, silently watching me as Aiden binds her hands. Something about her blank face feels more fearsome than if she was openly enraged.

I check that my legs are still firmly over her own so she can't knee me between the legs or somehow get them up around my neck again. I'm still impressed by that last move she pulled. It's hard not to be.

I've seen it a couple times during training exercises in the northeast, but I've never seen another recruit master that level of flexibility before. Did she train in Jadeya at some point? She looks Felshanian, but with as little as I know about her, I'm not taking it off the table just yet.

My curiosity is fully piqued. Her skin burns under my touch, and I realize I'm smothering her as I try to keep her contained. I lean back, giving her ample space to breath, free from what must have felt much like a stone atop her chest.

Aiden finishes tying the rope, and I slowly release her hands and lift my legs off her own one at a time. We each take a side, a hand under each arm, lifting her from the ground. She's sturdier than she looks. I much expected her weight to mimic that of a lone feather. There must be more muscle forged in her frame than her clothes expose. Color rises to my cheeks at the thought, the inappropriateness of what her clothes do and don't expose.

I inhale deeply, allowing composure and logic to return. "We are simply looking for a thief who stole from Sir Reynauld at the market. After we've questioned you and cleared your name, you're free to go," I tell her.

"And if I am the thief in question?" she asks.

I give a sideways glance in her direction. Is she admitting to it? I gesture toward her horse, and we begin walking the short distance.

"If you are the thief, you will be commissioned to return what was stolen to Reynauld plus ten percent, and maybe a few nights in Turin's jail. If you can't return what was stolen, you spend more time locked up, based on how much was taken, plus some kind of recompense for the person you stole from. Some kind of work and labor toward the bereft, left to the discretion of the Court."

"What if what was taken wasn't Reynaulds to begin with?" she asks. Everytime she speaks I wish she'd say more, her mystery quickly becoming something I want to unravel. I look at Aiden who raises an eyebrow and gives the slightest shrug.

"Can you prove that it wasn't?" I respond.

"Can you prove it was?" She stops and looks up at me as we reach the horse. She's smart. Most would give any information they could to a guard. But she seems more determined to fight me than anything, whether with fists or with words. I tense at our close proximity, trying hard to shut down my undesired delight.

I'm betrothed to the princess. It's Lena my heart belongs to.

But even as I think the words, the lie sinks low in my gut. There's no romantic love between us. I've tried to unwind her own feelings, and as far as I can tell, the platonic feeling is mutual. It has been easy up to this point to keep myself focused on my job and my future, to keep women and love at a distance— but my body wants to get closer to the girl next to me. I find myself wanting to know more about her, to ask questions and uncover the riddle that encompasses this thief.

"Why would you defend Sir Reynauld? He embodies all the things that are wrong with this world. Why help such a man?" There's real pain beneath her words, allowing me, I decide, a rare glimpse beneath her cloak of indifference and her impenetrable exterior.

The torment I feel that she believes me capable of condoning this vile man's actions, someone who would try and thwart those who would fight against his cruelty, feels deeply unsettling. There's more to it, I want to tell her. No honorable person would side with Reynauld, least of all me. My debt to the kingdom, to the king and queen, is the only thing that moves any cooperation forward with that man.

I help him because his family brings in half the wealth of the country, and without it this land would crumble. I do his bidding at the request of the queen, because she's on shaky ground after breaking the betrothal between Lena and Lady Davenport's son. Amiable ties with the Kotarans are a necessity if Felshan is to have any sort of future.

The words fall flat against my throat before I can even open my mouth to speak them. I know it's not enough, the explanation seeming like mere ramblings of a rich boy who wants to continue hoarding his gold. I want to make her see my side, to see how my hands are tied. But my lack of response sets her lips firmly together, the fortress of her mind shut tight once again.

I turn to Aiden. "I will stay here with Miss..." I trail off, waiting for her to fill in the blank. She looks forward, her expression blank once again. Ok—not going to get her name tonight. I try not to feel a little disappointed. "I will stay here with the prisoner. You go grab our horses, and we'll tie this one up," I nod to her horse, "behind Red. The girl can ride back to the palace barracks with me," I say, looking towards the thief.

"Yes," Aiden says, nodding once before running back into the trees. The girl and I are alone together once again.

"If you give me more information while we wait, I might be able to help you once we return to the palace. If you cooperate, I could convince the jailer to spring for a nicer cell as we sort all of this out." It's meant as a joke, but her blank expression shows just how far it missed the mark.

A defeated smile appears to cross her lips, completely devoid of humor. "You are all the same."

"Who is all the same?"

"Guards. Royalty. Anyone with power to control the life of another. To make the rules."

"And what, exactly, is the same?"

Her gaze moves to meet mine, a fire rising beneath the emptiness. "You want what you want, detached from the truth. As long as your pockets and egos remain full. You don't care about the people you trample to get high up on your pedestal. You just want to get it done and over with so you can move on to your cushioned seats, expensive wines, and beautiful women at your every beck-and-call."

"If someone is guilty, don't they deserve to be punished?" I ask, trying to remain calm. Part of me understands her frustration and distrust, the other part of me is loyal to the job and title bestowed upon me.

"But the process of finding guilt is biased. It's always guilty until proven innocent. You don't have any idea if I took whatever it is this moron says I took. But I'm guilty nonetheless." She motions with her restrained hands, unable to sweep her arms out in her frustration.

"Did you take what I think you took?"

She stops and looks at me. "Maybe."

"Yet you are trying to argue the moral high-ground?"

"Yes. Because if I did take it, it would be for a very good reason. A reason anyone and everyone should be concerned about, no matter their status. But no one cares. Or at least, no one is willing to care. To take a dip in their coffers." Even in the dark, I see the blood rising to her cheeks. "It's all good when the people you lock up are the poor ones. The ones that can hardly put food on the table and keep their kids alive. No one puts up a fight. You put the *guilty* in prison *where they belong*." Her sarcasm rings through the night.

"But what about the wealthy ones? The ones no one wants to look at? Because if they are the culprit, it won't be so cut and dry. The wealthy in jail will cause a rift in the system. It will mean a shift, a change— and no one wants to deal with the rift if the wealthy are found guilty." She is breathing hard and heavy once she finishes, her indignation clear as her chest dramatically rises and falls. "And most of them are," she whispers.

I can feel a knock at a familiar door in my mind. The door that holds all the questions I never get to ask. And now in my position, I don't want to ask. This country is my home. The king and queen, and Princess Lena— they are my family. I protect my family. And now that I'm going to be marrying Lena in only a few months, I feel the familiar swirl of dizzying confusion and loyalty.

Logically, I know this girl doesn't deserve the explosion building in me, but the more I try and hold it back the more I can't seem to stop it. "It's easy to blame everyone else but yourself, isn't it? I'm not saying the rich shouldn't distribute more of what they have. But that isn't a pass to accuse innocent people, and excuse yourself of misdeeds simply because someone *deserves* it."

My emotions, once again running unchecked, have gotten the better of me. I barely know this girl, yet she knows exactly how to push me.

"Thank you for making it so easy to hate you, sir," she declares through gritted teeth, yet her voice seems oddly devoid of its previous anger.

"I don't care if you hate me," I say, a shiver running through my hand as I grab her arm and nudge her forward. Sometime during our yelling match we stopped to face each other, our caged and careful rage hitting each other full-force.

She stands her ground, refusing to budge. "I can carry you if you'd prefer," I declare, and grab her arm more forcefully.

Before I know what's happening, my legs are out from under me, and I'm staring at the bits of night sky I can make out through the thick forest above. I scramble to my feet just in time to see her dash away into the trees. The rope from her hands lies on the ground at my feet, trampled underneath me as I take off after her. Admiration is again tugging at the corner of my mind, but my frustrations snuffs it away. How in the Four Kingdoms did she untie her hands without me knowing?

"Aiden!" I scream, but in the dark and cover of trees, I know my scream is futile.

So is the subsequent, "Stop!" and, "come back!" I yell after the fleeing thief. She doesn't strike me as the type to cower in fear that I can simply yell loudly.

I chase after her fading form, moving in the direction from which we just came. A few branches claw at my face as I sprint through the foliage, hard enough that I know thin welts will soon form in their place. I trip on a thick tree root at some point, cutting and bruising my knee as I land on a rock.

Her path follows a winding circle. Why is she leading me back to the clearing? What are you doing little thief?

Realization dawns on me like a brutal punch to the stomach—her horse. How could I be so stupid? She wouldn't leave her horse. I dig in my heels, another burst of speed propelling me forward, turning to retrace my steps as I attempt to hit the tiny meadow first.

I'm smarter this time, keeping my arms up to ward off stray branches, keeping my eyes on the ground to avoid rocks and roots. I hear a whinny not too far ahead. One last boost of energy has me break through, just in time to see her mount the horse.

"Wait!" another bellow from me as I keep running toward her. I know she won't stop, but maybe just hesitate enough for me to catch up or for Aiden to get here.

"Maybe next time, guard," she calls to me, her victory glimmering in the moonlight. "Yah!" she yells atop her horse before the beast spurs into action, taking off through the trees. My feet stop mid-run, my burning lungs gulping for air.

All I can do is stare after her. She got away. I'm not going to wake from a dream. Roan Montgomery, Captain of the Guard, thwarted by a petty thief.

My breathing begins to steady as I hear Aiden calling. "Captain? Captain!"

"I'm here!" I yell back, shutting my open jaw as I walk in his direction.

He comes through the trees. "I couldn't bring both horses. The trees are too dense." Red follows close behind him. He looks around, realizing I'm alone.

"Yes. I know. She's gone," I say. Aiden raises an eyebrow. With the energy of the last few minutes finally wearing off a laugh bubbles up my throat, the shock still not planting me back to reality.

"She got away. I don't even know how." Another chuckle. Aiden just stares, looking as if I just crossed the threshold of madness. His brow wrinkles, concern pulling his face inward.

I hardly notice Aiden at all as I replay the night's events, piecing together a mystery that doesn't want to be solved. Somewhere along that puzzle is my earlier admiration for the thief who bested Reynauld, now having bested me as well, along with the clear thought of *what in Haythen just happened*— all mixing together to create the brilliant pot of perceived madness that Aiden now sees in me.

As much as I try and stop, the laughing continues. "Wow. We had our work cut out for us, and we didn't even know it."

"What happened?" asks Aiden.

"Really, I'm not even sure. One minute we were yelling about moral high-grounds, and the next I was on my back while she took off into the forest."

"She got out of the rope?"

"Yes." I reach my hand for Red as he nuzzles into me, grounding me and slowing the laughter. "She circled back around for her horse and took off."

A few moments of silence pass. "That was a huge fail, Captain," Aiden says, A single raised eyebrow relaying my thoughts at his obvious conclusion.

"A huge fail," I return, clapping him on the shoulder. She got through me, in more ways than one.

My amusement turns to icy determination. "Now that we know what she looks like, let's go catch us a thief."

10

THE PRINCESS

T HE EVENING'S EVENTS ARE passed in almost complete silence, except for the lone member of the kitchen staff who saved us from the heat of the night with a sweet, fruit infused drink. Roan stumbles onto the balcony just as my parents move to start without him.

Aunt Margaret gives an annoyed huff, dramatically folding her arms to further relay her distaste for the delay.

Roan smiles in response to her unhappy sentiment, turning toward my parents and each of us in turn. "Apologies, King Cassus, Queen Amelia, Lady Margaret, Princess Lena. There was a matter that needed attending to." He shuffles to my side, his hair disheveled and clothes tousled.

"We understand," my father says, weariness having a constant pull at his features.

Roan plants his feet by my own, his arm brushing up against my mine. "Late? It's so unlike you," I whisper nudging him gently with my elbow.

The corners of his mouth tick up ever-so-slightly. "You know how I love to make an entrance."

"Is everything... ok?" My eyes flash to his, trying to read any hint of what he's not going to tell me.

"It is." His lips are a firm line, his muscles tense.

He releases a heavy breath before gently taking my arm and weaving it through his own. I try not to flinch as he touches me. It's the gentlemanly thing to do, of course, to take my arm in his. A few years ago I wouldn't have batted an eye at the gesture. But now? Everything we're supposed to be to each other, betrothed and soon married—it's strange to associate my friend as anything other than, well, a friend.

"You look beautiful in green," he adds, his face softening as he takes in my appearance. My dress is simple yet elegant, as Mother likes to say. The neckline follows the curves of my chest, framed neatly by thin straps that lay just off my shoulders. The full skirt flows to the ground, a few large pleats adding texture to the smooth, lightweight fabric.

"A drink, sir?" says a servant walking from the far corner, holding up a tray to Roan, a lone cup resting on its shiny surface.

Roan eyes the tray. "I think the princess should go first, don't you?" The woman's eyes go wide.

"We already had our refreshment, Captain Montgomery. While we were waiting." I give as pleasant a look as I can muster, trying to unburden any guilt he might feel toward his lateness.

He nods his head. "Ah. Of course." He turns to the woman. "Thank you, miss. But I'm not thirsty." The woman continues to hold the tray up. Perhaps she doesn't understand.

"It's ok. You can take it away. Let whomever prepared it know it was delicious," I say, motioning her dismissal. She looks at me, seemingly flustered at his refusal. But after a few moments the servant simply nods, lowering the tray away and taking her place back in the corner.

My parents light the ceremonial lanterns, a thousand more dotting the ground below us in response. Roan bends down to our own with a long match, setting the wick inside ablaze and handing it to me before I release it into the abyss of the dark sky. My hands shake as I let it go, the tremor reaching through my arms and to my heart.

My friend stands beside me as we watch it float away. I dare a glance up to his face as the flickering glow trails through the sky. Flecks of dirt and pieces of twigs scatter throughout his hair, a brown smudge settled across his cheek. His lateness and somewhat haggard appearance leaves me with so many questions. I want to press him further about where he's been, but I know he will simply shrug and tell me not to worry. It seems nobody wants to speak the truth to me anymore. Not even Roan.

A tear escapes the corner of my eye. That single droplet holds so much— my stinging resentment of the role I must play in my brother's absence, as well as the sadness in those peaceful, floating lights as they disappear high into the darkness one by one. *I don't want to do this. Please don't make me do this.*

I miss you.

My thoughts quietly thunder by, drifting alongside the subtle glow of lights as they weave through the inky sky.

I look at each of the stilled faces standing on the balcony. *Are you enraptured by the beauty Mother, or frozen with grief and regret? Do you enjoy the beauty this night represents Aunt Margaret, or do you dread it each year as I do? Father, do you secretly wish he were here instead of me?* The last thought throws me out of my internal reverie. I know better than to ask questions I don't want to know the answers to.

We file off the balcony and back into the palace one at a time, our masquerade of indifference coming to a close as the last lantern disappears. Our family prefers to grieve in private, managing this day each year and its meaning in our own ways. Not even Lady Davenport from Fort Kotar and her daughters were invited to light the lanterns on the top balcony, instead sending theirs from their own private landing from the floor below.

My parents turn down the king's corridor, leaving Roan, Aunt Margaret, and myself to continue down the hallway toward my room. A wave of dizziness overwhelms me, threatening to pull me down. I reach out to the wall beside me, steadying my feet before it passes as quickly as it came.

"Lena. Are you alright?" Roan's deep voice curls around me. My aunt wraps a hand around my shoulder, peering around to glimpse at my condition. I've always been a little annoyed at the fuss, everyone dropping everything to be at my beck-and-call. But tonight it feels unbearable.

I turn to face them both. "I can find my own way. Everyone must be tired and eager for bed. No need to hold my hand the rest of the way."

My aunt looks exhausted, her red-rimmed eyes half-closed already. Her forehead bunches in concern, but I don't think she'll put up much of a fight tonight.

"I would prefer to walk you to your room. It wouldn't be right to leave you here." The duty in Roan's voice makes me recoil, taking a step back as if someone struck me.

"Right or not. I want to be alone," I say, trying to keep a tremor out of my voice. I'm exhausted in every sense of the word. Everything this day has been, everything it means, I can't hold up the facade any longer. *Don't cry yet.*

"Lena, darling. I know you're hurting. Let Captain Montgomery walk you the rest of the way, and I'll let your maid know you'll ready yourself for bed this evening," my aunt tells me.

I nod. After a brief hesitation, probably warring with her duty to see me safely on and her desire to melt under the covers of her private chambers, she finally kisses my cheek before turning to walk back the way we came.

Once she's out of sight, I set my gaze to Roan. "There's no law that says you must walk me to my room. I understand your obligation and duty as captain to protect the royal family. But I assure you— I'm perfectly safe behind these walls. Unless, for some reason, there's a lack of confidence in the men you helped train to guard this palace?" I know I'm being rude, hitting him exactly where his pride will strike deep.

"Lena." He reaches for my hand and threads his fingers through mine. A small flicker in my chest threatens to explode. "I don't protect you just from duty. I don't walk you to your room simply because I'm Captain of the Guard and it's my job."

We lock eyes, the blue of his conflicted with what to say next. My own pride ruins whatever tender moment we might have shared. I jerk my hand from his grip, his lingering silence allowing time for my mind to convince me once more that this will never be the love that the little girl in me always dreamed my marriage would be.

"I order you to go away. To return to the barracks, or wherever you stay every night, and whatever other responsibilities your captainship calls from you." A rogue tear falls from my face.

"Lena," he whispers my name again, his hand moving to wipe away the tear dripping down my face.

"Don't. Just go." I step out of reach, pointing down the hallway like a parent sending an insolent child to their room. He doesn't move, however, staring at the ground before bringing his gaze back to me. I refuse to listen to any more words of feigned caring or witness anymore gestures imitating tender devotion. When he doesn't move, I release a huff before my overdramatic exit, flying down the hallway to make my escape, a resigned captain simply staring at my shrinking form.

He doesn't come after me. Not that I expected him to. So many things run through my mind. Love for a man who is more like a brother. Regret for my cruel actions just now. Longing for the freedom of a role I never wanted. Anguish that another year has passed without seeing the smile of my most beloved brother. Anger that he was taken too soon. Sadness at all of the above.

Tears fall openly now, dotting the bodice of my green dress. Once I'm sure Roan won't follow me, I sink to the floor of the long hall, pulling my legs to my chest, and wrapping both arms around to hold them in tight. What a mess I must seem. How has my life gotten to this point?

Years of unshed tears fall to my knees, soaking a small patch of the soft skirt of my dress. A deeper exhaustion slowly envelops me, and I fear if I don't get up, I will fall asleep on the cold tile of the hallway. That would be an interesting site to explain to the maids.

I try to stand, my legs and bottom stiff from holding their awkward position. Black dots blur my vision as another wave of dizziness crashes into me like before, only this time I feel as if I'm standing on a ship instead of inside the palace. I wobble to and fro, falling down to my knees. Confusion whirls around me as my limbs forebode complete atrophy in a matter of seconds.

This is not a natural process of simply being overwhelmed, or an ordinary response to a taxing day. This is more. My pulse beats wildly. Was I bitten by something outside, or did I ingest something not quite right?

I search for a cause, a moment in time that could explain what is happening to me. Before the hall, I was on the balcony with my family. We had been outside waiting for Roan, and before that— my mouth drops open. One of the servants brought us a drink. I wasn't hungry so I took none of the bite-sized morsels of food, but the warm night led me to the drink she had provided. Poison?

"The drink!" I tried to yell, but only garbles escape my throat. "Help!" Another failed attempt to voice my fear.

Was it the servant? Or the cook? Or had someone else entirely made their way in, tainting our food and water before anyone had the sense to notice?

No wonder Aunt Margaret was so easily swayed to let me go on without her. She was suffering the same beginning throes of infected exhaustion. Everyone must be passed out by now. Everyone but Roan, who came after the deceptive drink and turned it away.

My heart steadies when I think of him, standing just a few turns away.

"Roan!" My mouth only forms the words, total silence in its wake. "Roan!" I try again, no sound escaping my lips.

I claw and scrape my way, but I hardly move. My body is sprawled across the floor in a last attempt to drag myself to safety. One by one, my limbs completely overcome to the paralytic effects of whatever I ingested, my dress a heap of wrinkled mess all around me.

I rest my head on the cold tile floor as unconsciousness finally wins the battle. My last thought is of my single lit lantern floating away into the darkness above.

11

THE THIEF

T HE FOREST HAS ALWAYS been my friend. But finding my way out in the middle of the night was quite a feat. A few scrapes and minor cuts line my arms and legs, the only evidence of my struggle. Nothing too deep or wounding, thank Haythen.

The memory of throwing that infuriating man, that guard, right on his back will fuel me for days to come. Relaying the look of shock in his eyes as I mounted Prue and rode off is a priceless reward for having to suffer through his ignorance and mere presence.

The inn is bustling downstairs, serving breakfast to bleary eyed one-nighters and a few regulars, like myself. I reach under the bed to grab my things, beating off dust and cobwebs from a lack-luster cleaning crew before swinging the small bag over my shoulder and tucking in my shirt.

The smell of food hits me hard, a low grumble coming from my stomach. I swipe a piece of bread and small hunk of cheese before I square away my bill with the keeper, grabbing a coin from my pocket to tip the maid who got the dirt and grass stains out of my clothes late last night.

The hired woman is busy wiping down tables to make way for the late crew about to stumble from their rooms. Watching the action sets a warm memory into motion—my mother in the kitchen, cleaning off the crumbs and scraps of food left behind by her children. Always with a smile on her face. At the time I was her only biological child, but the children she housed were always referred by her as her own. We had little to our name, but it didn't stop her from doing her part. At the expense of our own comfort on most occasions, our doors were opened to any child in need.

The icy breath of reality knocks me back into my senses, the pleasant glow of remembering bleeding into bitter truth and leaving a chill in its place. I drop a coin on the table. The maid nods her head in acknowledgment of my gratitude, clearly not used to patrons noticing let alone thanking her efforts.

The weight of the sun hits my face as I exit the building, and I throw my hands up against its brightness as my eyes adjust from the murky lodge.

Most of my morning is spent walking the tables at market since I had to cut short yesterday's perusal. Spring and autumn push the limits of the square, vendors and buyers alike swarming the ever-expanding display.

As much as it's growing, it feels like our pockets are shrinking. How is it possible for our people to look so prosperous, but simultaneously be scraping by? Simply surviving each day, instead of living in moments this good fortune should be bringing in spades?

As I round the corner of the square, my line of sight resting upon the stables, I see three men hovering around a stall— the stall holding Prue. Their red and gold uniforms glimmer in the sunlight. *Oh no you don't.*

I almost drop my bag as I move into a full sprint. My heart is pounding, teeth clenched, eyes fixed on these vermin who would dare touch my horse. They've already taken so much from me, and I refuse to let them take anything else.

A small notch from the neighboring stall works as leverage, my foot digging into the groove as I leap high into the air. They don't see me until I land a kick hard into the first man's back, while my elbow finds the second man's nose. The third fellow draws his sword while I swing my bag at his head, landing him to the ground, his sword flying out of his grip. I drop and roll away, grabbing the dagger from my boot, landing to survey the damage and lingering threat.

The second man leans his head back, blood dripping down his face—hopefully from a broken nose. Wicked delight fills me at the sight of red, satisfaction bleeding through me. The first man glowers in my direction, and the third walks toward his sword, his eyes fixed on me.

"What in the Four Kingdoms just happened?" the second man says, muffled from his pinched nose.

Typical guard cronies— easily beaten, easily duped. I continue to smile from my position, showing no teeth in the gesture, holding up one hand and waving them forward. I see the first man take a step in my direction with narrowed eyes. He wants this too. *Good.*

The third man speaks up before the other closes the distance. "Enough, Bowden!" He shouts loudly in the direction of the first man, giving the second one a pitying look before handing him a mostly clean handkerchief.

"We aren't here to fight." He looks at me now. A hint of recognition crosses his face as his fierce blue eyes bore into mine—eyes I remember staring up at me just last night.

Seeing him in daylight, decked in his full red and gold regalia, further taints my opinion of him, if that's even possible. "Didn't your mothers teach you not to take things that aren't yours?" I growl between my teeth.

"We don't want to take her. I promise you," the blue-eyed guard says.

"I'm not going with you. In case you forgot from last night." I tilt my head to the side, my smirk directly focused on the man I tussled with not even half a day ago.

His lips are firm, but I swear I see a gleam in his eyes as I remind him of our interaction. "We just want to talk. Right here." he says, motioning a single hand toward the ground.

"Then talk."

"We are on orders to find you and were given a description of you and your horse. We were simply discussing who should stay behind with the beast in case you came back before the others returned," he says.

"And why are you looking for me?" I eye each man directly before returning them to the spokesman, the guard from yesterday.

I need some time to think, a distraction to get myself and Prue out of here. My periphery scans the area, looking for anything I could use to divert and disarm. Something to give me an advantage.

"We are here on behalf of Lady Margaret."

My scowl eases at the mention of my patroness, and I stop my search for a way out. The guard waits for me to respond. When I simply raise my eyebrows, he continues. "She needs you to come. Immediately."

"Come where?" I ask. I know where Marg would ask me to meet. But these men could very easily be leading me to a trap. If he says anywhere but the back door entra—

"The back door entrance of the kitchens, at the palace." I let out my held breath, taking another deep inhale and exhale before I stand up, sheathing my knife back in my boot. Marg has never sent anyone to fetch me before, and our usual meeting is only a couple days away. What couldn't wait until then?

I stand, walking toward my horse, giving the men no more of my attention.

"Will you go then?" he questions, turning with my movements as I walk to Prue's stall.

"What do you think I'm doing?"

He eyes me warily. "I'll let her know you're on your way."

"She'll know when I get there before you and walk through the door." I glare at him as I untie Prue, mounting her before we're fully out of the stable. The hard expression never leaves his face, but I swear I see the corner of his lips twitch upward, his apprehensive, surly veil dropping temporarily.

He bolts away in what I assume is the direction of his own horse, my "Yah!" ringing through the vicinity as I dig in my heels just enough to spur Prue into a full gallop.

The wind loosens strands of hair from my braid as I move toward answers and away from the self-centered man now left in my dust.

12

THE CAPTAIN

S OMEHOW LADY MARGARET AND this thief know each other, and that's as disconcerting as to why Lady Margaret summoned her in the first place. Less than half a day ago I was trying to arrest her, and now I'll watch her march onto the palace grounds, invited by the king's sister herself.

Crisp morning air clings to me as I approach the back entrance of the kitchens, Red trotting through a patchy road of firm dirt interspersed with boggy mud. The thief is dismounting her horse, tying the animal to a small pole off the gate as I approach.

"How does it feel to be beaten by a thief, and a woman at that. Twice?" she quips, a small glint in her eyes.

"You had a head start. It's wasn't a fair race." I keep my features impassive, unwilling to yield even an inch of applause. But it's hard to deny that I'm impressed.

The girl places her hands upon her hips, her heart-shaped face tilting up to meet my gaze. "Today, perhaps. But I wouldn't call being unarmed with bound hands a head start."

"I have a strong feeling only one of those statements is true," I reply, looking at her boot where she sheathed her dagger earlier. The corner of her mouth twitches up just before she turns to walk inside, her braided hair swinging across her shoulder.

She pays no heed as she passes through the doors. I follow a few strides behind, brows crinkling as I watch her. She seems at home here. How does she know exactly where to go?

The bustle inside the kitchens is the same as any other day. The staff don't even look up as the thief passes by, completely ignoring her. Does she do this regularly?

The girl turns into a small room. As I follow around the corner, I bump into her after only a few steps inside. She lets out a *humph* in my direction as she steadies herself, and I sheepishly sidestep around her.

My chest and arms are thrumming where they touched her, my heart dancing when I notice her looking at me. I twist my fingers back and forth in an attempt to dispel the feeling, straightening my shirt and checking the sword at my side as I ignore her heated gaze.

Lady Margaret is waiting in the corner of this tiny room. She has none of the fanfare and fancy dress that usually accompany her and her self-admiration. Instead, she's wearing riding pants and a plain tunic. Her light, aging hair is pulled up into a bun atop her head. Bloodshot, drooping eyes confess her clear fatigue.

We stand in an awkward quietness until Lady Margaret takes a deep breath, releasing a dejected exhale before opening her mouth to speak. "I know this is an unorthodox way of going about meeting with you two, and I'm sure you are both, at this point, very confused."

Isn't that the understatement of the day. Between being pulled from sleep by a loud, frantic knock at my door within the barracks, a very frazzled first-year telling me I had been summoned to the palace immediately, and a distressed Lady Margaret giving me an order and description to find the girl who very clearly was my thief from last night— I definitely have a few questions.

"I won't waste any more time." She hesitates, darting her weary eyes to me briefly before she continues. "The princess... has been taken."

My limbs freeze at the declaration, trying to make sense of her words. My once dancing heart now hums like a brazen waterfall.

"What do you mean, taken?" I exclaim. I can't quite take a breath, as if that waterfall has sucked me completely under. All my senses tunnel toward Lady Margaret and the words that surely aren't real.

No, no. It's a joke. It has to be. Something to keep me on my toes. An exercise that will end in Lena's laugh reaching my ears as I find her hidden in a barn across Turin.

But she doesn't smile or make some demeaning remark about my gullibility. "I mean what I said, Captain Montgomery." The thief glances sidelong at me with Lady Margaret's use of my title, but I hardly comprehend the movement.

I can barely think. Barely breathe. My body feels foreign— as if somehow I've managed to completely separate from it and am watching myself from somewhere else entirely. "Why am I just learning of this now? I'm Captain of the Guard! I should've been alerted the minute—"

Lady Margaret holds up a hand, halting my building voice. "Because I knew you'd be upset. And I didn't want you compromised when I sent you in search of *her*." Her gaze now rests on the thief.

Again I don't move, or follow her eyes to the girl beside me. I keep my full focus planted on Lady Margaret. But instead of her face I see nothing except Evander's soulless eyes staring back.

I blink away the image. "I don't care who you wanted me to find. This is unacceptable. I'm Lena's—" I look to the thief, then back to Lady Margaret, my words dissolving in my throat.

"Stop your rampage, Captain. I understand how you feel about how I handled things. And nothing can be done about it now," Lady Margaret says calmly.

The tiniest bit of air escapes me, my mouth forming the only words that will come as my fire ices over. "Who took her?" I whisper, my voice raspy and almost unrecognizable.

"We don't know." Lady Margaret's words are quiet but firm, her eyes briefly glazing over as she stares off into the wall. A handkerchief is squeezed between both her hands, the cloth beginning to thin at the area of repeated movement as she twists it in her grasp. It's Lady Margaret's distress more than anything that finally proves to me the legitimacy of what she's saying, and my nerves unravel the more I realize she's truly not toying with me.

"What we do know," Lady Margaret continues after clearing her throat, eyes snapping between my shaking hands and the unmoving thief, "is that she was taken sometime after last night's affairs. After you walked her to her room. When her lady's maid arrived early this morning, the bed and room lay untouched. Princess Adalena nowhere to be found. I still have Palace Guards scouring the city. But as far as my sources have told me, she's gone."

My stomach drops. I didn't walk her to her room. She demanded I leave her alone, and I complied. Stupidly, foolishly, carelessly— I complied. I run both hands through my hair, threading my fingers together behind my neck as I begin pacing the small space. Would she have gone on her own? Run away maybe? No. Never.

"I have to ask, Captain. Did you see anything amiss after I left her in your charge last night?" Lady Margaret asks, her eyes searching my face for any hint of a lie or foul play.

I grind my teeth at the implication. "No. Nothing was amiss." I meet her stare for just a moment before darting my eyes to the wall behind her. "But..." I hesitate, knowing my fault before I even speak it. "I didn't walk her to her room. She demanded that I leave her. Commanded me to go. So I did." Lady Margaret pinches the bridge of her nose at my revelation before taking a deep breath.

She looks somewhat composed as she shares the rest of her information, but I don't know how. Lena is more like a daughter to her than a neice. Suddenly, her red eyes make sense. "We questioned the guards stationed at each gate. Those on the north, east, and south entrances saw nothing, relaying everyone who passed through in the night by name, description of their person, and where they were headed." Nothing seems off by this report. My men having followed protocol to exactness.

"Except for the west gate. When I arrived to question the night patrol, they were all asleep."

"Asleep?" I almost yell the word.

Where before I couldn't breathe, now I only see red. My men, asleep at the gate? Never. I shake my head, rubbing away the throb at my temples as I try to make sense of it all.

"To be fair, it seems they were also drugged. Groggy and incoherent as I kicked them awake," Lady Margaret says.

"So why do I feel like a child about to be admonished?" I ask, not bothering to hide my growl.

"There were two empty bottles of wine at their feet. Which means they not only accepted it from one of the conspirators, they decided to drink it on duty." There's a flicker of satisfaction while she tells me this news. My men failed. And therefore, I failed.

"You could've led with that information, as it now seems obvious which direction they traveled." I frown, my sudden need for fresh air sending my head into a brief, dizzying spin. When the room straightens, my gaze takes in her mud covered shoes for the first time.

"Not exactly. The other three gates also received this gift of wine from a mysterious patron. They just didn't accept it," she says.

Three out of four. Not the perfect report it needs to be, and will be in the coming months.

"So they tried to take out each gate, but the west is the only one that fell for it. Giving them the perfect exit." My words are said to no one in particular, more for the benefit of saying my thoughts out loud as I desperately grasp for answers. "I'm assuming you scoured the palace and surrounding forest," I say.

"Of course." Lady Margaret's annoyance shines through her answer. "I found some footprints at the edge of the west entrance, loose dirt and burnt bits of wood further down in the forest."

"Did you follow the path, find anything that would signal Lena was with them?" I ask, impatient.

"No," she admits.

"Why? Why didn't you follow it through, Margaret? She could've been just around the corner!"

My lack of title isn't what earns me a fiery rebuke. "Don't you dare scold me, Roan Montgomery." She sticks a lone finger to my chest. "I'm reeling with this, just as you. Trying to make sense of it. Trying to understand just what in the Four Kingdoms happened here last night. How someone could have gotten passed the Palace Guard and into our home. That alone should have been impossible." She pauses— an equal, burning glare emanating from us both.

The palace guards begin as a recruit in my program, but finish their training under the direction of Lady Margaret. She personally picks each one, most of them cousins or other relations to the lords and ladies who are in support of crown and country. It's both strategic and diplomatic, helping to indoctrinate a love and genuine desire to protect the royal family, while also maintaining financial and political backing for House Chattan.

I have a couple years with these guards before they're taken. But after they leave my barracks, it's rare for them to come under my direction again. The conspirators' infiltration into the castle is a personal hit on Lady Margaret and the Palace Guard. For the first time this morning I realize the circles under her eyes aren't only from lack of restful sleep. They monumentally failed. And most likely have a traitor among them.

The thought sends a shiver up my spine, and my frustration softens ever so slightly. "If you take into account the gate they used to exit, and keep moving in the same direction of the footprints and doused fire, the West Passageway seems their most likely course. They are headed to Fort Lowsan. And maybe to the border of Thenstra." My mind is moving faster than my words can keep up with.

"Most likely." The worry in her face instantly doubles.

Felshan's ties with Thenstra are riddled with difficulty. The king of Thenstra abruptly shut down the border without word or reason. We've all heard the story. Only few people alive today can boast having visited the country, let alone give us any great details of the land that might help to find Lena. "It must be someone in good standing with King Brekan, if he's even the one still in power. That's the only way they'd be able to cross the border."

"That's not exactly true," the thief speaks up, her voice firm but emotionless. Lady Margaret and I turn to her in unison, waiting for her to explain. "I don't know how reputable this is, but I heard that Thenstra has a black market. Some people were whispering about it. I don't know if it exists. But if it does, there has to be a border opening somewhere in order for that news to have reached Felshan."

"I have not heard such a thing," Lady Margaret says, perplexed.

"Nor I," I reply, my focus now resting solely on this thief.

"I don't have any details. Like time or place," she says. "But if it is real, it might be their ticket across the border, and ours to follow if they get that far." Heavy contemplation fills the air.

"They won't get that far. Captain Montgomery, they must have her hidden somehow. It's at least a week's ride to the Thenstran border, twice as long in a wagon and even longer on foot. They won't want to draw attention to themselves while they are still within the borders of Felshan. And a kicking, screaming, or knocked out girl across a horse would definitely draw attention," says Lady Margaret.

I finish her thought. "Which means they are in a wagon, and will have to ride steady." The wheels are turning wildly in my head. "They have maybe a half a day's lead, assuming they rode all night. Probably minimal breaks since they know we would catch on and start the search by early morning."

"I don't mean to be insensitive," interjects the thief, "but you don't need to follow; they will make their demands known soon enough."

Lady Margaret glowers at her briefly before attempting to cool her features. "I agree. Which is why I will be staying back and waiting for a demand. You both," she states, pointing at the two of us, "will find her and bring her home."

Shock, then annoyance clings to me as I look from the thief, then back to Lady Margaret. "With all due respect, I don't need any help. This thief will only slow me down. Give me three days, and I will catch up to this scum and bring Princess Lena home safely."

The girl rolls her eyes at me. "First of all, I have a name, and it's not *thief*. And second of all, I've bested you twice in less than a day. If anything, you'll slow *me* down." Her top lip curls back as her eyes flick to mine.

"You don't even know the princess. Why would you risk anything to try and save her? I would give my life for hers without a second thought." My voice rises with each word.

"Which is why Marg has asked me to find her. I won't let my emotions get the better of me," the girl says.

"I would never do anything to compromise Princess Adalena's safety, *thief*," I exclaim, anger continuing to move up my spine, one vertebrae at a time. Who does she think she is? I would never let my family get hurt. Never again.

"Then you better sheath your pride and get ready to be schooled by the thief you *almost* captured, *captain*," she replies. We are standing toe to toe, anger radiating off us both.

When I open my mouth to retort I am abruptly cut off— "You are the best tracker I know," Lady Margaret says to me, holding a hand up to silence us both. "But Ari can steal the fur right off a bear's hind legs. So if you can both shut your mouths for two seconds and pause whatever this is," she waves a hand between the girl and myself, "there may actually be a shot of bringing Lena home safely, without suspicion or fanfare to blast around our incompetence." She leans against the wall as she finishes. "I will stay back with the king and queen and attempt to assuage their panic at her disappearance while continuing to maintain the kingdom as best I can— waiting for any word or ransom to come to the palace. Otherwise, believe me. I would be coming alongside you."

I have heard rumors of Lady Margaret's glory days. Normally a princess would find an advantageous marriage for the good of her country and crown. However, being the king's favored sister, she was apparently allowed to represent the Crown all across the continent, learning many colloquial trades and skills as she went. Some slightly more scandalous for a princess than others, if the rumors are to be believed.

Lady Margaret continues, "Silence is of the utmost importance. Everyone already knows, to some extent, that the kingdom is on rocky ground since the prince died. The king and queen all but abdicating their responsibilities. But even without that knowledge, people can tell things are different, and not in a good way. If they learn that the princess has been taken it will leave the doors open for rioting and mayhem, allowing anyone to invade and attempt a takeover during the upheaval. From the outside," she pauses, a wave of fatigue clearly running through her, "or the inside."

As much as I wish she were completely mistaken, the truth of her words ring true. The guards have had to move in twos everywhere they go just to watch each other's backs. And not from foreigners, but from our own people. It's no secret that things have fallen into disrepair both in spirit and tangibility in the last few years. The discontent is palpable.

"You know I will go. Lena is my family. I will be ready within the hour, and I give you my word that I will bring her home." A calm washes over me once the promise locks into place.

Lady Margaret turns to the thief. "If you aid in bringing her home, I will consider all debts paid. You will be free of this, Ari. You can have your horse, and a sizable donation for settling down, or traveling Felshan, or traveling all of Haythen if that's what you want." The girl's eyes go wide before quickly composing herself again.

Ari. I say the name over in my mind.

The girl hesitates before speaking. "Of course. I will go." She eyes me sidelong, straightening her posture and clearing her throat so her next words will be devoid of her obvious disdain for me. "I will aid Captain Montgomery in bringing home the princess."

"Good." Lady Margaret visibly slumps, the weight of responsibility released and passed to another.

"I would like to bring Aiden and Bowden," I quickly interject. "I promise you they will be an asset to our journey. Ari," her name feels strange on my tongue, "may be the best thief in town. But Aiden has a sixth sense for direction and geography and is more than proficient with a bow. And Bowden is the one of best swordsman in the entire Guard."

Ari scoffs at the mention of these men. "Oh, come on Marg. It's bad enough you're going to make me work with one guard, their leader of all people. But three?"

"There's a chance they aren't going to Thenstra. It could be a ploy to have us searching in the wrong direction. They could've gone to the Western Seaport, south to Venes, or northeast to Jadeya. It would be helpful to have a pair to split off on another trail should we find one," I counter. I understand the girl's dislike of me after last night, but why disapprove of Aiden or Bowden?

"Done," replies Lady Margaret, not even taking a second to mull over our words. "Tell them to keep quiet and ready themselves to leave immediately. I will grab a few supplies from the palace and meet you in the yard before the breakfast bell." The thief—the girl—Ari—takes a deep breath, the scowl never leaving her face. But I don't care. Not now. Not after everything I've just heard.

Lena is gone. I'm still struggling to fully comprehend it.

I will bring her home, Evander. I will bring Lena home safely.

The promise rings through me like the unwavering rise and fall of the sun.

13

THE THIEF

I CAN LEAVE, OR stay, or do whatever I please— as soon as I find this princess and bring her home. Marg will give me Prue free and clear and erase any debt to her I still carry for her generosity and training.

Before, my freedom was *years* into the future. I hadn't given much thought to what I would do with it. It has been so long since I've seen and hunted the men who took my mother. Maybe I could devote my time to permanently free the world of those men who would hurt an innocent woman.

Or maybe all I would find is dust as I did before.

I feel my heart *thump, thump, thump*. The metal bars of my cage are groaning in preparation. My true desires have been imprisoned for so long, and I feel my body stretching with the promise of being set free. All I will need is the slightest scent of my enemy, and I will finally be able to devour them instead of searching the city from behind a locked enclosure— Marg's wishes always taking precedence over my own.

She trained me well. I know I can do what she's asking. It's this *captain* and his men I don't trust. If there's one thing that's certain, they will do whatever they want, whatever is best for them— just as the Guard always does.

The briefest image of my mother flashes through my mind.

I don't know Princess Lena, but I do know Felshan will fall if she isn't brought back safely— the final footing pulled right out from under us and a collapsed kingdom in the aftermath. I owe Felshan nothing, yet I can't turn my back on those suffering as I once did. I won't leave them to fend for themselves.

The sneer of Reynauld, the slap of the boy ringing through my ears, bony fingers digging into my skin, the fear in the boy's eyes as I handed him the bag of coin— anger is a familiar emotion, one I know how to handle well. I let its familiar energy fill me.

Those who take whatever they want, who don't care who gets hurt in the process— they don't deserve a happy ending.

I grab my few belongings from the stable, discarded there after my tussle with Captain Montgomery and his men. My stomach goes sour at the thought of these guards. They are a means to end. A necessary evil for now. I can do this last thing for Marg and for the people of Felshan.

There will be time to figure out the rest. Time for my savage desires to be satiated.

I swing my leg over Prue's saddle, adjusting my feet in the stirrups, my decision firm. "Ok, lady. Let's go save a princess."

I look in the direction of the captain, but he says nothing, unmoving as I make my approach. He is methodically packing food and supplies on the back of his chestnut stallion. Our fourth companion hasn't arrived, but the other is standing patiently, awaiting orders like a good little guardsman. He seems innocent enough, like the tendrils of greed and power have yet to wrap him in their grasp.

I see flecks of dried blood dotting this young man's nose. He looks to be close in age to me, his short, sandy hair giving him more of the look of Venes blood rather than Felshan.

"Sorry about that," I tell him, mirroring a gesture to my own nose. I'm only partly lying.

"Don't worry about it. I told the men I was in a fight with four Kotarans. If anything, you did me favor," the young man says. "And seeing a girl take down three guards at once— it was quite impressive to watch. You know, once the stinging from that elbow jab to the face stopped long enough for my tears to clear away."

I smile at his candidness. Maybe I don't completely hate this one.

"She didn't take us down," the captain replies, overhearing our conversation. "We weren't trying to hurt her. In a real fight, I'm not sure she'd be able to handle a single guard let alone three." I sigh heavily, attempting to mask my face in boredom. Hoof beats in the distance deter any spiteful response, instead focusing my attention to the rider approaching.

An older gentleman, graying roots speckling his hairline and marking him my senior by at least double my own years, if not more, heads toward us.

"Captain," he says, tipping his head before turning his attention to me. "So this is the thief," says the man as he dismounts, nodding in my direction. I raise an eyebrow at the captain, and he barely shrugs in response.

"My name is Ari. And if I am a thief, it's only because those I stole from *deserved* it." I direct my statement to Captain Montgomery, reiterating our conversation from last night, but I barely receive a huff in response.

The older man walks toward me, his unwavering smile crinkling the corners of both eyes. "You seem a bit familiar, have we met before?" the old man asks me. I don't smile, but the corner of my lips tick up ever so slightly. No, we haven't met before. But that sense that he's seen me, that feeling of déjà vu, is the mastery of shadows, of blending in, of becoming one with my surroundings. He may very well have seen me, many times, like a ghost haunting the streets. They feel it, but they just can't see it.

"Check her pockets, Otto. A few trinkets in there might seem familiar too." The captain's voice is hard, and the muscles in his jaw tense. I narrow my eyes at his degrading remark.

"Oh wait, I do have something," I say, sticking my hands in each pocket, trailing them out slowing with a choice finger raised on both hands. "Although I'd say these belong to you, *Captain*."

Otto gives a good hearty laugh. "I'm intrigued, Ari. I do hope you'll honor me with your story on our journey." Confusion dots my brow at the older man's words, and I can see the surprise on the captain's face as well. Seems the fourth rider will be this man. Better than Bowden. He seemed even more insufferable than the pigheaded captain beside me.

The old man holds his hand out to me. "My name is Otto." I don't want to take it, but something about him feels so genuine I can't help it as I clasp my hand in his.

"What happened to Bowden?" the captain asks, walking away from his task.

"He's not up for the journey. So I volunteered," Otto says.

"Volunteered?" The captain eyes the older man with a raised brow. "You mean you made him step down."

"I can't let you go off and have all the fun. Besides, I think his pride was a bit hurt by the girl." The older man, Otto, looks in my direction, and I'm surprised to see a bit of respect pass through his gaze. "Bowden is plenty capable of taking over for a few weeks while we're away. This may be the last adventure I have. You wouldn't take that away from an old man, would you?"

"Old man? I'm pretty sure you could outrun all of us here and wrestle a damn bear to the ground if he so much as wrongly glanced in your direction," declares the captain.

Otto just smiles his agreement, lowering his voice for his next words. "You know I love Lena. Anyone who knows her loves her. Let me help with this, Roan." The captain grabs this man's shoulder, squeezing gently as he nods.

The older man busies himself preparing his bag and horse as Marg rides into the yard. "Parker Aldren is missing," she says before she even dismounts. "Every palace guard is accounted for except him."

"Did you check the barracks, the surrounding villages?" he asks.

"Yes."

"Our traitor," he coolly replies. It wasn't hard to guess whomever took her was an inside man, but at least now it's confirmed.

"Do you remember Parker?" she asks, grabbing onto his arm.

"I do. I saw him just yesterday. He was good, from what I recall during his training. Strong, dependable, learned fast."

Marg spits on the ground in front of her. "Bring him back alive if at all possible. I want him rotting in the dungeons for the rest of eternity for what he's done. But don't hesitate to kill him if it means bringing Lena back unharmed. The same goes for any other scum that were in on this."

The captain nods in answer before turning to face the rest of us. "We are taking too long. We should be on the road by now. Get to it!" he yells.

He moves to his horse, arranging buckles and straps, checking that everything is in place before situating himself in the saddle. Everyone follows suit, the five of us mounted and positioned in a circle around the yard, awaiting the go-ahead.

"We don't know what awaits us out there, but as far as we know," begins the captain, "the princess was taken up the West Passageway. We imagine they have around half a day's head start, are carrying her concealed in a wagon of some kind, and will need to pass through Fort Lowsan before possibly entering Thenstra, or less likely, to the Western Seaport or over through Jadeya. We don't know who took her, but they are trained enough to get through a palace almost undetected." I can sense the distress in his voice as he addresses our group.

"And what if we are wrong— what if they aren't headed to Thenstra?" I ask.

"I have groups getting ready to head to Port Riga, Fort Kotar, and Fort Frennin just in case we are wrong," Marg tells me. "To get anywhere else in Haythen they'd have to pass through one of those four major cities within Felshan."

The captain looks at each of us in turn, his gaze unrelenting. "Our only hard objective is to bring back the princess alive and safe. There is no mercy for those who took her, and none will be shown if it comes to a fight. We need to be quick, silent, and efficient," he says. He's not wrong, but I don't acknowledge it with a nod like the others. I won't give him the satisfaction of seeing me agree with him.

"We've been balancing on sandy foundations for longer than I care to admit," Marg says. "Our princess— our Lena— is the promise of stability, strength, and permanence to the future of this kingdom. We need her back." She whispers the last part as if speaking the words aloud is too much for her nerves to bear.

I may not know Princess Adalena, but I know the pain of longing for someone who is gone. My heart breaks a little as I watch this once grand lady all but beg us to find the girl.

"Any word of this gets out," Marg continues, "and it will be the straw that breaks the horse's back. Felshan will fall, I promise you. Our prince is dead, and our princess is missing. Our kingdom is ripe for the taking. And right now, she's our final prayer— you're our final prayer." Tears form in her eyes, brimming but not spilling over.

She runs a hand over her sleeve, smoothing out any kinks. When she looks forward again her face is polished, the princess underneath shining through. "If it's a ransom they want, I'm sure a demand will be made soon.

I will stay behind. The king and queen are in no state to handle the affairs of the kingdom and a kidnapper's potential power play for their only daughter and last remaining heir." She pauses, steadying herself with a hand on her chest.

After a breath, she looks over at Captain Montgomery. "Go quickly and bring her back, Captain. Bring her home."

He nods sternly. "I will." He motions to all of us. "Our first break will be at high-day. Head out!"

I make last contact with a haggard Marg. It seems all her energy has left her as she says, "Be safe, Ari."

"Always." It's all I can say before I nudge Prue into a full gallop and head down the road after the guards.

14

PRINCESS ADALENA

A COOL BREEZE DRIFTS across my face, pulling my languid mind to consciousness. The last dregs of sleep bring only confusion as I stare up at a cloudless sky.

Why am I outside? Did no one notice and wake me, or did I drift off only moments ago? A heavy jolt sends my body down against something hard. The groan of wood against metal fills my ears as realization takes its time to dawn in my mind.

I'm moving. Is it me? Or is the ground itself moving beneath me? I try to roll over, but I'm wedged between something solid and unforgiving. As I bring my hands to shove against the object both of my palms rise in unison. A rope rests in and around both wrists, binding them tightly together.

I stare at them a moment before my senses return like a bucket of cold water has just been poured over my head. This is not home. I did not willingly climb aboard whatever is moving. I am not cozied up safe in my bed while I simply reorient myself like coming out of a curious, albeit nightmarish, dream.

I have no idea where I am.

Someone has committed treason. They have kidnapped me— have taken the princess of Felshan against her will. At least I think they did. My memory is foggy, still trying to restore itself after a heavy sleep as I try and open my eyes. But they feel so heavy. Too heavy. Perhaps I'll keep them closed a little longer.

I begin to think of my mother and father, my aunt, and even Roan. Do they know I'm gone? I don't know that Mother's frayed health can withstand the loss of another child— her last living heir. And Father— would he completely succumb to his grief when he learns of the disappearance of his youngest child? His last hope at redemption and joy in this life, taken from him like a day's ration of food swiped away from a starving family. All in the same breath as the anniversary of my brother's death.

"I think she's stirring," I hear a distant voice say. It sounds female.

"She's tied up, Onah." A deeper voice this time— definitely male. "You don't need to babysit a girl who probably hasn't lifted more than her own satin gloves since the day she was born. She'll sit nice and tight, won't you, *Your Highness*?" His mocking tone sends a shiver up my spine.

My head threatens to split in two, the remnants of a powerful drug still lingering inside me, making it difficult for my vision to move into a singular focus.

Of all the training I have received since the moment I could walk and talk, not once did a tutor cover the topic of defending myself. Not a single book titled *How to Escape a Kidnapping* ever crossed my desk.

Why did no one take the time to teach me how to take care of myself? As the thought rolls across my mind it's more an angered statement than a question. Of all the absurd lessons I've sat through— sipping my tea like a lady, addressing those of lesser station, genealogy of past royal lines, arranging flowers. Why did none of those lessons show me how to hold a sword? How to run long distances when my life depends on it? Or how to negotiate with traitors? I grind my teeth together. I will need all of those attributes in order to escape this. None of which I have.

My chest tightens at the same time a single tear escapes down to the hard floor beneath me, but not just for the misogynistic approach to my education. Oddly enough, I picture myself standing beside my brother. *If you had not died, no one would care about me enough to take me in the first place. You should have been there to protect me, to have handed the heads of these traitors to our father on a silver plate.*

And then I'm next to my aunt Margaret. *Father used to tell me you were the best swordswoman in all the Four Kingdoms. He told me stories of your adventures, of the masters you trained with. Why? Why did you never bestow that knowledge to me?* My pain is deeply misplaced, I know. But I can't stop the thoughts and blame from curling inside of me.

"I think the lass is crying," the female voice says. "Not used to living like the other half, eh?" Her obvious disdain hits me hard. *Not a friend.*

The male speaks again. "Imagine if you woke up in a palace, surrounded by fancy plates and flowers on every table. You'd cry too when you realized your snuff had been confiscated, utensils were required at every meal, and your teeth needed brushing everyday." An actual growl escapes from the woman at her accomplice's remarks. Are they not friends? Or maybe they are simply good enough friends that such a comment would garner forgiveness as the day wears on.

Tree limbs pass overhead, providing brief shadows from high day's sun and subsequent heat. As the instinctual, paralyzing freeze of fear begins to thaw at each limb, and the slightest movement shows me just how caged I truly am. My feet are tied at the ankles and something hard in front and behind prevents me from rolling off to either side. I try to rise, my elbow and knee digging into the hard wood of what appears to be a wagon bed.

A strong hand pushes me back down, and I flop against the unforgiving floor.

"Not so fast, Princess," the male voice calls down to me. "I can dose you with more valerian root if I need to. But if you'd prefer to remain with your wits about you then I suggest you stay put."

"Don't use her title!" the venomous female voice whispers.

"The princess! Everyone see, we have a princess tied up in the back!" he shouts. A brief tussle ensues, followed by a light-hearted chuckle. "In the name of Haythen, I think you left a bruise." I imagine a deep scowl forming on the ornery woman's face. "Keep your horses bridled. There's no one in an hour's ride in either direction. The spring market has garnered most traveling vendors, and it's too blasted hot for everyone else."

"You'll be the reason this mission fails," the woman cooly replies.

"Thank you for the boost in confidence, Onah. You're my guiding star, as always," he says. *Definitely not friends.*

If I didn't know any better, I would think this man couldn't give a flying rats tail if I'm a princess or not. Just a random stranger being paid to take a helpless girl. Maybe his lack of caring could be used to my advantage? If he's out for money, well. The heavens know I have plenty of that. My mother and father would pay any of his demands.

The afternoon is spent in silence, finding comfort in the companionship of the shapes I make out in distant clouds passing above me. The man and woman no longer speak as the speed of the wagon picks up, drowning out any sounds beside the clopping of hooves and the creaking of the wheels as they hit jutting rocks in the road. The position of the sun tells me we are moving northwest. At least some of my education has proved useful.

The wagon begins to slow, more voices drifting through the breeze. My muscles tense, freezing in place. It's a strange feeling to be afraid of what will happen next, yet already having succumb myself to whatever fate these people have set in place for me.

"The stars are bright today," an unfamiliar voice says as we come to a stop.

"The jewels of the sky," the male voice says from our wagon.

The stars are bright today? I turn my head slowly, the sun shining high overhead. It's mid-afternoon at least, not a star in the sky. My eyes squint as I try to make sense of their words.

We are stationary, but the wagon begins bouncing around as if these men are purposefully shaking it back and forth. I keep my head down, listening carefully to the sounds around me. Horses. People walking, crunching through the twigs and rocks where the road meets the forest edge. Lowered voices. More movement. Laughing.

"It's done. More will meet you this evening to switch the horses out," a man says. My body shivers even though the sun is weighing heavily on the day. I peer up, the smallest glimpse of tawny hair and a dark tunic reaches me before I quickly duck my head back down.

"We will keep an eye out for any... wayward travelers," says another, and the group laughs together.

"We appreciate your help. Don't we, Onah?" the familiar male voice says. Onah is the female companion I now realize.

"Shut up and let's go," she says. My skin prickles at her tone.

"See you on the other side, boys," the familiar man says before a crack of a whip sends the wagon back into movement.

It's a strange feeling—to have the memory of yesterday, wishing for any fate other than being queen. A position and title I've come to loathe and dread, only to wake wishing for the simplicity and safety such a role would bring. Tears spring again to my eyes at my childishness. How ridiculous it now seems to have wished away such an easy future.

It appears the heavens granted the demands of a foolish, entitled girl. How they must be laughing as they see me now.

15

Captain Montgomery

W E RIDE MOST OF the day, stopping with just enough light in the sky to make camp and cook dinner. Everyone is tired and stiff from the long ride, working through our kinks as we gather wood for a fire.

I told Lady Margaret I needed three days to find Lena and bring her home. After today I realize how wrong my estimation could be. We rode hard, pushing ourselves and our horses as far and as long as we could go. And there wasn't a single clue hinting that Lena, and whomever took her, had ridden along this road.

The long stretch of day and monotonous clop of hooves gave ample time for my mind to run away from me, imagining all the places they could have taken her. Is she ok? Is she hurt? If Parker Aldren is indeed her captor, why did he do it? What does he have to gain from such a thing? An emotional crack has formed inside of me, one that I feel might burst into a full panic if we don't come across something soon.

I will go to the ends of Haythen and beyond if that's what it takes, Lena. Just hold on.

We pass the time silently as we eat our small portion of fire roasted rabbit, courtesy of Aiden's skill with a bow, while also stretching our saddle-molded legs. The river Rashan rushes in the background. The West Passageway follows along the river's flow until we hit Fort Lowsan. Its blue sputtering fades easily in the background for everyone but me.

My eyes shut tight, and I pinch the bridge of my nose as the cresting memory of that fateful First Hunt, of Evander resting weightless in the water, eddies and ripples through my mind. A sudden bout of nausea has me taking deep breaths, an attempt to avoid losing the food I've already eaten.

I take small bites, even through the dizzying queasiness, knowing not every meal will include fresh meat. My body will need its nourishment in the coming days if I'm to find Lena. If we must search beyond Fort Lowsan, game may be harder to come by. The North is a mystery, very few having ever explored the land around and within Thenstra. So savoring this victory, no matter how sour it might taste, might be the very thing that bolsters me through the uncharted and formidable peaks of the Prythan Mountains. *Whatever it takes to bring her home.*

I hope everyone is prepared for the grueling days ahead, because I won't slow down for anyone's comfort.

A few rogue stars, the brightest in the sky, have started to pop through the darkening blue. They sprinkle above me as I unbuckle Red's saddle, laying it on the ground to give him a reprieve from the heavy thing.

Laughter breaks out on the edge of our camp, and the sound scrapes against me. It's disconcerting to hear such joy when the anxious unknown is grinding through my thoughts.

"I've visited every major city in Felshan, including Roan's origin city—Port Riga. In fact, I remember meeting him when he was just a boy, before he moved to Turin. And I'm so good with a sword, I've never received any major wounds or battle scars. My instincts are as fierce as the cats of Venes, and my blows like the solid hammers of a Turinian blacksmith," I hear Otto say, my interest piqued when I hear my name attached to Port Riga.

"Have you forgotten I've seen you with your shirt off, Otto? Your back is as scarred as an overripe melon." Aiden raises a brow, unsatisfied with his mentor, but also pleased with himself.

"Then let the girl answer, boy," Otto replies, mock annoyance clouding his merry features. He turns to the girl. "Alright, Ari. Your turn."

"Let's see," she says, tapping a finger against her chin.

Her small leather vest and belt lie discarded on the ground next to her bow and quiver, her unhindered shirt billowing with each breeze that drifts through our camp. The heat of the day has yet to wane with the setting sun, and I decide to follow her lead and remove the leather from my arms and torso, letting the flowing wind cool me down.

"Alright. My father is a fisherman, and he taught me the name of every single fish in Turin's waters, as well as how to cook them all to perfection. And I would rather sleep on the ground than in some fancy bed," she says to them, leaning forward with her elbows propped on her knees.

The fire is dying down, its faint glow sharply highlighting Ari's devious expression. No one moves to add another log to the flames, the already warm evening providing more than enough heat for a pleasant sleep.

"Ok. Let's look at this objectively," Aiden responds. "Your father could do any number of things— leaving a large hole for dishonesty. Although, who wouldn't want a fancy bed? One is too specific, the other too obvious. Which one would you go for, I wonder?" His leg bounces rhythmically as he stares at Ari, unblinking.

"Your father isn't a fisherman," Otto chimes in. "Some of those lavish beds have so much time spent making sure the lace is sewn on just right, they forget that comfort is why they exist in the first place." He looks to Ari, unwavering in his stare. "I'd rather sleep on the ground instead of one of those things too."

My brows kiss as I try to decipher their conversation. Scars, fisherman, Port Riga?

Ari's blank face spreads into a wide smile. "Indeed. My father is not a fisherman."

"Tally-ho!" Aiden slaps his knee. "Nothing slips by this old man." He bumps Otto's shoulder, all of them chuckling quietly. "So what does your father really do?" Aiden asks, turning back to Ari.

The wide smile on her face fades to a lifeless grin, shrinking further to a thin line, her hesitation silencing their game. I'm too far away to navigate the look in her eyes, but not so far that I can't recognize the void of emotion written across her features.

"He may be a fisherman. I don't know. I was raised by my mother." It's all she offers, and no one pries further. Her blank expression lasts a few more breaths before turning back to subtle contentment. "My knowledge of fish was given to me by Lenny, the orphan boy working down at the docks. He's a great teacher, if you ever want your seafood to be a work of art." Her words are quick as she tries to brush past the uncomfortable truth. She grew up without her father.

"I, for one, love a good fish stew," Otto says instantly. "If Lenny is up for a lesson, he'll have a student in me when we return." He winks at her before turning to his left. "Alright, Aiden. You're up." If there's one person you want navigating an uncomfortable situation, it's Otto. He's never been one to linger in awkward silence and always seems to know what to say to ease any tension.

Part of me warms to the thief, to Ari. She may have questionable morals, but it would be difficult to grow up without a father.

My own was vital to my childhood and long after I outgrew him in size. James Montgomery is a force to be reckoned with, in the best way. His care for our home, our family trade and employees, my mother, my brother and sisters— it shaped the very foundation of who I am and everything I hope to be. My father's example taught me strength, compassion, and determination. He would walk down the village road and garner the attention of everyone. Not from fear, but from veneration.

I asked him once why everyone would quiet and stare as he moved by. He told me, "I demand much but expect little. Every person in this city will struggle at some point, and they know I will be on their side when they do. When they are basking in good-fortune again, they will pay it back."

As I aged I asked him how to become a good leader. Before betrothal to Lena and the loss of the prince, my plan was to return home. To take up our family trade as my father did, and his father before him. "You must govern people with sternness and compassion, and use discernment for which of the two is appropriate for the moment." I shudder to think what would have become of me without him.

"Ok, Ok. My mother disowned me when I entered the Guard, and I've never killed a man," Aiden tells their huddled group.

"I hate to break it to you Aiden, but we can smell a mother's favored son from the top of the highest summit in the Kotar," Ari says straight faced, before her and Otto erupt into more laughter.

"There's nothing wrong with the love of a mother and her son, Aiden," Otto says in between his bellowing amusement.

"A mother's favored son, what? No. I could kill a man with my bare hands. I'm strong and fierce!" I hear him say, trying to shout it above their amusement. Aiden has long since shed the physical traits of youth, his sharpened features boasting that of young man instead of a boy. But something about his innocent nature still betrays his age. He's no stranger to the difficulties of being a guardsman, but he hasn't let any situation harden his demeanor.

"It's unkind to tease him simply because he loves his mother," I interject. The laughter dies off as their eyes turn in my direction, unknowing that I eavesdropped on their conversation.

"Aye, Captain. We weren't trying to carelessly tease the boy. Just lifting our spirits with an innocent game," Otto answers, glee still in his eyes. "Why don't you sit and join us?" He waves me over, scooting to make room beside him.

Ah. A game. More than most I understand the need for distraction— the need to uplift the spirits of your men and women, especially in the most dire of circumstances. A reminder of what, exactly, we are fighting for.

"Your opponent tells one truth and one deceit," Otto continues, "and you must decide which is which. Our boy over here just happens to be easier to read than Ari and myself." His happy demeanor is untainted by my mild rebuke.

"I'm not a boy." Aiden throws his hands up, irritated by the repeated torment of his age.

Aiden is the youngest in the Guard, but he more than makes up for it in talent. His use of the bow may just be the best in our entire unit, and he hits as hard as many of the seasoned men. He hails from a great family, and I've gotten to know his mother and father well. Aiden seems to be enjoying himself despite Otto and the girl's ribbing remarks. I nod for them to carry on as I turn to leave.

Ari sighs loudly before turning her focus back to the other two. "I don't think your captain's station allows him to tell a lie. Or perhaps it's the truth he's incapable of?" She lowers her voice, but purposefully keeps it loud enough for me to hear.

Heat rises to the surface of my skin, any empathy from the knowledge of her father forgotten.

My honor has been questioned more times in the last two days than in the last two years combined. I pride myself on my composure, having to work with the dour Lady Margaret, or those like the nefarious Sir Reynauld. But with everything that's happened— the anniversary of Evander, a traitor within the Palace Guard, Lena being taken— my cool control continues to evade me.

"Excuse me, *my lady*." Two can be gruesome in a verbal battle. "Pray tell, how much truth do you speak on a daily basis, in between your spying and thieving and whoever knows what else for the Lady Margaret? Maybe before you accuse others of the own faults you yourself carry, you may look at the hypocrisy you're drumming."

The girl doesn't look the least bit frazzled at my statement. Instead, she begins to laugh— an incongruous gesture to the words I just spoke. My frown deepens at the sound. "You speak of hypocrisy, yet you are head of the most duplicitous organization in our whole city, maybe the whole country. You mask your face behind honor and protection, only to expose it with neglect and destruction." Her laughter fades, her eyes going somewhere dark.

"I don't know what you speak of, or what past hurt you are bringing forth to the present to lay on my head. But I assure you, I wear no mask." I want to dispute whatever accusation she is making against me, but I don't know what, exactly, she is accusing me of.

She stands, walking from her perch around the warm fire to face me directly, our toes nearly touching. The flush of her cheeks matches the fire in her eyes. "That is certainly true," she says, her calmness making her meaning even less clear. "Your colors will always shine through no matter how much you try to hide them." This time her words are only loud enough for me to hear.

She reaches a hand to rest gently on my chest. What is she doing? Her warmth bleeds through my shirt, mixing with my own. Instinct tells me to step back, to let her hand fall away. But another force, something foreign, compels me to stay put. Her hand begins to glide down my ribs and to my side, landing at my waist.

"Red," she continues, twirling a finger around the hilt of my sword, "the color of desire, blood, and death. Gold, the color of wealth, superiority, and greed. Perfectly fitting to represent the Royal Guard, is it not?"

Every sword forged within Turin has a hint of these colors etched and welded into its hilt, the blacksmiths embedding each weapon with a love of our country. Of course you can commission one without the customary red and gold, but its unique construction will cost you.

Ari looks to our two other companions, their gazes honed in to our interaction. They both look over at their swords and the royal colors inlaid there, neither one understanding how the night could have shifted so suddenly. Hell, I'm trying to work through it myself.

A tug pulls at my waist. Before I fully comprehend that she means to release my sword, I grab her wrist. She doesn't look surprised nor does she try to break loose, as if she knew what my reaction would be. Our eyes lock, the space between us electrified with our shared fury.

I force my pride down in one quick swallow, forcing out my next words. "I don't know what I've done to offend you. But if you won't tell me, then at least take my apology." My gaze stays firm, but my grip softens.

"Would you accept an apology as debt paid from the men who took your princess?" she counters, poking a finger from her free hand into my heaving chest.

My muscles tense as I close the remaining distance between us, our noses almost touching. "Their lives will pay their debt."

"Exactly," she whispers. Her teeth remain clenched even through her quiet response.

Silence stretches between us. Tears prick at the corners of her eyes, magnifying the blaze that rages within them. For just the briefest of moments, I see the girl behind her stubborn, impervious facade.

My face continues to soften the longer I look at her, recognizing the anguish behind those tears. How long had anger prompted me forward after Evander's death? The guilt and shame I felt swirled into an intensity I couldn't understand for many years, still haunting me if I'm not careful, much like is radiating from the girl in front of me.

"Ari, I..." I'm at a loss for words, unable to figure out how to ask someone I barely know about all the things that have brought them to this point, about the misery that creates people like us. But something snaps her back to the moment, her distant focus returning to me. She tugs on her wrist, still wrapped within my grip. I want to hold on, demanding her to tell me everything, but I know how ridiculous it would sound coming from me, a stranger to her life.

She rips herself from my grasp, inching toward the forest edge. Her anger no longer festers on the surface, instead replaced by something else entirely. "I'm..." She tries to talk before shaking her head, looking between a confused Aiden, a concerned Otto, then back to myself. Our penetrating stares seem to push her further away until she finally turns and runs into the cover of the trees.

Aiden stands, moving to run after her. "Let her go," Otto says, putting a hand on his shoulder to stop him.

"Something isn't right," Aiden replies, looking between his two superiors.

"Sometimes all we need is a little space to sort out our thoughts," the old man tells him before turning his attention to me. "Good grief, Roan. What have you done to her to make her hate you so much?"

"Whatever it is, she can keep her hate. As long as she stays true to her word and helps us find Lena, I don't much care how she feels about me."

But a small part of me does care. A tiny corner of protectiveness folds softly into the story of this thief. I push it away, unwilling to investigate what it means. "If she's not back by the time the owls sound, I will go find her," I say, directing my words to a worried Aiden.

I rub at my hand, the heat from her skin still scorching my own.

16

ARI

I was old enough to remember every detail.

Sometimes I wish I had been a small child, and the natural obliviousness of the life around me would have muted the images in my mind. But no. My recollection is as sharp as my dagger's tip, pouring salt into the wound of my grief each time I allow the memories to surface. And tonight those memories won, melting through my mental shield.

Once I'm out of the camp my tears flow freely. I don't go far. Even through my fissure of self-control, I'm not so stupid as to wander off in a foreign forest when night is quickly approaching. The faint light of the fire and rhythm of voices still reaches me as I drop to rest against a large tree.

My body shrinks in on itself. I pull my knees in tight against my chest, dropping my head atop my arms now folded across them. Staccato breaths hiccup out of me, and I struggle to catch enough air with each inhale.

I shut my eyes tight, praying it's all a dream. But all I hear are my wild screams as they drag my mother away, the disjointed walls and cold hearth echoing my pain throughout our home. Her warm brown eyes are a mix of fear and resolution as they take her. The swirl of red and gold brands in my mind, its mark fresh and poignant.

And here I am, breaking bread with those who stole my mother from me. Playing games with them. Laughing with them.

Aiden, the captain, Otto— they might not have been the one dragging her away while I begged and pleaded for them to let her go. Screaming of her innocence as I cried and pounded my fists into the walls. All while no one even spared me a second glance. But they represent the very people who would destroy a starving woman and her child for no other crime than simply being hungry.

Fresh tears are hot against my skin, pooling at my chin before I can wipe them away. My mind takes advantage of the open gate to my emotions, tugging at anything it can find to prolong my suffering, even going to the blank space of my father. He rarely takes up room in my thoughts, but tonight his void feels excruciatingly unfair.

My mother only spoke of him when I prodded her, asking for even the smallest token of information. Anything was acceptable— anything I could take to conjure his image, filling what I thought was a hole left by his lack of presence in my life. I felt entitled to what my mother knew of him, blind to the pain it brought her to talk about him.

She told me his hair was dark— a contrast to my soft, pale brown. His eyes were a mix of forest greens. I was proud to have his eyes. Now, I would give almost anything to see my mother's golden brown hue reflected in my own.

I spent my time with her foolishly. If I had known how little of it I had, I wouldn't have passed one moment talking of my father.

My head pounds. I'm not sure how much time has gone by, but my tears finally run dry. The emptiness left behind feels foreign and weak, so contrary to the effervescent anger that usually thrums through me.

"We should go look for her," I hear a voice say in the distance. Somewhere inside I register the three men I left in my tantrum. Normally, I would feel embarrassed that I behaved so recklessly— letting my emotions overpower me as they did. But even as my thoughts tell me I should be ashamed, nothing comes. There's no energy inside of me to care tonight, my tears and grief draining everything from me.

I try to pull at my hatred, striking the match that will surely give me the strength I need to walk back to camp and face the men there. But again, nothing surfaces.

"I love you, Mother," I whisper, unsure if I actually spoke or if my thoughts did the talking.

I lie down among the fallen leaves, feeling the comforting cradle of the earth below me. My eyes wander around the forest floor, noting the scuttling of small creatures, the moss growing up the trunks of the trees, the light breeze pushing around the fallen debris around me, and finally catching on the stars above.

Their ethereal force pulls me away from the pitiful shell of a person I've become in the last few moments. I let them swallow me into the vast, darkening sky— getting lost in their grandness and savoring their shimmering patterns. I give myself over to them, allowing them to fill the emptiness inside me.

The twinkling lights weave together, gifting me with the image of my mother— a healthy, strong, and happy version of her. She smiles at me as she pushes a piece of stray hair behind my ear. I reach out to wrap my arms around her, to pull her close, to feel her heart beating against me and listen to her steady breathing. Before I can touch her, she fades among the shadowy blue hues of night.

An ache throbs deep in my chest. A bottomless sorrow. A longing that will never be quenched. I want just a few more seconds with her before the tendrils of a cold world wrap around me yet again. But her image is gone. The blended stars settling back into their fixed perch.

Emptiness finds its way back to me.

It has been years since I grieved for my mother and allowed the torrent of emotions to break through my stable shield. Years since I've mourned for the child in me that was lost that day, my waterfall of anguish always evaporating into the heat of determined fury. My vow that I would stop the injustice of our city, that no one else need suffer as I had, has pulled and pushed and molded everything about the girl I am today. I won't give up my aching hatred anymore than I will forget the atrocious events that were its catalyst.

Traveling alongside these men, finding their princess— they are a small price to pay in order to get what I want. Once I'm free of Marg, of doing her bidding, I will be able to seek my vengeance without anyone else hindering my plans, or telling me no.

Part of me feels guilty for brushing Marg and her impact on my life away so heartlessly, but I lock that part of me up tight. There's no room to care for those who may get in my way or try to change my mind.

And I won't stop now, simply because a few guards have a spark of kindness. Tonight, I will let my longing and sorrow stay. Tomorrow, I will let vengeance and determination sing through me once again.

I find my footing, rising from the ground and stretching my stiff muscles. Slowly, I make my way back to our camp, finding my bedroll before collapsing onto it. Otto sits near me, stoking the fire one last time before laying out his own blanket.

"To be human is to experience the pain of this world, lass. The more you acknowledge it, the less power it has over you." The old man's words don't push through my numbness tonight. I simply close my eyes, wishing for both a dreamless sleep and one filled with the soft laughs of my mother.

The gentle hum of a waking forest stirs my consciousness, a pleasant transition from a deep sleep. The sky is still dark, but I sense the rising sun is not far off. I shift my position on the ground, my sore muscles screaming in protest. Full days of riding and sleeping on the ground will take some getting used to.

My stiffened body isn't the captain's fault, but I throw a glare his way nonetheless. I stand and stretch, concentrating on each body part until I've unfolded my wooden joints into a flexible human again. Each movement rustles the tranquil morning, and the ripples of displaced air begin to wake the men around me.

"It can't be morning yet," I hear Aiden mumble.

Mornings are becoming less bothersome as I grow older. I do prefer the dark of night, especially in my line of work. However, beyond simple light and dark, there's something about the first rise and last fall of the sun that holds a piece of magic in my heart.

My mother would sometimes wake me early, much to my chagrin as a child, just to watch the colors shift in the sky. The ache in my heart reopens as the memory of her breaks through my morning grogginess.

"What should we make of the new day the heavens have created for us?" she would ask me.

"We should start with breakfast," my grumbling stomach would prompt me to say. Now, I wish I would have said a thousand other things.

The men finally wake, packing up our camp with silence and swiftness. I keep to myself, following my resolution from the previous night. These men, our task— it's merely a means to an end.

Nobody has mentioned last night, leaving me to the truth of it. I'm grateful for that at least. We start another long day of riding just as the tendrils of morning chase away the shadows of night.

"Four younger sisters?" It's hard to keep the astonishment from my voice. Thus far in the day I have succeeded in keeping to myself, distancing from these men and any friendliness or camaraderie. But my shock at Aiden's revelation, the size of his family, breaks my vow of silence.

"Aye. Four. They are wild little things. My poor mother." Aiden beams as he tells me of his family, his voice projecting the protective air of an older brother.

"So you are the oldest of the brood?" I rhetorically ask, my vow continuing to crumble with each word I speak. Mentally I kick myself, affirming after each interaction that it will be the last.

"When I left for the Guard, my mother was beside herself. At first I thought it was because she would miss me. But then I realized it was because I was the only one who could tame their unyielding spirits long enough for her to get any work done, or even to rest."

"Our mother's favored son indeed," Otto adds. A smile crinkles my eyes before I school my face back to impassivity.

But my body leans forward, wanting to know more. I have always wondered what it would be like to have a brother or sister, someone older to teach me their wisdom. Or a younger little one I could guide with my own.

"And you, Otto? Any family?" Aiden asks the older man. Again I chastise myself for wanting to hear his answer. *I'm not here to make friends.*

"My father lives near the barracks, thanks to the captain." Otto nods to the front of our group towards a quiet Captain Montgomery. "But I never settled down. Never had children of my own. Too much unknown and moving around— it would be hard on a wife and children." My respect for him begins to grow at the revelation, but I decide to break the stem before it flourishes.

The captain holds up a hand to silence our conversation, pointing to the edge of the road. My focus snaps to our surroundings, listening intently for anything out of place while we quietly change our course. Prue follows my direction, moving behind me into the cover of the trees. I stroke her forehead to ease any nervousness once we're off the road.

"I recognize this place," the captain says, muffling the decibel of his voice as if the forest is listening. "There's a message outpost around this bend. I've used it occasionally to check in on the Royal Guards stationed in Fort Lowsan. The king and queen use it for communication between our two cities. Private businesses pay to use it as well. It's been a while since I've been up this way. But as far as I know, it's still up and operational." He pats his horse on the shoulders. "I'm going to ride ahead. Check in to see if anyone resembling the princess or Aldren has come through here."

"So, why are we hiding in the woods?" Otto asks. It's hard to keep a straight face as Captain Montgomery sends him a pointed look.

I sometimes wonder how he and Otto became such good friends. I know it's usual for a master to warm up to a flourishing student, but it seems these two men could not be more different if they tried. Captain Montgomery— the brooding, irritating, arrogant, prig. Otto— the charming, humorous, astute old man.

"Because a party with three guardsmen and Turin's best thief sets off alarms." The corner of my mouth ticks up as the captain admits to my skill. I wonder how much of his ego he had to clip off to actually say something nice, even if the compliment wasn't given directly to me. "We need to stay inconspicuous. If you remember, half the mission is bringing Princess Adalena home safely, the other half is to do so without kicking up dust and alerting half the kingdom's power hunters to the fact she's been taken," the captain says, annoyance running through his words at the obvious answer. "So, like I said previously, I'll go ahead. You three scout out the surroundings and stay hidden."

"I'm going with you," I say, moving to stand beside him while handing Prue's reins to Aiden. I don't trust myself to stay with the other two. It's easier for me to hate the captain— going with him will give me time to buoy my mental and emotional shields.

"I can go on my own. You stay back with Ot—"

"It's best if we stay in twos," I cut him off, my mind already made up. "Isn't that why you asked to bring your men in the first place? To pair off if needs be?" My cool words leave little to argue against. "Besides— women are less threatening. We might get more information if I come along."

"Less threatening," Otto laughs under his breath. "Guess not too many men have come across the likes of you." He tips his head toward me. Aiden shares an agreeing look with his former master, while the captain looks like he just tasted rancid soup. *Definitely easier to hate the captain.*

Whether he likes it or not, I'm coming. "It will be easier if you don't argue with me, and faster if we just get going," I tell him, sending a muted glare his way.

I face forward as I walk away, not deigning to even look back, making sure my intentions are clearly unnegotiable. I'm not staying.

A deep groan rumbles out of him. "Otto— you and Aiden stay hidden in the tree line with our horses. Ari— it would be best to leave our weapons here," he says from behind me, his frustrated annoyance clear in his tone. "As civilians of Felshan, we wouldn't be traveling with a sword, or a bow." I slow my walk, turning at his words. He unwraps his belt, handing off his blade. It's a few steps before he catches up to me, holding out his hand for my bow and quiver.

A growl rises in my throat.

"Don't worry." Aiden takes a step forward. "We will be watching. If anything seems amiss we will come." His face is firm, his lips a thin line. He looks older when he gets serious, and it almost makes me smile. The oldest brother in him is hard to tame it seems, just as his younger sister's wild spirits.

It's strange to feel his caring gaze. Another crack forms in last night's vow, and I attempt to mend it as I relax my face into indifference. I hand the captain my bow, not sparing a parting glance to our other two companions.

Our steps are deliberate. Walking over fallen branches and logs while stifling the crackling dead leaves and twigs underfoot. Our steady breathing adds to the cadence of the mid-morning forest.

The breeze rustles through the green surrounding us, the trees clustered tightly enough that we must weave through them every few steps. Wild flowers poke through random patches of grass and weeds, growing only where stray rays of sunlight break through the ceiling of the forest. The scent of spring swirls around us as we move, while all variety of birds flit through the branches above, adding their song to the air.

"We will say you're my wife, and we are traveling to Fort Lowsan for your brother's wedding," Captain Montgomery says, breaking the forest's trance. "It would make more sense to travel in regards to your family, since when we married you'd come live with my family."

His deep voice reverberates the atrocity down to my very bones. His wife? I would rather willingly burn my hands in tonight's dinner fire than pretend to be anything of his.

I open my mouth to rebuke his absurdity, but he must already sense my objection. "You don't have to like it, but it protects us both if we pretend to be married." His sleeves are rolled to his elbows, his tanned forearms swinging gently at his side.

"So, in order to travel as a woman I must be married?" Heat rises in me, but I soften into it.

"Obviously not. But it offers less questions. Many husbands and wives travel together and leave little to be wondered— or remembered— which serves our purposes well." His tone is matter-of-fact, paired with a slight edge of irritation.

My indignation makes it difficult to keep my voice quiet. "If we have to be related, can't we just be brother and sister?" It's a genuine question. If I have to be bound to this man, even a counterfeit relation, at least brother and sister would imply minimal touching. It wouldn't even imply love, as I'm sure many siblings hate each other. And it would take very little effort to play the part of loathsome sister to the man walking beside me.

"Do you have to argue with everything I say?" He asks. His eyes are wide and his jaw rigid, strong arms outstretched to either side of him.

"When it's ridiculousness you're peddling— yes, I do." I begin to roll up my sleeves, the heat of day reaching me as a few beads of sweat form on my brow.

A deep breath fills his chest, his arms falling back to his side during his exhale. He rakes a hand through his dark hair, a few strands falling back into his face. "And what would be our reason for traveling outside of Turin as brother and sister?" His voice is steady now. "Most civilians die having never traveled more than a few minutes away from the home they were born into, let alone having traveled to a completely different city."

My mother never left Turin, I realize, and I've only visited the outskirts of the city. His reasoning is sound, but my stubbornness won't let me yield so easily. "You seem to have a grand imagination. I'm sure you can come up with something," I answer, not bothering to look his way to navigate his reaction.

The captain stops, his ocean-colored eyes fixed on me. "Alright. You win. Be my sister," he says. "And watch the greedy eyes of any man inside roam over you like you're fresh meat to be roasted over the fire." And his eyes do just that— looking from my worn leather boots, to my leather belted waist, grazing up my shirt, until they slowly reach my gaze.

His glare is like winter, much different from the summer flames that resided in them last night. It's a look I'm not used to, and I stare back as I try to make sense of it. I've seen darkness in men before, a coldness like we lived at the top of the frigid Kotar in the middle of winter. But this is different. His intense gaze is focused solely on me. Not on my body, not on my weapons, not on what I can give him or how much he could sell me for— just me.

"I've handled feral men most of my life," I tell him, talking through the unsettling feeling burrowing into my stomach as he continues to stare at me. "Just point a knife at their throat and they become much more respectful."

He says nothing, turning to face forward once again while we walk.

As we get closer, the building comes into view. Although, building may be too strong a description. It looks more like an oversized hovel, boasting little room for more than a couple beds and a place to prepare a meal.

We enter into a small clearing, breaching the property of the outpost. The captain and I walk carefully, taking in our surroundings, listening and watching for anything out of place. Nothing seems amiss until the stable comes into view.

"Something isn't right," the captain says under his breath, looking from the stables to the outpost building and back again. Every stall is full, plus at least half a dozen more horses tied to a makeshift wooden rail. They lazily graze on the grass surrounding them, almost bored by our approach.

"I didn't realize this place would be so busy." I meet the captain's gaze as a familiar buzz awakens inside of me.

Everything around me sharpens. The tiny blue flowers surrounding my feet. The smell of a coming storm. The sound of bees flying around their hive. With my next step, I feel for the familiar anchor at my ankle, my blade still securely in place. My heart immediately eases. I may have handed over my bow, but I wouldn't be caught dead without my favorite weapon in tow and a way to defend myself should the need arise.

Each step is careful and meticulous as we make our way to the entrance. My fingers tick as I wait for any reason to unsheathe my dagger. We stop just outside the front door, crossing under a small hanging sign that reads, *Mail Outpost*.

"Sister." The captain nods at me stoically as he reaches for the handle.

"Just open it." I roll my eyes at him as I stand up straight, smearing as close to a genuine smile on my face as I can for whomever waits inside. A creak peals through the air as the door is pulled open. We step through the frame, the door closing with a loud *clang* behind us.

And a dozen pairs of greedy eyes greet me.

17

CAPTAIN MONTGOMERY

THE SHARP ODOR OF unbathed men and sour ale fills my nose. I raise a hand to my face to stifle the smell.

"Brother," Ari twines her arm through mine. Her entire demeanor shifts as the door closes. She looks more like she's in the company of her favorite uncle than a band of potentially dangerous strangers. Gone is the biting thief from Turin, and in her place is— well, I'm not really sure. The girl next to me seems completely at ease, her focus honed on the room like a cat listening for the rustle of a mouse.

I turn my concentration away from her, sweeping my gaze through the space. A few small tables line the area, men surrounding each one. They are packed in as tightly as they will fit, like clothes stuffed into every crevice of a drawer, requiring great effort just to close the thing.

No light comes from the back of the tiny establishment. There's a great chance the only entrance and exit lies within the door we just walked through, only a couple paces behind us. A row of swords are lined against the side wall, matching the same number of men crowded into the tiny room. Between Ari and myself we may be able to keep a few of them disarmed, but eventually our line would break and we would be in trouble.

We are outnumbered six to one.

"I apologize. My brother isn't the social sort." Ari takes a step forward, maintaining her grip on my arm. Her eyes are calm like a glossy sea on a windless day. "We are looking for a little help. Our horse slipped a shoe earlier this morning, and we are hoping to buy a replacement beast after seeing that your stables are overflowing. You're welcome to our horse, of course— just half a morning's ride southeast toward Turin. She's tied up just off the road."

Ari's broad smile doesn't seem to soften the stiff faces staring back at us. She pinches my side. "Smile," she quietly says, somehow without moving her lips.

All I can do is glare at the thirst in their treacherous eyes. It takes every effort not to choke the life out of the man sitting closest to me, his eager grin directed toward Ari. We may hardly know each other, and I may have wanted to tie her to the nearest tree and leave her there ever since we left Turin, but she's still under my protection.

Ari releases my arm and steps toward the closest table of men, her cooling absence from my side making my nerves jump in response. "What are you drinking, sir?" she asks, lifting the nearest cup to examine the contents. She doesn't wait for an answer before throwing the cup back and gulping down whatever is inside. A few drops escape down her face before she finishes, and she wipes an arm underneath her chin to dry the gathered stream.

What did she just consume? The empty cup is slammed against the table before she offers another wide smile to the room.

"Jaren— why don't you grab another chair," a man says, the corners of his mouth ticking up as he stares at his now empty cup.

The man's tawny hair is combed back. Its thick, clumpy sheen highlights little flecks of white that dot through his scalp while its length flows over his shoulders and curls lightly at the ends. His eyes look like the color of murky water reflecting gray clouds. A dark tunic wraps around him, lining his hefty arms and torso before disappearing underneath the table he has squeezed into.

"Any woman that can drink like that deserves a seat at my table." The man's face is alight with pleasure, yellowing teeth escaping through his lips while he waves a hand toward one of the men in the back. The one I assume is Jaren stands, dragging his own chair across the floor before fitting it next to the man who previously spoke.

As Jaren steps away from us, a flicker of familiarity trickles through me. Have I seen him before? I can't quite place him, but recognition pulses through me. I watch him retreat to his spot in the back of the room, irritation tugging at me as he shimmies between the tight space of men.

"Perhaps your brother would prefer to wait outside," the tawny-haired man says to Ari, his attention never wavering from her form.

"Corin may be a bit of a killjoy, but he's harmless. Come, Corin. Come sit by your sister." There's humor in her gaze as she waves me over. She winks at me before turning back in her seat to face the man. "I'm Calla, by the way. And you are?" she asks him. I scoff quietly to myself as I move by her side, closing the distance in only a couple steps.

Another man gives up his chair so I can sit. The chair won't quite fit around the table, so I'm forced to sit a pace behind her, sticking out like a wing among pigs.

"I'm Silas of Fort Kotar." The tawny-haired man, Silas, reaches out a dirty hand which she gladly accepts. My frown deepens as his hand lingers around hers longer than it should, but she appears completely unaware. I may not know Ari well, but I know her well enough to grasp that she is, in fact, well aware of his advances.

She wasn't lying when she told me she'd been dealing with men like this most of her life. It would seem practice makes perfect. Her act is so tight I can't tell where Ari ends, and Calla begins.

"Well, Silas of Fort Kotar. You're a far way from home," she says, her sweet tone pulling him in closer. At least one of us seems to be enjoying ourselves.

"As are you, Calla of... Turin?"

"Aye. Turin." Ari, or maybe Calla is more appropriate here, takes on a bit of Aiden's accent. "Our father went to care for an ailing uncle up in a small town just off Fort Lowsan. Seems he got whatever illness his brother was battling, and he himself is now fairing poorly. We are hoping to bring him back so he can heal within in his own home."

Her story is flawless— a perfectly fabricated narrative. I close my jaw before anyone can see my shock, which would most certainly unravel the thread of her deception. How many times must she have done this to become so good at it?

"What is a man of Fort Kotar doing in charge of a small mail outpost between Turin and Fort Lowsan?" she asks. Her countenance is so enchanting, I half expect her to be invited to sit on his lap. I grind my teeth as the revolting image crosses through my mind. In fact, I'm so distracted by the pair, I forget for a moment that we are here for Lena.

"We are just passing through. The one who runs this station was kind enough to let our horses rest while we take a small respite from our travels." Silas grins.

Disgust fills me as I think of the real fellow in command of this outpost and where he truly is in this moment. Perhaps they let him go. Or more likely, he's rotting away in a shallow grave out back.

My fists lay clenched in my lap, each muscle ticking the more I have to sit here listening to this man. I try to relax, instead observing the room and leaning back into everything Otto taught me. Watch. Listen. Wait for a change in the air, for the hair on my arms to stand on end, for the unmistakable aroma of trouble. But no matter how hard I try, my focus always returns to Ari.

She converses with Silas so effortlessly, and I can't yet tell if it's part of her act or if she truly enjoys it. I don't know whether to be impressed or nauseated. Something unfamiliar gnaws at me as I see them interact.

No matter. It's hard to neglect that her tactic seems to be working. And since we are here for Lena, I swallow my distaste.

Silas leans forward the longer they talk, his eyes only leaving her when inspecting me. His apprehension seems to seep away with every sentence she speaks. If Ari can get a lead on Lena, I'll sanction whatever she needs to do in order to get it— even entertaining this moron.

I turn my focus back to the room, trusting Ari to get whatever information she can. If this doesn't end well we are only a few steps from the exit. Once we made it outside it would take only a few moments for Otto and Aiden to see our distress and come, evening the odds to a winnable chance. Or at the least, an escapable chance.

A few of Silas's men appear to be in conversation, but each one also seems to be keeping an eye on our interaction. There's no change in the atmosphere, not yet. But I can't shake the feeling that trouble is on the horizon.

The men are getting restless with their foreign company, a few gazes drifting to their weapons against the wall. Their swords are out of reach, but no one dares move toward them. *Hurry, Ari.*

Jaren catches my eye again, a scowl on his features as he stares at me from the corner of his vision. Not only do I know this man from somewhere, but his regard is more than the wariness of a stranger. It's almost malicious in nature.

I watch him interact with his table. His brown hair is slicked back, his dark eyes sizing me up while he pretends to be engaged by his companions. If I stare long enough, maybe my mind will finally reveal where I've seen him before—

"Your brother, Corin. Does he speak?" My eyes flick away from Jaren, landing on Silas as he acknowledges me. I force away a grimace, hoping not to deter Ari's efforts in gaining his trust.

"Don't mind him. His wife ran off with one of his closest friends just a few days ago. He hasn't spoken much since," she says through a pitying frown, trailing a finger down the side of my face in what I expect is supposed to be an intimate gesture of affection and comfort. "It's ok, brother. We will fix you up and find you someone else." She pouts her lips, talking to me as if she were talking to a child. I almost roll my eyes, breaking the pathetic character she's conjured up for me.

Instead, I narrow my eyes, annoyed at how I've somehow come to be the quiet, pitiful one in her story. She is biting back a smile, trying to keep the facade of doting, sorrowful sister on the tip of her tongue. But the humor still reaches her eyes, a slight shimmer among the hues of green.

The men chuckle to themselves, and my jaw tightly clenches. I wonder what it would feel like to knock Silas right out of his chair. The image brings me the slightest bit of satisfaction.

"Say," she turns to face Silas, "we've been trying to locate exactly where they went. She took a few things that belong to our family, and it would be nice to get them back. We thought them long gone, but perhaps you can help us." Ari shifts in her seat almost imperceptibly, the only indication of the true thief underneath her facade. "Have you seen anyone come through here, or on the road of your travels, that may have been her and her lover? Brother," she turns to face me, "why don't you describe your betraying former wife and sordid friend to Silas." She's laying it on thick, but a glance at Silas shows me he still believes every word.

I clear my throat, turning everyone's attention on me. "My wife— she has light colored hair, like that of a pale sunflower. Her eyes a soft brown. She's a little shorter than Calla." I look toward my supposed sister before turning back to Silas. "And my friend— he has dark hair, similar to my own, reaching to his shoulders. He likes to keep it pulled back. His eyes are equally dark, and he's built well. They would obviously be traveling together," I tell him, doing my best to keep as heartbroken a look through my countenance as possible, playing to Ari's story.

The man's once velvety demeanor turns rigid. The room quiets, all eyes moving from Silas, to Ari, and then to myself. All my senses come to life, my body fringing on the precipice of staying put to see this through, or grabbing Ari and lunging for the door. Only the smallest chance that he will tell me of Lena, give me any clue to where she may be, keeps me in my seat.

A few beats pass before Silas speaks, putting me further on edge. "I can't say I've seen anyone that fits that description." He leans back in his chair, his hands meeting together in front of him as his icy stare slips between me and the girl.

He knows we are lying. But how? Up until I described Lena and Aldren, Ari had him eating from her hand.

My shrewd companion doesn't miss a breath. "That's too bad. Looks like today is not our lucky day after all. Well, Corin," Ari looks to me, something akin to both victory and loss playing across her face, "we should be on our way if we want to get to Father in time."

"Don't you want a horse?" Silas asks her. "That is why you came in here after all." Unconsciously, I reach for the handle of my sword, my body sensing the unease around me, but I'm met with the reminder of its absence.

"I can see there are no horses available here," Ari replies. She stands, her chair scraping out behind her.

Everyone in the room rises, mirroring her movements, except for Silas. I stand slowly, my full height reaching above any other man here. The man closest to me looks me up and down, a frown pulling at his face.

Ari smiles as she looks around, a fierceness within the gesture that signals the end of Calla. "Such loyal men you carry with you, Silas."

"Down to the death." His hateful grin is potent, taking over the putrid scent of the space. Thundering silence follows, everybody waiting for the other to move.

"When I give the signal, run," I breathe, loud enough for only Ari to hear. The only response I get is a mere twitch of her finger.

I inhale deeply before lunging wildly to the side. My fist closes the distance toward the man nearest me, connecting to his jaw and sending him backward into his table. My gaze turns toward Silas, my pent-up annoyance itching to give him the same fate.

But twelve hungry men swarm us before I get the chance.

I turn just in time to see the door swing open, Ari running through the only exit. The clamor of unsheathing swords reaches me, spurring me to follow her. I duck and twist my way out of the grasp of several men.

Silas sits in his chair, watching the scene stumble around him, his face cloaked with indifference. Knowing men like him, he saves his vengeance and serves it slowly. More than ever I regret leaving my sword behind, desperately wanting to feel it glide into his chest and watch his malevolent grin fade away. But I made the stupid decision to leave it behind, lending me worthless against the steel heading my way.

The light and heat of early afternoon reaches me as I sprint out the door, the clamor of footsteps rumbling close behind me.

18

ARI

I'M NOT AFRAID OF a good fight, even one where I might be outnumbered. In fact, I welcome a challenge.

But I know the openness of the forest and road beyond the outpost will give us the ability to maneuver around these men. In such a tight space within the building, we would be easy prey to fall upon.

I dart through the exit, several footsteps following after me. Everything was going smoothly with Silas until the captain spoke. Did he know I was lying the entire time, playing me for the fool? No. I would have sensed it.

A *thump, growl,* and subsequent *clang* reaches my ears. I'm halfway across the clearing when I turn around, finding Captain Montgomery fighting off three men, another two coming up close behind him.

He moves with exactness, the need for a sword rendered almost moot as his body becomes the essence of a sharp, cold weapon. His fist connects to the side of one man's face, knocking him back into two others before they all fall over. The captain grabs the man's sword from his hands before he even hits the ground.

His movements are devastatingly graceful as he twists around, counter-attacking another man coming at him from behind. His arms ripple with the impact of jabbing the sword's hilt into the man's stomach, his other elbow swinging across his opponent's face before an explosive kick lands the man to the ground. The captain's advance is relentless.

Without thinking I pivot, charging to protect his back from yet another coming at him from behind. Another line of swords come barreling out of the threshold, wielded by their now emboldened owners. I dip low, retrieving my dagger as I move to meet them, joining the fray at the captain's side.

Something whooshes past my ear before a gurgling noise erupts from somewhere close by. I'm taken aback as I see the shaft of an arrow protruding from a man's neck, a small drop of blood dripping down his skin. Silas's group hesitates, gaping at their companion.

Another whiz fragments the air. Another. Then another. Three more arrows find their target in three more men. One lands in an arm, another in a leg, and the last one in a side. These subsequent hits aren't killing blows, but they will be painful, hindering the men and aiding us greatly in our escape.

"Run!" someone screams. Otto bursts through the tree line mounted on his horse, my bow in his hands.

My periphery catches more movement. Aiden rides forward, another arrow nocked and ready to fly, aiming steadfast for any of Silas's men who dares move forward. It causes just enough pause for the captain to free himself from the bulk of the assault, his size clearly marking him as the greater threat. I don't have time to scoff at their naïve assumptions. He runs for his horse, spurred forward by the safety of Aiden's cover.

Jaren, the man who gave up his chair at Silas's request, notes the momentary lapse of focus, darting forward with his sword raised, chasing after the captain regardless of Aiden's threat. I grab the tip of my dagger and launch it across the distance, landing the cold metal into the soft heat of his flesh.

It embeds deep in his side. His cry of anguish and outrage echoes through the clearing, his pain bouncing off my impervious skin— now as well-built and hard as the Turinian steel jutting from his wrenching wound. The captain turns in stride, pulling my knife from the man's torso. In the same motion he kicks Jaren square in the chest, knocking him flat on his back.

My vision tunnels as I race for Prue, grabbing the reins from Otto as I leap atop her. When I turn to locate Captain Montgomery, he's gone. The pounding in my ears grows louder, my breathing shallow and ragged. I search the ground, tensing to dismount and find our fourth companion.

My gaze is drawn by sudden movement. I flick my focus to the back of the property, the captain running from the stables. A held breath releases from me in huff, my shoulders dropping as I see him. Horses shoot from every direction, sprinting left and right past their riders and deeper into the forest. The captain cuts the last one free, grabbing the reins of the chestnut horse before climbing onto its back and barreling toward us.

He's smart, scattering any chance that Silas or his men will be able to follow. A few of the horses may return by the end of the day, confused and directionless, but we will be long gone.

A glint catches my eye as Captain Montgomery rides closer, and I realize my dagger is still in his hand. I spare one last glance at the mail outpost, just in time to see Silas step outside. My victorious smile greets his darkened gaze.

Aiden nocks one more arrow. His concentration and skill paint over the boy who started this journey with us only yesterday, molding him into the man now in front of me. The arrow's point lands only a finger's breadth from the head of Silas just before we disappear down the road.

The building and wounded men are now only a trace in the wind as it blows through my tangled, sweat dampened hair.

Rain falls around us in sheets.

Otto ties a small tent between the trees, hardly big enough for two of us let alone four, while the captain releases the extra horse acquired earlier.

Each movement I make pulls my soaked shirt away from my body, its weight a heavy suction, exposing more of me than I wish to bare to these guards. I undo what's left of my braid, wringing out my hair in a futile attempt to keep it from matting while I sleep. My skin prickles as I accidentally nudge into the captain.

He turns toward me, his gaze trailing down my dripping hair. "Thank you," he says, quieting his voice in our close proximity. "I believe this hunk of metal may have saved my life today." He hands me my dagger, now cleaned of any remnants of Jaren.

I suck in a breath at his description. My dagger is a sleek piece of art. "This hunk of metal, as you say, has saved my life more than once. It's no respecter of persons, living up to its purpose well." I avoid meeting his gaze as I take it from his hands.

I did save his life today, without question. In my dreams I've never saved a guardsman, let alone the Captain of the Guard. A good day would be watching their barracks burn to the ground, even better if it was by my own hands. The idea of saving Captain Montgomery's life only a few days ago would have been absurd, not to mention riding as a companion to two other guardsmen. I would have thought myself gone mad if I could go back and relay the last two day's events.

My hate has driven me these last five years, taking me for a heavy ride as I mastered my craft with Lady Margaret. Where would I be if I let it go? What other purpose would my life hold? It anchors me to this life— one I choose to spend in the murky clouds so others can see the stars.

My muscles relax when I see that true gratitude rests in his blue eyes. Water drips from the captain's touseled, sable hair, trickling down the hard planes of his face and falling to his neck. I let my thoughts drift away with the steady drum of beating rain, watching the drops of water as they disappear beneath the fabric of his shirt.

"Our fortune couldn't be better," Otto says, looking out toward the rain. "This will greatly deter Silas and his men, covering any remnants from our path today." His words are meant for no one in particular, being as our entire group is squished together like the corseted torso of a wealthy woman.

"Did you find out anything about the princess? Or Parker?" Aiden finally asks, turning his attention to the captain and myself. Our tent grows quiet at his question, a small echo of thunder sounding in the background.

I don't know if he's speaking to me or to the captain, but I answer anyway. "They knew something. Did you notice?" I turn briefly to the captain before explaining everything that transpired while we were separated. "The moment Captain Montgomery gave the description of the princess and Aldren—"

"Roan," the captain interjects. I pause, my gaze meeting his own. "You can call me Roan. There's no need for formality out here," he says. My skin prickles again, but a quick check shows I haven't touched him since the last time.

I call him captain not because I'm uncomfortable using his name, but to remind myself to keep my distance. To remind me of what he represents. And to hell if I'm going to cozy up to the likes of him or anyone close to him. I try to scoot away, leaving some distance between me and him, but end up bumping into both Aiden and Otto. No matter where I move I will be touching someone I swore to hate for my entire lifetime.

The captain notes my movement, but says nothing.

How did I wind up sandwiched between three men? Not only three men, but three guardsmen at that? I release a deep exhale, rubbing at my eyes to try and clear away my irritation and obvious lack of judgment. I may have agreed to come along of my own free will, but I didn't agree to become bosom friends.

"Once Captain Montgomery gave the description of the princess and Aldren," I continue, trying to take away any friendliness from my voice, "Silas immediately clammed up. He went from willing to personally escort us on our journey to Fort Lowsan and home again with our supposed father, to ready to slit our throats in mere moments."

"He recognized the description," the captain adds, not even flinching at my refusal to use his preferred name. "He knew we were looking for Princess Adalena."

"You think he was involved?" Aiden asks.

"If not directly, he at least knows something. That outpost was made to house only three or four people. The keeper and some stable hands, along with a few horses. Those men were out of place, hiding and keeping off the road during daylight." The captain looks distressed as he speaks, his voice low and gutteral. His vision goes distant as if trying to fit all the pieces together that seem odd-shaped and askew.

"We may not have solid proof that the princess came this way, but I'd say it's a decent breadcrumb that we're heading in the right direction. It's too strange and coincidental to ignore," I state.

Otto nods at my speculation. "Aye. I agree. Roan, would you conclude the same?"

The captain is expressionless, his voice dry as he says, "Yes. I would agree."

No one says anything for a few moments, all of us silently contemplating. Why would so many need to participate in order to take one young girl? There's more to it than just kidnapping a princess. There's more to their plan. Whoever they are, do they want to invade Turin? Overthrow Cassus Chattan, and put another in his place?

I wouldn't care much if they did. Although, I'm sure many lives would be lost. And most of those lives, along with the suffering inflicted from such a move, would be paid for by those with the least amount of power to change even their own circumstances.

The captain clenches his jaw, the muscles there tightening, his hands toggling between balled fists and openly flexed, distracting me from my reflections.

"We should have stayed and fought," he whispers, although everyone hears.

"We were outnumbered," I respond.

His eyes are cold, their brilliant blue muted to the navy darkness building within. "With Aiden and Otto, we could have handled it. We could have grabbed Silas and questioned him to our heart's content, gotten details of Lena and where they're headed. Instead, we are following some obscure path we simply *hope* they're on," he replies.

It feels as though he's talking to himself rather than to our group. But his dejected voice seems to bring us all to wonder if we could have, or should have, done more—won a dozen against four, and gotten more concrete evidence to guide us. Perhaps earning us the knowledge of the path and direction to follow that would definitively stop with Lena at the end of it.

Our conversation dies off, leaving nothing to do but stare at the clouds and their deluge wreaking through this part of the land. The water has cooled away the steamy afternoon, leaving a bit of chill through the air, sending a shiver up my spine.

"There's no use in arguing the shoulds or shouldn'ts of the past. It doesn't get us anywhere but more frustrated, and expending the energy needed to solve our current problems," Otto states, his bold tone directed at us all. "I say for now, we follow the West Passageway to Fort Lowsan. We can meet up with the Santanas, and—"

"No. We cannot involve the Santanas," the captain interjects, cutting Otto off from his next words. The history and High Houses of Felshan families are not my strength. The name Santana doesn't jog any memories, but I'm not surprised. I had no use for such things outside of Turin. Why spend my time learning the names and history of the wealthy, those who literally have everything, when my time could be put to much better use supporting those not born to privilege?

"The Santanas have always been friendly to the Crown. If the princess or Aldren went through Fort Lowsan, they would be able to provide that information. I've heard they run that city like a prison yard. We might be able to receive something vital to our quest," Aiden responds.

"They do run their city like a prison yard. If they knew we were in Fort Lowsan and our purpose for being in their city, we would be swallowed into the cell of Lord Santana's *hospitality* until all trace of Lena or Aldren disappears," Captain Montgomery tells us.

"But I thought you were friends with Lord Santana's children? Weren't Tess and Liam close with the prince?" Otto asks.

The captain stiffens, and a long pause accompanies Otto's question. "They were," he finally replies. "But in case you've forgotten, the prince has been dead for seven years. Lots of friendships waiver during such a long period of absence." The captain's eyes are hard, but not because Otto questioned him. No. There's something deeper there that I can't quite point to.

"Maybe it's time you remind them of their affection for Evander, and their fealty to the Crown," Otto counters. Something passes between the master and his old student, silent words passing to and fro, neither one breaking eye-contact.

"We go into Fort Lowsan without making our presence known. The Santanas are not to be told of Princess Adalena. If anything changes, I will let you know." And with that the captain lays down in our cramped space, signaling the end of our discussion. I've never heard of Tess or Liam Santana, and keeping to myself has always been my way, so steering clear of their family is no great disappointment.

Otto turns away, clearly not agreeing with his captain's assessment. He swallows his defeat rather quickly, patting Aiden on the shoulder and offering a warm smile as he joins the captain on his overlapping bedroll. "Best get some sleep. Tomorrow will be another long day, especially if this rain keeps up," Otto says.

I don't realize until my three companions are nestled on the ground that I somehow got wedged next to the captain. Maneuvering my way to the corner, I attempt to evade the stream of water seeping through the edge of the tent. A quick tug on my bedroll brings further misfortune as I realize it's tucked underneath Captain Montgomery. Do I risk letting him know that I'd rather sleep in the pouring rain than curl up beside him? Or do I sleep in the muck?

A quick manipulation of my position lends me a clean space for my head, curling my legs up against my chest to keep them as dry as possible. Only my boots and the bottom part of my pants sink into the wet dirt. It's not the worst place I've ever slept.

One night won't kill me.

19

Captain Montgomery

I WAKE BEFORE SUNRISE, the first few fingers of light brushing through the sky.

A warm weight drapes across one leg, its comforting weight leaving me within the in between of sleep and wakefulness longer than usual. I finally open my eyes, blinking as consciousness sharpens my vision and awareness. Ari lies nestled next me, her head pushing against my thigh and her arms entwined around and beneath my legs. She looks so peaceful, her chest rising and falling with each steady breath, in and out. Her soft brown hair lays sprawled out beneath her while her eyelashes cast the barest hint of a shadow beneath her eyes.

I unwittingly clear my throat. The harsh, gutteral sound rattles through our small space. My inadvertent movement jostles her from sleep, and I move my body away before she knows of her precarious positioning only moments before. She sits up, her heavy-lidded eyes resting on me, their softness molding swiftly to annoyance.

My feet sink with each step as we pack up our meager camp, mud coating the bottom half of my boots. The ground is mushy from last night's rain, and the clouds above threaten more before the morning melts into afternoon.

"Let's pray to Haythen we find the princess in Fort Lowsan," Aiden says. "I've heard the Prythan Mountains are similar to the Kotar— taller in some places if you can even imagine. If their spring season is anything like ours, it won't just be men like Silas we will need to keep an eye out for." He stares into the sky as he walks his mare to the road.

"What do you mean?" Ari asks, tilting her head to the side.

I've never seen the Prythan, only heard stories I assumed were mostly fictitious. The kind used to add drama to the tale to keep the listener entertained. Many liken the Prythans to the Kotar, Felshan's mountain range that boasts some of the highest, most dangerous peaks in all of the Four Kingdoms. But if the stories boasted any truth, then while the Kotar Mountains— which I know well from my training in the Guard— are dauntless, the Prythan Mountains are indomitable.

"This rain, while we are on flat ground, is more of a nuisance," Otto replies to Ari's question, his eyes gentle as he looks toward her. "It may cause us to slip around, slow down, and coat our bottom halves in a good deal of mud. However, all this moisture—" he pauses, looking out into the north where I swear I see a faint, shaded outline pushing through the clouds onto the horizon. "Up in the Prythan. Well." He shrugs, and his eyes glaze over for a mere moment before he forces a grin.

Ari's brow still lays furrowed, her confusion adding to my own bewilderment. I thought with all her training with Lady Margaret, she would have at least been exposed to the lower of the Kotar. The mountain front that, when compared to the full range, look more like rolling hills. But Ari appears oblivious to the plight of the mountains, even the smallest Felshan has to offer.

Otto catches on to her confusion quickly, not allowing her ignorance to create any embarrassment on her part. He finds an earthworm inching its way across our path, picking it out of the saturated dirt of the road and laying it gently on the back of his hand.

"Think of us as this worm here," Otto says. "If I tilt my hand, the worm can still make its way up and over. My hand is dry, so there's good traction. If I add a little water," he jogs to the side of the road, grabbing and emptying the gathered rain water from a cup-shaped leaf overtop the worm. "The worm moves around a bit, and may get washed away if he's in the strongest part of the run-off. But for the most part, he has no problem staying aboard my hand— finding his footing again, so to speak.

However, the water mixed with dirt," he bends, digging his hand into the soft ground, and plopping the contents overtop the creature on his tilted hand, "will push the worm clean off without any notice or hesitation." The worm drops to the ground with the heap of mud.

Ari raises an eyebrow at Otto's now filthy hands. "I'm not a child, Otto. I think I could have kept up with a verbal explanation."

"Now, where's the fun in that?" Otto winks at her as he finds more cupped leaves to wash away the grime from his visual representation.

"Summer is really the only pleasant time to spend up in the mountains," Aiden adds. "Autumn leaves the threat of early snowfall, making the journey three or four times longer and killing those who don't have enough supplies to last that long. Winter boasts temperatures so cold you'll freeze overnight if unprepared. And spring— impassable roads from winter snow run-offs and extra rain, or being buried in a mudslide."

"It's no wonder we don't all live in the mountains," Ari sneers.

The gates of Fort Lowsan loom ahead of us.

We urged our horses to go as fast as they could, driven by Otto's vivid explanation of the danger of the mountains and our hope of avoiding the northern fort altogether.

Parker Aldren must have ridden day and night in order to evade our rescue party. I think of the last time I saw him, standing guard outside the throne room. He had talked to her. I heard him conversing with Lena from where I stood around the corner. A growl rises from my throat as I imagine him plotting against her, against my family.

I knew Evander better than I know my own brother, and the king and queen treated me as their own son. The treachery this family has endured... A tightening pit forms in my stomach, clenching and churning my insides. Not only for Aldren's treason, but my own part in their pain. I may not have directly killed Evander, but I may as well have been the one who shot the arrow.

I push my guilt aside for something deeper— the pledge I made all those years ago. The one I whispered while clutching onto my best friend's lifeless body, the Rashan swirling around our forms, its crystal blue water tinged with Evander's blood. For as long as I lived, I would personally make sure King Cassus, Queen Amelia, and their daughter, Princess Adalena, were protected. That I would never leave their side. I would do what Evander no longer could. Whatever dreams I may have held for my future were reforged that day into a polished sword of promise, one even stronger than Turinian steel.

I see that sword digging deep into Aldren as I watch the life leave his eyes. It's not pain and anguish that I will feel. No. It will be satisfaction and honored vengeance. My promise fulfilled without any remorse.

20

ARI

A S WE APPROACH THE entrance of Fort Lowsan, everyone's spirits drop at the sight of dozens of wagons waiting at the south entrance.

A checkpoint of guards, swords sheathed but at the ready if the need should arise, line around the large metal gate from both below and a cove above. It's a dark, heavy, monstrosity of a thing, built not to keep out simple farmers and tradesman, but apparently armed giants. Additional soldiers stand on the massive wall surrounding the Fort, bows in hand— archers awaiting a command from their leader.

"We need to split up," Captain Montgomery says, dismounting his horse a few paces back from the line while turning around to face Otto, Aiden, and myself. "I know the Santanas. They have eyes and ears all over the city searching for anything out of the ordinary— and four armed Felshanian soldiers," he eyes me, tagging me half-heartedly into the category, "are definitely out of the ordinary. But if we separate, go in one at a time, we might pass through without any red flags raising to their spies."

"The Santanas work for the Crown. They wouldn't dare stop business of the Captain of the Royal Guard," I declare.

"We are a far ways from Turin, Ari." There's a minuscule pause before he says my name. He still has to intentionally think through what to call me, the contempt of *thief* still wanting to cross his tongue. "The Santanas are loyal to the Crown, but to themselves first and foremost. If we are to keep our assignment private and expeditious, keeping our tails out of their sights and a gilded prison in the process, we need to blend in."

"What did Parker do? It's pretty obvious to have a girl passed out in the back as he crossed through. Would they have gone around the perimeter to stay out of eye-shot?" Aiden asks.

"It would take too long. Aldren is smart. He would have found a way to hide her, not daring take the extra day around," the captain says.

"Are we sure they are going to Thenstra? He could be going to the Western Seaport. Side-step entering Fort Lowsan altogether," Otto questions.

"He could," says the captain. "But it's unlikely. The Seaport was used to trade between Thenstra, Felshan, and Venes. Once Thenstra shut its borders, it no longer stayed the most lucrative option. We can trade with Venes easier by land. There's hardly anything at the Western Seaport anymore. A small town, a small garrison of guards keeping what order they can."

I turn and roll my eyes. I'm sure those guards are keeping order, as long as that order fills their purses.

"If he wanted to throw us off, he could take a boat from the Seaport up to Thenstra, instead of going through the mountains," I say. The geography of Felshan's northwestern border isn't something I ever studied closely, but if it's less traveled like they say, it might appeal to Parker Aldren. Stay off the beaten path. Less likely to be seen.

"Hmm. It wouldn't be a bad plan. But he'd still have to pass through Fort Lowsan," the captain replies. "The north gate of Fort Lowsan bridges where the northern Kotar Mountains and southern Prythan Mountains gather the melting snow run-offs, creating the river Villar which heads toward the western oceanfront, and the Rashan, winding down toward Turin and the eastern oceanfront. The water flows around the city and underneath it, building in aquifers. Eventually, they empty into one of those two rivers."

The captain bends, drawing in the soft ground. Triangles mark the Kotar, a square for Fort Lowsan, and the flowing lines of the Villar and Rashan moving away from the city.

"In the spring, the waters of both rivers overflow at their meeting point. The warm weather melting the snowfall from both mountain ranges. Fort Lowsan is built higher than sea level, saving the city from flooding. However, the only passable bridge at this time of year is the northern gate of Fort Lowsan. Aldren wouldn't be able to cross to the seaport unless he went through the Fort."

The captain's drawing and hurried potamology lesson squashes any theory that Aldren might have gone another way.

"So, his goal could still be the Western Seaport. But we might find him in the Fort before he makes his way out. Especially if they indeed have a wagon in tow, and a girl to hide within it," Aiden adds.

"Yes," is all the captain responds.

"What about these wagons here waiting?" I ask. "Princess Adalena could be in any one of these. We should send someone forward, someone who knows Aldren and could spot him, while keeping an eye on the cargo of each. See if anything seems out of place."

"In order to move to the front of the sequence, I would have to declare myself. My title is the only thing that would give me that opportunity," says the captain.

Otto meets his statement with a raised eyebrow. "Don't go straight through the gate. Just wiggle yourself in with a group at the front when no one's looking. Come on, boy— get a little creative." It's clear Captain Montgomery isn't fond of being called boy, even by an old mentor like Otto. Aiden doesn't seem too distraught about it, maybe even a little pleased to not be the only one referred to as *boy* in our group.

We dissipate into the waiting crowd, each one moving a little closer to each wagon, surreptitiously checking the contents when we can. My eyes meet with Aiden and Otto once I've checked the last cart in my vicinity, no longer able to see the captain from where I stand. As far as I can tell, none of us have found her.

I hold Prue's reins, feeding her a small apple from my bag as we wait for our turn in line.

"What is your business in Fort Lowsan, woman," a soldier asks me after I cross the vast, metal threshold with Prue.

"I have an aunt in need of help with her children. I've come to aid her for a time." Do I look like someone good with children? A dress would've solidified my story, but maybe women in pants aren't as uncommon in Fort Lowsan.

He nods and moves me forward out of the entrance.

"And your name?"

"Seneca. Seneca Smith." He jots my name down on some paper.

"And your aunt's name?"

"Fiona Smith." I smile to myself. Seneca and Fiona. Some of my better aliases. Although Calla and Corin weren't half bad either.

"Ok, Miss Smith. If you stay longer than a month, you'll need to file for permanent residency."

"Permanent residency? That sounds like a daunting process." I joke, just enough to seem trustworthy, but not enough to be memorable.

"Aye, it is."

I only wanted to make idle conversation, but now my curiosity is piqued. "What must one do to be granted permanent residency in Fort Lowsan?"

He looks annoyed with my question, but he answers it all the same. "You must prove you have a place to live, ties to the city, and a way to provide for yourself. If you are a woman, you must also show proof of marriage, or have a guardian sign for responsibility."

"So can my aunt come sign for me?"

"The guardian must be male."

"Of course. Heaven forbid a woman has any rights over her own life." I can't seem to help the quip. While women of noble birth are seen as parallel to their male counterparts, as evident by the princess being heir to Felshan's crown, the lower born don't have the same privilege.

The guard eyes me up and down, his patience clearing fading. I undeniably just went from a forgettable nobody, to a notable, and irritating, somebody.

He puts a hand on hilt of his sword just as I hear a familiar voice in front of us.

"Oh my beautiful girl, there you are!" says Otto, rushing toward me. His face is painted with genuine excitement, wrapping me in his arms, bumping the guard out of the way in the process.

I was the last of our group to cross— Aiden, the captain, and Otto passing through before me. Luckily, these guards don't seem to pay much attention to the patrons passing through the gates, at least the unmemorable ones.

Thank you, old man, for keeping your mouth shut better than I ever seem to.

"Hello, Uncle... Stewart," I say.

"Yes, yes. Your uncle has come to rescue you my girl. Come here. Your aunt—"

"Fiona," I whisper rapidly.

"Your Aunt Fiona is waiting down the road!" He sells it enough that the guard hands me a *temporary residence* paper, Seneca Smith smeared across the top, and sends us on our way. I don't know which comes first, the relief that we all made it through, or the disturbing idea that I would need a man to obtain permanent residence in this city.

Captain Montgomery meets us a few paces down. Otto runs ahead, and a brief whisper passes between them.

"Cousin! So good to see you!" He runs up to me and picks me up in a strong embrace. I stiffen as both his arms remain wrapped around me. His warm breath settles against the side of my face, my hands reaching around to the scruff on his neck.

"The guard is still watching you," he tells me softly through what sounds like a smile.

Of course I get the thorough guard. I smile wildly, pulling both my arms tighter around the captain, then lean back to lightly peck his cheek. If the guard was close enough, he would see that both mine and the captain's reaction to that intimate gesture wasn't in line with family that had known each other their whole lives.

He releases me almost instantly, and my feet thud back to the ground. The captain leans back, his joyful features hiding the search in his gaze, his eyes questioning my own. I'm unsure what to do next so I plaster a smile on my face, hoping we will be able to still pass as long-time-no-see cousins.

Otto breaks the awkward tension. "Come on, you two. Fiona will be wondering where the hell we've gone if we dally any longer."

He doesn't break character for even a moment until we are far out of sight of the gate and its keepers, asking me about my travels and even taking the reins of Prue to give me a rest. He must have actual cousins this has played out for in earnest, or witnessed enough reunions to commit it to memory.

Everyone seems mostly unscathed. Aiden had apparently been detained when a patrol saw his sword, questioning his weapon and what he was doing. He sold the story of being a Palace Guard on leave, going west to visit the sea.

"You don't think that raised suspicions, Aiden?" an uptight Captain Montgomery asks, looking around our immediate vicinity.

"What else would you have me say? I needed a reason to have a sword within the city walls, none of them would recognize me from the Fort Lowsan Guard so that was off the table, and I figured they'd be less likely to question a guard from Turin. One look at the steel of my blade, and I was released." Aiden's explanation only earns him an eye-roll from the captain.

It was quick thinking on his part, Turinian steelwork is hard to miss. I give Aiden a little pat on the shoulder to shove off the captain's disapproval, earning me a hint of a smile.

After searching Fort Lowsan for most of the day, we stop to feed our aching stomachs at a local tavern on the outskirts of the city.

The old man and Aiden aren't the messiest eaters I've ever seen. However, the captain looks as though he's taking supper with the king himself. Not that I've ever eaten with the king, or learned proper etiquette for that matter. But watching his careful bites, the precise breaking of his bread, the evenness with which he drinks his water— it's almost disconcerting.

"Are you trying to impress the bar maids?" I ask the captain. His brows kiss as he scans the room for the maids before returning his gaze to me.

Instead of explaining myself, I mimic his movements— sitting up straight, gently sipping my water, breaking off a tiny piece of bread that I chew at least twenty times before swallowing. I glance side-long at his raised brow before bringing a reasonable spoonful of soup to my mouth.

His face relaxes as my meaning sinks in, but the scowl never leaves his face. "I'm not an animal, so why would I eat like one?" he responds, more a statement than a question, before turning back to his meal. My shoulders square as I raise my chin a little at his clear annoyance.

"This might be the best stew I've ever had. No offense, Otto," Aiden mumbles through a mouth filled with food.

"None taken. I'm about to go ask the wench who made this to marry me," Otto says, his serious expression proof of the truthfulness of his statement.

"And what if she's mean and smells like the pigs this place is named after?" I ask, a sign outside literally marking it as *Hog's Place*.

"Then, I make sure I'm only home for supper time." He winks at me before putting another spoonful in his mouth, and I let out a huff in response. If men actually used their head when choosing a wife, there would be much happier couples roaming the country.

Once our minds have cleared from the turbulence hunger brings, Captain Montgomery brings us back to business, as always. "With no signs of the princess here, I think we should move on."

"Fort Lowsan is a decent sized city. We only had time to roughly scan through it today. She could still be here," Aiden replies.

"She could. But I don't think she is," the captain says. "The Santanas may wish to run their city separately from the Crown. However, they would never sanction or allow the princess to knowingly be taken. It would make more sense for Aldren to simply pass through than try and hide her here. Lord Santana would find out soon enough, and put an end to their plotting." Otto opens his mouth to speak, but must think better of it, staying quiet instead.

"The sun will be setting soon, but there's enough daylight to continue forward for a little longer," the captain continues. "We passed through the south entrance of Fort Lowsan. If they are taking the princess to Thenstra, they will need to head out the north gate."

"And if the Western Seaport is their goal? We never did see that theory through." Otto interjects, locking eyes with the captain.

"It makes sense they would be headed to Thenstra, from a logical stand-point. To a more neutral and unknown territory. Whether they go north through the Prythan Mountains, or, perhaps, west to the sea," the captain concedes. "They could potentially sail to Thenstra from the seaport, and cross into the country through one of their ocean ports—"

"None of this is neutral, and none of this makes sense. Kidnapping a princess, for what? They must've known we would come after her. What does taking her accomplish exactly?" Aiden quietly exclaims.

"It brings confusion and fear. With the prince gone, and the princess now taken, the country is vulnerable. Could be for money, political gain, power, revenge." Otto replies. "She's a priceless bargaining chip for whatever their plans are."

The Captain stiffens, his face an unreadable mask. If it weren't for his unsteady breathing, I would guess him to be the most life-like statue I've ever seen.

"Who's to say they didn't just pull one over our eyes, turn around somewhere and head to Jadeya or Venes?" I ask. "There are a thousand places she could be right now."

Captain Montgomery holds up both hands to silence us, our thoughts and theories getting jumbled together as we all try to speak. "All we have are the few clues Lady Margaret found and the logic I know Aldren to possess. He's no fool. He thinks like a leader. Initially trying to throw us off, poisoning the guards at each gate, that made sense. It could easily be done without detriment to travel, speed, and time.

Once they had her, he knew I would be coming. Like I know Aldren, he knows me. He knows we would come for her, as Aiden said. There wasn't time to take the chance that they could throw us off. It became all about how quickly they could move her out, and get her to their planned destination. Lady Margaret said she sent more guards to investigate paths they could've taken to Venes or Jadeya. We have been tasked with Thenstra."

He makes more sense than I want to admit.

"Why don't we split up then?" I suggest. "Two of us go north to Thenstra, two of us go west to the sea. Since those are two of the most logical places he could take her. Marg— Lady Margaret— didn't say she was sending anyone to the Western Seaport."

There's a moment of quiet before Otto speaks up. "It's not a bad plan."

"And if something happens to one of the pairs?" the captain asks.

"And what if we all go together in the wrong direction, and we don't find her? At least this way we cross off two possible destinations," I reply. The captain pauses, my question clearly hitting against his good sense.

A few more moments tick by in silence as we wait for his final word. "We will split up," the captain says. "Otto— you and Aiden will go west to the sea. The *thief* and I will go north to Thenstra." I try not to let a smile cross my face, but I can't help it this time. I don't even care that he used the demeaning term, its label starting to grow on me a little bit anyway.

The bar maid comes to clear away our dirty plates, and Otto hands her a coin.

It takes a moment for the idea to sink in that I will be traveling the next few days, or longer, alone with Captain Montgomery. My earlier smile wavers.

Why couldn't I spend my time with Otto, filled with stories that make me laugh? Or even Aiden— he could talk about his sisters all day and I wouldn't be annoyed.

They may all be part of the Royal Guard, but the latter two are decent company at least.

"Any opposition to our new arrangements?" asks the captain, eying each of us separately.

"None," Otto says, Aiden nodding in agreement.

"And you, Ari?"

I stare at the table a moment before reaching his gaze with my own. "I've always wanted to visit Thenstra."

21

PRINCESS ADALENA

A FEW CRATES LINE the edges of the wagon, *Turin Coastal Company* stamped on their side.

My chin rests on the junction of my knees which I hold tight against me. The rocking of the wagon sends the bottom of my face knocking against the solid bone, but I don't move it. Its rhythm puts me in a trance as I keep watch, each passing tree and rock eventually fading into the distance as the day drones on.

The empty road paired with my submissive silence earned me a chance to sit up, to relieve my aching back and sides from the hard bed of my wheeled cell. We passed through the last northern city of Felshan just before dawn, the first ringlets of morning bouncing across the horizon as we left the final gates of Fort Lowsan.

My disappointment has come to be my friend over the last several days, my hope smashed each time I feel the seed take root. There were no Santana spies to question the old woman who traveled beside me through the city. In fact, no one even had a chance to see to me. Her knife stayed shoved against my side as we traversed the dark, abandoned streets, threatening a painful death if any noise escaped my lips.

Onah— the literal and figurative pain in my side. She's quite a peach, if one likes a spiky, thick skin giving way to sour, rotten fruit underneath.

Tess Santana and her brother, Liam, came to visit the castle many times when we were younger. Hope clung to me when I heard my captors reference our approach to the hilled city. That hope was diminished with every completed turn of the wheels underneath me. I recognized none of the faces that escorted us through what I gleaned was Fort Lowsan, and I began to wonder if the Santanas were somehow involved.

How would we get through Felshan's northern settlement, arranged to be the front line of defense from a Thenstran invasion, without House Santana's approval? An icy chill runs through me as the realization of betrayal buries deep in my veins.

"Princess Adalena, do you have a nickname? Something that rolls off the tongue a little easier?" My male captor asks, pulling me from my thoughts. I don't speak, keeping my same, unmoving position as if I didn't hear.

"*Parker* never garnered much to work with in the way of shortened names. My mother just called me *son* when she could only be bothered to speak a single syllable. It's highly unoriginal, I know," the man says back to me. He keeps talking, and I get the impression he greatly enjoys the sound of his own voice. "My sister, Wren, on the other hand. My mother was smarter when it came to naming her. Although, I myself find *Wren* to be such a boring name."

The man is insufferable. I have a feeling Onah and me can agree on this one, tiny thing.

"Do you *ever* stop talking?" she says.

"I'm just making friendly conversation. You should try it sometime. Do you have any nicknames, Onah? Anything dear old mum might have called you before you became the hardened woman I see before me?" The woman snarls, clearly unamused, but doesn't give him the slap that his offensive banter typically evokes.

Instead, she gives a cool response, as if she were telling someone the news of the day. "I don't remember my mother. Probably a whore down at the docks. But from what I hear, your mother is very nice and very pretty. Perhaps I could have her make up a nickname for me. One day soon I may just get to meet her, and I can ask her myself."

The air behind me stiffens, Parker's flippant demeanor instantly turning to ice. I hear him take a slow, deep breath. All hint of amusement leaves this cramped wagon space.

He's talked about his mother several times over the last few days. But when Onah brings her up he acts like a dog backed into a corner, whimpering in submission. So strange— how quick he's been to mock her, and how abruptly she seemed to put him in his place with only the mention of meeting his mother.

The two take turns in the wagon bed before we stop for a quick bathroom break in the afternoon. If today is anything like the past few, we will ride well into the night before stopping for a few hours of rest.

Onah takes the first shift, lying down a bedroll next to me and snoring after only a few moments. How she can sleep so soundly with every jolt and bump is beyond my understanding.

When Parker comes to the wagon bed next, he sits with his back against the side instead of lying down, focusing all his attention on me. This is the first time I've been able to see his full face, only catching glimpses of edges and corners of him until now. His unwavering stare prompts me to shift around in an attempt to avoid it. After a while I think he might be doing it on purpose, to try and make me feel uneasy or catch me off my guard.

"Can I help you with something?" I finally ask the man— Parker, if the story of names is actually true. A few moments pass without an answer.

"Onah isn't enough of a person to irritate, now you must come do it to me as well?"

My words snap him out of his trance, and a warm smile covers his face, showing a straight array of white teeth. "You know, I think that's the most I've heard you say in days. She still has a voice!"

Onah turns to glare at the man who is once again shouting as if we are the only people left in the world, but I hardly register the decibel of his voice. His onyx hair is tied back, and those deep brown eyes— something about them registers a spark in my mind. I squint as I take them in, my head tilting off to the side.

"Pardon me, Princess. I've spent so many years in the employ of the king and queen and all the formalities that come with the job, it seems odd indeed that I'm sitting in the back of a wagon with their daughter," the man says to me, no hint of warmth in his tone.

The memory slams into me like I fell into the Rashan in the middle of winter.

The guard. He's the guard from the hallway. The handsome guard Roan teased me about. The one who offered to walk me after I left tea with my mother, aunt Margaret, and Lady Davenport. My mouth hangs open, my pulse quickening as realization dawns on me.

"You're the..." I stutter, pointing a finger at him as I struggle to wrap my mind around this truth.

"I'm the," is all he replies, exhaling the words. His face is blank, no amusement that the helpless princess figured it out, nor malice like I would have expected at such a revelation, poking at my ignorance.

"Onah was also the servant that drugged your water, up on the balcony." A hiss sounds from somewhere behind me, a sharp voice following the noise. But all I can do is stare at Parker. His face never falters from his vacant expression except when answering back to the biting voice and whatever words were muttered from the old woman.

It only takes a few moments for the shock to twist into unadulterated anger, a flurry of scorching tears gathering at my eyes.

I close my mouth into a thin line, color rising to my cheeks as I let the fire burn within me. "How dare you." My voice is eerily steady, but my words are filled with more fury than I thought myself capable of feeling. "How does it feel to now be a traitor, with the Princess of Felshan tied up in the corner? After you swore an oath of protection, to watch over me at all costs, even against the pain of your own life?" My teeth grind together, my heart pounding as a single tear plops down my face.

I want my words to fly at him like daggers, but he seems to have turned them into tiny pebbles instead. Only a minor flinch betrays any kind of remorse from Parker. He lowers his voice, an unusual frown pulling down his features as he leans toward me. "How do you know this isn't me keeping an oath?"

"I think being held against my will in the back of a wagon in the middle of nowhere unravels that theory," I say, my breathing fast and shallow. The rope tied around my hands and feet is the only thing keeping me from pouncing— from clawing at him like a cat attacking its prey.

He simply shrugs in response, his frown now a memory as his usual smirk slides back into place. "You make a fair point, Princess. Now, this oath-breaker is going to take a little nap. It's tiring business, breaking promises and kidnapping members of the royal family. My body could really use the rest." And after his snide remark, he lies down and closes his eyes, wadding up his jacket to place underneath his head.

I would give just about anything for this rope to give me more leeway so I could kick the smugness from his face while he sleeps.

The next few days drone on, one replacing the other with the same drudgery and schedule. Men meeting us with fresh horses, riding through the night, watching Onah and Parker sleep only inches away from my reach. The only time the thick, scratchy rope isn't digging into my wrists is my two minute bathroom break in the afternoons.

A minuscule joy fills me when I notice the wagon slowing down. "Alright, Princess. I've come to rescue you from your misery," my kidnapper jokes. Parker Aldren is much too happy for his own good. Onah, the onery old woman, is his opposite in every way. It's as if Haythen knew they were both needed to balance out the other's presence in this world.

He's mostly kept to himself since his true identity came to light. No more regaling us with tales of his family, or bantering with Onah.

A stray lock of his hair falls into one eye. As he rakes it back, he holds out his other hand to help me down. "Thank you," I say as I step to the ground, and I berate myself for my politeness. The traitorous guard deserves no gratitude from me. I rip my hand from his the moment my feet find the steady earth below me.

For the sake of modesty, Onah is usually the one who takes me out a little ways so I can go to the bathroom. It's as embarrassing as one might imagine, peeing in the presence of not only a stranger, but someone who hates you for no reason other than the station you were born into. I've never tried to befriend her during our brief time alone— not like it's easy to do so while you're squatting in the dirt anyway. Her scowl and petty remarks about *how far I've fallen* are enough to deter me from the prospect as it is.

This time, however, it would seem Onah is asleep. Her rattling snores are hard to miss. Parker makes a quick decision to let his ill-tempered partner keep her sour attitude in the dream world, instead accompanying me behind a cluster of trees.

I open my mouth to mutter another *thank you* for saving us all the heartache of Onah's consciousness, but decide thanking my captor for kindness only gets to happen once a day. And only because I was raised to be a gracious woman.

"Now, you're going to have to do something you hate," Aldren starts. *You mean besides being held against my will?* "You will need to hold a conversation with me. I would prefer to give you some privacy, but in order to do that I need to know you're still behind that tree. It seems the lesser of two evils, talking to a man you despise versus having that man watch you relieve yourself. So, which would you prefer, Princess?"

"I have a name. And it's not *princess*," I sharply respond.

"I do know. I apologize," he says, dipping his head ever so slighty. His words sound oddly sincere. "Old habit I suppose. What would you like me to call you? You never did clarify."

"Lena is fine. I'm princess of nothing out here, and I loathed the title even in the safe confines of the palace." The corners of his mouth twitch upward and his brow furrows as he takes in my answer. Something betwixt, *why wouldn't you enjoy being a princess?* And, *aren't you so glad I saved you from that miserable existence?*

"Why not *Adalena*? It is your given name after all."

My brows knit together as I let myself study his face. I forget this man once silently served by my side. The reticent statue. The watchful sentinel to never be seen or heard. What did he learn in his time at the palace?

He stops me in front of a large oak, motioning for me to walk behind. I obey, walking around until I'm out of sight, lifting my skirts and crouching down, always the compliant girl I was raised to be.

Looking around me I see nothing but the beauty of the forest. The trees swaying freely with the breeze, bushes and grass and flowers growing unencumbered. The sun shines effortlessly to the ground, bouncing through the umbrella of branches and leaves from above.

I'm so tired of being the agreeable, submissive, dutiful daughter. Of feeling helpless. Of always being in another's control. Something inside of me snaps. I forcefully inhale as the reverberation thrashes through me, my eyes glistening with the unfairness of it all.

My next words spill out of me as if they have a mind of their own, finding a home where there once was nothing but conforming, disciplined space. "That name, *Adalena*— it's such a mouthful. It belonged to a great-grandmother that I never knew. I always felt like it imprisoned me into a future I had no control over. I'm a descendant of proper royal names, and proper royal women, who step flawlessly from one role to the next. Never questioning their place. It's an ever-constricting noose around my neck." My hands rest against my throat, rubbing away the ghost of pain throbbing across my skin.

"I'm part of a legacy of royals who accept the unspoken agreement to support their husbands, bear children and heirs, and on the rare occasion, to lead. Whether they are prepared or capable or even want to means nothing. Nobody asks. Nobody objects. Like a puppet, the strings are pulled and everyone complies." My sarcasm and frustration melt together seamlessly.

I'm bearing my soul to a complete stranger. The handsome, treasonous guard. Words which have hung inside me since Evander— since I abruptly went from child, to woman, in a matter of minutes. I didn't even realize they existed in me until now, the awareness of their presence exploding out of me. A truth that can no longer stay hidden inside.

Parker shows no emotion at my revelation. I take a deep breath, color surging to my cheeks. Why did I tell him this? The dishonest guard couldn't care less about me and my privileged woes. Roan hasn't even heard these inner most thoughts. Not that he wouldn't understand. I'm sure more than most he would. But after my brother died, something shifted in him. We are friendly, and I care for him deeply— but somehow it no longer feels like we are on the same side.

Parker Aldren doesn't seem to have a side. Or maybe he does, and he's good at hiding it.

It's just the loneliness, I tell myself. If there was anybody else to talk to, I would shut my mouth to the man next to me. The one who forcefully took me from my home. Someone I should hate and despise until the end of time. Someone who deserves to stay in a dungeon for the rest of eternity. But the anger at these facts never seems to surface. I wait for it— even desire it to come. But looking over my shoulder, his back to the tree to give me even more privacy, the fury only comes toward the name and title I never wanted.

I stand, smoothing my skirts and wiping at my eyes before I walk back around, preparing myself for his judgment— a reply about how good I have it. How I should be grateful. That my life is prized and coveted by all who lay their eyes on me. But that never comes either.

Where I've only seen sarcasm and cold eyes, now I see genuine warmth. As I study his face, I realize Parker isn't that much older than me. And I'm loath to admit it, but I can't even remember when he first arrived at the palace. How long had he been a guard? How many times did we interact, and I didn't even notice him? *A good leader knows who has her life in their hands.*

"I don't know how I would fend, having my future planned for me. Given everything you've experienced, I'd say it makes sense that you feel this way, Lena." My heart skips a beat, though I don't know why.

Gone is the cheekiness I've come to expect from him, and in its place an unexpected kindness. There has always been an emptiness behind his use of *princess*, but with my preferred name there is a glimpse of sincerity. Is this the trick of a criminal? Warm up to their prey before they stick a dagger in their heart? I stand awkwardly across from him, arranging a wrinkle from my sleeve as if I'm not surreptitiously trying to figure out what's below the surface of Parker Aldren.

At some point while I was knocked out from whatever concoction servant-Onah gave to me, I was changed into a plain, muddy colored garment. It's comfortable enough, maybe even more so than my normal stiff, layered attire. My lips remain in a firm line as we begin our walk from the privacy of the trees. I refuse to let Aldren know that I don't mind my new clothes—maybe even like them.

My eyes flitter again to the forest around me. How easy it would be to run. All I would have to do is make a decision, and start moving my feet.

"I wouldn't recommend it, Lena. I may not look like much, but I'm fast. And I would rather not have to break a sweat this afternoon." He reads my thoughts with ease. Am I that predictable?

I look him over. He would most definitely catch me if I tried to make an escape while he was standing so close to me. He isn't as tall as Roan, but his pants are stretched to accommodate thick, sturdy legs. His sleeved shirt is rolled up just passed his forearm, revealing a strong grip and what I imagine to be chiseled brawn underneath the rest of his clothes. Parker sends a wink my way when he catches me staring, obviously unaffected by my perusal.

I scowl at his arrogance. "I'm not stupid, Aldren. I have no idea where we are, no sense of which direction to even run, and I have no food or water. I wouldn't make it far even if I tried." I may not make it very far, but I'm fully aware that braving the wilderness is leaps and strides above being forced and tortured into a prison. Parker has given little away as to where we're going, but my gut tells me it's nowhere I want to call home.

We start our short walk back to the wagon, me taking the lead so he can keep an eye on me. Our conversation silences as we focus on the short task of returning to the road.

I shouldn't have spoken so much to him, revealed so much about my distaste of royal expectations. Our quiet steps leave plenty of room for the soft hum of embarrassment to echo around me. *Stupid girl.*

The ground is littered with small plants and fallen trees, making our path in and out of the forest irregular and scattered. I'm sure I take the longest way, both from inexperience in the outdoors and a desire to stretch my legs as long as possible.

There are mere moments before we break through the tree-line when I hear a cracking sound and an accompanying *oof!* afterward. I turn to find Parker on the ground, his foot somehow wedged in a small crevice of two fallen trunks underneath him. He pulls a couple times, unable to effortlessly break free from nature's trap.

He laughs uneasily. "Well this is new," he mumbles to himself. "Lena, would you—"

An idea forms quickly in my mind. I look to the road, confirming Onah's sleeping form still crumpled in the wagon. There may be only a single breath before he's free.

"Don't," he states, all his jollity wiped away in his penetrating stare. All his features pull into a seriousness that I've yet to see on Parker Aldren. He looks fierce, like a panther stalking its game. *A trapped panther.* My stomach leaps in wicked delight.

I turn and run.

"Lena!" A determined scream follows after me.

I don't turn back. I don't think. I focus on my surroundings, making sure each pounding step finds firm ground. A sudden energy pumps through me, tunneling my vision and concentration. Stray branches and thick shrubbery pull at my skirts, scratching along my arms and ankles. One swipes across my face, the sting making my eyes water. I quickly blink it away, numbing it against my intense concentration.

My heart is throbbing in my chest, the unusual exertion and anxiousness building into heaving breaths. *I'm going to do it. I'm going to make it.* I will move deep into the woods, then figure out the rest. There's no plan, just a profound need to be free. Free of Onah and Aldren. But as I push harder and harder, that need evolves.

I want to be unchained from everything, from everyone. I want to make my own choices, to choose things for myself— not because I'm supposed to, or because my parents find it in my best interest. I know there's a country, people depending on me and my family, people outside of myself that need a good leader. But is it too much to ask— too much to even ask me if I want it? Years of unshed tears and emotion tug somewhere deep inside.

Footsteps sound behind me, pushing me over the edge. *No. No. No.* I shake my head, willing it to just be my fear wanting me to slow and give up. How could he have caught up so soon?

I will never be free, and that thought alone leadens my feet. The chains of royalty and duty will hold me for the rest of my life. The bondage of someone else's demands.

Evander left me here alone, pushing me into a position I never wanted. And that single idea, blaming my dead brother, someone whom I would pay any price to hug and touch and talk to one last time, pulls the final thread of anguish looming under the surface.

The tears don't stop.

Parker is close enough that he no longer needs to shout. "Lena, stop. Please," his voice pleads.

Hopelessness halts my progression through the woods. No matter how hard I try, I will never get away. A moment of hope and independence will always lead back to chains.

Leaves crunch underneath me as I fall to the forest floor, unable to hold back my crushing heart as my hands and knees give way underneath me, landing me sprawled in the dirt. Twigs and stems mold into my soft skin. With each hiccuping breath I take in the fresh smell of the woodlands— its scent both grounding me back to the moment and reminding me how I will never have this small moment of freedom again.

Warm arms wrap around me as my tears continue to flow unhindered. Fingers swipe away the wet, plastered hair from my face and dust away the debris of dried leaves, dirt, and bark. These hands are both calloused and soft, a contradiction that I don't try to make sense of. I pull on the shirt of the man in front of me as I bury my face into his chest as far as it will go. Sobs wrack through my body, and I feel the warm arms pull me in tighter.

It feels like I've been crying for hours before calmness finally reaches me, and my tears run dry. An aching head and dry throat are left in the aftermath. I want to apologize, to make an excuse for my untoward behavior. But I don't have the energy left to open my mouth, or to care about how I must appear to this man. A defeat I've felt only once before— losing to death as I stood beside my brother's grave— fills me once again.

"We need to get back before Onah wakes. Can you walk?" Parker asks me.

I nod, trying to separate my face from his hard chest, his shirt sticking to my cheek as I pull away. I try to stand, but my shaking legs give way, and I stumble forward onto my hands and knees. He wraps a hand around my arm, gently lifting me as I try again. Once I'm upright, his arm sweeps underneath me, picking me up and cradling me against him. The fight in me has been replaced by exhaustion, and I don't protest. I rest my head against his shoulder, closing my eyes as he makes our way back through the trees. I hardly register the walk back, drifting in and out of my groggy misery.

"What happened? I woke up to you screaming the girl's name," Onah pries as we move back into sight of the road. Everything is bleary as I attempt to open my eyes at her voice.

"A boar came out of nowhere, scared her half to death. She has a few cuts and scrapes as she tried to get out of its way. I'll attend to her while you drive," Parker tells her.

The lie comes so easily out of his mouth. He lays a blanket down, prompting me to lie and rest. He washes each scrape from my arms and ankles, moving to the larger gash on my cheek last. My gaze rests on the clouds moving slowly overhead, watching each puffy formation effortlessly cross through the sky.

"Eat this." The male voice doesn't register in my mind until I feel something pushed into my hands, alerting me again to his presence. My eyes meet his, a sweaty brow and frown greeting me. His stern gaze bores into me, the unsaid and said between us creating a connection I never wanted, but don't have the strength to push away.

I don't know what comes next, so I focus on what is right in front of me. I eat the piece of bread Parker gave me, sitting up to catch the breeze on my face as I chew. A tiny drizzle of honey sends a pang of sweetness across my tongue with each bite.

"Bread with honey is my favorite," I say, voicing my thought to no one in particular.

"I know," Parker replies, a hint of a smile pulling at his lips as he watches me eat. "I bought a small bottle from one of the men in Fort Lowsan."

I say nothing in response.

A war begins in my mind. I don't want to be queen, but I was born to this privilege. I am unsure if I will be a good ruler, but now that the chance has been taken from me, part of me wonder what it would be like. My tears are all dried up, and in their place a spark of resolve and determination lights up the darkness.

I will get out of this, and I will make my own choices. Nobody gets to decide my fate. And if I become queen and marry Roan, it will be because I choose it.

I just have to work past Onah, and past the one whose eyes have yet to waver from me—Parker Aldren.

22

CAPTAIN MONTGOMERY

I T'S DECIDED.

Otto and Aiden will move to the west, checking the Western Seaport for any signs of Lena, while Ari and I will head up north to Thenstra. Our small group leaves the *Hog's Place*, the Prythan Mountains highlighting the northern horizon, Thenstra lying nestled between them.

Seeing their daunting peaks spread across the distance solidifies my decision. Otto is the strongest man I know, but the elevation and speed with which I plan to travel would not go over as well as he declines to admit. And Aiden— he's the best of the best, but I'm not sure how he would fair in a fight with Aldren. He can hold his own to be sure, but fighting someone you used to have drinks with at the end of the night— it does something to a person. I don't want him to go through that if I can help it.

Ari has definitely proven she can take care of herself. And as far as I can tell, would have no problem taking Aldren down if it came to it.

My mind is moving in circles as I continue out of the exit of the tavern. *Save Lena, no matter the cost.* I'm last in line as we move onto the street, heading to our horses as we make final preparations to split our rescue party.

"Roan Montgomery," an icy female voice says somewhere behind me.

My feet stop, freezing in place. Each part of me registers the sound of my name from a tone that I haven't heard in almost eight years. *No. No. No.* My eyes close as I take a deep breath, willing it to be anybody else. We were so close— just minutes away from passing through the final gate of the city. I attempt to soften my hard expression of disbelief and dread, turning to face the woman I would know anywhere.

"Tess Santana," I reply, forcing a grin.

Tess stands with her arms folded, amusement on her face like someone just fell drunk off their horse, or told an off-kilter joke. I get the impression that joke is on me.

Her dark hair is pulled high atop her head, twisted tightly into a bun, showing off her high cheekbones. Golden eyes are a gleaming contrast to her thick eyelashes, perfectly lining their almond shape. I would recognize her full lips anywhere, one of the many temptations she threw my way whenever she visited the palace growing up. Her fierce features pull together into something devastatingly beautiful.

She was always exquisite, but it seems the last few years have added even more to admire. And for many men, to lust after. Tess knows the effect she has on men and uses it to her advantage whenever the need arises. I wouldn't be surprised if half the dozen guards flanking her have been lured in by false assumptions of interest and baited charm.

Tess walks toward us, her smile only faltering when she spots Ari to my right, noting how near we are standing. Had the thief been following so closely beside me, or did she move to my side once she heard my name from Tess's lips? It would take only the smallest movement for our hands to entwine, and our warm proximity isn't lost on the woman approaching.

"A little bird told me you were in the city, but I didn't believe it. What would Turin's premier captain, renowned leader of the Royal Guard, and firstborn of the Port Riga Montgomerys be doing so far from home?" Tess continues her approach, stopping so close to me I can see the shining specks of yellow, gold, and brown dotting through the color of her eyes.

Ari takes a step back, but not out of fear or deference, or even because she's trying to be polite. I've been around her long enough to know none of those are true. The way she places her feet and positions her body mimics that of a lioness right before she attacks a potential threat to her cub. Does she think I need protecting from Tess Santana?

It's almost laughable. If she only knew the girl, I suppose now a woman, standing before us. Tess always hooked another into doing her dirty work, like a siren calling to the lost sailor. If she's walking into a pit of vipers, a fiery end will certainly be planned and eagerly waiting to strike from the bushes.

Out of my periphery, I see Ari's hand nearing the handle of her dagger. It's hard not to conclude that she cares for our mission, for saving Lena, at least in a tiny measurement— enough to fight off a woman with almost a dozen trained soldiers behind her. Or maybe it's the more likely scenario. My life stands between her and what she really wants— freedom. Freedom from what, I'm not wholly sure. She doesn't seem to hate Lady Margaret. But upon learning that she'd be released from her employ, Ari agreed to come without complaint.

Tess's full, pouting lips are only inches from my own. Otto looks almost bored at our interaction. However, bored is too docile a description for Aiden, who has fixed his eyes on the woman approaching me, an eagerness on his face that betrays his interest. It's a stark contrast to the hard scowl strewn across Ari's face.

I've never seen Tess in action, other than flirting her way to anything she ever wanted. How quickly would Ari be able to incapacitate her if she deemed it necessary? Maybe Tess has taken it upon herself to finally learn skills in close combat and would be able to hold her own in a tussle with our thief. Tess does seem daunting in her tight pants and top, their contrasting cream and black matching the woman's many, variating guises. But Ari is clearly as unimpressed as me with her sharp appearance.

If I wasn't so put-out at the disposition Tess's presence has brought us, I might even laugh at the reaction these two women illicit in each other. Both so different, yet so similar.

"Maybe my dearest childhood friend has an assignment in Fort Lowsan. But, of course, House Santana would have been notified of your arrival, if that were in fact the case. And I would have been anxiously awaiting your beautiful blue eyes to walk through my gates." Tess's finger traces along the side of my face and across the stubble of my jaw, her hands as soft against my face as I remember.

I hold back a snarl rising in my throat. "A little bird told you we were here?" I eye her with a knowing skepticism. "Nobody here knows me but you, Tess. How did you spot us?" I get straight to the point, unwilling to play in her games.

"I do know you, Roan. Which is why I'm so hurt you didn't plan to stop by and say hi." Her voice raises a few notes, her bottom lip dipping in her feigned approach to being emotionally wounded. "How long has it been? Six? Seven years?

"Eight," I reply, my voice stoic.

I've witnessed all the ways she tries to manipulate the people around her— used to getting what she wants from her performances. I'm confused that she hasn't taken into account that I know the woman that exists under her dramatics, the glimpses of Tess that only a close few have ever had the pleasure of seeing.

"We are in a hurry— simply passing through. You know I would have stopped if time permitted," I add, keeping my voice and breathing in a steady rhythm. It's not a complete lie. But I've learned to be so precise with my time that I can always find more pressing matters than visiting Tess Santana.

"Such a hurry that you can't come see an old friend? How I've missed my partner in crime these *eight* years." She looks up at me from underneath her dark lashes, the corner of her mouth curved in one of her most alluring smiles. Luckily for me, I've become immune to her flirtatious charms.

Tess and her twin brother Liam came to visit Turin almost every year, tagging along with their father and his men to give the yearly reports from Fort Lowsan. Those few weeks every year were held with both dread and enthusiasm. Some of our best work happened when Tess came to the palace, leaving disorder and irritation in our aftermath.

Most of it was harmless— putting a few spoonfuls of dark pepper into the chocolate cake batter when the cook wasn't looking, earning the choking coughs of everyone at the dinner table. We were only eleven for that one, and Evander tried his best to deter Tess and me from the antic. He ended up being the one to sneak into the kitchen, proof of how much sway and persuasion the girl was able to conjure up.

Turns out he was madly in love with her, but was, like most young boys, too nervous to speak up. I seemed to be the only one resistant to her glamour, and in response it spurred her into her own infatuation that, unfortunately, wasn't toward a love-sick prince.

I lower my voice so only she can hear, which isn't hard given how close we're standing. "What do you want Tess? You know the quivering lip and contrived flattery doesn't work on me." I don't hide my irked tone. Nothing has changed since I saw her last, and it's in this brief indifference that her facade drops for only a moment, giving way to her displeasure.

"It seems your directness has grown even more as you've matured. How much that little talent helped you all those years ago." She doesn't lower her voice to keep with my own, talking loudly for everyone to hear. Typical Tess— always the flare, always the underhanded motivations. I can't help but flinch at her remark, doing my best to hide the effect by bringing a hand behind my neck and rubbing at my tense muscles. I never wanted to hurt her, but I couldn't pretend that I had felt for her what she had felt for me all those years ago.

She turns from me, walking over to Aiden with her same flirtatious edge. He's new meat for her to sink her claws into. "Besides, it seems you've brought a few unfamiliar faces into my city. I do love getting to know a handsome stranger."

Tess holds out her hand and Aiden snatches it up, placing a gentle kiss on its back as she sends a wink and wide smile to Otto. The old man shifts on his feet, while Aiden can't take his eyes from her. I don't blame him. If I hadn't become unaffected by her polished grace as a young boy, it might be hard to look away from or ignore her awing effect, a glistening magnificence that hovers in the very air surrounding her.

An audible growl escapes from Ari, her heated glare directed toward the scene between Tess and Aiden. "And apparently," Tess glances sidelong at Ari, "a girl who would've stuck a dagger in my back already if there weren't twenty armed men surrounding you."

Ari stands tall when Tess's eyes move to her. She folds her arms, chin raised, all the charm from the Santana woman lost on this thief of Turin. "I'm no more a *girl* than you," Ari says, her upper lip curling.

Twenty men? I let out a huff of air as I look around. Sometime during her little speech, more Santanan soldiers crept up from behind, creating a wall around our retreat. My mind races, trying to come up with a plan, anything that will get all four of our group through the blockade of soldiers unharmed and as swiftly as possible. Lena's life depends on it.

My determination is fortified at the thought of her, and I hold up both hands in a gesture of surrender, stepping inside Tess's line of sight. "I will be passing through Fort Lowsan again soon. Plan on me staying a while— we can spend a few days together, learning what the last few years have brought. For now, we have urgent business that requires we leave, immediately."

The woman moves away from an entranced Aiden still clutching her hand, reclaiming her intimate stance in front of me. Her tall frame leaves only a few inches from the ever-shortening string of my composure.

I hope the girl that once held affection for me is still in there somewhere. I rest my hand beneath her chin, tipping it slowly so Tess's gaze reaches mine. Guilt tugs at me as I knowingly play against her emotions. "You know me, Tess. You know if I say I'll be back, I will be. Please. We are on our way out and will do so peacefully."

"What urgent business, Roan?" Tess plays back, pushing my hand away, knowing the upper-hand still lies with her.

I take a deep breath, my patience for her fraying at the edges. My eyes go hard, any softness from our past shriveling as I think of Lena getting further and further away.

"That's for the Crown to know and their appointed captain to take care of. Or should I send word to King Cassus and Queen Amelia, telling them the Santanas stood in the way of their word and request being carried out?"

"Tsk, tsk, tsk." Tess clicks her tongue. "No need to get worked up, *Captain* Montgomery. I've learned so much in the last few minutes, and my interest is fully piqued. I'm sure a quick word with my father will clear this whole thing up. And you can be on your way." She turns to walk toward the armed men in front of us.

"Tess, there's no time for th—" I take a step after her, but my words are shoved back down, a sword drawn by the soldier closest to me. In only half a breath's time, its sharp edge lingers only a hair's breadth from my neck.

Another familiar face stands that sword's length between us.

"Liam," I dare only one word, afraid any other movement will nick the blade against the soft tissue of my throat.

"Roan. You finally recognize me, eh?" Liam Santana lowers the tip of his weapon, just enough to allow me the range of motion to look him straight in the eye.

"Your sister likes to command all of the attention." My remark only elicits a chortled sigh from the boy I once knew.

"She does, doesn't she? We both know our strengths, and we use them well," Liam states, his smug countenance floating between us.

A swirl of movement sends a small whoosh of air toward me, the sound of unsheathing metal dancing around me.

"I suggest, sir, that you move away from the captain if you'd like to leave here still breathing." Liam and I turn in unison toward the voice.

Ari holds a raised dagger to the back of Liam's head, another pushed up against his side just below the ribs. In all the flurry of Liam's quick, unexpected approach, we missed the nearly invisible play by the woman beside me. Somehow, she not only grabbed her own dagger, but mine as well.

Liam lifts a brow, clearly not used to being the one taken by surprise. Carefully, he lowers his sword from my jugular. "And you are?" His head movement is limited, his gaze shifting sideways in an attempt to get a better look of the woman putting him in a rather precarious situation.

"I'm the one who will gladly slit your throat and watch you bleed out right here if you don't lower your sword," she retorts, giving him a menacing smile as she pushes the knife a little deeper into his side.

Liam gives a shaky laugh, mostly to cover his groan of pain. "However did you persuade this one into your company, Roan? She's too lovely to be caught up with the likes of you."

"I suggest you lower your sword, Mr. Santana, or you'll get to see firsthand how lovely I can be," Ari declares, her eyes honed in on his every flinch.

"I think I would like that," Liam smiles, venturing a twist against the sharp blade in order to see her face. Both eyebrows raise and a short whistle escape him as he takes her in. "Good grief, Montgomery. I'm impressed. How did you land a vixen such as her? If she belonged to me, we'd never leave the house." It would seem he's taken a few lessons from Tess when it comes to flattering a mark.

A deep grunt rumbles through him as Ari kicks behind his leg, landing him to his knees against the stony ground. "I belong to no one," she barks in his ear, moving the blade from his side and tossing it back to me before grabbing a fistful of his dark hair. She yanks back his head while moving her dagger to rest flesh against the now easy access to his neck—one swipe and he'll be lying in a bloody heap on the roadside.

"Alright. That's enough." Tess announces. "Tell your warrior princess to stand down." She waves flippantly toward the dicey scene playing out between her brother and the mysterious Turin woman. "You're outnumbered, Roan." She raises outstretched arms, reminding us of their advantage and prompting me to survey the Santana's Guard in a wide, arcing circle. "You can follow us peacefully, or we will take you forcefully. Your choice."

Otto stands with both arms folded, wholly disinterested in the repartee, and apparently unconvinced of any danger as he's made no attempt to enter the fray of our shaky reunion. Aiden's gaze follows Tess, but the boyish grin has finally fallen from his mouth.

Good.

I need all the players if we are going to win this game.

23

ARI

I'M SITTING IN A room unlike anything I've ever experienced.

It stands looming over me— a steep ceiling, gold flourishes touching every inch of the space, grand windows with their adjoining thick, flowing drapes, and a bed that would easily fit six grown men. I don't want to sit down, afraid I will muss the linens or the elegant, velvety upholsteries. My discomfort is as wide as the space before me, unused to such finery and enclosed spaciousness.

Out the windows is a vast, open courtyard filled with, at the moment, an array of people. Some look to be servants and workers of the estate, moving to and fro with their afternoon chores and duties, keeping the grounds and living quarters up to the prestige and status of the Santanas. It reminds me of Turin, only an orderly version that shows a devoted concern for the well-being of the employed people.

I desperately want to hate Tess and her condescending, over-reaching brother, Liam. I've yet to meet their father, Lord Santana, but already I feel a tiny smidge of respect for their family. What I see from my limited view is nothing short of inspiring. Everyone has a purpose and a place, something grander than their common upbringing to contribute toward and feel proud of.

It's suddenly clear why Marg wanted the kidnapping of Princess Adalena kept between us— there are very capable families within the realm, skilled leaders that would meet very little resistance should they make a move for the Crown. Felshan's monarchy is fragile, a strong wind able to turn the Chattan-Sinclair line to rubble and seat another more proficient and equal to the task of rebuilding our atrophied kingdom.

Part of me wants to slip the information to the Santanas, the thought of light and life brought back to the people of Turin urging me to move forward with the idea. Could I turn my back on the princess? On the three men I started on this venture with? On Marg?

The first two hold little sway, even if they seem up to the task of personally changing the future trajectory of our suffering city. But Marg— her image won't leave me. After the prince died, her life's mission became entwined with Felshan and its capital city of Turin.

Could I betray her work? Her dedication to Princess Adalena taking the throne? Marg has hindered my own gain, but also given me the ability to seek the vengeance I've wanted since my mother was dragged from our home. I may never find those who took her from me, who made her rot in a cell without any proof of her crime, but I know their kind. Satisfaction will be such a sweet reward as I slowly inflict their suffering. And because of Marg, I can. I will.

My resolve cements into place. I won't forsake my teacher and her efforts.

Don't fail me, Marg. My silent prayer dissipates within the spacious walls of my temporary room.

A knock at my door startles me away from my vantage point. "Come in," I say, unused to having to carry my voice so far in order to be heard.

"We are to attend dinner with the Santanas tonight." Captain Montgomery stands at the entrance to my room, his face pulling into an almost pitying look. "Tess sent... clothes for us to change into." He steps out of the way, a rosy-cheeked woman moving in his place.

"Hello, my lady." The older woman curtsies. "My name is Larisa. I'm here to prepare you for tonight's dinner party."

"Prepare me? Am I to be one of the courses?" Genuine confusion knits my brow.

"She's here to help you become more... presentable." The captain is doing his best to be diplomatic, but I frown at him anyway.

"What's wrong with my presence?" I ask, my fingers tapping against my crossed arms.

Larisa moves through the doorway to stand across from me, grabbing my hand and pulling me around as she assesses me front to back. "Perhaps a nice bath, and good wash of your hair and scrub of your nails." She pulls the tie from my braid in a swift movement, the ends unfolding from their confinement.

"I can bathe myself, thank you," I say, a single eyebrow raised. Unused to such personal attention leaves me flustered as she continues her way into the room, dropping a heap of fabric on the over-sized bed. "What is that?" I ask, dread forming in the pit of my stomach.

"Your dress for this evening," says the woman, honest excitement lighting her face. My stomach twists and I hold back a gag as I stare at the layers of pastel fabric.

I lift the thing from the bed, taking in the low-neckline, lack of sleeves, and lace trim. "I would cut off my own foot before I would ever pull this hideous costume over my head." I turn to face Captain Montgomery, continuing my outrage. "I'm not wearing this." I move across the room, pointing a finger into his chest. The corners of his lips twitch upward, but his eyes stay wide as he takes in the monstrosity crumpled in my arm. "You go find whoever picked this out and tell them they can choke on my fist."

My ill-mannered remark earns an open-mouthed expression and audible gasp from the old woman now standing behind me, combing out my braid with her fingers. Larisa gives a congenial whack against my shoulder, leaving me perplexed. Are there years of time I spent with this woman, time that I've somehow misplaced that would secure this kind of familiarity?

"That's no way for a lady to speak," she admonishes, my head pulling back as she catches on a few knots. I can't remember the last time someone else brushed my hair, even rudimentarily in this manner.

"I, madam, am no lady." My remark is lost, her one-track mind given a task that she's determined to see through to the end.

"Now, there wasn't time to bring a tub up to your room, so we will need to walk down to Lady Tess's bath chamber." She walks to the ornate dresser against the opposite wall and opens one of its giant drawers, pulling out a plain, dress-like garment to accompany us down the hall.

I want to dig in my heels, refusing to adhere to the obnoxious wishes of some wealthy standard. But the thought of washing away days of grime from my skin is tempting enough for me to cooperate with this woman. For now at least, I can get on board with a warm bath. But someone comes within arms-length with a dress and regret will reign their life from that moment on.

We walk past the captain still standing at my door, heading for the tub of tension-relieving hot water. "I'll come back and check on you in a little bit," he tells me, reaching out a hand as if to touch me. But he must think better of it as that hand soon rests back against his side.

"Oh stop the fuss and go change. From the smell of it, you could use a bath yourself." Larisa remarks. "The girl is in good hands with me. Now be on your way, Lord Montgomery."

The use of such a title catches me off guard, sending a questioning look toward the man. Lord? Since when did he become a lord?

"It's captain, madam. Not lord." She looks confused at his correction, but moves past him as if she can't be bothered to figure it out or hear an explanation. "If you need me, my room is just down the hall, with Aiden and Otto." I nod to him, glad to know where our other two companions are holding up, before turning my attention back to the promise of a bath.

The abruptness of Larisa brings a coy grin to my face as I follow her, watching Captain Montgomery out of the corner of my eye as he pulls out his shirt and sniffs, a look of sour agreement sending him back down the hallway to his own bath.

I'm exfoliated from head to toe, any prude notions pushed far into the corner of the room as Larisa and another younger woman, Katya, scrub every inch of me. My skin is covered in about eight different fragrant oils, and my hair is washed in a concoction of blended soaps before being rinsed with water steeped with primrose, peonies, and hyacinth blooms. Or so they tell me. A towel the size of a blanket is handed to me to dry off before I'm wrapped in the slim garment Larisa brought from my room, hitting me at the knees and tying off in the front.

"So there's a woman underneath the dirt after all," a familiar voice chimes.

Tess walks into the bathroom dawning a form-fitting dress that hugs her hips and accentuates each curve— ever the picture of affluent delicacy. Curls bounce around her face, some pinned back while others spring freely— a stark contrast to her rather severe presence this afternoon. I want to scowl, but her beauty and harmless appearance leads me to a raised eyebrow instead.

"I heard there was a bit of a disagreement toward the ensemble chosen for you." She sits down next to me, staying clear of the two women working through my hair.

"I will wear the clothes I brought, or I will walk out of those doors right now. And anyone who gets in my way will come away wishing they hadn't."

"What a treat for the men outside, to see your pretty legs waltz out in your bathrobe." Her face dances as she looks me over.

Of course I wouldn't leave in this thin shift that leaves little to the imagination. I roll my eyes, not bothering to hide it. This woman, Tess— she wants me to be uncomfortable. Maybe she even delights in it. My eyes narrow toward her while my mouth remains in a tight line.

"Oh, come on. I won't make you walk around in that frilly eyesore Larisa laid out for you. You can borrow some of my clothes while yours are getting cleaned downstairs," she says. My head whips around to face her.

It wasn't hard to miss during our interaction earlier that she and the captain had once had some kind of relationship— the extent of which I'm unsure. There was still a reverence in his eyes when he spoke to her, even though it seemed that she had liked him more than he had liked her. But I don't understand it. She's one of the most dazzling women I've ever seen.

Tess walks back through the adjoining door, showing off the deep plunge in the back of her dress which exposes almost the entirety of her back. Her muscles aren't well-defined through her soft skin, but that's not surprising. Most wealthy women prefer a sedentary lifestyle; Marg is the only one I know who has gone against that pattern.

Tess seems a perfect candidate for a wife: stunning, soft, and rich. If she preferred the captain, it would seem he had a silver platter handed to him, and he denied it, denied her.

She enters the bathroom again a few moments later with a stack of neatly folded clothes between both hands. "I'm a little taller than you, so the pants might need to be cuffed at the bottom. But I think the rest should do nicely.

After you've dressed, you can meet us downstairs in the great hall. Larisa, if you wouldn't mind showing her the way."

"Of course, my lady." Larisa dips her head.

"If you need a place to wash up while you're here, you're welcome to use this bathroom." Tess's facade drops for just a moment, another kindness showing through that I didn't expect. She must feel it too, because she adds, "But, make sure to knock— wouldn't want to walk into anything too scandalous, now would we." Tess's dark dress swishes with each step as she again retreats back through the door to her bedroom, a gentle *click* officially closing our brief conversation.

Larisa shows me downstairs, walking the length of the house before the looming doors of the Great Hall come into view. Tess's clothes fit me almost perfectly. The dark, gray pants needed a slight adjustment at the ends like she said, but the deep green top feels like it was made just for me. Is this what it feels like to have money? To have clothes that fit and feel like butter against your skin?

My hair is down, something I rarely do since it always seems to get in the way. Larisa and Katya convinced me that all their work would be best showcased without my usual braid. Instead, one side is twisted around the back, pinned underneath the bulk of my long wavy hair, with white and pink Bougainvillea blossoms placed in its folds. I almost look like the lady Larisa originally thought I was.

Arguing voices greet me as I approach the doors.

"I can't. Why in the Four Kingdoms would we come here to hurt House Santana? We've always had a respectful trade and relationship between Fort Lowsan and Turin," I hear Captain Montgomery say as I enter.

He is sitting across from Tess and Liam, a full plate of food untouched in front of him. His expertly fitted dark jacket and pants blend perfectly with his neatly tousled hair, his blue eyes popping against the contrast.

Between him and Liam, I'm not sure who seems more red faced. "Is this a Montgomery talking or a Chattan- Sinclair?" Liam throws back, earning a glare from the captain.

"It's all of us, Liam. None have a reason to go against you and your family!" Roan declares before the movement of me walking through the doors catches his eye.

He turns to look at me, and I feel his gaze peruse my new appearance, looking me up and down before resting on my face. If he approves of my new clothes he doesn't show it. Otto sends a wink my way, while Aiden looks as if he has taken his first full breath of the night.

As I take in the Great Hall, I realize it is great indeed. The room is large enough to fit at least a hundred people. It is a perfect fusion of whites, grays, and earthy browns. The table is long enough for three or four people lay atop it without touching. It's smooth surface has been painstakingly polished and sanded so a subtle shine emanates from the wood.

"Oh, Ari." Tess stands, a wide smile crossing her face as she follows the captain's attention to the door. "So nice of you join our little debate. Your companions could use the level-headedness of a woman on their side." I walk toward them, noting the absence of Lord Santana.

A plate of food already prepared for me sits next to the captain. His stare never leaves my face, pulling out my chair for me as I get closer. I've never seen him quite so poised and proper. As I move past him the faint smell of fresh vanilla and woody citrus float around me. I unintentionally lean in to him to inhale more. His eyebrows raise ever so slightly as he marks the gesture, and I snap forward as I move to sit down.

Tess and Liam are situated at either end of the table, a rigid Aiden sitting to Tess's right, sporting a well-tailored gray tunic. Otto is a cleaned version of himself and seems to be the only one eating— opting to engage with the meal in front of him instead of the squabble playing out with the rest of the group.

Tess follows my survey of the room. "I do apologize. My father can't join us tonight. In all the excitement of seeing my old friend," she gestures toward Roan, "I forgot he's out of the city and won't be back for a couple weeks." The captain lets out an audible grunt. He clearly doesn't believe in her selective memory.

"Your companions have told us they aren't here to spy on us. But tell us, Ari," Tess continues when I sit, her focus still resting on me. "If you aren't here to observe and report on House Santana to the Crown, what could you possibly be doing in Fort Lowsan? Anything honorable would have been set forth ahead of time. And seeing as none of you have ties to our city, I have nothing else to conclude except something deceitful in nature."

I don't have a chance to answer before the captain opens his mouth. "For the last time— lives are at stake, Tess. The longer you keep us here, asking us the same questions that I already said we're sworn by the Crown not to answer, the more responsibility you heft onto the shoulders of House Santana for the innocent you are jeopardizing."

He leans forward against the table, resting his hands on either side of his plate, a deep grimace directed straight to the woman across from him. He ventures to even out his heated voice before continuing. "Please. We grew up together. If that meant anything to you, I implore you to let us go." His eyes convey all the pleading he can muster.

"I liked you better before the prince died," Liam says, straight-faced. Captain Montgomery clenches both fists atop the table, his jaw closed so tight at the remark that I wonder if any more pressure would shatter a few of his teeth.

Tess narrows her eyes at her brother, softening her gaze when she looks back to the captain. Is that pity in her eyes? I realize the prince is dead. The blanket of grief hanging over Turin for the last seven years is hard to miss. But what relationship did our captain have with that prince exactly?

Liam's sister flicks her gaze to me. "Ari, maybe you can help us out. The others in your party keep moving us in circles. You say you aren't here to spy and take back sensitive information to Turin. If you can't tell us why you're really here, how are we to believe that the former isn't true?"

I may not know political tactics and those subsequent advantageous maneuvers, but sometimes telling part of the truth is enough of an appeasement when one doesn't wish the other to know all their secrets. "I would say the former is, in fact, true. I am here to spy." The captain turns toward me, eyes wide, tilting his head as his puzzled gaze searches me.

Tess leans in a little closer, while Liam scoffs. "I knew it. I told you, Tess. We can't trust them!"

"What I mean is," I interrupt, sending a glare toward Liam, "I am a thief and spy. Commissioned by the king's sister, Lady Margaret, as a way of keeping Turin safe and functioning smoothly until Crown Princess Adalena can assume the throne." The captain's jaw falls as I give away my secret. "And in doing so, the whole of Felshan has also run more efficiently." Part of the truth mixed with the idea that we are, technically, all united under one roof. Maybe playing the compatriot card will soften their distrust.

"And what have the Santanas done to warrant Lady Margaret's eye, sending her spy to Fort Lowsan?" Liam has lost all of his former charm, his gaze now stern and cold as he looks at me.

"The Santanas have done nothing." I do my best to hold a steady mask of calm composure as all eyes are now resting on me. "A palace guard has betrayed Lady Margaret, earning retaliation from his outraged former captain," I wave a hand toward the man next to me, "and the sending forth of the lady's most talented tool at her disposal." I raise a finger pointing it back to myself.

My presumptuous comment earns a nod from the woman sitting across from me. Silence follows as the siblings contemplate my words, and I dare a glance at the captain, who doesn't look as put out as I imagined he would be with me disclosing this information.

"I'm intrigued, Ari— commissioned thief and spy of Lady Margaret's." Tess's attention flits between Captain Montgomery and myself. "I have an idea. A test, if you will. And, if you pass, you are all free to go." Her light-hearted tone leaves me leery of her next words.

"What kind of test?" Aiden asks, resting an arm on the table, flicking a short glance my way.

Tess displays a mischievous smile, staring at Roan. "Do you remember Sir Crane?" The captain takes a deep inhale. "He owns a few orchards through-out Fort Lowsan," she says, looking back in my direction. "There was a rumor that he siphoned an orange tree sapling from Venes, attempting to grow oranges up north. Our weather— it makes it difficult for an orange tree to grow. Which is why most of us in Fort Lowsan have never tried the sweet citrus fruits of Venes. Rarely do our people get to make the trip to Haythen's southern country, and it's difficult to keep the fruit from rotting before it's transferred up here. So, you see, oranges are a delicacy up in these parts, Ari."

Each time Tess says my name there's a prominent gleam in her eye. She shifts, turning her sights once again to Captain Montgomery. He is still sitting beside me, one arm folded across across the table and the other supporting the side of his frowning face. All his attention is focused on Tess.

Where is she going with this? And why on earth are we talking about oranges? I just admitted to illicit behavior, and here we are learning about Haythen geography and agriculture. I'm trying to solve a puzzle that I nei-ther have all the pieces for, nor a clear picture of what I'm trying to piece together in the first place.

Liam seems to have mastered the look of boredom mixed with the desire to slit someone's throat, sitting lazily back in his chair and fiddling with a

knife. Otto appears to be asleep in the corner, while Aiden is quietly searching between the faces of everyone gathered at the table, looking as confused
as I feel.

"Our royal captain here visited one summer with his parents. How old
were we, twelve?" she continues, glee melting off of her every word.

"Thirteen," Roan corrects, the lines on his forehead deepening.

"Thirteen." Tess nods a couple times, looking up at the ceiling as if overcome with nostalgia. "We decided, the three of us, that we were going to
sneak into Sir Crane's orchard and search for the orange tree. Roan was the
only one who had tasted one before. Which, I suppose, is what happens
when you grow up in a palace." She winks at him, earning her a scowl in
return. He grew up in the palace?

"The way he spoke of its perfectly sweet, sharp taste, and its bright flesh
and fragrance as you peel that top layer away—as if it were touched by the
heavens and given its taste by angels themselves. Well, it sealed the decision
for me. We would steal an orange from Sir Crane's secret orange tree." Tess
clasps her hands out in front of her, resting them on the table as she leans
into its side.

"We planned for days, hitting every angle and avenue a bunch of thir-
teen-year-olds could possibly imagine. The only thing we didn't plan for
was what to do if we were caught." Tess laughs at this, as if the whole
experience was some big joke between the three of them. But Liam's smile
doesn't reach his eyes, and Captain Montgomery is as still as a statue, his
eyes never wavering from Tess and her reminiscing. I wonder if I pushed him
off his chair if he would shatter into a million pices?

"It's not hard to guess what happened next. Caught red-handed by the
surly Sir Crane himself," continues Tess.

"I would be surly too if a bunch of kids broke into my estate," I mutter,
unacknowledged as Tess seems to still be caught up in the memory.

"You know, I'm fairly certain that was the first time my dashing good looks didn't work on a man," she says.

"Yes, but your name did," Liam remarks. Tess is so proud of wherever this is going that she hasn't stopped beaming through the entire story. I shift in my seat, for once stumped at the finale this cavalier woman has in store for the four of us.

"Once he learned who we were, he didn't dare take it to the Guard, knowing they'd drop the charges immediately— being under the command of my father. But he still demanded payment. Lucky for us, at only thirteen, we didn't carry much around with us in the name of valuables. So, he took whatever we had on us, thinking it was worth enough to us that it would at least hurt a little." She stops, turning her sights to her brother. "What did he take from you, Liam?" Tess asks.

"The queen from my chess board. I'd just won my first game against Father the night before. I carved my initials into the bottom. L.E.S. Liam Elias Santana."

She doesn't waste any time. "And you, Roan?"

The captain hesitates, taking a deep breath before gracing her with his answer. "A leather cuff, studded with brass buttons. My sister had given it to me for my birthday the previous winter."

"Mine was a ring," Tess says, continuing the revelations. "Beautiful white stone carved into a perfect circle. A Jadeyan tradesmen had just made his way through Fort Lowsan a couple weeks before. It was the most magical piece of jewelry I'd ever seen."

"It's been great going down memory lane, but what does this have to do with us?" Aiden speaks up, the allure of Tess beginning to wane as the night goes on.

"I'm so glad you asked." She places a kiss on the side of Aiden's face, bringing back a sliver of his previous captivation. "Ari is going to steal back our things from Sir Crane."

My eyes shoot to meet her own as she claps her hands together in satisfaction. Her bright, scintillating smile after this final announcement is the only proof we need of her delight toward this *test* she's conjured.

"No," the captain says, immediately following her last words.

"You really are no fun anymore, Roan," she replies, turning her attention back to me. "But I think this one is up to Ari. If she really is the grand thief and spy she says, this will be nothing more than an evening stroll for her."

"And what does it prove besides that?" Captain Montgomery stands up, his chair groaning loudly as it's pushed out behind him from the sudden movement. "There's still no proof we aren't here under ominous orders. It will take more time than we have to spare. Tess, listen to yourself. Why are you doing this? What is going on?"

"Maybe I want my ring back."

"Then go take it back."

"I'm a spiteful woman, Captain. If he's going to embarrass me, then I will embarrass him in return." Roan is taken back by her response, searching her face for more than she's saying. There's more to this story, but our limited time doesn't leave much space to flush it out.

"I'll do it," I say, earning the stares of everyone in the room, including the once sleeping Otto.

"You won't. We are walking out of here right now, and no one is going to stop us." The captain steps around his chair, pushing it in before buttoning up his jacket.

"The sun is almost set, Captain. We couldn't leave now even if we wanted to. Besides, what's wrong with a little good faith opportunity to unite old friends, and new," I reply. Maybe I can play the pawn of intrigue after all.

I will play the cards she's laid bare while searching for the ones she's hidden deep up her sleeve. It could very well be a trap, but it's nothing I'm not used to. The last seven years have been spent searching around corners and watching my back. Why would this be any different? People are devious and unreliable by nature. And friend or not, Tess is as conniving as they come.

My smile now matches Tess's. "I have a couple conditions."

"Name them," the delighted woman says.

"When I bring you back these knickknacks we are free to go, no questions asked."

"Of course."

"And we must make it happen tonight. No delays."

"Done." Tess doesn't even hesitate.

The captain closes his eyes, running a hand slowly through his dark hair. "What aren't you telling us, Tess? This is absurd, and you know it." His voice is calm, quieted from his previous tone.

"Can't a girl just want her ring back?" She does her best to play at sincerity, but her simulated innocence is hard to miss. Do men really fall for this?

The captain rubs at his temples, shaking his head. He doesn't like that I agreed to this. But he must see like I do that it is the path of least resistance.

Liam stands, a smile on his face that finally reaches his eyes. "We better get started."

24

CAPTAIN MONTGOMERY

"Get what you need, then meet me in my room," I say, cornering Ari as we walk out of the Great Hall and away from Tess and Liam.

"What just happened in there?" Aiden catches up to us.

"Tess being Tess," I say, returning my focus to the thief in front of me. "You aren't doing this. We will gather our things and walk out, immediately. We are four of the most skilled soldiers of Turin, trained in the militant capital of Felshan. We will fight our way out if necessary."

"And risk being hurt? Unable to continue looking for Princess Adalena? Or thrown in their dungeons? No thanks. I've spent enough time nursing wounds and escorting people to a dark cell to know I'll take an alternative when presented with one," Otto chimes in, coming up behind us. Ari winces at his words.

"Ari was right when she spoke in there," Aiden begins. "We can't leave now anyway. If she can pull this off in a single night, we can leave at first light and be on our way. We lost a day, but we can make it up, as *free, unharmed* men... and woman," Aiden finishes, stumbling as he almost forgets his female counterpart.

"I can do this, Montgomery," Ari says. "We have her word that we can go if I do this. So let me do it. And let's get the Four Kingdoms out of here."

"And if the whole thing is a trap?" I respond.

"If I don't come back, go on without me," she replies as if she's simply telling me the weather outside.

"I don't like this. She doesn't care about some stupid ring from almost a decade ago," I say.

"So, let this play out. We know the pieces don't fit. Let's find the ones that do and turn this in our favor." Ari gestures toward our small group.

I am so close to her that our arms brush, our hushed voices calling for a close proximity to keep the Santanas out of our plan. My heart beats loudly, the rush of it drumming through my ears.

"I agree with Ari. I say we see it through. Nothing else to do right now anyway but wait until morning," Otto says.

I'm reluctant. Untrusting of the motives of Tess and Liam. But my resistance releases into acceptance, mostly so I can finish this meeting and compose myself once again.

I hate the idea of Ari going into that house alone, not knowing what lies inside. But I can't see another way. I nod, the last of our group to give my approval before we break away from our hallway exchange.

I continue to wrestle with it as I walk the remaining distance to my room. Ari can't risk herself like this— for some stupid trinket and some ridiculous revenge plot. I need her. I need her help to find Lena.

Lena. Lena. Lena.

Rustling around with Sir Crane is going to make some noise— a spotlight I've been trying to stay clear of since we left Turin.

When my breathing steadies once again, I make my decision. Fear will not run my actions. I will stay by Ari and keep her safe, and we will move once again to find Lena, our whole group intact. The best move at this point is to let it play out.

A pawn can still trap the queen.

The sun has fully set, the only light coming from a waning moon with its accompanying cacophony of stars dotting through the darkened sky.

Sir Crane's home is only a short jog away from where me, Ari, and Tess crouch in the grass. Stubby, bush-like trees in varying sizes line the rise and fall of the land, stretching as far as the eye can see. The large hills and their appending valleys color the landscape for miles, marking the distinct land around Fort Lowsan, making it easy to stay hidden and out of sight as we move closer to Crane's house.

Calling it a house might be an understatement, as its vast outer walls display a villa closer to the magnificence of House Santana's grand courtyard and adjoining residence. Who knew growing and selling fruit could be so lucrative?

The late evening hour has left the building quiet, asleep within the shadows of the looming exterior. Wagons, crates, boots, and random metal tools lie scattered throughout the rows of greenery, abandoned at the close of day as if the people just disappeared when sun made its last call on the horizon.

"Sir Crane's office and personal quarters are on the far right side," Tess tells us, pointing toward the far section of the home.

"How do you know? Were you inside? Personally mapping out that section?" I ask, still sore from her obstinance.

"He would be so lucky." Her calm tone clearly didn't hit the mark I was aiming for. "The front and back entrances are kept locked from dusk til dawn. You may have to break a window to get inside. Or here," Tess rustles around in a small satchel hanging from across her shoulder, "I borrowed these from Larisa. She says she uses them if she ever gets locked out of the manor, or she can't the find the keys to a random cupboard or wardrobe."

An array of short, thin metal rods with various hooked ends lie in her grip. The maid knows how to pick a lock? People are truly a mystery, even when I think I've sized them up well.

"I don't need lock-pics," Ari claims, returning her focus to the house, analyzing her first obstacle to retrieving the items.

"Well, then here's a rock for the window." Tess grabs a large stone lying beside her, almost too big to hold one-handed.

"Good grief, Tess. Who is the thief here? I don't tell you what angle to hold your head to give the best view of your fluttering eyelashes, so stop trying to tell me how to best break in to someone's home," Ari mocks, earning a raised eyebrow of surprise from Tess and myself. I do my best to suppress a smile. In any other circumstances, these two might just be friends.

"By all means, let's see the master in action." Tess winks at Ari, now settling into a silent, watchful position. For a moment, I forget we are here against our will, in one of the most nonsensical situations I've ever found myself a part of.

Ari looks in my direction. "Remind me what I'm looking for again."

"A white, stone ring. The queen from a chess piece, letters L-E-S carved into the bottom. And a leather wrist cuff with brass buttons inlaid. It covers around a thumb length's size of your arm, a small clasp on the underside. It's been so long, I don't remember much else to help identify it, other than Sir Crane doesn't seem the kind of man to wear leather jewelry. So if you find it, it's most likely the only one in his possession," I respond. My earlier compliance unravels the longer we linger in the orchards.

"I'm going to move around the back, get a better layout of the property." Tess nods at Ari's words.

"I'm coming with you," I state, shifting to follow after her.

"And I will move around to the other side, keep an eye from that vantage point. If I see anyone running, I will move toward Aiden and Liam waiting at the road's edge." Tess declares.

We left the two men with a solid view of the home and instructions to come to the rescue with our horses if we need a quick getaway. Otto opted to sit this one out, something about being too old to become Sir Crane's object of torture.

Ari and I run through the woods, stopping periodically to make sure no men securing the home are making rounds through the rows of silhouetted trees. We find a centered clearing, perching down as we scan the immediate area.

"You don't have to do this, you know. I don't trust Tess and Liam. It's not too late to turn around and make run for it," I tell Ari once we've stopped.

"And what about Otto, probably fast asleep in his bed? Are we to just leave him behind as we *make a run for it?*" The reminder sets me back on edge, my hands arcing from my face up through my hair, until they clasp together under my stubbled jaw.

"If I'm not back within the hour, leave. There's no need for all of us to be under his thumb if this doesn't go as planned." I don't nod or agree with her statement in any way, my face fixed toward the tranquil household blanketed within the eclipse of night.

Out of my periphery, I see her hand reach toward me, wrapping an oddly steady hand around my arm. "I'll be ok. I've done stupider things than this, and always seem to come out of it on top. We will make it out of this. We will find the princess. Trust me." Is she trying to comfort me?

I stare where her hand rests against me, moving my focus to her shadowy green gaze. My muscles tense under her touch, the heat rising from me a stark contrast to her cold fingers. I don't pull away, instead inadvertently inching closer to her. She lets go, her gaze suddenly refusing to meet mine.

Pull yourself together.

Regret crawls through me, my wayward body still pushing against my better judgment as the memory of her touch still scorches my skin.

"I will be right here. If you are in trouble, come to one of these back windows. I will be at your side as quickly as I can," I tell her. There may still be a small desire to stand in her way, holding her back from the danger that surely lies ahead of her. But I know my duty. Lena is my future, and I will not abandon her for anything, or anyone.

Ari nods before turning to run through the length of the yard.

Let her be ok. She may be the most unbearable woman I've ever met, but I want her to get out of this unscathed. It's not betraying of my set future to wish for her safety.

At least, that's what I tell myself in this moment.

25

ARI

A STURDY TRELLIS WEAVES its criss-crossing wooden beams up the stone wall to the back of the estate. My feet find their first hold, the earthy material carrying my weight with a muffled groan, the ascending vines absorbing most of the sound. *Thank goodness.* I climb the steep, makeshift ladder to the third-floor terrace, jumping the distance between the edge of the lattice and the sturdy framework of the extensive home.

I land with quiet precision, having played out the same position entering a residence uninvited at least a few dozen times over the years.

The balcony gives little to hide my approach, a few chairs and a small table off to the side. If someone were to open the doors or look out the window, I would be laid bare for them to see. Being in the open sends my nerves on full alert, a mix of excitement and uneasiness rushing through me. I move toward the doors, giving one last look over the edge to the captain waiting in the cover of the neighboring fruit garden.

A pull on the handle and a short *tick* confirms what I hoped to be true. No one locks the balcony doors, the trusting nature of an elevated room. Carefully, I slip through, opening it just enough to slide inside. A quick survey shows that I'm alone, an unused bedroom sitting before me.

Blending into the monochrome shades of night is easy, compliments of Tess's endless wardrobe. I move silently down the hallway of the home, encompassing Sir Crane's personal chambers as Tess said.

I've walked through inhabited rooms before unnoticed, but knowing hardly anything about this man keeps me on edge. Is he a light sleeper? Does he go to bed early, or work well into the night? Is he adept with a weapon?

Normally, I would trail and analyze the person for days, even weeks, before entering their house. Even then, I would get a feel of the layout, walking the adjoining rooms and halls before actually looking for, or taking, anything. This time that luxury won't be mine— the analysis and taking happening all in a matter of minutes.

Where would a wealthy fruit merchant hide random trinkets from a bunch of children? The idea that he would save such things after so many years is a little ridiculous and highly improbable, but I continue forward nonetheless.

I move from room to room, greeted by more unoccupied bedrooms. A set of stairs carries me to the second floor, finding much of the same. The rooms are well-kept— no dust, debris, or clutter of any kind. But also, no signs of life.

Is he gone? Maybe to a summer home? I know many of the wealthy keep multiple residences. But it would seem the warm weather and upkeep of such lands would keep him around during this time of year.

My heart skips a beat. *Something isn't right.*

I move carefully, the emptiness of my surroundings ringing through my senses. As I get closer to the center of the building, faint voices come from a distance. I slow my movements, coming cautiously to the door that separates me from whomever the voices belong to.

"We have enough of the city on our side. We can move as early as next week," someone says.

"The Santanas still have support. What about those who don't wish to see them step down?" another asks.

"Are you questioning me, brother? The work we've done leading up to this moment? We are days away from bringing the last seven years into focus, of claiming what is ours." More voices speak, too muffled, and I struggle to make sense of what they are saying.

Silence follows. I lean closer, my ear now flush against the door.

"With Lord Santana away, their foothold will falter. No one will fall behind his impetuous children when public opinion sways toward us. The final payment is on its way, the package safely in transit. By week's end, the Guard will be in our purse. It will be the final straw, tipping the scales in our favor. Our task is done, gentlemen. It's time for a new reign to enter our city. The dynasty of Crane." A few muted cheers erupt at these words.

I'm frozen. Are they are conspiring to overthrow the Santanas? What package in transit? My mind is racing, trying to piece together the little information I overheard. My breath catches in my chest, an invisible weight making it hard to breathe. I'm caught in the web of a vicious scheme that has little, if anything, to do with me.

A loud crash bellows through the hallway, snapping my attention toward the noise. The room in front of me goes quiet, the sound of shuffling bodies coming straight toward where I now stand.

Mere seconds remain before the flurry of action reaches me, exposing my eavesdropping and my unwelcome presence. I only heard three talking, but who knows how many more are soundlessly present to this treason. Three against one is questionable if it comes to a fight. Not impossible, but enough to set my teeth on edge.

Another clatter sounds, softer this time, from the part of the house I've yet to explore. It spurs me into action, retracing my steps to an adjoining broom closet I cleared just minutes ago, only a few steps from where I stand exposed. Silently, I enter, just as the door with the voices bursts open and spills out its occupants.

A moment of dread fills the empty closet as multiple sets of footsteps charge through the hall. *More than three.* I duck down, pulling on my knife to make sure it's in place for what's to come.

"Check the rooms. Check the house. Seal it down." A male voice reaches through the darkness.

More footsteps clamor by, but no one enters my space. I shift my feet around the cramped closet with barely enough room to stand against the wall next to my exit. When the sounds of running and shouting cease, I peer out the door, checking the dark hall. Rustling comes from the left wing of the home, but my immediate vicinity is clear.

The door inaudibly swings open with my gentle force as I move out of hiding. It takes a few breaths before I reach the end of the hall, stopping short of the stairway. More voices trickle down from the third floor, one of them distinctly female.

Each step upwards is nimble and swift. It's not my first time investigating a skirmish that isn't my own, but the first time I can't see any benefit from it. I don't work for the Santanas, hardly knowing them at all. Yet, I've been brought into the middle of their political misfortunes.

Questions threaten to overpower me, but I lock them away. There will be time for answers and confrontation with Tess and Liam. For now, I'm drawn to the voice that mentioned a package and a payment.

I can't put my finger on it. But a feeling, an understanding that I have yet to uncover, keeps persuading me to go forward. To push against my survival instincts that want me to turn and run. There's something to discover, something nagging in the back of my mind that refuses to make itself known.

A buzz starts low inside of me, spreading like water tipped from a glass until a low-level hum radiates from every part of me. *Danger.*

Yes, my profession is perilous by nature. But when a threat is imminent, when a fatal blow lies just around the corner, or behind the next door, or at the end of a hall—my entire body sings with vigilance, strength, and focus. I become the threat. This nobody from the streets of Turin, the prey that is reviled, becomes the hunter to be feared.

I approach the room. The distinct female voice registers louder as I get closer. "Did you think you'd get away with it? You will lose your life for this treachery," she says.

"Is reality not sinking in, my dear? You two are outnumbered. And it seems you've given me a great gift. It's not against the law to kill trespassers if your life is in danger. When the Guard investigates and sees the weapons that were in your possession, I will be cleared of any wrong-doing. And with both of you out of the picture I will be able to step into the light without any resistance," the male voice says.

"When our father returns, you, sir, will be hanged for your crimes against House Santana," a familiar male voice spits across the room. Liam.

I lie back against the wall just outside the room's entrance, listening intently to the exchange. What is Liam doing inside? He's supposed to be with Aiden. Is Aiden ok? My mind is swirling with more and more questions—spinning to make sense of what is happening.

"There will be nothing left for your father to return to. You and your whorish sister won't, unfortunately for you, make it through the night. Your father's lands will be seized by tomorrow afternoon. An emergency viva voce will commence as early as the evening, temporarily placing me in power in the absence of Fort Lowsan's governing house, until I call for a dissipation of House Santana after your father never comes home. Your entrance to my home tonight has saved me a lot of trouble. I couldn't have planned the sequence of events better myself," says the male voice.

Someone yells, the sound of fury reaching me as if there wasn't a wall between us. Heavy steps, the sound of grunts and bone against flesh leaving little to the imagination. I step from my hiding place, the distraction of the fight enough for me to peer into the room. Five unknown men, one of them most assuredly Sir Crane with his graying hair and drooping features, along with Tess and Liam Santana, occupy the space.

Why would they be here? I was supposed to be the one in the house. They were supposed to...

Realization soaks through me as if caught in a summer storm. I was supposed to be the distraction— my retrieving of three worthless items. They must have assumed my presence would divert Sir Crane. He was supposed to be in one of those rooms, my searching and presence alerting him. And my subsequent interception from the man would have allowed Tess and Liam to come unnoticed.

The picture begins to take shape, the obscure pieces finding their place. They never counted on me retrieving the items. Or me being able to sneak in undetected. Tess didn't think I could go unseen.

Part of me is impressed by Tess's cleverness, sending me in as the decoy. It almost brings a smile to my face. I knew there was more than meets the eye when it came to Tess Santana. But the other part of me wants to strangle the woman. She thought I lied about who I was, or at least embellished my abilities. And because of it she used me as a pawn in her game, and I walked right into it. My lips curl downward. And what a stupid game it was. They have been caught red-handed by the one person they wanted me to inadvertently entertain in order for them to avoid.

These siblings are not adept to fight off these men on their own in the middle of the night. Where is their backup? The twenty men that met us outside the tavern? Another glance into the space shows a now bloodied

Liam, red oozing from his nose, and Tess backed into a corner by the heftiest of Crane's company.

"Maybe we don't kill this one right away. The night is young. Let's have a little fun first," the burly man says, ravenously fixed upon the Santana woman. I stifle the snarl rising within my throat. This man will be the first to die under my hand if it comes to a fight.

Tess draws a knife from her waist. "You come near me and I will cut off your most valuable asset." The men only laugh at her remark, the kind of sound a starving hyena makes right before devouring their fallen prey.

There's nothing I would love more than to let the Santanas figure this out on their own. If they are going to throw me to the wolves to get whatever it is they are looking for, then I should return the favor. But something about the way these men were talking earlier, how they're talking now— it feels as though it affects me as well. I don't know how and I don't know what my role is in their schemes. But for some reason it feels important.

I should turn and run. Save myself. But when have I ever been sensible?

The smell of death hovers close by. These men would have no problem watching the life slowly drain from Liam and Tess Santana.

I can't take all these men out alone. Liam doesn't look completely helpless, but Tess looks like a baby bird that just fell from its nest. Her long, graceful features would master a ballroom, but will do little to help her here without some basic training. She will be a liability in an all out brawl should one arise.

I'm about to step into the room, even lifting a foot from the floor to grab my dagger as I enter, when one of the men begins to speak. "Almost a decade in the making, Phillip. Can you believe we're finally here? And we didn't even have to lure the mouse in with the promise of cheese." I freeze at the declaration, my brows scrunching together. Almost a decade? Almost a decade making what exactly?

The same puzzlement lies on the features of Tess. Liam is preoccupied with what is most likely a broken nose, either unable to respond or completely oblivious to the conversation.

His sister can't help pulling at the thread. "What do you mean?" she asks, focusing not on the man who threatened her only moments ago, but the one who spoke of their premeditated plan.

"Let's just say taking over one throne of power is no different than another. The stepping stones become easier to lay," the man says. I grasp at the edge of understanding.

"Now, now. They may be living their last moments, Tamen, but there's no need to give away the whole farm," responds Sir Crane.

My eyes focus, taking in a deep gulp of air as all reservations leave me. *Trust yourself, and you will win them all.* Marg's words ring through me as I step across the threshold.

My body moves in one fluid motion. I step carefully, hoping to make it as far into the room as I can before being noticed. But a noisy floorboard creaks underneath me, my once soundless path now giving away my presence. Tess spots me immediately, unsure of what to make of my appearance— neither joy nor fear crossing her face.

Before the horde can react to the noise, I jump behind whom I suspect is Phillip Crane. As the head of his house, his life would be most valued, and his word followed by whomever stands by his side. And if it came down to it, I wouldn't hesitate to cut off the head of the snake slithering in front of me.

My blade is already in hand as I kick against the back of his legs. His feet fall from under him, landing him on his knees just as I wrap my arm under his own and secure my hold at the back his neck, rendering his left arm completely useless. The edge of my blade rests against his throat, the push and pull of my precarious hold solidifying that I'm no stranger to a killing blow. Every time he tries to back away from the pinch of metal against his sensitive flesh, he's met with the resistance of my hand behind him.

He opens his mouth to talk, but I cut him off. "I don't think that's a good idea *Phillip*, unless you don't want to ever speak again." I smile down at him, a maliciousness in the gesture that earns me a continued scowl from his men.

They advance on our position. "One more step and you'll watch his life disappear before your feet." I tighten my control on Sir Crane. An involuntary grunt escapes his lips, triggering him to raise his free hand to stop the progression of his men.

A small lantern lies broken on the floor in front of a large desk, centered toward the far wall. Glass shards are shattered in the area, scattered around by the chaotic steps of clumsy confusion. A large map is spread across one wall, dark wood accents claiming the majority of the space. For being a fruit grower, I see little to do with orchards, upkeep of land, or industry and commerce in what appears to be Sir Crane's personal office.

I stare toward Tess, lying awkwardly in the grip of the burly man. "Now, Phillip. Why on earth would Tess and Liam Santana want to break into your home?" I ask. Tess looks between us, her chest heaving.

"Seems to me," I continue, "that if there was something they wanted from you, their station would only need ask you." Sir Crane's men look toward the Santanas, Liam still attempting to stop the blood spilling from his nose. "Which leads me to think you have been a naughty man, Phillip Crane." Tess looks at me, the color draining from her face. She struggles against the burly man's grip, earning her a sharp tug back toward him. One look at the fear in her eyes, and I make my decision.

"Now, here's what we're going to do," I announce to the room after my quick survey, settling my scrutiny on the man holding Tess. "You're going to move out of the way so Liam and Tess can proceed to the door." The burly man doesn't move. His eyes narrow as his mouth turns downward.

"Oh Phillip. It looks like you might need to convince him," I whisper down to Sir Crane, but loud enough for everyone to hear.

He gives a hectic wave with his free arm, motioning for the man to step aside and let the woman pass. The burly man releases a growl, his stare honed directly on me before he lets Tess go. She moves without hesitation, walking to her brother and grabbing his hand, a few folded papers in her strained grip.

Sir Crane's men reluctantly part so they can make their way to the exit, both still able to walk without trouble. *Good.*

Tess stops in the doorframe before turning back to me, an anxiousness and relief battling across her features as her eyes meet my own. We need a way out. Preferably a way that leaves us mostly uninjured.

"Alright, Phillip Crane. I hope you can keep up with me. I know those knees are probably not what they used to be. And I would hate to spend my morning cleaning blood out of my clothes. So for your sake, and mine, I need you to be a good boy and scoot toward the door." Another groan escapes his throat, and I can't decide if it's the noise of a *yes, I understand,* or a *I'm going to kill you the second you let me go.* Most likely the latter.

We begin our shimmy— Sir Crane inching his way across the wood floors, me backing away slowly, my knife still planted firmly against him and his arm still twisted up through my own. Once we reach Tess and Liam, I turn my hushed words to her, while my focus stays on the four men now baring their teeth at me. "Go out the back entrance, and get our horses ready."

"Should I find Roan and Aiden?" she asks, her quiet tone keeping with my own. Her breathing is heavy, an anxiousness thrumming through her as she looks between me and her bleeding brother.

"No. They won't have gone far. They will see you running toward our exit point. That's all the confirmation they'll need that it's time to leave." Tess agrees with my response, a thumbs up and deep inhale readying her for the sprint. "Liam, can you still fight?"

"Yes." He nods, the blood now crusting along his lips and chin.

I lean down until my head is flush with Sir Crane's. These words I mean only for him. "If you follow us, or try to harm us in any way, I will personally make sure you regret that decision."

Of course he will follow. His men will do everything they can to intercept us. But this previous warning will alleviate any lingering guilt if I end up killing one, or all, of their group.

I look at Tess and Liam in turn, signaling the chaos about to follow my next action. In one quick motion I release the man from my unpleasant grip, kicking him hard in the back. I don't wait to see how hard he falls or how quickly he gets back to his feet, bolting as fast as my legs can carrying me.

Tess and Liam head for the closest stairwell to escape the back exit from the first floor. Instead of following them, I head down the long hall, finding the far stairs and heading back up to the third floor.

Footsteps and shouts flow out of the room, a few streaming after the siblings and the others following me. They're panting breaths chase me, their close proximity shutting everything else out of my mind. *You're almost there. A little faster.*

I run across the third floor, finding my way back to the unoccupied bedroom I first entered, not daring to look behind me at the furious trail of men. *Just run. Just breath. Stay calm. Stay focused.* If I can lead them outside, it will be easy to hide within the veil of night and pick them off one by one with the help of the captain and Aiden.

In seconds I'm back on the terrace, taking a running leap onto the trellis. *Please hold. Please hold. Please hold,* I chant to myself before I bound off the edge.

My feet find their footing, the wood unmoving under the force of my body as I hurdle into it. Another shout steals my attention, a man leaning over the balcony as he reaches for me. I descend as quickly as possible, skipping holds and falling the last few feet in my haste. I'm tunneled purely into my escape, unsure if he plans to follow down the wall. I'll find out soon enough.

Just as my feet land on solid ground a heaviness knocks into me, pushing me brutally to the ground. One of the men, the burly one who held Tess, straddles me before I can get upright, pinning my arms to my stomach, his weight crushing into my small frame. A failed attempt to swing my legs up and around him sends a broad fist into my jaw, causing my body to go limp for a brief moment.

The blow isn't the first time I've been hit square in the face, and it certainly won't be the last. But the sharp, painful pressure brings a nauseating black to my vision. The agony burns through my lower face, a fire that spreads up through my head. Its disorientation leaves me vulnerable, open for whatever this man has planned for me.

I've barely had time for the scene to come back into focus when a familiar blue gaze comes into view. The captain barrels into the man binding me with his weight and strength, his elbow meeting the side of the man's head. He slumps down hard, knocked out in that single impact from Roan Montgomery. The captain holds out a hand, pulling me to my feet. Unspoken concern radiates from him as he reaches for a better look at my face. My jaw will be purple by morning, but at least it's not dislocated.

"I'm fine. We need to go. Tess and Liam—" My words are cut short at the sound of clashing metal. We turn in unison, seeing two of the men parring with an injured Liam.

Phillip Crane and another man rush out of the back entrance, the old man spotting me almost instantly. A snaking smile tangles through his face, not even bothering to acknowledge the obviously capable man looming beside me.

"The girl is mine," Sir Crane tells his companion before unsheathing his sword, my mere blade a shadow in comparison. I suddenly long for my bow, kept behind so I could maneuver without its bulky presence wrapped around me.

The two men walk toward us. Captain Montgomery runs at the man beside Sir Crane, using a loud bellow to throw the other man off. They meet with a loud bang, weapons swinging through the air, the dance of conviction and dedication.

It's not hard to see the thousands of hours, the months and years of devoted practice, of mastering the skills of defending himself and his people. Roan moves with precision, his body knowing the steps, the moves, the places to swing and the time to retreat— a rhythmic waltz of prowess that will soon render his inferior opponent unconscious, or more likely, dead.

"I'm going to enjoy this more than you know," Sir Crane says to me, pulling me back to our imminent confrontation.

I criss-cross the space, circling the old man. Otto has proved that age doesn't negate your ability to fight and fight well, so I don't count the man out before I've had a chance to see for myself. My vision channels on Sir Crane, analyzing every action, every flick of his hand, every movement of his eyes. I can't help but be reminded of Silas as I stare at the man, the same darkness behind their gazes, the same brazen greediness greeting me.

A pair of hands wrap around my neck from behind. I'm caught off guard, unprepared for the second man from Liam's match to abandon his initial target in favor of me. I step a leg back, twisting my torso around and wrapping my closest arm up and around his own, trapping them tight and unmoving against me. The heel of my free hand busts up into his nose before I wrap my arm up and around the back of his neck and send my knee into the soft tissue of his stomach. The man doubles over in pain, giving me the extra leverage I need to use my full weight to throw him to the ground.

The distraction is enough for Sir Crane to close the distance between us, knocking my legs from behind and resting the edge of his sword against my throat as I land on my knees. The reversal of our position isn't lost on me.

A malevolent chuckle scrapes through the air. It's not lost on him either, apparently.

Roan sends his man down with a final jab, his opponent unable to get back up for another round. He turns in stride, facing my rocky position, only a few running strides away from where I kneel. His focus remains on Sir Crane as he closes the last few steps separating us.

"You hurt her. You die." Roan's husky voice betrays no emotion beyond his tenacious desire to shove his sword into Phillip Crane's chest.

The old man doesn't have time to return a threat before the gargling noise of death reaches my ears. Phillip Crane's sword goes slack against me. I turn in time to see Aiden standing beside him, a dagger lodged neatly in Sir Crane's side. He has only a few, painful minutes before his punctured kidney and lung suffocate him from the inside out.

Aiden's fierce gaze boasts nothing of his earlier innocence. Blood trickles down his hand, more splattered across his shirt. I nod to my rescuer, the only show of gratitude I can offer as I turn my concentration back to the stage of Phillip Crane's defeat, crawling over the grass until I can look him in the eyes.

"What did you mean earlier— the package, the money, the decade of planning, the mention of thrones?" There's an edge to my voice. A desperation to hear the truth, while also praying that my instincts are wrong. That desperation folds haphazardly into dread as I wait to hear my fears confirmed.

A dying man's thoughts go one of two ways: relieving himself of his guilt and wrongdoings in order to pass this life with a clear conscious, or holding his secrets close in one last victory against those who wronged him.

Sir Crane picks one last defeat. "You'll never... find her." His whispered words are garbled with blood, but the truth that flows leaves me speechless, frozen next to him as I witness his last few breaths.

His vicious grin settles into a frigid line. Aiden stands a few paces away from me, confusion pulling at his brows as I kneel over Sir Crane's body, staring at his now lifeless face.

I have lived the last few years of my life with nothing to lose. A life that simply lived day to day, taking care of myself, never being tied to anything more than Marg's wishes. When did my indifference to Felshan, to its crown, turn into something more? When did tendrils of affection for this princess plant themselves inside of me? No, no. It's not affection, just a desire for my own gain. *Right?*

But my heart still drops. Feeling slowly leaves my limbs, one by one, as his words sink into me. I want to scream, to release the panic building inside of me. He was somehow involved in the kidnapping. He knew something. All this time, answers were right here. I turn, finding myself alone.

The captain left when Sir Crane was incapacitated and is now standing next to Liam as they finish the last of Crane's men. He traps the man in a firm hold, signaling Liam to take the killing shot.

"Wait!" I yell, attempting to stop their final blow.

He's the only one left to spill their secrets. To help us discover vital information about the princess. To bring her home safely.

"Don't kill him!" I scream, leaping to my feet and meeting them across the yard. "He knows something. He knows something about the princess." I'm out of breath, hardly able to find my voice. I recognize his face from Sir Crane's office. I think he called the man Tamen.

The captain's face goes rigid, looking down at the man struggling to break free. Liam only stares at me, and I realize too late that he has no idea what I'm talking about. There's no time or room for secrecy. The house has likely been alerted by the commotion, and who knows how many more able bodied men will come ready to fight. Someone could have already notified the Guard of our intrusion.

"Crane told me we would never find her. What did he mean? Find who? The princess?" I try not to spit at the man, but in my haste to make him talk it's hard to keep my emotions in check. My nerves are pushing up against our last, fraying moment to find answers.

"Go to hell!" he screams back at me.

Roan twists Tamen's arm behind him, holding it in such a way that the smallest movement will break it, the position itself causing excruciating pain. The man yelps in response, his face twisting in agony.

"The girl. The girl," he relays through the pain. "They needed passage, undetected through Fort Lowsan. We helped them get through," Tamen says through paining breaths.

"Who was with them?" Roan asks, understanding clicking into place.

"I don't know. A guy. An older woman. And a younger woman." The man squeals as the captain pulls his arm tighter. "I told you, I told you! That's all I know!"

"Which way did they go?" Captain Montgomery asks.

"I don't know. I swear. We just had to get them out the north gate without the Guard noticing."

"What did they mean inside, that this takeover was almost a decade in the making?" I ask, my body feeling as if it might explode at any moment. The captain only stares at me as I relay what I overheard.

"Taking control of... of... Fort Lowsan." Tamen's hesitation is evidence of his lie, my many years of interrogation highlighting his deception.

"Liar. Someone said taking over one throne of power was no different than another. The stepping stones were easier to lay. What did he mean?" I shout at him, no longer able to play the cool, collected interrogator.

He flinches, but is unyielding. Roan pulls his arm to its breaking point, the agony pushing at the man's resolve. It takes all my willpower not to slap him unconscious.

He looks as if he will pass out at any moment as he begins to sway. "The throne of Turin, the whole of Felshan," Tamen huffs out.

I step back, Roan meeting my gaze as shock and disbelief share the space between us. Liam stands to the side, his eyes going wide as the words spoken around him click into place.

More questions swarm my mind as I turn my attention back to the groaning man. Shouts ring from around the house, lights springing to action inside. *Just a few more seconds.*

Roan turns his attention to the house coming to life, a few shouts reaching us from where we stand. Before I know what's happening, he snaps Tamen's arm, sending the man down to the ground, unconscious from the pain. *What— no, no, no...*

I scream, "What did you do? He was about to tell us everything!"

Roan stands rigid, the smolder of ten thousand fires bottled inside of him. I move to release my disbelief with more yelling, but am stopped dead by his appearance. It looks as if he's been intensely burned, but his skin remains flawlessly intact. The pain in his eyes. The contorting of his face down through his body. I'm almost afraid if I touch him, my hands will blister from the heat.

Torches light up the night, the shouts and noise of more people filing in from around the house. "It's time to go." Aiden comes up from behind, an urgent tug on my arm, the captain somehow already in motion and pushing me along. It takes a moment for my feet and consciousness to pair up and move with intention away from the scene.

Concern accompanies Aiden's gaze toward Roan, the invisible flames surrounding him smoldering into coals as he takes a step forward. He carries a pitying look as he passes Tamen on the ground, but not for the man himself lying unconscious at our feet. No. Something more like disappointment and a resistant resign.

Tess breaks through the tree line, our horses in tow as she gallops through the manicured lawn. Her gaze lingers for only a moment at the men dotting the ground around us, most with fatal wounds. I hesitate, wanting to bring the passed out Tamen back to the Santana's home. There's more we can get from him. More he can tell us.

Roan follows my gaze, sensing my thought. "There's no time. We need to go, now. If we're to avoid a fight we won't be able to win." Just a moment ago I could have sworn he was about to explode into a million pieces, but his now doused demeanor is almost begging me to move toward the horses.

"Let's go!" Tess yells, jumping down to help Liam up onto the saddle. Aiden grabs onto the nearest horse, hoisting himself on its back. The captain and I are the only two left on the ground. We leap for the only horse left.

"We'll ride together. Come on," he declares, motioning for me to get on first.

His warm body presses against mine as he climbs up quickly after me. The closeness is an odd comfort after everything that just happened. The shock of Tamen's revelations. Tess's deception. They are still roiling through me.

Hands wrap around my torso as I grab the reins and prompt the horse into a gallop. Tears prick my eyes as we race through the night. Aiden saved my life. Roan saved my life. So much could have gone wrong. The captain sacrificed the answers we were desperately searching for in order for us to get away unscathed. I don't have to like it, but I can understand why. Before I can think better of it, I wrap my own hand over his, squeezing once. He squeezes back, holding onto my hand tightly. Roan's breath is warm and heavy against my hair, but he stays silent during our retreat.

He must be reeling from this as much as I am. We may have different reasons for wanting this mission to succeed, to find Princess Adalena, but the truth seemed to take us equally off guard. Someone is planning a coup against the royal family, against Turin and the rulers of Felshan. Against the people he grew up with.

The warmth of the captain behind me does little to assuage the cold reality laid before me. For who knows how many years people have conspired against the royal family, against Felshan. Does Marg know? Are the people of Turin safe? Was my mother somehow a casualty of this treachery?

My furious, heart-broken tears are wiped away from the whipping wind of our escape.

26

Roan Montgomery

"**E**XPLAIN. Now." Outraged is too small a word to express how I feel in this moment. "What just happened back there was never about any ring or stupid chess piece." I knew Tess had been lying about her reasoning for Ari to retrieve the items, but I wasn't expecting what actually ensued.

Tess stands facing me, her arms folded tightly across her body. Gone is the flippant girl who forced Ari to get back a mere ring out of sheer pleasure. In her place is a rigid, straight-forward woman who seems to have little remorse. We've all just spent the better part of the night fighting and running for our lives, and I want to know why.

"He was conspiring against House Santana," Tess begins, her words breathly and quick. "My spies told us he was planning something. There were no details, only strong suspicions."

"What suspicions?" I ask, my chest heaving.

"It seemed everywhere I went, everywhere Liam and Father went, there was a Crane close by. Just that feeling of someone watching me, watching us. We even lost a pile of merchant and employment contracts, a few invoice copies from our vendors. It seemed a simple misplacement at first. But about a week later, we noticed an exodus of close to one-third of our people.

One-third, Roan." I rub a hand across my face as I listen to her story, the energy inside of me urging me to pace.

"I had no proof, only my gut that something sinister was afoot. If I took it to the Guard and I was wrong, or they found no truth to it in their investigation— I would have either shredded ties with one of the wealthiest merchants in Fort Lowsan, or given him time to move the operation somewhere I would never find— always waiting for an imminent attack on my family and wondering when it would come," Tess says, her eyes red and drooping. Did she look this tired before, and I just hadn't realized until now?

All of us stand around the kitchen, confronting the Santanas at our first point of entry into the safety of their house. Each of us is covered in a thick layer of sweat with dirt smeared across our skin and clothing. A bruise is already developing under one of Liam's eyes, and Aiden's lip is swollen where one of the men landed a fist. Each of us boasts dried blood blotting across our bodies, either our own or someone else's.

The space is lit with a yellow glow as someone lights a few candles. Otto and Larisa were woken as the yelling and commotion started, seating them within our impassioned confrontation.

"Well, everyone is alive. So that's a good start," Otto says, earning him the narrowed eyes of us all.

"You put everyone's life on the line for some half-baked plan? Why didn't you just tell us, Tess? We could've come up with something— together. Something solid. Something that didn't leave us running for our lives." I try to keep my voice even, but I fail miserably.

"Maybe the better question to ask is, what is going on with the princess?" Liam asks, his bloodied chin raised as he stares at me through slitted eyes.

"Lena? Is something wrong with her?" Tess asks, looking between our silent stares. Somehow, despite how the evening progressed and her clear fatigue, she looks as regal as ever.

"The man, there at the end. Tamen. He talked of a girl they had to get through Fort Lowsan. Who is she?" Liam's arms are folded, staring daggers between Ari and myself. "If we're going to judge each other's secrets and motivations, might as well lay them all out onto the table," he continues. Aiden's confusion quickly turns to understanding, looking wide-eyed between Liam and myself.

"The difference, Liam, is that we didn't lie about why we were here. We told you up front we weren't at liberty to discuss it. You blatantly mislead us at the threat of our lives!" I throw back at him, also trying to deflect his question.

The energy of the fight is roiling through me, setting the stage for my hot-headed reproach. In actuality, as much as I want to hate the Santanas in this moment, I understand their distress, and why they did what they did. I will do whatever it takes to retrieve Lena, no matter the cost. There's not much difference between me and my old friends, but I don't have the energy to tug at that thread tonight.

"You didn't answer my question, Roan. Who's the girl? And why did Ari mention that he knew something about Princess Adalena? What is going on?" Liam asks, arms still folded as his gaze never leaves mine.

"What happened to Lena?" Tess questions again, louder this time as she takes a step toward me.

I rub circles on my forehead with the heel of my hand. "I can't tell you. I'm sorry." Liam pinches the bridge of his nose, shaking his head at my answer. "I gave my word." Liam scoffs as I finish. My glare does nothing to make him unwrinkle his frustration. I made a promise, and I won't go back on it. And after everything that happened tonight, I don't feel any guilt keeping Lena's secret to myself.

Tess takes a steadying breath before she speaks. "We understand. Please let us know if we can help." I know she wants to say more, her eyes boring straight into mine. If she's anything like the girl I remember, she wants to back me into a corner and refuse to let me leave until I answer all her questions.

I stare back at her, unflinching under her gaze. "Listen. I know you're angry with me," Tess continues, "and you have every right to be. But when Liam spotted you walking through the gates— I could've wept with joy. With your help I knew we could make it work. We could figure out what Sir Crane and his lackeys were up to. But then you said you were just passing through and couldn't stay." She pauses, turning her attention to Otto, Aiden, and Ari in turn. "I'm sorry for the deceit. But I needed you. We needed you. I thought you were lying, Ari. You look the part of thief and spy, but not many actually live up to their word."

I can't help the *pfft* that escapes me and the subsequent eye-roll that accompanies her last words. But Tess doesn't stop her discourse. "I didn't actually think you'd be able to get in and out unnoticed. The house is so big, and those things could have been anywhere. I just... I couldn't leave Fort Lowsan in the hands of Phillip Crane and his horrible family. And it was the only way I could think of that wouldn't have you marching through those doors and out our gates."

She turns back to face me. "In fact, I'm still surprised you didn't. You were never one to follow orders." A friendly grin plays at her softened face, a plead for forgiveness as she plays to our past together.

Ari has been quiet up till this moment. "What did you take from his office?" Her face is even, almost bored. I make a fist as the thought of her hand squeezing mine as we rode away resurfaces.

"I was reading through some papers from his drawer when the handle of my lantern broke and the glass shattered to the floor. Guess I should check the hardware of my reading lights before breaking and entering," she muses to a somber room.

"And...?" Ari prods, her mouth closed into a firm line. Though I swear there's a gleam in her eye as she watches Tess squirm beneath her detached stare.

"I just grabbed whatever I could wrap my fingers around. Some receipts from the look of it. The travel summary of my father and his trip to Fort Kotar. And it looks like reports about different guards, their locations around Fort Lowsan and their salaries. I think it will be enough to show that something was going on. These aren't exactly contracts for a fruit merchant," says Tess, pulling the rolled up papers from a back pocket. Ari holds out a hand, and Tess passes them over to her.

Aiden chimes in. "Sir Crane is dead on his own property. How do you plan on explaining that to the Guard? You may be in charge here. But if they feel foul play was afoot, they will take it straight to the palace."

"I will tell them I went to confront him. I had suspicions of a plot against my family that I wanted answers to. He attacked me, and I defended myself," Liam says. Definitely not an answer that would fully exonerate the Santanas from an investigation, but also one that might prod more into Sir Crane's business dealings and surely uncover his illicit activity.

"You should go report this immediately. His family could be there burning documents and packing up evidence against the Crane's."

Liam nods at my statement. "I know. I'm going to head over there now." But he doesn't move.

Instead, we stand in silence. Liam looks me up and down, his scowl eventually softening into a grimace. The only noise between us is the rustling of papers as Ari searches through the documents Tess grabbed.

"I'm sorry, Ari," Tess sputters. "I know. Using you as bait was..."

"Kind of brilliant. Had it actually worked," Ari says, not bothering to look up as she continues to scan. If anyone has a right to be upset, it's her. But she hardly even seems bothered by it. She was moments away from dying, more than once, and she's acting like nothing was amiss.

Tess blinks rapidly, her mouth slightly ajar. "W-what? I thought you'd be furious?"

"Oh, I am. You and your brother got lucky. Very, very lucky. You planned for me to get caught. An extremely poor plan, might I add. And because of your mistakes you almost killed us all. Next time, have someone who actually knows what they're doing come with you. Or better yet, stay behind." There's an edge to her voice now, her lips twisted into a frown. Liam hisses at Ari's words, but she doesn't even glance in his direction.

"I know, I know," Tess replies, closing her eyes as she shakes her head. "If it weren't for you, my brother and I would most likely be dead. So, I guess I'm trying to apologize. But also, say thank you." Tess drops her gaze to rest upon Ari. "You didn't have to come back for us. After what we did. You had every right to walk away. But you didn't. And, I'm... I'm very grateful. Thank you, for saving our lives."

Tess's eyes glisten as she walks over to the thief, holding out a hand. Ari looks at her and her show of gratitude and respect after all that happened, before slowly reaching out and grasping the hand of the girl who just toyed with her life. A shaky acceptance branches between the two women.

It will take a while to forgive what happened here tonight, but my anger no longer boils on the surface. Instead, I focus on Lena. She came through Fort Lowsan, and the Crane's helped them move through unnoticed. *She was here.*

"I promise I will make it up to you, in any way I can." Tess turns to the rest of us. "I thank all of you as well. Because of your efforts, my family is safe tonight."

"I did work really hard," Otto mumbles, resulting in a glare from Aiden, and a huff from Ari.

"Now. How can I help you get on your way? I can gather some supplies and make sure your horses are watered and fed by daybreak."

"Thank you," I respond. Her kindness doesn't make up for the last few hours, but it will give me the space to plan our way toward Thenstra. And Lena.

The room is still tense, but Tess's attempts to appease our anger has taken the edge off. Ari hands back the clump of papers. "Nothing jumps off the page. Send word if you find anything else," Ari tells her.

Liam turns to leave, giving the rest of us silent permission to do the same.

I lie on the floor, a snoring Otto on the bed and a shuffling Aiden across the room. The image of Lena being escorted by Sir Crane, his malicious eyes perusing over her, won't leave me. Parker Aldren dragging her from her home, keeping her tied up and doing who knows what else.

"The girl. The girl. They needed passage, undetected through Fort Lowsan. We helped them get through."

The man's words play over and over in my mind, blurring the irrational with reality. I'm the only one that can protect her now. It's just me. And I refuse to let another hope of Felshan lose their freedom and their life on my watch.

I roll over in my bedroll. *Whack.* My head hits the side of the wall. Sleep must have finally found me. I'm not used to sleeping on the floor, but figured Aiden and Otto deserved a bed last night. I've never taken the west road to the sea before, and I don't know what awaits them.

Although, I suppose I've never taken the journey past Fort Lowsan up to Thenstra either. Maybe I'll soon wish I had the memory of a good night's sleep here.

"Is someone attacking," I hear Otto mumble through his not quite awake, but not quite sleeping state.

"If they were, you'd be dead," I reply, attempting to rub out the painful throb on the side of my head.

"Then let the killer approach and shut you two up so I can sleep," Aiden interjects.

The sun hasn't risen, but it's not far off, apparent through the tiny bit of light streaming through the large windows. Once the birds begin their morning alarm, sleeping becomes futile.

"We should get going soon. I'll bring back some breakfast," a snore vibrates through the room, "while you two finish whatever exquisite dream is keeping you from acknowledging your captain." They don't budge. "Or maybe instead of breakfast I'll just bring back the bucket of ice the cook keeps downstairs." Otto at least grunts at that remark, and Aiden waves an arm in acknowledgement. I pull on my boots and pack up my makeshift bed, heading out the door to wake Ari.

I find her room, tracing my steps from yesterday and knock softly. "Ari," I whisper through the door. "It's me, Roan."

She doesn't answer, so I knock louder. "Ari, are you awake?" I bring my voice to a normal level this time, but still no response. I find the handle, checking if it's locked. When it doesn't budge, I put a little weight behind it. But it still doesn't move. My stomach clenches as I take in a sharp breath. "Ari!" I yell against the door. Nothing.

I stand back from the door a little ways, ready to break it down if she doesn't answer me in the next few seconds. I square my shoulder between the frame, readying my feet to leap toward it with all the strength I have.

"Shhhhh!" I hear from behind me. "You're going to wake up the entire house with your bellowing." I take a full, stable breath.

Ari walks down the hall, wet hair dripping down her neck and back, dampening her shirt before trailing on the floor behind her.

"You're soaking wet," I say sheepishly. The bruise on her jaw blooms bright even in the shadows of morning. I cringe, thinking of that man on top of her, hurting her before I could get there.

"No kidding. That's what happens when you're taking a bath and hear your name being shouted from the rooftops before dawn. Not really time to dry off properly." She walks over to her door, unlocking it and stepping inside.

The way her clothes are sticking to her, she must have jumped straight out of the bath and threw them on while still literally soaking wet. Her face is glistening with water as she passes me. I feel stupid now for making such a ruckus, but I would do it again if necessary.

My companions are my responsibility. Their safety and well-being is under my hand. I watch Ari pass in front of me, her light brown hair darkened from the dregs of water still clinging to each strand. Her emerald eyes stare me down before she backs up and sits on her bed.

I stand in her doorway, brushing off imaginary dust from my shirt as I try to think of my next words. "I take it you are... alright?"

"Of course I'm alright. Unless you think someone was hiding in my bath water to murder me, and I am the spirit of a now dead Ari come to haunt you."

"I wouldn't rule it out. Being in your presence for more than five minutes might just be enough to give someone the motivation." A deep glare from Ari stops me from moving further into her room. But I can't help the hint of a smile that tugs at my mouth.

"I concede," I say, holding up both hands in surrender. "You're a lovely person." Her glare turns into a quirked eyebrow. "I mean lovely as in I wouldn't want to hide in your bath water to kill you. Maybe just to maim." My heart quickens as she continues to look at me, and I realize we are talking about her bath water. What am I even saying?

I cough loudly and turn away, a deep red burning at my cheeks. I take a deep breath and mask my features before turning around. "We need to get going before the streets are crowded with their morning market. I will go find us some breakfast and meet you at the stable," I say.

She pinches her lips together, looking me up and down before answering. "Yes Captain." She mimics the Guard salute in mock veneration.

"I might change my earlier answer to less than five minutes in your presence," I respond before turning to leave, her boot hitting the door as I shut it.

"Leaving without saying goodbye?" a voice asks from down the hall. Tess stands against the wall, a thin satin robe draped around her and tied in the front, her dark hair pulled to the side in a loose braid.

"We need to get on the road as soon as possible," I reply, closing the last few steps between us as she stands in my path to the kitchen.

"I don't suppose you'll tell me where you're going?"

"North."

"There's nothing north, Roan."

"Maybe. Maybe not," I respond, still sore from her deception last night.

Tess has been my friend since her first visit to the palace, but it has been eight years since I've seen her. I still feel the pull of friendship, but it has faded into a ghost of what it once was. It would be easy to remove the veil muting who we used to be to one another, letting the bold pigments of our relationship come into view once again. But now isn't the time for renewing my platonic affection. Not with the urgency of Lena gnawing through my mind.

I move to walk around her.

She reaches for my arm, gently stopping me before I pass. "I realize it has been a while, and people change. But the boy I knew, the one who couldn't wait to see his family each summer and talked of nothing but a future in Port

Riga— what is he doing as Captain of the Guard?" Her eyes search me, but I don't meet her gaze.

"I know you were there when Evander passed, and I don't pretend to know what that was like. But don't forget, Roan. It's ok to want things. To keep living. It's ok to pave your own way. His family won't break without you."

I tense at her words. "They are already broken, because of me," I whisper.

"Why are you punishing yourself? It wasn't your fault Evander died. Roan, look at me," she guides my chin with her slender fingers until I'm staring into her dark eyes. "It's ok if you want a life outside the palace. If you want to go home."

Her words dig at a wound, one I didn't expect to have to acknowledge this morning. One I've become a master at ignoring.

I can only answer her with two words, "Goodbye, Tess."

She doesn't stop me this time as I move past her.

Once I come back with a few slices of bacon, Aiden and Otto need no more convincing to get up and moving.

I try not to think of Tamen's words— of how the Crane's helped transport Lena secretly through Fort Lowsan, of overthrowing the throne, and there-fore, King Cassus. My heart throbs in my chest, my hands shaking if I give my mind over to what all of this could mean. People were conspiring against the Crown, and not even a whiff of it ever reached my ears. I'm Captain of the Guard. And this treason, apparently years in the making, was going on under my nose. Obviously taking Lena had something to do with their plans, but what it all means still isn't clear.

I should go to the Crane's and demand to speak to their family. But after killing all those men, cousins and fathers and brothers, they will put up a fight. A fight I don't have time to try and win. The longer we wait, the further away Lena becomes. She is my number one priority.

We pack up and meet Ari at the stables, preparing our horses and giving out last orders and instructions.

"You should hit the sea before we hit Thenstra. If there are no leads or traces of the princess, head up to the Prythan Mountain Pass," I tell the two men. "It will take us almost twice as long to trek through the mountains than you to the sea. If we find her and begin back, we should meet up with you quickly, and we can return together."

"And if we find the princess?" Aiden asks.

"If you find her, then head back immediately and send word to the Santanas. At that point the princess should be home safely, and it won't matter that they know. If we don't find her within the month, we will return to Fort Lowsan."

Tess walks out from the kitchens to hand Ari a bag and pile of clothes while mumbling a few instructions to her. The girl's face is wild as Tess talks, looking like she wants to refuse her gift. But the lure of the soft fabric beneath her fingers is too much to push away.

Ari loads the clothes in her saddle bag before mounting, handing the bag of what I assume to be food to Aiden to put in his. Tess turns her head toward me, giving me one last nod of farewell. My stomach churns as I think of how I left things with her, but I brush past it. There will be time later to make it right.

"Be safe my friends," I finish, grasping Aiden's hand firmly and patting Otto's shoulder.

"And you, Captain." It's still strange to hear Otto call me that, when it seems like only a few months ago I was his subordinate. I turn to leave, but he keeps my hand gripped firmly in his.

Startled, I turn back. "That girl is smart. I know you don't fancy each other. But Ari might just surprise you if you let her," Otto says.

I glance at the thief, knowing already that he's right. I may never admit it out loud, but Lady Margaret knew what she was doing when she demanded the girl come along.

Her and Tess are laughing, something Aiden said setting off the shimmering noise. Aiden has a light-hearted countenance, and he isn't bad to look at. He's a good man, deserving of a good woman. And the more I get to know Ari, the more I would describe her as a good woman. Seeing him interact with the girl, making her laugh— it would make sense, the two of them.

A subtle pain springs low in my gut.

I'm suddenly very happy that Aiden will be splitting off today.

27

Princess Lena

"WHERE ARE YOU TAKING me?" I ask Parker Aldren.

My heart is beating out of my chest as I wait for his answer. He doesn't look as surprised as I thought he might at my question. His jaw clenches just before he takes a deep breath, probably biding his time while he decides what lie to tell me this time.

After I tried to escape the other day, we spent the rest of our day riding in silence. He hardly looked in my direction at all. And when he did, there was fire in his gaze. I wasn't sure if he was angry that I tried to run, or frustrated that I even had the chance at all while under his watch.

I figured the next days would be spent in a similar reticence. However, when we woke up the next morning, his easy-going manner had returned, making jokes at Onah's expense and telling me more ridiculous tales from his childhood and the antics his mother had to put up with.

Once the road began to climb upward into the mountains, my seat in the back became more and more optional. When Onah took her turn to nap during daylight, I was allowed to sit in the driver's seat next to Parker.

"You remind me a little of Roan, you know," I tell him.

"Captain Montgomery? Oh goodness. I hope not. All seriousness and tension, that one. He seems good enough. But definitely not the type you want to go bet on the horse races with after a long day. You know?" Parker responds. I chuckle at his fairly accurate description, accidentally bumping into his shoulder in the process.

There's a side to Roan many haven't seen. Roan Montgomery before his best friend, and my brother, died during the First Hunt. And for whatever reason, that's how I still choose to see him. Happy, mischievous, charismatic, full of dreams.

"He wasn't always so serious," I say in his defense. "He used to be the biggest trickster in the palace. One time, him and my brother dressed up as their most loathsome tutors, coming to dinner pretending to be them. Even memorizing their mannerisms and particular idiosyncrasies. I thought Mother would be furious. But they had everyone in stitches by the end."

Parker smiles, a single laugh huffing out of him. "No way. You lie."

"I promise you, I don't." I smile alongside of him.

"Captain Montgomery? Are you sure we're talking about the same person? Mister three practices a day, early to bed and early to rise, perpetual scowl man?"

"Yes. That one."

"Huh. Well, I guess the saying is true. You never really know someone until you really know someone." It seems a redundant phrase, but it also makes an odd amount of sense.

Our conversation dies among the methodical *clop, clop, clop* of the horses' hooves as they pull our wagon. We continue up the mountain road, our bodies swaying back and forth each time we hit a rut or uneven terrain. It's definitely a marked path, but one that could be easily missed for those who weren't close enough to see it.

"Do you want to marry him?" Parker asks me.

At first I think I've misheard him. No one has ever asked me such a forward question. If it were any other situation I would have admonished whomever asked me such an personal thing. But the longer I'm away from Turin, the more I realize just how stifled I have been. I tense, rubbing my fingers together one by one as I take my time to answer. There's no reason not to answer. I doubt Parker Aldren even really cares, more likely just filling the time with something better than the sound of rocks hitting against our wagon's wheels.

But it's an honest question, one a friend might ask if they were concerned about my well-being. Is Parker my friend? No. I don't think a captor can really be my friend. But something inside me wants to open my soul to him, this thieving stranger, if only to clear away the truth built up inside of me. To release it into the world to someone I know doesn't care what answer I will give. And if I'm being honest, I don't think I've ever had someone I could confide in, someone that didn't have ulterior motives and biases toward my feelings, not even Aunt Margaret.

I speak before I've come up with a polished answer. "Roan is a good person. I know it wouldn't be wrong to marry him. He would make a great king consort, and I know he wouldn't love another once we said our vows."

"Being a good person doesn't mean you want to marry them," he replies, his eyes firm as he finishes, "or that you love them." He looks ahead as he says it, not even side glancing my way. "Do you? Love him I mean."

My eyes go wide. "What?"

"I could be wrong. But it sounds as if he was a pretty flower your parents picked for your table. Not someone you actually love." Blood rushes through my ears, drowning out every other noise except for Parker's voice and my breathing.

How dare he. How dare he try to tell me what I do or do not feel.

As I speak my voice is eerily calm, but somehow it makes my meaning blast louder than if I screamed it at the top of my lungs. "What is it to you?

Whether I do or do not love him? Why do you even care? In a few days, or weeks, or months— you will be rid of me. My heart and where it belongs will no longer be your concern." I feel stiff after I say the words, like my body doesn't know what to do after finally speaking my mind.

When my brother died, my parents grappled for whatever normalcy they could find. Roan grew up with us. I think they really just wanted to keep as much of their family together as they could. He had become family. And in a small way he took away the pain of my brother's loss.

Nobody has ever asked me if I wanted to marry Roan, let alone if I loved him. And I've never talked about it. My mother and father told me we would be wed on my eighteenth birthday, and I was taught never to question their authority. Roan is comfortable, and I know he would be a wonderful husband when the time came.

"But if you decided you didn't want to— that you didn't want to marry him— could you tell them?" Parker asks, unfazed by my anger. His words take me by surprise, his ease after my admonishment. The heat rushing through me doesn't dissolve, but a curiousness tugs at the corner of my mind.

"I'm... not sure." And that's the truth. I want to tell them, and might if I was actually there. Really, I want to demand that I have a choice. Not that Roan is a bad choice. I just want to decide for myself— now that I've had time to paint my own future with the small taste of freedom I've been given.

A soft laugh escapes me. When did I start to see being kidnapped and tied up in a wagon as freedom?

"I was originally betrothed to Rebecca Davenport's son, of Fort Kotar," I randomly tell him, but I don't know why. "They own a large percent of the ore in Felshan. And the Kotar mines give us some of the strongest steel in all of the Four Kingdoms."

"Turinian steel," he replies.

I nod. "And the alliance with the Davenports would have been a good one for my family. My mother went to great lengths to break that promise in order for me to marry Roan. That's how important it was to them. They were willing to destroy our ties with the Davenports to make it so." I fidget as the words take hold.

"That doesn't answer my question," he replies, daring yet again to ask, "Do you love him?"

But I know he already knows the answer. I stare off at the great Prythan peaks in the distance. "No. But maybe if given enough time, I could have," I whisper, his exhale the only confirmation he heard my answer. His body hardens beside me, not missing the insinuation that my life has been inherently shifted from any trajectory that would have allowed me the chance to love and be loved.

He has taken me away from that life, from a place where I could potentially muster the courage to defy traditions that have taken away my liberties—to choose my place, my husband, my position. It almost makes me laugh as I realize how ridiculous everything has become in only a short amount of time.

I'm just imprisoned in another way, sitting here beside him. I suppose there are worse things than sitting by a handsome kidnapper. A blush rises to my cheeks as if Parker can hear my thoughts.

I clear my throat, shaking away my embarrassment. "You never answered my question, either. Where are you taking me?" I ask again, feeling more determined to retrieve an answer.

He hesitates for only a moment. "I have orders to take you to Thenstra."

"Thenstra?" My surprise is hard to mask. I have zero sense of direction I've come to realize, so he could be lying. But what would be the point now? He could have said Venes or Jadeya, and it wouldn't have made much of a difference.

Except no one has come in or out of Thenstra in over twenty years. I hardly know anything about it, and that's as frightening as sitting here with two people who had the gall to take me from my home against my will. If it had been Venes or Jadeya, I would have had a little comfort. I know those places. I've visited each several times. I know their people, but not Thenstra.

"Thenstra," he repeats.

I bite onto my lower lip as I look north. "Well. Who ordered you to take me there?" My hands are shaking before I clasp them together to mute the spasms. But he says nothing in response.

"Was it your idea to take me in the first place? Why take me at all? What does anyone have to gain from taking me to Thenstra, of all places?" My questions are boiling over, brought on by my ever growing anxiousness and profound desire to be free.

He continues to face forward, a frown pulling his features inward. "It wasn't my idea. And I don't know why they want you."

"They? Who's they?" I'm almost yelling now, leaning forward in my seat as I speak. Parker turns to me, wide-eyed, motioning to the back of the wagon at Onah's sleeping form.

"I can't answer these questions, Lena. I'm sorry," he quietly tells me, shaking his head.

My jaw tightens at his reluctance. Suddenly, I remember I'm not just shooting the breeze with a friend. Parker has been kind and friendly toward me, especially as of late, leading me to forget his true purpose here. He's my enemy. He's taking me to someone who most definitely doesn't want my best interests to come to fruition. I scoff at him, folding my arms and matching his now forward gaze. So many things don't add up.

"I will do whatever I can to help you, I promise," he says after a few moments, finally facing me.

"Let me go then," I reply. I raise my chin, now refusing to look at him.

He rakes a hand through his air, closing his eyes as a deep sigh escapes him. "I can't do that."

"Then your promise falls flat. Because doing whatever you can to help me would mean letting me go." I look at Onah asleep behind us, and I lower my voice. "You could take Onah. Goodness, I could probably take Onah. Just give me one of the horses, and a little bit of food. I'll find my way just fine."

He chuckles a little. "You obviously don't know her very well. Or your lack of navigation and outdoor survival abilities." I glare at him even though the insult is valid. But I decide I'm unamused as to whatever Onah-fighting knowledge is rolling around inside his head, not his truthful quip. He spots my fiery stare, losing all the humor he had before.

He lowers his voice to match my own. "I know I seem like a monster. What kind of man would steal some girl from her bed in the middle of the night, taking her across the country to who-knows-where against her will? But I have skin in the game too. People depending on me to see this through. No matter how badly I feel about it."

He has skin in the game? What a ridiculous excuse. I bury my face in my hands, not wanting to acknowledge him in the smallest bit.

"You can think of me as the oath-breaker, and I deserve it. You can hate me until the end of time, and I would deserve that as well. And you definitely don't have to trust me. But I promise you— if I could let you go, I would've a long time ago. In fact, I wouldn't have taken you in the first place. I don't want to hurt a princess any more than I want to cut off my own arm," he says.

There's so much more I want to ask, but I know time is limited as another snore carries from the back of the wagon. I try to unclench my teeth as I pry for more answers.

"At least tell me who ordered you to take me. If it wasn't your idea, if you want me to comply from here on out, I need to know who told you to do this. Otherwise, I'm going to assume from now on that you're a princess stealing fiend who finds joy in taking innocent girls away from their families," I say, although my surface-level threat definitely falls short.

My mind has teetered on panic since the moment I awoke in the wagon, discombobulated and afraid. That paired with the complete unknown of what lies ahead of me has pushed me against my breaking point several times. And I'm ready to shatter if I don't get something, anything, to calm my mind. Just knowing a name, any name, somehow feels as if it would relieve the tension building inside of me and threatening my sanity.

"Silas." A single name. But one that will be burned into me forever. "I think he's just a middle-man. But there you go," he whispers.

"A middle-man. A middle-man to whom?"

Parker rolls his eyes. "You told me to tell you where my orders came from. They came from Silas."

"Silas who? And who does Silas work for?" I pry.

"You realize if anyone knows I'm telling you this, it's my head."

Somehow this knowledge feels powerful, like it's is my ticket out of this. I try not to seem too pushy and desperate, bringing back the cheeriness from our earlier banter. "Then you better hurry before Onah wakes up. We wouldn't want anything to happen to that pretty head." I wink at him.

Reluctance crosses through him, looking as if it feels physically painful to both stay silent or to tell me what I want to know.

Just then, Onah rises from her wooden bed. A deep frown and blood-shot, bleary eyes accompany her as she sits up. My hope of answers smashes into a million pieces.

"Stop. I need to pee," she rasps.

As Parker brings the horses to slow, I attempt to breathe in the scenery of the mountainside, letting this new information lose its edge. Large, rolling mountains give way to grand, jagged peaks in the distance. I stare at their beauty as my own craggily thoughts move from spike to spike. We stop on the side of a hilled meadow, the air slightly more cool than the day before.

Silas. Silas. Silas. I let the name roll through my mind. It may be the only lead I have, but I commit it to memory nonetheless.

Parker studies my face, concern covering his own. Not the kind of concern shown after he brought me back from my attempted escape. The kind that comes when you're wondering what someone is thinking, or when you know you've said too much. I plaster a soft smile to my face to throw off the scent of my true thoughts.

I don't know what I can do from here with only a single name. Parker is right, and I hate to admit it. I wouldn't last a day out here if I did somehow escape. I'm supposed to be one of the most powerful women in Felshan, but I'm powerless to change the course these people have put me on.

At least my anger can be directed away from Parker. I don't even know why I want my hatred funneled away from this man. People are usually kind to me, so that's not necessarily something new. Maybe it's just the comfort of his presence during a time of great alarm and fear. Or perhaps that his kindness is genuine and not because he fears a royal repercussion if he acts otherwise.

He did the physical taking of me from my home, yes. But from the way he spoke, it seems as if he himself was backed into a corner. Can I fault him for that? Maybe. Maybe not.

Silas. Onah. Parker. I repeat the names inside my head, my imagination running rampant at who the first man is and why he would want a princess. Onah because I know she isn't the mastermind of this scheme, but she's here— why? What is her motivation?

The last because, I just don't know what to make of Parker Aldren.

28

ARI

I T's BEEN TWO DAYS since we left Fort Lowsan.

We aren't yet to the highest peaks of the Prythan Mountains, the biggest obstacle between us and Thenstra. But we've hit their rolling foothills. And I can't help but feel that each step brings us closer and closer to the princess.

The captain and I have hardly spoken of what Tamen said a few nights ago. He talked of overthrowing the throne of Felshan, basically unseating King Cassus in the process. With Silas involved as well, I can't help but wonder who else has had a part in this. Maybe someone else altogether has been pulling the strings?

Crane and his men have planned for almost a decade. Fort Lowsan was merely a stepping stone. Silas and Phillip Crane and whoever else are obviously the ones behind Princess Adalena's capture. But what does it all mean?

It's as if I've gathered all the necessary information, but I'm trying to navigate in the dark without a map. I'm struggling to make sense of it all. What do they gain from taking her halfway across our continent of Haythen?

If all they wanted was to replace King Cassus, wouldn't killing her gain them less problems? Obviously, I would never condone killing an innocent girl. But it would make more sense than a kidnapping.

I don't know Princess Adalena. But as time goes on, the more I think of her, the more her fictional place in my mind becomes a substantial presence. There's a desire to see her safely home, but I'm still rumbling as to whether that desire exists outside the question, *what's in it for me?* Maybe it's the way the captain talks of her and her family, or simply that she's taking the shape within a protectiveness I feel toward the people of Turin.

Night is approaching quickly, the chill of mountain air closing in. Pockets of brightness pop through the trees as the life of twilight bridges the sun and moon. The darkness brings with it the rhythm of a starry sky. And the voices of the mountain erupt around me in an exquisite cadence that paints the shadows with its harmony. The aromatic melody of fresh summer flowers and pine needles swirl through the air, but my mind is too jumbled to relish the dazzling scent.

Captain Montgomery sits across from me, rummaging through a bag before throwing it to the side with a *thump*. The warm fire in the center of our camp casts an orange glow, its deep shadows accentuating his frown.

"What are you looking for?" I ask, my forehead wrinkled in genuine curiosity.

"I can't find my straight-blade, and I need a decent shave." He rubs a hand under his chin and around his face, the sound of his sprouting beard against his fingers getting lost across the crackle of our fire. "I always nick myself when I use a knife. I should've done it at the Santana's before we left, but I chose sleep instead of a clean face. Oh well. There are worse things I suppose," he softly adds, throwing another log into our fire.

I shuffle around on my log perch, staring at the shadows and light dancing across his face. "Do you want some help?" I finally ask. "I wouldn't say I'm the Four Kingdom's gift to a perfect shave, but you might come out with fewer cuts."

"Do you shave often?" he asks, an eyebrow raised.

I roll my eyes, standing up and pulling my knife from my boot. "No I don't shave often. But I do have some practice. I used to set up a shaving booth at Market to earn a few extra coins for the week. And by booth, I mean standing off to the side yelling at men as they passed. I got a few bites. Most of them turned out ok," I say, twisting my knife between my fingers, my lips turning up in a grin.

The captain doesn't relax his raised brow, pondering for a moment before waving me over. He lathers a soap concoction around his week's length stubble, his jaw now covered in a thick, sudsy froth before turning his attention to me.

"Is it sharp enough?" he asks, looking at the knife in my hand as I move next to him.

"It sunk into Jaren's side well enough."

The captain rubs at his eyes, taking a full breath as my words permeate, obviously not too keen on sharing a blade with Jaren. "Besides," I continue, unable to help myself as I watch his queasiness, "only one man lost his life with this one. Such a sharp blade next to such a soft neck. All it took was a small cough, and—" I slice a finger across my throat. My flippant remark now earns a bored stare from the man in front of me as he has clearly caught onto my game. "I sharpened and sterilized it last night. Now close your mouth and let me do it," I say. He releases a sigh before complying, tilting his face upwards.

I place a hand behind his head. My thumb pulls his skin taut as I start from the edge of his jaw, sliding effortlessly toward his chin. With each swipe, I wipe the remnants of soap and cut hair onto a small cloth draped over his shoulder.

After a few more strokes, I'm suddenly aware of how my body is pushed close into his. Our legs are oddly entwined, and his hands could easily close around me and pull me in with a single motion. I feel his warm breath on my neck as I work, and a shiver drives up my spine.

"So, Captain. Where does the name *Montgomery* bear from?" I ask, breaking the quiet.

Silence doesn't bother me necessarily. But being so close to him— noting the different hues of blue dotting his eyes and the tightly drawn muscles around his face. He's never affected me this way, and I don't know what to make of it. It now feels necessary to focus on something else entirely.

"Port Riga. Northeast Felshan," he responds.

Port Riga. I've never been there, but then again I've never been anywhere other than Turin and its outskirts. I continue to pry, giving me something else to gather my thoughts around rather than my racing heart each time his breath hits my skin. "Are your parents alive? What do they do for work?"

He looks at me now, and I pause my blade so he can fully answer the question. "Yes. They are alive. My father, well. He does many things. Trading. Marketing. Fishing. Building. Contracting. Gardening. He loves it all, and he seems to be good at all of it. I guess that's common though, for a son to think his father can do no wrong."

I nod, wondering what it would be like to grow up with such a man. "And what about your mother? Does she help him? Take care of children? Do her own thing?"

"My mother is always up in whatever my father has going on. Equals in everything. Sometimes he stayed home, taking care of me and my siblings while she was out at the market with vendors. Other times she was home, attempting to teach her boys some manners while my father was out on business. Both have their own assets to bring to the table, and they take advantage of their strengths together."

I can't help but stare at him. I don't blink, mesmerized by his descriptions, more questions springing with everything he tells me. What would it be like to grow up with both parents? To learn trades? To be taught manners and watch the joy grow around you?

Mother did her best, and I always knew she loved me. She only spoke bits and pieces about my father, what I could pry from her anyway. Now that she is gone, I wish I had some direction. Some idea of who I am and where I come from— everything that Roan seems to have. It's hard not to feel the tiniest bit of envy.

"How many siblings do you have?" I ask.

"Three. A younger brother, and two younger sisters."

"Your mother had four children?" I say, more in exclamation than a question. He nods, his eyes alight.

I remember Aiden's family and all his younger sisters. It's not that large families are rare, but most avoid children as much as they can. Too many mouths to feed with too little food to go around. "What in Haythen? I think I need to meet the strongest woman in Port Riga. Learn her secrets." This earns a laugh, a real laugh from deep within the captain. It's the first time I've heard the sound, and I don't hate it.

I continue, "So, what does your mother think of her oldest son, *the captain?*" His laugh stops, the chuckles dying out like ripples in calm water.

I thought such a lady would be proud. It's no small feat running the entire military of Turin, training those throughout many of Felshan's other cities as well. I know Marg likes to have more say in the Palace Guard, but if she were gone, he'd be in charge of that too.

"I think... she misses her son." His voice is quiet, his gaze gone distant. Sadness shows from behind his usual, stony features, and I want to both close the door to it and bring it even more to the surface.

I can't help myself but ask, "Why does she miss her son? Do you not get home often?" I've stopped any movements completely at this point, my blade hanging in the air above his face. I didn't realize until now how little I actually know of him and his life.

"No, unfortunately. I don't. There's not a whole lot of time off from a position such as the one I hold. I used to spend summers home when I was younger. But— I haven't been back in almost four years."

Four years. If my mother were alive, I would see her every chance I had. I wouldn't let a single day pass without giving her a hug, listening to her voice, helping her cook and prepare our food each morning. It would be my life's mission to be with her as much as I could.

"Why don't you spend summers home anymore?" I ask, sure that he will soon tire of my questions, or that I will finally hear enough and move on.

"I lived at the palace as a boy. Raised up with Prince Evander and Princess Adalena. The plan was always that I would return home after my royal education. Take over the family business. But things don't always turn out the way you think they will. I became captain and... that was that."

I picked up bits and pieces from Tess and Liam. It's not shocking news to hear he spent time at the palace. But it would seem he spent quite a bit of time. More than I knew.

My curiosity wins over my better judgment. "So you were friends with the late prince? The one they hold the lantern memorial for every year? And Princess Adalena?"

His body stiffens at my question, and I realize too late how insensitive it must seem. My heart pounds, waiting for his firm dismissal and my subsequent embarrassment to spill over.

A few moments pass, and I desperately wish I could take it back. *Nice going. Bring up the man's dead friend.* I return my blade to his face, attempting a few more even strokes while I inwardly roll my eyes at myself.

"Yes. We were friends," he eventually says, startling me.

"That's nice," is all I can seem to muster in response. My stupidity earns no more questions from me. In my defense, I don't have a lot of friends to learn social normalities. Marg isn't much of a chatter box, and most of my interactions with others include running or silently observing.

After a few quiet moments and a few more strokes down his face he turns the tide toward me. "What about your family? Parents? Siblings?"

I've never been good at the details of my childhood. Mostly I don't want to relive it, and each time I have to tell someone, the memories are as fresh as the day they happened. Not that I have had many people to tell, and Marg asked only once. But he answered all of my inquiries, the least I could do is offer the same.

"I never knew my father. My mother died when I was twelve." His blue eyes dart to mine, looking for emotion I purposefully armored away. The pain of my loss, of the distance between me and Mother— it's too over-whelming when I open that door.

He reaches a hand up as if he wants to touch me, to soothe away the truth. But he must think better of it because he slowly drops it away. My face heats as he continues to stare, and a rare discomfort edges its way into my mind. Was I embarrassed that an almost stranger wanted to comfort me, or am I upset he didn't?

He isn't an almost stranger, I suppose. We have been together longer than I have been with anybody, besides Mother and Marg.

I'm reminded of that first night in the woods when he walked from the trees, his muscular form and blue eyes highlighted in the moonlight. Our tussle the next day as I thought he was stealing Prue. Those eyes full of fire when I said he wasn't capable of telling the truth, and then as I tried to unsheathe his sword. His strength as he fought off Silas's men, and fought with Tess on my behalf. The way he saved me as I fell from the trellis at Sir Crane's estate.

Letting our time together replay in my mind has made me feel more uncomfortable than I was before. I shift on my feet, clearing my throat as

I begin the delicate work of shaving around his neck, leaving little room for talking.

When I finish, the last swipe of my blade leaving its final soft streak behind, he hands me the small cloth from his shoulder. The air around us feels heavier somehow, my breathing a little more labored. But I pretend it is as it always has been between us, merely tolerating each other at best.

I wipe away small bits of soap from my fingers, then turn to use the clean side of the cloth to wipe away any left-over residue from his face. But the strangeness never leaves, as much as I wish it to. It's as if those personal glimpses into our lives has shifted something between us. I glide my fingers across his face, feeling for any roughness that I may have missed. But his skin is warm and smooth, my hand moving effortlessly across his jaw and neck.

He follows my gaze as I finish, and I'm again brought to the realization of how close we are. Roan reaches up, not shying away this time, tucking a stray piece of hair behind my ear, his thumb lightly brushing against the yellowing bruise on my jaw. My breath hitches against that brief, heated graze against my skin. His fingers skim my neck, trailing my arm until he finds my hand. A dizziness drags through me, and I have to close my eyes until it passes.

"Thank you," he says, taking the towel from my grip. My mouth won't even form words in response.

Neither of us move after that, his eyes darting briefly to my lips, then back up to meet my own. Something inside of me tells me to wrap my hands around his neck, to run my fingers up through his hair just to see how it feels between them.

I hated this man just a few days ago. Everything about him. Everything he stood for.

Is it possible for one powerful emotion to swing so rapidly to its counter-part? For hate to become... to become what exactly? No, No. I barely know the man. And he's someone I still despise in so many ways. But I can't deny that something has sprouted inside of me. Something hot, forceful, and persuasive. Something that has nothing to do with hate at all.

I try to take a steadying breath as the storm of his presence threatens to pull me under. His eyes swirl with a fire that is neither anger or anguish, but something else entirely. Something similar to only a couple mornings before when he was banging frantically on my door at the Santana's.

The way he looked at me then— I thought it was a softening, a tolerating of my presence where before there was only annoyance and frustration. But now... now I wonder if it was something else completely.

Part of me wants to jump headfirst into the blaze I realize, as I unknowingly move my face closer to his. Some invisible tether pulling me toward him without my conscious consent. The heat of his breath mixes with my own, and another wave of dizziness has me reaching out for something to steady me. His hands slide around my waist, gentle but sure, a mighty pillar to keep me from falling over.

"Are you okay?" he asks me, his voice bringing me back to reality. My imagination is a tenuous link to what's happening between us, but his words anchor me back to the moment.

His hands are strong as they grip me, and my traitorous body is responding to him in a way that is both disturbing, as I've sworn to hate this man forever, and alluring. An impulse wants me to lean into him, to his touch. My heart is beating wildly as he keeps his hands planted on my hips, even after the dizziness has waned. I'm taken over by something other than logic and reason as I continue to stare into his eyes, their blue gaze sinking me deeper and deeper the longer we stay unmoving.

It feels like hours have past, but only seconds exist in this moment. Each breath moves us closer. I suddenly wonder what it would feel like for our lips to—

Prue whinnies in the distance, startling me and pulling me from my passionate trance. Realizing how intimately our bodies are settled into each other, even closer than before, has me taking a quick step back, his hands falling from me as I jump away to put some distance between us.

What in the Four Kingdoms just happened?

"Well then," I examine his face from afar, "no cuts." I twist the dagger in my hand, a shaky laugh escaping from my pounding chest.

"I'm sorry. I never meant to..." he begins, slowly standing.

"No, no. Don't apologize. It's my fault. I... I don't know what came over me. I felt a little dizzy, and... well I'm fine now," I say, a bit of color rising to my cheeks. We stand across from each other, toggling between staring at each other and trying to find anything else to look at.

"I will go see if I can find us some breakfast for the morning," he finally says, a sternness to his voice, his muscles tense. He grabs his bow from his pile of things, crunching through dead leaves and forest debris. "You should get some rest. It will be another long day tomorrow." He walks off into the distance, leaving me alone with my idiocy.

When I find movement in my frozen limbs, I grab my mostly dried bedroll, having been soaked the night before from yet another rainfall, and move it away from the fire so the cool night air can work against the flush of my skin.

I want to both relive what just happened, and forget it entirely. But I guess I opt for the former. I replay the events in my mind over and over. The way he moved my hair and put his hands around my waist to steady me.

And it wasn't just me. I hadn't just thrown myself toward him. He had moved of his own accord.

I curl up, wishing I would blend away into the forest floor and erase the last few moments. Do I want them gone? I don't even know what I feel, or what I want right now.

The last thing crossing my consciousness is the fire burning in those deep blue eyes.

29

Roan Montgomery

MY ARCHERY SKILLS NEED some fine tuning, but I manage to spear through a couple rabbits before the sunlight makes its last debut. *Where's Aiden when I need him.*

My mind is racing as I scan the trees, a breeze bringing my senses slowly back to me. What had happened back at camp? I was in control of myself, but I wasn't. One moment she was offering to help me, and all the sudden I wanted nothing more than to grab her. To untie her loose braid and run my fingers through her hair.

Hunting seemed the only excuse to get away and compose myself. I had wanted to kiss her— wanted to feel her against me. To feel her lips on my own. To feel her skin beneath my hands. The more I think about it, the worse I feel. And the more I want to go back and do it again, but finish what I started.

Perhaps the thief simply wanted to lower my defenses, to see where I was weak. If so, she succeeded. I've never met anyone that could upset my ability to stay calm and patient, analyze the situation, and respond accordingly. Something about her is simply infuriating and... enchanting.

And what about Lena? I'm betrothed to Lena. I'm going to be with Lena. I love... Lena.

Guilt bulges inside of me as I relive those moments with Ari, and for the lie I keep trying to pass as truth.

I want to love Lena. I want to. But in the almost fifteen years I've known her, I've never once felt what I felt in those few seconds with Ari. I need to shove away the memory, to remember my place in this world. I can't be with her when I'm promised to another. I just... can't.

I start the trek back to camp, rabbit in hand, newly emboldened to keep my composure around this girl. The last dregs of light disappear into the horizon before I find my way back, making it difficult to see my footing as I walk.

A few loose roots wrap around my feet, throwing me off balance. I'm able to right myself each time, but my steps remain clumsy. I try to be more careful, stepping around the inanimate claws gripping at me. It almost seems as if they want me to fall, want to catch me unbalanced. To watch me tumble down. I won't let myself get caught up, to falter. I won't.

My mind is so focused on my surroundings, it's a welcome reprieve from the turmoil of these two women— one I'm on a path to save and marry, and one whose touch seems burned into me in a way I'm not sure I can forget.

I take a few more careful steps before a scream echoes in the distance. *Ari...*

I drop the rabbit, my hand already gripping the hilt of my sword, running as fast as my feet will take me. My chest is pounding as I make it to the foliage at the edge of our camp, my steps slowing as I head toward the rustling voices from up ahead.

Three men rummage through our bags, and another pins Ari to the ground. Her face lies hard in the dirt, her hands wrapped around her back and held by the weighted grip of the man on top of her. His knee digs into her leg, his other hand pushing into her upper back to keep her flush against the ground. She bucks against him, clawing at the dirt as she tries to roll herself over and out of his grip. But he stops her with a single motion. A knife lies at the side of her throat, its sharp edge threatening to slice into her soft neck if she attempts to move again. She stills, the icy breath of rage searing through her eyes.

My jaw clenches tightly at the sight, my breathing coming in heavy waves.

"Get off me, and I might decide not to kill you," she snarls through gritted teeth. The man leans harder against her back, his weight pushing against her lungs, a swift grunt of air escaping against the pressure. The men surrounding them chuckle as they throw our stuff around.

"It would seem the easy target you found us is putting up more of a fight than you thought, Jaren," one of the men laughs.

Jaren— the one holding the knife to Ari's throat and pinning down the woman half his size. *Jaren*. Silas's man. And... someone else's man. The cool familiarity crawls through me once again. I've seen him before, and not just with Silas. Where have I seen him? I stare, willing my mind to open and share the secret of this man. Jaren looks to Ari, pure hatred seeping from his dark eyes. Those eyes...

My memory hits me like a punch to the gut. My jaw drops open as I realize where I saw him once before. He was at Sir Reynaulds that day. The afternoon before Evander's observance when I went to assist Reynauld. He was there. Jaren was with Reynauld. A low snarl bubbles in my throat, but I swallow it back in order to stay hidden.

Is Sir Reynauld somehow connected to all of this as well? He must be, mustn't he? I haven't seen Reynauld since that day, nor thought of him or heard his name since then. Is he part of this treachery too? I've yet to see any other connection to Reynauld. But if he is involved— I will find out. And I will gladly pay him back.

Silas could be working for Reynauld. Or him for Silas. I look around for the greasy, tawny-haired man, but see no one else beside these four. His men are doing his dirty work. I'd expect nothing less.

Jaren does have a reason to hate us, the memory of Ari's dagger lodged in his side rolling through my now sharpened memory. But he wouldn't be here without his master's demand. And who exactly is commanding Silas? I plan to find out.

My senses are on full alert. The anxious thrill of a fight swaps thought and reason for instinct and strategy.

The other three men come into focus. The one dumping out my saddle bag is the same man I knocked over before leaving the outpost. The other two rummaging around I don't recognize.

No doubt Silas has ordered these men to take us back alive, if I sized him up correctly. He personally wants to watch death creep upon us, the light dimming from our eyes, relishing in our demise. Silas will regret this night. Jaren will regret this night. I vow it to myself before I cautiously step out of the bushes and into the clearing.

"Gentlemen. How nice of you to join us this evening," I say, stretching a smile across my face. They startle, turning to look at me without any hint of friendliness.

I look directly at Jaren. "Is that any way to treat a lady, my friend?"

"She ain't no lady, and I ain't your friend," Jaren replies, disdain dripping from his lips.

Tsk, tsk, tsk. I make the clicking sound with my tongue as I try and mirror the collected confidence of Tess Santana. I wag my finger at this man about to lose his life. I briefly make eye contact with Ari, her eyes fixed on me, before turning to the other men.

"I ask that you release me, my horse, and my supplies. And I won't report you to the Guard." The men look at me incredulously.

"What about your *lady*?" one of them asks, thinking he's caught the upper-hand.

"While I've greatly enjoyed her company," I wink at Ari, and she proceeds to roll her eyes, "she's proven more trouble than she's worth. You can have her, her horse, any of the supplies she was carrying and be on your way." They look at each other, then back to me. My lack of caring for the woman under Jaren's knee is not what they were expecting.

"He's not serious," Jaren growls, his eyes never leaving me. "They are working together. He defended her against Silas."

"Oh, I assure you sir. I'm being very serious." My cool composure backs up my words as I fold my arms across my chest.

"Except we're the ones who outnumber you, boy. We are the ones who are going to make the demands here," an older man says. His use of *boy* makes my skin crawl. I tolerate it from Otto, but only out of respect for his friendship.

"I'm no boy, I promise you that," I assert, my tone low and controlled. I steal another glance at Ari, her eyes hardened on me. If I set her free at this moment, I have no doubt she'd come straight for me— after Jaren met his end of course. I glance at the man continuing to push her into the dirt, a little too comfortable atop of her.

My teeth grind together, making it more difficult to keep my voice calm. "You may have the numbers, but you lack the training," I say. I snap my head back to the other three, pulling my sword from its sheath, running my fingers down the expertly crafted steel. The glare from the fire bounces an almost perfect image of these men back to them in the reflection of my sword.

The smallest of the crew takes an almost imperceptible step back. "Turinian steel."

"Ah, yes. Turinian steel. Made from the purest metal. Mined from the great Kotar." I grip the handle firmly in my hand. "Steel engineered impeccably by master blacksmiths who train their entire lives to make swords of this caliber. Swords found only in the depths of Felshan's militant capital, whom Thenstra no longer trades with." I take a shot at their nationality, swinging my sword in a quick loop. Its *swoosh* through the air is like music to my ears.

With a slight bend in my knees and my weapon pointing in their direction, I ask, "Do we have a deal? Or would you prefer to spend your last moments with the edge of my blade?"

The one who has yet to address me steps forward, drawing two knives from a leather strap across his chest. "I know you think your fancy toy will make us quiver in our boots. But I was the best knife handler in Thenstra before you were even born, *boy*." He spits out the word *boy* again as he raises both hands, twisting the knives around each finger in his own elaborate show of skill.

Three on one isn't the worst odds I've ever faced. A smile crosses my lips as I move toward him, lifting a hand to gesture him forward.

He charges at me, a single-minded determination to end this fight before it even begins. A knife whirls through the air, blocked and deflected to the ground by my leather clad wrist. I move on him before he can throw the next one.

Our weapons slice through the air, metal meeting metal as I block his advance. His footwork isn't polished, and after a few fumbles I can see the rhythm of his errors. The next few moments are spent lunging, my fist connecting to his jaw, and a complete knockout as the man hits the ground with a loud *thump*— not a single cut on either of us. I laugh, the lighthearted sound being met with gnarled lips and seething eyes from the three remaining men, Jaren included.

"This is the best that comes out of Thenstra? No wonder King Brekan hides atop the mountains," I taunt.

"We are no Thenstrans." The older man draws his sword slowly, looking to me as if I'm fresh meat in the starved sands of Venes.

"This can end now if you just let me go. It's a simple trade," I say.

The man who was about to charge looks disbelieving, but my logic starts to win out as his anger softens to annoyance. He looks to Ari, then back to me. "We can keep her?"

"You can keep her," I reply, raising my right hand in a gesture of truth and promise.

I steal another glance at Ari and where I expect to see fire, I see cool resolve. Silas would still consider retrieving only her a win, since her deceit ran much deeper than mine. If they were truly his men, they would know this and cut their losses.

The older man nods. "Fine. Go. Quickly." He hooks a thumb over his shoulder in the direction of the road.

I nod, sheathing my sword as I begin gathering up my things. Everyone watches me carefully, the steady rhythm of cicadas rising in the once noiseless camp. I strap the saddle on Red, and I check my bag, sighing loudly as I rub my temples.

"What is it?" the leader snaps at me, breaking our silence, his sword still drawn.

"She stole my map. The little thief must have taken it when I left to find food. I need it before I go. If you wouldn't mind sitting her up for a moment so I can check her for it." I keep my true desire from my face, nailing a blank mask of slight annoyance on it instead.

The leader narrows his eyes. "You said we could keep her. That includes anything on her."

"Yes, yes. I understand. But you see, that map is very important to me. If you just let me take it back, I will be on my way with no further incident." Ari struggles against Jaren, and he pushes her face harder into the dirt. The slightest wince pulls my body backward, but luckily everyone is too transfixed on the struggling girl to notice.

"Stay still little lamb. The meat doesn't taste as sweet when you panic," he says, leaning down toward her ear. She turns her head as much as she can and spits straight into his face. I can't help the smile that buds on my lips.

His features twist into fury as he wipes the slime away. Raising his free hand, he lands it swiftly on the exposed side of her face before he shoves her, again unmovable between his weight and the ground. The last bit of air forces out of her in a grunt. I grind my teeth as his blow lands on her already bruised jaw. The energy humming through my limbs demands to be released, and I draw my sword once again.

"Lift her up, Jaren. Now." Effervescent energy courses through my body as I see a red welt forming on the side of Ari's healing face.

Jaren eyes the older man in their group, who in turn narrows his gaze toward me. A glimmer passes through the man's eyes, the corner of his lips turning up almost imperceptibly. He looks me up and down before shifting his gaze to Ari. "Lift her up," he says, the full force of his stare boring into me once more.

At first Jaren resists the order, scowling at the man who gave it. But eventually, he begins to lift himself up, peeling away the pressure holding her in place. I can't help the satisfactory tug at my lips as I watch him, not bothering to hide it from the man watching my every move.

"Goodbye, Jaren." I mouth in his direction as he fully releases his weight from her back.

Like a feral cat released from its cage, she springs into action. Twisting her body around in the dirt and lining up her feet with his face, she uses the full force of her legs to swing around and land a kick square to Jaren's jaw. He falls back to the ground, face bloody from a broken nose and what appears to be a few loose teeth. He releases a high-pitched growl, spitting blood from his mouth, more blood dotting his shirt as it would appear the wound at his side is obviously still unhealed.

The two remaining men are frozen, mouths slightly ajar as they stare at her, then down to their companion's bleeding form on the ground. "You'll regret this," the older man spits out between clenched teeth.

"I don't think I will," I respond before charging the two men.

Ari knocks Jaren out with another swift kick to the head, taking the knife sheathed at his chest and running to my side. She moves to take the smaller of the men, dancing around him as he tries to strike her. One. Two. Three. Ari ducks, rolling around him as she swings a leg back, catching him off balance.

I focus my attention on the older man who clearly has more gumption than his other companions. We parry for a few moments, blocking each other's blows, ducking fists, and moving steadily around the clearing. The subtle crackling of the fire blends into the song of our fight. The man lashes out, grazing my arm, a sharp pain shooting through the wound. A quick glance confirms the cut is minor, and I charge with renewed fervor.

The clang of metal rings through the quiet of darkness. Ari moves around the camp behind me, crossing my vision once or twice before I hear an *oomph* and the sound of a body hitting the ground.

I turn in a panic, looking in the direction of the noise. Ari stands over the man now splayed across the forest floor, his still form staring off into the trees. I've stopped being surprised that such a small woman can bring down a man twice her size. She is quick, clever, and carries a deathly precision that no one would expect, giving her the advantage in a fight. I smile when I think of how naïve I was that first night at Sir Reynauld's estate, believing it would be like cutting through butter to bring her in.

Distracted, my opponent rushes me. I'm knocked hard to the ground, pain radiating from the back of my head as it collides with something hard and unforgiving. Before I can stand again, he's on top of me, sword at my throat.

"Women are a weakness," he spits down at me. My sword is on the ground, too far for me to reach. His knee crushes against my arm. The blade against my neck is enough incentive not to move.

He laughs down at me, as I can do nothing but stare up at him. "Unfortunately for you, you won't get to live long enough to remedy this weakness."

The firelight is blocked by his body, his shadow casting a dark blanket over me as I try to keep my focus away from the pain in my head. He raises his hand to strike his sword through my neck, the satisfaction bleeding through the glint in his eyes. But before he can strike, I hear a guttural sound escape his mouth, his face going rigid as pain and confusion darken his features.

An arrow protrudes from his chest, and his sword goes limp in his grip. I push him off, rolling him to the side as I jump to my feet. My head swims, a light-headedness pulling me down, and I drop to one knee to keep from falling over.

Ari stands across the way, bow still raised, her focus intent on the now lifeless form sprawled into the dirt. A calm impassivity encompasses the air around her, all except for her eyes. They reflect the blazing fire in the center of the mayhem, glistening as she lowers the bow.

"Are you ok?" I manage to ask, looking at each of the four men lying on the ground before landing them again on her.

"Yes. We should go," she says sternly. "Now." I nod in agreement as I try to rise again, successfully this time.

I shake away the dizziness as we busy ourselves gathering up our things, rapidly throwing whatever we can find into bags and saddling her horse. I stare at the woman as she grabs the reins, leading her horse out of the clearing. A blank expression rests across her face. She doesn't glance my way as we head out, leaving the dead and unconscious men in our wake as if it never happened.

It feels like hours have passed, the energy of the night waning into a deep and draining exhaustion. "We should avoid the main roads as much as we can for a while," I state once we are well away from Silas's men.

She says nothing, the only noise around us coming from the subtle crunch of leaves and twigs underneath our feet and the slight breeze blowing through the trees.

"Ari?" I stare at her blank face, noting the same trauma among my men after their first true fight. I quicken my pace until I'm beside her. "Ari. Was he the first man you killed?"

"No," she says matter-of-factly, her features even and steady, still facing forward.

I want to break through her trance, to get her to look at me. She seems as though she's sleep walking, her body making the movements, but her mind is completely shut down. "It's normal to want to distance yourself from a situation such as this. But it's important to remember that defending your-self, or another person from harm, isn't always a heinous act. Sometimes it's brave, courageous— and a right all of us have. To preserve our own life. Our right for safety and security. The shock can feel overwhelming, but—"

She begins to laugh, cutting me off as if I had just told her the funniest joke she'd ever heard. The girl stops walking and falls to her knees, the sound bursting from her in waves until it seems that's all she's capable of. There's a sorrow to the sinisterness of it— a mask to her pain, I realize.

I've seen many reactions from men and the shock that follows after killing someone or witnessing death, even if it's someone they don't know or par-ticularly care about. But I've never seen someone convulse with laughter in this way. It might be eerie to anyone else, but I've learned that everyone deals in their own way and their own time. All I feel is an intense need to wrap my arms around her.

"Ari," I try to get her attention, crouching down in front of her, concern weaving through my very bones. I put my hand on her shoulder, gripping it gently, attempting to catch her attention. *Just look at me,* I want to shout.

She stills at my touch, her eyes flicking to my hand resting on her. "You think I'm in shock?" When she finally looks up at me, her face is contorted with rage. "I wish I could go back and run your sword through both of the remaining two who still live. I'm offended that their hearts are still beating. That they will get to wake up and go about their lives, threatening and hurting whoever gets in the way of what they want. They should die a thousand deaths. And I will gladly go back and bring that upon them if I could find my way." Tears are streaming down her face as she finishes.

Her voice turns into a whisper as she says, "What do you make of the girl who wishes death on her enemies? Of the thief that has no problem killing any threat against those she cares for?"

Anyone else might be taken aback by her words, but I find only understanding as I listen. "I think she's probably afraid, and anger feels easier than fear," I whisper down to her.

Sobs wrack through her body now. She slumps, the final string of her self-composure snapping underneath her. I reach for her, putting my hand on her other shoulder to steady her. She is shaking, the cooling air and exhaustion finally reaching her.

I stare at her, remembering the look in her eyes as she watched the man lying motionless at my feet. Gone was the thief who brought me to my knees the first night we met. Gone was the woman who defended Prue at the stables, leaving me and two of my best guards bruised and bloody. Gone was the emotionless force of a lone warrior— and in her place was a girl. A girl whose instincts crumbled into the insatiable need to stay alive. A girl who knew the consequences of ending a life.

I know, because in many ways I'm still that boy. I'm still just a child watching his best friend take his last breath. A boy pretending to be Captain, watching as I condemn another to suffer for their crimes.

My head is telling me to leave her be. Give her space to let her emotions roll out and not intervene. Just walk away and let her have her moment. But every thread of my heart wants to console her— to bring her into me. *Comfort her. Hold her. Give her somewhere to rest.*

I reach out, brushing a tear from her cheek, avoiding her red jaw from where Jaren slapped her. The same hand trails down her arm, pulling her in close as I move my body toward hers. My arms circle around her as I lean in. She lays her head into my chest, tears now spilling out heavier than before.

She is cold against me, and I hold her tighter to transfer the warmth of my body. Her braid has come loose, subtle waves of hair trailing down her back. I run my fingers through the wavy strands, pulling them away from her face and winding them through my hand so they don't stick to her wet cheeks.

The tremors soon begin to subside, but I keep myself wrapped tightly around her, stroking her arm.

I don't want to let her go.

30

ARI

I AWAKEN WHEN THE first residue of dawn spreads through the morning sky. The grogginess of sleep still clings to me as my senses orient me back into consciousness. Tess's gifted shirt is soft against my stomach, but my pants are twisted awkwardly, my legs feeling distorted and oddly trapped in their grasp. The smell of soap and leather fills the air around me. Something warm and supportive rests underneath my neck, and its comfort attempts to prolong my tranquil state. For a moment, I follow the urge to succumb to its spell and let myself be lulled back into sleep. But a nagging feeling of unfamiliarity stirs within me, unsettling my peace.

The feeling pulls me awake. The final string of sleep unravels its grip as that warmth pushes against my instinctual unease, and I open my eyes to find two familiar arms enveloping me from behind. Those arms are still wrapped in leather, a few gashes leaving discolored lines across them. A leg, one that doesn't belong to me, rests next to my own. His breath is hot against my hair, and my neck prickles in response. I lick my lips, looking around at what I can see without moving my head and alerting Captain Montgomery behind me.

His scent, soap and leather and morning rain, mixes with the heat of a rare thread of sunlight ringing through the leaves above. A war rages in my mind. Stay warm in this cool morning air within the arms of the captain, or save my dignity and roll away, immediately? I take a long, deep breath, letting myself have a few more moments of the peace and calm of his strength before I break his hold and sit up, putting a body's length between us. A shiver runs through me at the cold left in the wake of his body against mine.

I try to access the annoyance I felt for him only days ago, painting a frown on my face as best I can. If we did indeed sleep entwined all night, I can try to at least be irritated by it.

Except— I'm not.

I squint as I replay what happened last night. There was laughing, and crying, and then... his arms around me. Heat flushes across my skin as the details come back to me. I fell apart, completely— had a total meltdown right in front of him. I want to bury my head in the leaves beside me and not face the jabs that are sure to come my way when he awakens.

He stirs before opening his eyes, his groggy gaze landing immediately on me. "Good morning," he says, rubbing bleary sleep from his eyes.

"Morning," I choke out, attempting a smile before I remember I'm supposed to be irked.

I do my best to shake it off, busying myself with the current task at hand— my aching stomach. Prue grazes on a small patch of grass, and I'm to her side in five or six long strides. I pull a few slices of dried meat from my saddlebag, thanks to Tess, and an apple. I split the fruit and divvy out the meat.

"Here, Captain." I hold out my hand with the meager breakfast. His arms are braced against his legs as he sits on the ground, his eyes boring into me as he takes the food. They are questioning, roaming my face for any hint of emotion. I look away, unable to meet his gaze without another flush rising to my cheeks, remembering how he had comforted me— how I had *needed* him in that moment. His arms brushing through my hair. The intimate touch as he wiped away my tears with his thumb.

What must he have been thinking as I broke right in front of him? What must he be thinking now?

"You really can call me Roan." His eyes search mine as he says it, a hint of a smile playing at his lips. This is the second time he's asked me to call him by his first name.

My head is ringing. I don't acknowledge his statement, not sure how to approach him with so many of my mental walls breached. "We need to hurry and get moving. Those men should be awake by now. They will be hunting us down at first chance," I say, my gaze focused on Prue.

I continue to busy myself, hoping to evade his questioning eyes. Since we didn't set up camp last night, there's little to pack up, to my chagrin. I avoid all thoughts of what actually did happen, opting for the easier option of pretending it hadn't happened at all.

Distraction. That's all I need. A distraction. I hop on Prue, maneuvering her through the trees while the captain hurries to adjust the saddle still on his horse.

We decide the main road is still unsafe, so we continue traveling through the woods for the day, keeping the river Villar, a northern tributary of the Rashan, in our sights. As long as we follow closely to its banks we will be heading in the right direction, even without the view of the road.

The path we travel is too narrow to ride side-by-side. The trees, although young and small, are situated close together, and I'm secretly relieved that I won't have to deal with any prying questions. Or worse, sit in silence next to someone who witnessed a crack in my armor.

We break for the day with no sign of Lena, or Thenstra. It's not surprising since we can't travel on the main road, but I'd hoped we'd at least hear travelers passing in the distance. Thenstra's gates must truly be shut tight. I don't know if the captain has a plan to get through them, or if he has thought that far ahead.

I realize we've never actually discussed it. We should be strategizing and making plans, but I can hardly look at him let alone talk to him after last night.

The fire is warm against my face as I turn the rabbit, one I easily caught after we stopped for the day, making sure each side finds that golden brown hue. The smell of its blistering skin makes my stomach rumble.

The captain left a while ago to swim in the depths of the Villar, both to stretch his muscles and clean the layers of grime from his skin, he claimed. It has been days since Tess's luxurious bathtub experience, and while the water may be cold, my body yearns to wash free the events of yesterday. I'm anything if not patient for my turn, giving him his space to rest and clean up. My eyes wander between the trees and toward the water for a brief moment before returning to the fire in front of me and the roasting meat.

I stand, stretching taught muscles as I shoot a few arrows in a nearby tree at varying distances, aiming for a knot in the trunk. Anything to divert my mind. I hit close to the center, but never make my mark.

"Don't pull back until you're ready to shoot," a familiar voice says, coming up from behind. My body tenses, but I don't turn to acknowledge him. He moves until he's close enough for me to feel his radiating heat. The water must not have been *too* cold.

"It takes energy to nock an arrow and hold it back. Don't waste that energy as you aim. Your eyes know where the arrow needs to go. Trust your body to get it there." His voice is low, as if he's telling me a secret. A shiver runs up my spine.

"I trusted that my arrow would find the heart of the man trying to kill you last night," I sneer at him, masking that shiver. A smart woman would take his help— lock it away in her arsenal of knowledge and skill. But right now, that woman isn't me.

"Yes. My neck is forever grateful to you that it's still intact." He rubs at his neck, a grin running across his lips just before his austere demeanor steels back into place. "Your entire body changes when you're threatened. Your strength, stamina, and focus are intensified tenfold. During a fight, I've seen men attack and kill someone twice their size. Building that focus when you're not under threat will give you that much more of an advantage when you are in danger."

Captain Montgomery has come out to lecture me, it would seem. I want to roll my eyes and remind him I'm not one of his recruits, but I refrain.

When I only cock an eyebrow, he holds out his hand. "May I try?"

I hand him my bow, and he takes a step toward me. My breath hitches as he looms close enough that I can hear each steady inhale and exhale, close enough to see the smallest bit of stubble growing where I shaved only last night. The memory of his hand brushing my hair behind my ear before moving down my arm, the look in his eyes as he did it, floods a warmth through me that makes me wish I could jump in the cold river to wash it away.

He reaches over me, grabbing an arrow from the quiver at my back, his dark hair falling into his face. I scoff, rolling my eyes as he winks at me, trying to ignore how the blue in them reminds me of the oceans of Turin. Boy would it feel good to knock that smile off his face, if only to give myself something else to focus on.

He turns, spotting the knot in the trunk surrounded by my own mislaid arrows. Usually, I'm a great shot. I hit the mark when it counted, at least. He pulls back quickly, hitting the mass just off center.

My mouth gapes open as I take it in. "I thought you said Aiden was the best with the bow?"

"He is. He would have hit the mark dead center." He laughs a little as he goes to retrieve the arrow, also gathering my own and bringing them back with him.

I watch him as he walks, like seeing him for the first time. I knew he was strong, was never blind to the muscles bunching beneath his shirt and making his pants taut around the thigh. However, this is the first time I sized him up not as an opponent, but something else entirely. My heart is pounding as he catches me staring at him.

I await a snide remark, but instead he says, "You have the strength and ability for the bow. And you proved last night you can aim under pressure. Now you just need to practice your intention and focus."

Last night wasn't beginner's luck. A dagger may be my preferred weapon, but I'm decent enough with a bow. Today, however, I haven't been able to shoot a single straight shot.

Once he hands me my arrows, I nock one and let it fly, hitting at the edge of the knot. It wasn't perfect, but the closest I've gotten since I started. I prepare myself for the gloat of his teaching skills, but when I turn he is no longer in the clearing.

My eyes scan the trees. He probably just went back to camp, but I can't seem to help my continued perusal. Just as I'm about to finish the search, my gaze freezes on his bare chest. He is standing half naked in the banks of the river just off from my practice site. His shirt is bunched in his hands, his pants rolled up at the ankles. His chest and shoulders look like that of a statue— perfectly carved like he was made of stone itself. I may even believe he was if each movement didn't pull his muscles into a dance, rippling across his back and stomach like the perfected combination of an arabesque, pirouette, and relevé.

Roan rinses his shirt in the water, cupping more onto his face and body. It seems he's taking controlled inhales and exhales as he does it. Is the water cold, or is it something else? My focus hones in as the liquid sluices down his toned torso, my feet inching closer to the stream's edge. It isn't the first time I have seen his bare arms, but it's the first time I can actually appreciate how they match the rest of him so perfectly.

He spots me staring at him, again, a ridiculous grin forming on his wet face. I look away as if I hadn't been awkwardly gawking at him like a bird spotting a nice, juicy worm. "It's not very deep, but it's refreshing enough," he calls out to me.

I move to sit on the bank, no longer daring to look up, but also acting as if nothing is amiss. I've been getting good at pretending nowadays. My shoes come off, and I soak my feet as I pour water over my face and hair, doing my best not to look in his direction again, not even once.

"Would you like some help?" He's next to me before I have a chance to answer. His hands are much bigger than mine, bringing a steady stream of water over my head until I start to feel the relief of a clean face and dirt-free hair. My shirt is soaked once he finishes, but I know a few moments spent next to the fire this evening will have it dry in no time.

"Thank you, Captain," I manage to say after he takes a seat next to me. His arm brushes my own as he wrings out the remaining water from his shirt and dawns it once again. I finally relax a little when his skin is covered.

"You're welcome. And I told you, please call me Roan," he answers, grabbing his boots and lacing them up.

"Thank you, Roan," I reply sheepishly. The intimacy of using his given name was a bad call, his clear enjoyment of it knocking more pink to my cheeks. Do I look like a fool? I must.

I'm still unwilling to meet his eyes. Instead, I listen to the soft hum of flowing water, again trying not to think of everything I just saw. But the image of his tanned skin, the shadow of each muscle perfectly reflected

273

within the final fingers of light is burned into my mind. And a small part of me is glad for it. The other part is screaming that I should get away, to turn and run as fast as I can.

Don't use his name. Don't sit by him. Don't ogle his perfect shoulders and chest and...

I shake my head. I'm supposed to hate him, and I suppose part of me still does. Although it's getting harder to understand why. He didn't hurt my mother, or me. He's only a little older than me, probably wasn't even in the Guard when my mother was taken.

"We should get back. It's getting dark, and it would be wise to eat something before we sleep." My train of thought is interrupted by his words, the reminder of fresh meat pulling at my hollow stomach.

I want to scream to free myself from my racing thoughts. But the way he said before *we* sleep. Does he think I will sleep by him? Or is he saying he wants to sleep by me? I feel as if I'm going crazy. Of course he doesn't mean anything by it.

Roan—I mean the captain—offers a hand out to me as he stands. I grab it, my skin prickling where we touch. I pull my hand free as soon as I'm upright. But as I take my first step through the rocky riverside, my feet latch onto something strong and steadfast. They lose solid ground, and I stumble my entire weight forward. I'm falling before my mind catches up to what has happened and before I can stop it. My body crashes into him, hardly nudging the man backward. He grips me tightly, unwilling to let me fall.

"I'm sorry," I bluster, still trying to make sense of what just happened. Behind me lies an exposed tree root, my foot still trapped underside it and caught in its grip. I grasp at his shoulders, trying to unhook myself so I can stand independently once again. "Stupid roots blend in a little too well," I continue, trying to appease my clumsiness. I peel myself away from his damp shirt, my hand feeling each muscle as I move from him. It's times like these that I wish my memory wasn't so damn good.

"I'm glad I was here to catch you." He genuinely smiles. Not a smile like he's embarrassed for me and doesn't know what else to do, but a real smile as if he understands. "Just last month I fell over my own sword. Flat on my face. I'm not sure I'll ever live that one down."

"I suppose we wouldn't be human if we didn't act dim-witted on occasion," I say, trying to keep my traitorous smile and pounding heart at bay.

"Agreed," he responds.

I realize I'm staring up at him still, like a buffoon. He simply stares back, his eyes searching my face. I take a deep breath before untangling the last of myself from his arms.

It's like I'm an imposter in my own skin as another shiver rolls up from my hands. The ghost of his own gripping me still lingers even though we're no longer touching. I stare at them as I walk back to our camp, confusion as present as the heat raging deep inside me. I don't know what this is, and I'm as afraid as I am intrigued.

I'm almost done. I'm almost free. Don't screw this up.

Starting some side romance on a hunt for a princess isn't and never has been in my plans. Especially when I promised to hate the entirety of the Guard for all of eternity after everything with Mother. But it's hard to forget the way he looked at me before Jaren showed up. The way we spent the night. The way he closed the space between us. Waking up this morning cradled in his arms.

He's Captain of the Guard, and who am I? Daughter of no one. Friend of nobody. I don't even know my last name. The relationship would be short lived, a mere fling to stack in his memories of *that one time.*

I'm nothing near a proper lady— one who deserves a fine man, a fine house, and a bunch of little babies to grow up and carry on the family name. But I'm more than a book to be stacked on a shelf, never to be read a second time.

Each muscle in my face is taut as I roll through my options: continue on with the captain, spoiling whatever happy future I could possibly find. Or stay away. Find the princess, earn Prue and my freedom, and be on my merry way— finding those who took my mother from me, those who would hurt others for their own gain, and making them pay ten fold.

My mind is made up, and everything clicks in to place.

This won't happen. This can't happen. No more *almost* moments. No more intimate names. And definitely no more sleeping in his arms.

This is it. I will *never* touch the captain again.

31

ROAN MONTGOMERY

I RUN A STONE down the length of my sword, polishing the metal with each scrape and pass.

The fire is warm against my face. I stare into it, catching glimpses of Ari's sleeping form in between the wisps of flames. My body is exhausted, but my head is unwilling to shut down.

Why does being so close to her feel so good? Merely catching her in her fall, her form against mine for only moments, was enough to completely undo me. Could she see how my body responded to her in my arms? Could she see the things I was thinking in that moment? If I wasn't a gentlemen, those thoughts would have compelled me to keep myself wrapped around her for much, much longer.

Heat flushes across my skin as I imagine what it would feel like to kiss her— to feel her lips against my own, her hands gripping tightly around my neck, bringing me closer, wanting more. I close my eyes tightly, attempting to rub the images away with the heel of my hands. But when I open them again, she's still there. And not just her physical presence sleeping across from me. This infuriating thief has taken root inside of me, despite my attempts to keep her at bay.

An image of Lena pokes into the fray.

I love her. I truly love her. But the love of a brother to a sister, a daughter to her father, or a friend to a friend. And she is— she truly is my friend. I tried the last three years, since her mother and father asked for our betrothal, to see her as someone I could love romantically. But the more I pushed myself, the further away our love was pulled.

Bringing two great houses together, the Montgomerys and the Chattans, would be a great feat. And I have confined myself to the idea of a marriage of convenience. A marriage to please the people around me. A marriage for the alliance it would bring, and the resurrection of the son and prince everyone lost.

I always thought loving Lena would be much like painting. Layer by layer you draw, brush, and stroke the canvas. Each day a new detail is added, a new color, a blending of hues and shapes molding themselves onto the paper. Days, months, and years may pass as the design unfolds itself from something unrecognizable, mere pigmented dots and chromatic lines growing into a landscape of glowing intensity. Until we finally step back and witness the exquisite portrait of our lives together— a tapestry woven from time and choice.

It becomes a beautiful creation inspired simply by choosing each other in each moment. By showing up each day and stoking that friendship, we would watch it transform into a picture of a love we both wanted. I never doubted Lena and I could learn to enjoy our lives together, built from the years of our friendship.

Until now.

Guilt tugs inside my chest. I'm promised to one, but seem to want another. And worse, my promised person is rotting away somewhere unknown, in a country unfamiliar to her, with people who would use her and hurt her for her name and status alone. A tension rises within me as I think of Lena barely surviving— hurt, starved, waiting for life or death, but not knowing which will greet her. If her brother were here, if Evander had been around instead of me, I have no doubt she'd already be safe at home in the arms of her family. Breathing becomes more difficult as I think of her, and I know sleep won't find me anytime soon.

Ari stirs in front of me, mumbling words I can't make out. My eyes fix on her, watching each delicate movement. I don't know what I feel for this girl. Maybe it's simply lust or infatuation. But even as I think it, I know it's more than that. The surface of my understanding disappears into plunging depths that I can't yet put words or feelings to.

Wherever this leads, no matter what happens, I've had a taste of the real thing. It's not love, not yet. But now I know the ache felt in the absence of someone I care about. The hunger for more of them. The desire to be close to them.

I try to close my eyes, to let sleep overtake me. But even with my eyes shut, all I see is Ari.

My eyes are dry and red as the first light of morning fans through the sky, the rising sun still a ways away. The smoke and dry fire left their mark. I do my best not to rub at them, but I find myself mindlessly reaching for them nonetheless. My midnight revelations slowly come back to me. Once feeling courageous and true in the cloak of night, they now seem difficult and uncomfortable in the light of day.

My future may be unclear and rocky, but I know it isn't Ari's fault. None of it is her fault. If anything, she has set me free of mirroring my life to duty alone. Of giving me at least the desire to open the doors to my dreams once again. Dreams I long thought dead and buried.

A loud crack of thunder shoots through the sky, darkened clouds looming on the horizon. Boots crunch through the forest floor, my focus quickly returning to the person emerging in front of me. I can't help but stand and smile at Ari as she approaches. It's the oddest thing, how my spirit instantly lifts just by looking at her.

"Good morning," I beam.

The smile nor the greeting are returned. My brows knit together as I watch her cautiously gather up her things and pack them away. Perhaps she also didn't sleep well. "It sounds like we're going to get wet this morning," I add.

Still, she says nothing, only nodding briefly. I pretend to busy myself cleaning up my meager accommodations as if nothing is amiss. When she passes close by I can't help but reach out for her, moving directly into her path.

She cocks her head to the side, narrowing her eyes. "We need to hurry. It's already late in the morning, and the rain will slow us."

"The sun hasn't even risen yet. I'd hardly say it's late."

"Every morning we have been on our way long before the sun rises. But today, you decide your royal hide needs its beauty rest." My royal hide? I'm not sure who would ever consider a captain as royalty, but I can't help but grin at her snide remark.

"My hide is far from royal, but it does occasionally enjoy the benefits of a longer stretch on the hard dirt the outdoors provides," I joke. She rolls her eyes in response.

The wind picks up around us, whipping loose strands of hair around her face. The storm is moving in quickly, stronger than I anticipated at first glance. Her hair isn't in her normal braid, but pulled to the side and tied with a thin piece of cloth, her wavy strands rippling past her shoulder. *The influence of Tess Santana.* But my inward smirk at the thought doesn't reach my outward presence, nor do I tell her the look frames her face well.

"When did this turn into your summer diversion from the city?" she questions. Her gaze is swirling with something deeper as her words sink into me.

"Excuse me?" I ask. My defense is sparked, but I do my best to calm myself. I'm not sure in what world I would call eating dried meat, sleeping on dirt, getting soaked by rainfall every other hour, and being chased around by men with swords a summer diversion.

"Have you forgotten why we are out here, trying miserably to sleep on this *hard dirt*?" I narrow my eyes at her— another push against my composed demeanor. Another crack of thunder, coming in closer this time. "A princess is out there," she continues, "in the hands of who knows who at this point. Wanting her for nothing more than their own gain. She's scared. Alone. And some of us actually care about getting her back."

My jaw clenches and each muscle in my body is taut and alert. I'm not sure how the morning could have shifted so suddenly. Last night I could've sworn I saw her anger and annoyance fade away. I even thought maybe her clumsiness was because she had been as distracted by me as I had been of her. Now, looking at her seething form, I don't know what to think. Not only that, but she's accusing me of not caring for Lena, of this being something other than my entire being trying to get her back, and get her safely home.

I attempt to focus my vision on the trees behind her. The branches, and leaves they hold, blow wildly in the building wind. I manage a few breaths before I open my mouth to respond. "Don't say I don't care," I declare through softly clenched teeth, my voice the ice to the fire within. "Not a minute goes by that I don't think about her. That I'm not strategizing every possibility to get her back."

She holds her ground, her gaze meeting mine without any hint of melting away under my heat. I continue, "And why do you presume to know what she's going through? You don't know her. You've never even met her. She might be scared. She might be alone. But she's one of the strongest people I know. She's brave and courageous. She's one of the only good things this world has to offer." My final words take aim and fly from my grasp. "At least I'm not trying to find her as a means to escape my own life."

Ari stands rigid, her burning eyes fixed solely on me. "You would too if you were me. You have no idea what my life has held up until now. I tell you a few sentences about me and you think you've figured me out? Nice try. Growing up in your fancy palace with your rich family. What have you ever had need to escape from?" As she speaks she moves closer to me, her admonishment wanting to hit its mark as squarely as my words found theirs.

"Money and finery isn't all it's cracked up to be," I respond.

"Spoken like someone who has it."

Her green gaze storms heavier than the clouds above us. I don't break away from her, and she doesn't turn away. "Yes, I grew up with money," I say, all the heat suddenly gone from my voice. "And I was ripped from my family as a child. Sent somewhere foreign and unfamiliar to live out my days, seeing them again for only a few weeks each summer. Yes I was blessed that the family I had to live with was good to me. But my choices have rarely been my own. I was born with everything decided for me, and the more I tried to take my choices back, the more I hurt those I loved."

I try not to wince as I think of Evander, of his family grieving these last seven years. But I continue, "And the older I get, the harder it becomes to break away from that pattern. I'm a wolf caught in a trap, trying to determine if I should succumb to my fate or chew off my leg." It feels as if all hope has abandoned me. And I suppose in a way, it has.

The truth is that life can be shifted. But mine has always felt fixed. I let myself get here— never questioning or standing up for what I wanted. When Evander died, a part of me went with him. Watching light leave someone's body, someone I cared about— it transformed me in a way that nobody else can see. I was on my own. A boy of fifteen trying to figure out how to get over my role in the death of my best friend.

I busied myself. I entered the recruit program two years early, finishing my education in whatever spare time I could find. Never letting myself have a free moment to think or to remember.

It worked. Up until it didn't.

Maybe I don't deserve to ever figure it out, to ever not feel the swirling emptiness that sucks me away whenever I think of that day and the hollowness of a world without him. I would deserve nothing less.

But right now, standing across from Ari— I can finally see the distance I've put between me and my true desires. His death will never leave me, but maybe it doesn't have to. I can still live, even though he will never again. I let myself die that day too. And maybe that is a dishonor to his memory, of that young boy so full of life before it was ripped away too soon.

"At least you had people who cared about your future." Her eyes pull down at the edges, her earlier irritation subdued into a quiet sigh. I hesitate for a moment, my head unsure, but my heart yearning.

Our stories are different, but our feelings are the same. We desperately want to have a say in the future. To protect those we care about. To love and be loved. To be cared for. To see our dreams come true— to be able to have dreams in the first place.

Evander's last breaths may haunt me forever, and I don't know if I'll ever forgive myself. But does that mean I should never be happy? Guilt and yearning clash inside of me, water and fire furious with their approach. But I close the door to that fight, the searching eyes of the girl in front of me craving to be acknowledged instead. I can give that to her.

I want to give that to her.

I take a deep breath before I close the distance between us, cupping her face in both my hands. "I care about your future."

Tears slowly fill her eyes. "No you don't," she whispers, trying to turn away. But I wrap my fingers around the back of her neck, stepping closer.

"I do." I tilt her face until her eyes meet mine. "I'm truly sorry, Ari. I'm sorry for everything. I'm sorry for how I treated you when we met, and the days after. I'm sorry for the pain you've had to endure. I don't pretend to know the hardships you've faced in your life. They are so different than my own. But I want to know. Will you tell me?" Her eyes search mine, not yet willing to commit to something she's unsure of. I don't blame her, but I don't know how to help her see that I'm telling the truth.

I pause, shifting on my feet as the next words form in my mind. "I want you to help me find the princess because I can't do it alone. And I can't live knowing Lena is in harms way. But when it's done, when we've brought her home safely and we've returned to normal life— I want to keep seeing you." Her brows draw together at my words, her gaze frantically searching my own for the sincerity behind my words.

I continue, my hesitancy falling away as we move deeper into whatever this is between us. "I would like to know you. And if you'll let me, to laugh with you. I want to get to know the thief I met in the middle of the night. The one who knocked the breath out of me."

My life has been on the brink of shattering, and men have tried to end my life in more ways than one. Nights have been spent feeling as if complete destruction was about to take over me, and I wouldn't survive— nor did I want to. But never has my heart beat so fiercely. Never have my nerves been so wildly on fire. Never have I wanted anything more than I want her in this moment. Her green eyes, the golden flecks of her hair shining in the scattered sun above us. I want to be the one who makes her eyes dimple as joy reaches every point of her face.

A few raindrops begin to fall around us. Those penetrating eyes highlight her fear and her unsureness. But I stay firm. This is my truth. In this moment, this is all that makes sense.

Eyes locked, she pensively reaches her hands up to cover my own as they now rest aside her face. Her fingers move down each of my arms, erasing the tiny drops of water that found my skin from above. She makes her way up to my shoulders, searing a path to my chest.

I move my hands to her back, slow and deliberate, trailing them until they sit firmly at her waist. My gaze shifts to her lips, her chest heaving as much as my own. Her soft fingers reach up and around my neck.

It feels as if the forest is spinning around me, and Ari is anchoring me to the ground.

Her touch is like a dream. One I didn't dare to imagine until now. I want to grab on to any piece of her, holding on with everything I have so she won't float away from me. I pull her closer, the rain falling more evenly now. My grip tightens around her hips as the heat of our bodies mix together. The smell of her—like sweet summer berries and honeysuckle blossoms— twirls around me, my vision beginning to blur at the edges as I breathe it in. But it's hard to catch enough air, and all I can think of in this moment is tasting her lips with my own and letting that summer berry burst with its sweetness.

I lean down, feeling her breath against my face just before I close the final distance between us.

32

ARI

A STEADY BEAT OF rain falls around me, mirroring the fierce thrum in my chest as Roan leans into me. Water dances along my eyelashes, falling gently down my face as I close my eyes. One minute we are screaming at each other, and the next all I could think about was wrapping myself around him. I *needed* him, again. But this time I needed much more than just sleeping in his arms.

His mouth gently brushes mine, his lips warm as they meet my own. Roan pulls back ever so slightly, making sure he has my full permission before he continues. I don't wait for him to understand my answer as I pull him closer, the fever of our lips melting into one another. He is gentle at first, allowing an exploration of each other and each new element we find. My body folds into his, unaware of anything but his hands at my waist and his mouth on my own. I'm wholly enveloped in his frame, his scent, his presence— suffocating everything else out of this single moment. Our kiss deepens, moving from a calm searching of something unfamiliar to a frantic passion of need and desire.

I didn't know I *wanted* this, didn't know I *felt* this, until I heard him say that he cared about my future. And then something collapsed inside me—

something musty and old and powerful and... safe. But it wasn't safe. I didn't know what safety meant until I let him in, let him see and feel my pain. And he stayed. He still wanted me despite what he saw.

"If you only do what's safe you may never truly be happy," my mother once told me. It made no sense to me then. I thought for a while that working with Marg, everything I'd done for the last four years, was me relinquishing safety for happiness just as she had said. But now— now I know she meant this. Being here and not running away. Not pushing away. Letting my shield crumble. Letting myself be truly seen, even in a small measurement.

I'm burning from the inside out in the best way imaginable as heat builds wildly inside me. We move in unison to the rhythm of the vibrant rain falling through the veil of leaves above. Water drips down our faces, soaking into our hair and clothes. But I don't stop. We don't stop.

There's an urgency in each kiss, a surety to every touch, and strength as we cling to each other. The storm eases, its threatening downpour held at bay, dissolving into a steady drizzle.

Roan pulls back, his lips softly swollen, before tipping his forehead and resting it against my own.

I want to look up, to read his face and interpret every single thought that passes through his eyes. But a piece of me is afraid of what I will find. The vulnerability twisting through me makes me want to crawl out of my skin. So I stare at his chest instead as his fingers brush across my lips. He twists a piece of my hair, neither of us moving, our arms still wrapped around each other.

I don't dare open my mouth, to speak first. So we stand in silence, my hands resting against his chest, his own holding me close.

I almost laugh, wondering how my hate could have turned around so violently into something like this— something so soft and inviting. There's still a tug, a pull that wants me to step away, to put distance between us. I want to listen to it, but the comfort I feel standing here wins. And I stay.

Prue whinnies in the distance, the sound setting my heart at ease. But then another sound accompanies it— the crunch of leaves.

My body freezes, eyes snapping open as I pull back from Roan. The heat once raging beneath my skin arranges into cold focus as I scan the woods, each of my senses active and alert. Roan drops his hands to his sides.

"What's wrong?" He stares at me intently, his brows crinkled together.

"Shhh." I mimic silence with a finger up against my lips, standing still as I listen intently for a sound, any sound that doesn't belong. His features harden into a mask of concentration as realization dawns. He follows my gaze, joining me as I search the trees, while one hand grips the shiny gold hilt of his sword.

"Something isn't right," I whisper, a buzz running through me, goose-bumps forming up both arms. *Danger. Danger. Danger,* it tells me. *But where?*

"We should make a run for the horses," Roan replies underneath his breathing. Before I even have a chance to lift my feet, an arrow hits the tree closest to me, only a few inches from my shoulder. "Run!" he yells. Another arrow, whooshing between us this time, again disappearing without its mark. More arrows come as we rush to cover within the trees.

Our horses are only a few yards away, but the melee comes from the area behind Red and Prue. We scramble in the opposite direction, my legs pumping hard and fast. My heart falls as I move further away from my horse, now painfully within another's grasp.

"Don't lose them!" I hear a voice shout behind us. My fury, unfortunately, cannot melt the path of regret.

It's a voice I recognize.

Jaren. As I look behind me, I count more than the two we left unconscious in the dirt. It would seem a few more have joined their ranks.

Another shout. "If you don't run faster, you'll be the one who has to report back to Tamen!" This yell isn't intended for us.

Roan and I make eye contact for a mere moment, the surprise evident on his face as much as my own. My blood cools at the mention of this name, but I don't slow.

Tamen. The one who gave us vital information about the princess crossing through Fort Lowsan. The one who passed out as Roan snapped his arm. These men work for Tamen?

Had he been in charge this whole time? Even in Fort Lowsan? Did I get it wrong thinking Phillip Crane was the head of their treason?

"Follow me!" Roan yells as I throw one foot in front of the other as quickly as possible.

I have no weapons but my dagger, and that's no match for a quiver of arrows. Roan's sword is swinging in its sheath, clattering at his side as we weave in and out of trees, the storm above us finally opening up to her full glory. Sheets of rain cover our escape, slowing the men and their ability to find a straight shot. But it doesn't deter their advance.

"I get the girl!" I hear Jaren scream behind me. "You hear that, *lady*. Silas wants you very much alive!" His taunt rings through the trees, his laugh echoing around the woods in every direction.

The idea of my fate being decided by a slimy weasel like him, or Silas, or Tamen would make me laugh if I weren't devoting all my breath to darting up the side of a mountain. My chest and legs are burning, but I keep moving, keep pumping myself forward, faster and faster. I'm use to the flat terrain of Turin, and every inch of my body is yelling at me for it. I turn to see Roan struggling, but still able to keep just a few paces behind me.

"Don't stop!" Roan calls up to me, water soaking through his clothes and dripping from his fingertips. I look forward, demanding myself to keep pushing, pushing, pushing upward.

Their voices go distant, but I don't let myself falter.

"Tread carefully. The ground is soft," Roan says, brushing his sodden hair from his eyes. His voice is quickly drowned by the tittering rain, falling in its deluge. Water drips down every crevice of his face, falling sharply from his jaw. I swipe at my own face, the torrent above making it difficult to see as the rain seeps into my eyes.

I'm too tired to think. Too tired to argue.

My boots sink into the earth below me, slipping as I move. For every step I take, I lose half the distance as soft ground slides me backwards on the sloped mountainside. Mud clings to my arms and legs, my hands burning as I catch myself in yet another fall. Clean streaks of water tumble across my dirty skin as the rain continues to drop, unrelenting.

It feels like we've been climbing for hours, my legs crying for rest, when a tired hand grabs my arm. I turn to see Roan behind me, pointing to my right. Hidden next to us in the mountainside is a small lip of rock, moss and overgrown roots dangling around it. Roan sticks a hand through the foliage, meeting what appears to be emptiness on the other side. I leap forward, eyes darting from his face to the possible protection behind the veil of plants.

Darkness encompasses a small hole at its center. The possibility of refuge sends us both scrambling to get inside.

He climbs in first, moving through the veil of plants and disappearing right into the side of the mountain. As I enter behind him I stumble over his feet, catching myself on his outstretched hand, but still knocking against the back of the hollowed ridge. I rub my shoulder, aching from the impact, before I'm able to fully take in the space.

There's hardly enough room for one, let alone two of us. But I collapse to the ground anyway, my aching, anxious body thanking me for the reprieve. We do our best to arrange ourselves to fit in the space. Roan sits in front, his boot poking through the entrance. He reaches out to grab some nearby branches pulling them over to hide his shoes from the open air and any searching eyes. I wind myself up snugly against the back stone wall, my knees pulled in tight.

Our heaving breaths continue to rack the tiny space for a long while. Water drips off us, pooling onto the dirt floor into muddy puddles.

Gradually it becomes easier to breath, and the only sound comes from the steady onslaught of pouring rain. I stare out through a small hole in the vines at the opposite ridge, devoid of thought or emotion, lost in the beat of the storm. We are quiet for a long while, long enough for exhaustion to sink its teeth through my skin.

"How in Haythen did they find us?" Roan asks, talking his thoughts out loud. I say nothing, my mind still trying to make sense of everything, but coming up short.

"We need to keep moving," he continues. "The only reason we are alive is because the storm slowed their ascent and hid our tracks. They may be idiots, but they seem to be good at tracking. If we keep heading north, we should hit Thenstra in a few days. We can buy more supplies once we hit Vyre, its capital city."

I stare at him. "What about our horses? What about Red and Prue?" Tears threaten to prick my eyes, but I hold them back, swallowing the thick lump in my throat.

"If these men cared enough to follow us as long as they did, they will most likely keep following us. Once we aren't wet, starved, and half frozen we can make a plan to do the hunting instead of being the hunted. We will get them back. Until then, we move quickly and quietly." His voice firm. He's back in his full captain character once again.

"Marg gave me that horse," I start, a trance overtaking me. "I was fourteen and had never ridden a horse before. She told me the best way to learn was get on and go. So I got on. I went. And I never looked back. I vowed that day that she would be mine forever." My mindless words flow out of me until the end, when my voice moves deeper.

I must sound ridiculous, sharing the origins of a horse and a girl, but I don't care. And if Roan shares my sentiment of that ridiculousness, he doesn't show it. Instead, he remains serious, grabbing my ankle and squeezing it gently. "We will get them back."

I nod, cracking my knuckles before laying my head on my knees and closing my eyes. I can't remember the last time I felt this tired.

Roan releases my ankle before clearing his throat. "Ari, there's something I haven't told you."

I don't open my eyes. "What?" I'm barely able to get the single syllable out of my mouth. The thickness in my throat is so dense it's hard to take a breath let alone talk.

"I've seen Jaren before." His voice is even, almost monotone. "Before this. Before Silas."

My head snaps up, my eyes searching his face. "Where?"

"With Sir Reynauld. I went to his estate on behalf of Lady Davenport, his cousin, before the night you and I met. She asked me to assist him in finding... well... you, obviously. That's why I was bringing you in. Why I chased after you that first night." His eyes never leave mine. He told me as much when he tried to take me for questioning. But this is the first I'm hearing of any connection between Jaren and Reynauld.

"And, what? He was there?"

"Yes. Jaren was with Reynauld when I went to get the details of what happened. I went to talk to him, and Jaren was there. With Reynauld. I knew he looked familiar, but I couldn't place him until the clearing when he pinned you down. And then so much happened. It wasn't until now, seeing him again, that I made the connection."

So much has happened. My breakdown in the woods. Avoiding Roan. Seeing him in the river. Kissing him. My skin prickles, sending goosebumps up my arms. But my forehead wrinkles as I try to make sense of what he's telling me. Jaren was with Reynauld, the day before the princess was taken.

"So, what? What does that mean? Reynauld is involved with the princess being taken? With Silas?" I ask, more as a way to voice my thoughts then to get any kind of answer.

"It looks that way. Unless Silas had Jaren doing something else there on Reynauld's estate. But... it seemed like... Reynauld knew him. Like he was an employee of some sort." His hands silently tense into fists as he talks, and his voice turns raspy as he finishes.

I pinch the bridge of my nose. I don't have the energy to try and fit the pieces together. Not right now.

Roan kissed me, and I kissed him back. Then we were running for our lives as Jaren taunted me. Threatened me. They took my precious Prue. My muscles are still screaming at me from pushing up through the soggy mountainside. Too much has happened to try and make sense of all of it. And now this. Now Reynauld.

In this moment, I only have the energy to take care of what's right in front of me. I will do as Roan said. We will find supplies, and we will hunt. I will hunt.

I will get Prue back. And then I will kill Jaren. Then Silas. And if Reynauld was involved— him too. I don't care if he has family in high places. I will do whatever it takes to the rid the world of these men. Men who would take whatever they want without fear of retribution, without care of who suffers in the process.

And I will enjoy every moment of it.

33

LENA

"**W**HAT'S IN THERE?" I ask, biting at the inside of my cheek.

A large, dark hole looms in front of me. A cave. I've never been underground before, even if that ground was carved out of a mountainside. Each footstep feels heavier than the one before.

"The tunnel is short. The main gates through the Prythan Mountains are shut and haven't been opened since King Brekan closed them." I inch closer before a forceful shove almost trips me headfirst into the rocky terrain.

"Get moving. We don't have time to ease your soft mind," Onah spits at me.

Parker jolts forward to catch me. Once I'm again sturdy on my feet, his upper lip curls as he eyes the woman. But she pays no heed. "Like I was saying, this is a passage some of the more rebellious people created so they could still get in and out of Thenstra. There's a similar passage through the eastern Prythan Mountains, those bordering Jadeya, as well.

Last night we left the horses and wagon on the edge of the road, traveling the last leg of wherever this journey is taking us on foot. The rocky cliffs make it impassable for our large cart, and the smaller spaces are obstructive to our horses.

The weather up here is less stable. Last night a coat was almost necessary, and today I wish I could shed all my clothes under the stifling sun.

Parker passed the time with more tales of his family. The most intriguing one happened with his older brother as together they finagled a young, drunken friend into a canoe while he slept— waking to find himself in the middle of a lake with no way to get back but swim. I don't believe half of what he tells me, but it paints a comforting picture of love and friendship.

Part of me wants to ask where they are now— his friends, his family. But my gut tells me that story isn't as fun to tell being that he's here with me instead of with them.

I realize now how a piece of me has clung to the stories of his home. There was a normalcy to his words as he told me of his mother and sister, his older brother, of friends from a time that seemed only yesterday, but must in reality have been from a time long past.

I'm finally creating my own stories. Ones worth telling at least. I roll my eyes, letting out a heavy sigh as I'm once again pushed against the fact that I'm not just exploring the mountains with a good friend. Somehow, being near Parker, I keep forgetting that truth.

As I stare into the dark abyss in front of me, I hope there will be a story I eventually get to tell as well. One where I come out the other side without being swallowed whole by some cave dwelling monster. Or worse, murdered by a knife in the back, courtesy of Onah. The way she looks at me, I wouldn't take the possibility of that fate away just yet.

The woman marches past me, a makeshift torch in her hand. "This will be the last daylight you see, Aldren, if you don't get this girl to the other side of this mountain, breathing and at least mostly intact. I don't care if you have to listen to her scream the entire time while you carry her over your shoulder, or knock her out and drag her through. Just make it happen." And just like that, she disappears into the darkness.

"Motivational as always, my friend!" Parker yells after her disappearing form.

I've never been one to be afraid of the dark. But something about this— the tight, confined space. The unknown of what lies beyond it. Is there enough air to breathe once we're inside? What awaits me once I pass through? I'm standing frozen at its precipice, the claws of a shadowy strangeness reaching for me.

Parker strikes a spark a few steps away, lighting his own torch and holding it up to fend off the blackness inside. "If you'd like, you can hold the light. We can go side by side when it permits. And from there, I will go in front or behind, whatever you're most comfortable with. It's not long, maybe the time it might take for you to host a fancy dinner party."

A dinner party. Obviously he hasn't been to one hosted by my mother. They can go well into the night, and even to dawn depending on the celebration. It has been many years since Mother threw one of her grand parties, but I remember some from when I was a girl. It was truly awe inducing to watch. I always fell asleep halfway through, exhausted from eating and dancing more than I ever thought possible. Sadly, I won't get the option to simply fall asleep here.

He holds out an arm, and I link mine with his— not even questioning how absurd it is that I'm seeking my captor for comfort. My breathing is heavy and uneven as we begin, entering the rocky void with as much confidence as a beetle about to conquer a falcon.

The first half is as horrible as I imagined— cramped, narrow, and demanding single file progress. When I have to unlink my arm with Parker's in order to get through, I unintentionally grab his hand instead. He walks in front with his arm angled back to keep hold of mine. He doesn't complain though, instead gripping me just as hard. Somehow knowing I'm not alone in here is enough to keep me from moving into complete panic.

We continue slowly, crawling and climbing, letting go and grabbing back together as soon as possible, like magnets finding their invisible bond once again.

"How often do people use this?" I huff out, my gaze darting across the rocks and shadows.

"Fairly often. I've been through a couple times. Never run into anyone else though," he says.

"It doesn't seem like much could get through here. Not much could be transported anyway."

"Princesses seem to do ok." I can't see his face, but I know there's a smile there. "I'll have to send a note to the owner of this route and let him know." I turn my glare back to him, sending a dark chuckle echoing through the cave.

"What do they use this for?" I ask. Curiosity clears away the tension and fear, giving a brief reprieve from my shaking legs.

"Mostly trade. Although, like you shrewdly noticed, there's not room for much else than a person to fit through in some spots. I believe they have a system to get their goods in and out. Ropes and pulleys and such. Thenstra has a festival starting soon. This tunnel should be overflowing by next week to get everything in to prepare," Parker tells me.

Surprise lights my face. A festival? "Nobody in Felshan knows about this. As far as we know, everything has been completely shut off. I'm surprised at least a trickle of knowledge hasn't yet spread about this place. That not even the king of Thenstra has put an end to it."

"Oh, he would if he knew. That's why it's very hush-hush. Only a dozen or so people know, and they have strict orders punishable by death." He smiles again as he shares the information.

"How do you know all of this?"

"I don't. But it would make sense. I only know of it from Onah, and I'm not sure how truthful she really is," he says.

I turn and give him a shove in the shoulder, but it's like trying to move a brick wall. "Onah is right. You really do talk too much, you know," I say. He mocks an air dagger to his heart, feigning the pain of my words. "You're insufferable," I add.

"My words make sense, if you think about it. King Brekan closed all doors to neighboring kingdoms, and you think he'd be fine knowing there are tunnels connecting Felshan and Thenstra? Whoever built this did so on pain of death. There must be strict orders to keep it silent. They also must make quite a bit of money, because it looks well-traveled and taken care of."

I look around me, noticing footprints in the tracked dirt beneath me. Scrapes and marks from some kind of metal lay on the rocks of this cave. How does one learn to notice such things without another pointing them out? The detail Parker sees slips easily past me. Everything looks like random dirt, rocks, and darkness to my eyes.

We move into a larger area, the space opening around us, and we are able to walk abreast instead of single file. After a few moments, I notice our hands are still tightly clasped together as they were before. It's unnecessary now, but I don't let go. My stomach is still twisting as my eyes search the path ahead. My breathing is shaky and labored even though it seems we're past the worst of it.

My palms become slippery, and Parker grips my hand tighter. "For what it's worth, I think you'd make a great queen. If that's what you decided to do." His words take me off guard, and not just because they are moot at this moment in time.

He thinks I would do a good job? We've been together not even two weeks, and he thinks he knows me that well? He did have time to watch me in the palace, to see me in a way I hadn't realized. Color rises to my cheeks. I'm unused to such trust and faith in me.

I don't doubt his honesty. He believes me capable, as far as his knowledge has seen anyway. I don't know if I agree yet, but the thought doesn't make me cringe like it once did.

"You're a horrible captor," I tell him.

Our eyes lock, and for the smallest moment, I think he might lean down to me. To do what, I don't know. His gaze traces the lines of my mouth, and all the sudden it feels much too warm in here. The corner of his lips turn up, a grin blooming across them. But he faces forward, continuing our walk toward Onah and to whatever lies on the other side of this darkness.

"I wasn't lying when I said I would help you, in any way I can. It may not mean much coming from me. But I promise you, I will." He doesn't look at me as he says these words.

And truthfully, I don't know what to say back except, "Thank you."

My stomach has almost settled when I feel a breeze, the torch sputtering against it. As we turn a corner, light shines down the remaining rocky corridor, rendering my firelight unnecessary. But still I hold it in front of me, feeling some measure of protection in its flickering glow.

It takes a moment for my eyes to adjust to the brightness, holding my arm up to shield the sunlight from my face. My fingers are still interlaced with Parker's, and I give him a shaky smile. I have no idea what happens from here, but my breathing seems to have evened out some at least. He nods to me, his own smile reassuring me of his last words.

I'm about to open my mouth, to ask him what happens now, when a heavy force knocks me down and out of Parker's grip, pinning me to the rocky ground. A sharpness jabs into my face and stomach, and I claw at the loose rocks and earth around me as I try to move.

"Parker? What's happening? Parker!" I scream. Rough hands grab at me, tying my arms firmly behind my back, something hard and heavy digging into my shoulder.

"What are you doing? Where are you taking her?" Parker says, his frantic voice behind me.

When I'm finally lifted from the ground, tiny pebbles dot along my cheek and clothing. My eyes are watering from whatever sharp element was jabbing into me while I was pinned down. Parker Aldren is held back by two men, thrashing at them as he tries to move out of their grasp.

"This wasn't part of the agreement, Onah," I hear him say, his breathing quick and shallow. But his sharp tone seems to be lost on the woman. Her grin is vicious as she looks at my arms tied behind me, and back to Parker.

"You had no agreement to her welfare, Aldren. You had to simply get her here. You've done that. Congratulations— you're off the hook. Feel free to go retrieve your mother. I am so disappointed I won't get the chance to meet her first. Perhaps another time," the older lady says, smirking in his direction. His mother? What does this have to do with his mother? Retrieve her from where?

Something ghostly crosses his face at Onah's revelation, but it's quickly huffed out. "Lena. Lena. I'm so sorry. I had no idea. Please believe me," he tells me, shaking his head. His eyes plead with me. *Believe me. Please believe me*, they say, over and over, glistening as they stare right at me.

The gruff man holding me pushes me forward, and I trip on the rocks underneath me, landing down hard as they slice into both of my knees. A drop of blood falls down one leg, a sharp sting radiating through the wound. But there's no time to assess the damage, and no one caring enough to help me. No one free to do so anyway.

"Be careful with her. She'll walk if you ask her to!" Parker yells at the man, his words hitting my back as we retreat down another path.

I twist my body, trying to catch any glimpse of him. My gaze lands on his face—his dark hair pulling free of its tie, a few strands falling to his shoulders, and those dark eyes staring straight at me. Onah grabs my arm, shutting me between her and the man pushing me forward.

"Let's see how your soft feet fair without your lovesick bodyguard watching your back," she says, spit dripping from her maleficent smirk. Lovesick? Too much is happening around me to try and make sense of her words. "It seems you can take a man out of the Guard, but you can't take the Guard out of the man." Her gaze flicks back to Parker, his face now turned to hardened stone at her words.

After a few more steps I strain around again, turning my head to get one more glimpse of him. He struggles with the two men, attempting again to get past them. "Lena! Lena!" he screams after me.

The last thing I see is a fist colliding against his jaw and another to his stomach, sending a bloodied Parker hard to the ground.

34

ROAN

E'VE SAID NOTHING ALL day, carefully timing our breaths to keep from tiring ourselves too early.

The soft ground has laid our position for all to see, our steps clearly visible. We run to keep ahead of Jaren and his unearthly ability to track us. Out of pure exhaustion and fear of being heard, we move in silence. Clouds intersperse with the sun overhead, and I can't decide if rain will yet again become our savior today and cover our footprints.

Ari holds up a hand, signaling a few moments of rest. I turn in all directions, searching for anything out of place and anywhere we can sit that doesn't expose us to our enemies. We move to a cluster of large bushes that hide us from the open countryside as we catch our breath. Farms intersperse the land— some beginning to sprout little tiny seedlings, some sporting larger plants already blooming to make way for their fruit, and others untouched and bare.

All my senses are honed to spot Jaren or his companions, taking in the beauty around me in the process. Someone has spent years tilling this land, the rows of symmetrical greens and their colorful buds winding through the rolling hills. I've never seen mountains cultivated in this way, and its brilliance isn't lost on me. Oddly enough we've crossed paths with no one, as if these farms till, weed, and harvest themselves.

"What's the plan for getting through Thenstra's gates?" she asks me, the first words spoken today. Her voice is soft as we continue to search the horizon, neither willing to get too comfortable.

We have to be getting close, within a day at least. I've never been this far north, but I've studied plenty of maps. Ari braces her arms against her legs, leaning over as she waits for my answer.

"My plan is a work in progress," I say, earning a scowl from the girl.

"Wonderful. We're running for our lives without any direction," she says under her breath, but loud enough so I can hear. I don't blame her irritation, even directed at me.

"I've been in worse situations. I can't think of any right now, but I'm sure I have." My words don't bring a smile to her face, but her irritation seeps away. It's a small win, but I welcome it.

I take the lead from here. We are trying to outrun horses and well supplied men while we have no food, no water, and a perfect trail left behind us. We are sitting ducks here in the open. Jaren won't have any trouble picking us off if we let our guard down, even for a moment.

The sun is swallowed by the clouds late in the morning, and I take my first deep breath all day. I'm still damp from the last storm, but I've never prayed for rain harder than I do now.

A large cliff looms before us, the sight most unwelcome. It will take at least a full day, maybe more, to walk around it. Time we don't have. The mountain slopes sharply to a valley far below, the forest returning in the distance. If we can make it there, we will finally be out of the wide open spaces of the farmland.

"What now?" Ari asks next to me, releasing the words in a deep exhale, voicing both our thoughts. We stare at the vast canyon stretching as far as we can see. She walks away, moving to the side of the cliff, looking below at the sheer drop. "There's something here," she says before scooting to the side, her body dropping below the edge.

"Ari!" I yell after her, realizing too late that I may have just given away our position.

Her head pops up as I run over to the drop, and I bend down to pull her back to safety. She puts a finger to her lips, her head instantly snapping toward me when she comes into view. It looks as though she's floating against the mountain, and I can't help my open jaw as I gawk at the impossibleness of what I'm looking at. "There's some kind of road here, dug into the side. It looks like an old smuggler's path."

I'm still stunned as I look over the edge to see her feet resting on firm ground. Completely hidden from view lays a path perfectly carved into the side of the cliff, exposed only if you're standing right above it.

I turn around, scouting the area once more before I duck below the lip of land. This route should shave off at least half of the time it would have taken us to go around, and I can't help but pray Jaren and whoever else doesn't find it. It may finally give us a cushion of time so we can stop looking over our shoulders.

We move carefully, the trail criss-crossing back and forth on itself as the path slopes down. After a time, my stomach growls loud enough that I hear a tiny laugh bubble from behind me.

I turn my head, somehow grimacing and smiling at the same time. "I can't remember the last time I was this hungry."

"Go spend some time in the East Village. You'll get used to that feeling quickly." She says it with meaning, but I don't get the feeling she's admonishing me more than just telling me truths that I refused to acknowledge before now.

"Is that where you grew up?" I ask her, listening intently for her reply.

But before she can give one, the ground gives way underneath me.

I'm falling down the sodden mountainside as rocks, stray twigs, and branches cut through my shirt and pants, leaving cold, bloody streaks in their wake. Sharp stings ping across me from every direction.

Everything passes in a blur as I try to dig my fingers into the slick ground, grabbing at anything that might stop me. It's too steep and slippery to find anything of substance that will stop me completely. The best I can find will only slow me down for a fraction of time before I pick up momentum again.

Something gritty and bitter flicks into my mouth, and I frantically spit the thickness away. My eyes sting as I try to keep them open, looking for anything to hold on to, my vision murky as I try to wipe them free of muck. I slide down further and further, my body tumbling in every direction, my limbs aching as I fight to stay above the plunging mountainside.

It seems like hours before I begin to slow, but it couldn't have been more than a few, terrorizing seconds. Blood now steadily streams down my face. The red pops from underneath the layers of mud coating my body as I try to assess the damage. The pain of each fresh cut rings across my skin until I finally lie still. My mind is scattered, trying to make sense of what just happened.

I'm buried under inches of mud, the heaviness closing in around me. I attempt to move my hands, feeling each finger wiggle in response. As I look around, checking my neck for any injuries, I see only a giant brown pile with me as its centerpiece. Everything seems to blend into this surrounding brown abyss. I will myself to roll over, to uncover myself from the heaviness of the mountainside, to plant my feet into the ground and stand. But nothing happens. My legs refuse to comply.

My heartbeat stutters when I don't move. Is it the weight of being partially buried? Am I deeper than I realize? I try to sit up, but my head doubles back, feeling as if I will wretch all over myself.

When my vision clears back into one steady stream, I maneuver the only limbs that will answer me. I plant a hand firmly into the soft ground, pushing with all the strength I have, lifting my torso high enough that my body should pull free alongside it. My weight begins to shift, but there's no time for celebration. An intense pain shoots up my leg and through my side. Nothing but black greets me as my vision threatens to swim into nothingness.

I lie still, trying to keep my breathing in control. My hands fumble for the sword at my side. Maybe I can use it to give me the boost I need to get my feet underneath me again. But my grip comes back empty. Somewhere along the fall, it must have broken away from my side.

Ari. Ari? I search my surroundings, doing my best to keep my panic at bay. Did she fall? Is she ok? Nothing but walls of dirt and rock interspersed with what must be plants and tree roots dot through the mud. My arms reach out for one to hopefully pull myself free and unbury my legs, but it breaks almost immediately.

I try to yell, to see if she's hurt. But a deep inhale sends my side into agony once again. Something is broken, maybe a couple ribs. But a broken rib doesn't explain the unbearable torment in my leg, and my inability to stand or move. I search through the mud and debris with my limited mobility, turning only my head as I scan the area.

There's no sign of Ari. No sign of life anywhere except the starlings flying above me. I stare at them intently, noting their movements and patterns as they weave through the air— so graceful, so free. Is this how Evander felt right before he died?

Is this my end?

My focus snaps back. No. I'm not going to die today. I look down, my entire body blended perfectly with the endless brown. Exhaustion pours over me, threatening to pull my mind away from me.

Ari. I need to see if she's ok, to help her. I must get to Lena. I need to save her.

I'll give myself a few moments to rest my eyes, to let my body build back its energy. And then... then—

The world goes black.

35

ARI

I LOOK UP TO nothing, a gaping hole in front of me as if a giant hand came and scraped away the mountainside.

"Roan!" I yell, but it comes out more like a mangled cry. The path is completely gone. Just— gone. My legs are paralyzed for a single heartbeat before truth crashes into me. The soft ground. The rain. *Mudslide.*

I lean over the edge, frantically searching. My thoughts are screaming to stay away. Where I stand could fall away at any moment. But the terrified churning in my gut turns into tunneled focus, compelling me forward. Nothing but brown muck greets me as I look down.

I can't see him.

My eyes search wildly for a path, any way safely down to find Roan, but none appear. The gap is too wide for me to jump, and if I go back the way I came it will take me at least a day to get down there. He might not have a day.

I don't know his condition, but from the buzzing I feel running through me I know he needs help, desperately. My resolve breaks through any sense of personal safety.

"This is stupid, Ari. This is beyond stupid," I say out loud before grabbing my dagger and gripping it firmly in my hand. I take one more breath before I stick my blade as hard as I can into the soft mountainside, and leap myself into the sloped gorge.

The knife does its work, slowing me down as I slide toward the bottom, but not enough to save me from the force of the debris in my path. Something hard slices through my skin as I plunge, rocks bruising into my soft flesh. I move quickly through the grime, slipping effortlessly down, down, down.

The grip on my knife begins to waver as my sweaty hand mixes with the slick muck, wedging themselves between my hand and its hilt. I dig my elbow and heels into the thick paste to give myself time to adjust my grip. The hill steepens, hurling me harder and faster to whatever awaits me at the bottom. Brown, brown, and more brown greets me, making it difficult to assess how much longer I have to go. A few trees come into view. *Almost there.*

A glint just ahead of me catches in my vision. On instinct I reach for it, grabbing hold of something long and sturdy. I slam it alongside my knife into the soft ground, twisting myself onto my stomach. Slowly, but surely, it finds traction and my speed eases. I pull it from the mud after I stop completely, swiping away the thick murkiness to see what lies beneath. Roan's sword.

I stand, every inch of me covered in mud. A few scrapes on my arms burn bright against the brown as I scan the damage around me. I'm atop a large, thick pile of mud, its edges thinning out into the forest until green pokes through in the distance.

"Roan!" I shout, my voice booming through the quiet space. Only a soft breeze and silence greet me.

Where are you, Roan? Scream. Wave your hands. Just show me where you are. My feet sink in with each step as I move to scavenge for my... friend? I don't really know what Roan is to me, but I suppose it's the least of my worries right now.

More nerves rip through me as I see large branches and small trees sticking out from the rubble. The probability of finding him whole and unharmed is zero, I realize. He could even be buried underneath the vast remains of the fallen mountain, and I may never find him. My breath hitches and my eyes suddenly feel heavy.

Mother would have liked him.

The thought bubbles through my mind, drifting away like a fallen leaf in the Rashan. But wait— it's *my* thought. My truth. I grab it back, the idea turning from phantom smoke to something corporeal as I wrap myself around it. I allow it to take hold in me. I let its truth give me the energy I need to lift my foot out of the sinking ground, its suctioning *squelch* hardly registering past the ringing in my ears. *Find Roan. Find Roan. Find Roan.*

I move around the scene, my heart racing as each step gives me more of nothing. *Must move faster. Must find Roan.* My breathing is quick and shallow, my head spinning as the brown melts together into one endless pile. Have I searched here already? I don't know. No landmarks exist in this hell to help me keep track. I get the spindly sensation that I'm going in circles, covering the same ground over and over. I let out a cry, its radiating howl echoing through the canyon cliffs that surround me.

Another noise flickers through the scene. A groan, a cough, a whimper— I'm not sure. I whip my head around, my feet fumbling through the muck as I follow the direction of the sound. My legs ache as I continue to slip around, falling and picking myself up every other step.

"Roan!" I yell. "Where are you?" I continue to scream his name, hoping to hear any kind of response. But nothing comes. As I take my next step, I trip, falling hard. My hands sting as they land against the gravelly mud, but a groan just behind me dissolves away the pain.

"Roan!" I yell, turning and coming up beside him. His stare is blank, focusing on the sky above. "Roan, talk to me. Roan?" It feels like I'm screaming, but hardly more than a whisper come out of me. "Where are you hurt?" I ask, not fully expecting an answer, but hoping. Carefully, I roam around to feel for broken bones, deep cuts, and anything sticking into him that he may have picked up from the momentum.

"Evander. I'm so sorry," he whispers as I continue my assessment.

"I'm Ari. Roan, can you see me?" I snap a finger to catch his attention, the sound getting muffled from my dirty fingers. But his eyes don't move in reflex to the noise.

"It's all my fault." Another whisper.

He must have hit his head. My thoughts want to explode with his rambling, but I direct myself to stay focused on his physical injuries.

When I get to his legs, blood is pooled underneath his right calf as I wipe away the thick coating of mud. The slurping sound makes me wince as I lift it from the ground. *Please don't be broken.* I roll up his pant leg. A deep, long gash runs from above his ankle to a few inches below his knee. It's bad, but as far as I can tell it's not broken. *Thank goodness.*

"Roan," I say his name again, snapping again until I see his eyes flicker. "Can you move your leg? Wiggle your toes?"

He opens his mouth, releasing a garbled noise. When nothing else happens, I take that as my answer. *No.*

"Roan, focus on my voice. Can you move your other leg?" I shake his left leg, hoping the movement will find its separation from the pain of the other. He begins to wiggle the leg, then bending it at the knee as if to stand.

"Woah, whoa, whoa. You have a nasty cut on one side. Let's try to sit up first, then we can assess standing up." I crawl to his side, grabbing an arm to assist him as he lifts his head off the ground, my other hand sliding easily around his neck with the assistance of the mud generously coating each of my fingers. He screams, muffling the sound with clenched teeth before falling back down to the ground, the movement tugging me forward as my grip still holds firm on his arm.

I lift his shirt. Another thick cut runs from his hip to his ribs. Both his leg and stomach need to be cleaned and stitched, the muck already infiltrating both wounds. "Ok. We need to get to the road. Find some help," I say matter-of-factly.

He's completely covered in mud. The white of his eyes and a few specks of dark hair are the only contrast to the brown. He mutters to himself, too softly and jumbled to make out any words.

I move behind him. "I'm going to lift you, and you're going to support yourself up with your arms. Can you do that, Roan?"

He nods, the first coherent gesture he's given. A painful grunt rings through the air as I adjust him, but it seems his arms are in fine condition as they snap into place.

"Good. Good," I say after assessing him again. "Do you feel dizzy?"

"Not... anymore." His breathy, pained answer confirms an injury to a rib or two. "I think... I'll live," he chokes out.

A smile erupts on my face. I'm so happy he spoke that I hardly register his words. I want to hug him, the relief pushing me toward him. But I refrain. I don't want to hurt him any more than he already is.

"Save your breath. You need to stand. I'm not strong enough to carry you out of here." I look at him sharply, hoping the realization of my words is sinking in. "It's going to hurt, but I need you to stand."

His groan of protest doesn't stop me from throwing his arm around my shoulder. "Open your eyes. If you're going to pass out I need to know it," I tell him. We rise together, my legs burning underneath his weight. His breathing is ragged, his face contorted with pain.

"Ok. Now we need to take a step. Roan, can you take a step for me?" He leans on his good leg, limping forward in jagged movements. "Good. Keep going. I know it hurts. But we have to get to the road."

"I'm comfortable here, aren't you?" He turns his head toward me, our noses almost touching as an exhausted head rests against my own. And I don't know how he has the strength, but he smiles at me.

"It would be more comfortable if I didn't have to carry you the whole way," I counter, matching his smile with a grin of my own. He moves some weight from my shoulder, taking labored steps with a clumsy, strained stride.

"Thank you," he croaks out as we walk.

"Nothing you wouldn't do for me," I reply, realizing that it's not a lie.

I pretend I didn't almost lose my mind, worrying I may never find him. Fear threads its bony fingers through me as I glance behind at what could have very easily been a tragedy.

"If my distance is correct, we could hit the main road before sunset. You need help— help I can't give without the right supplies. I know it's not what we planned, but we need to cut our losses and take our chances with Jaren's madness. Who knows. Maybe he hates warm beds and hot food, and will stick to the forest instead. Or even better, maybe he already gave up."

A low grunt escapes him, and I realize it's a laugh. He's trying to laugh. *That's a good sign.* "It would seem your mental state is at least mostly intact," I respond.

"Stop. Trying. To make. Me laugh," he replies through ragged breaths.

"It sounds like you may have some bruised or broken ribs. While my rudimentary skills could stitch you up with some lightly mangled scars in your future, I can't set or mend bones." My brows knit together. "We need to find a doctor."

"Let's just... focus... on getting to the road," he says. I nod, looping an arm around his waist.

"I saved your sword," I say, pointing a few feet away. The only response I get is another deep grunt. *I'll take that as a thank you.*

313

This stupid weapon has been a pointless relic these last few days, but I hold it now with a new found reverence, and lug the once beautifully polished weapon up and around my waist.

The road appears in the distance.

It takes most of the day like I thought, all but dragging a man twice my size through the forest. My joy is dampened by the angst of having to travel, who knows how much longer, completely exposed. We need cover, as quickly as possible. With Roan injured, the odds of walking away from a fight with both our lives still intact have dwindled dramatically.

I watch Roan grimace with every step he takes. He needs a bed. He needs food. His wounds need to be clean, stitched, and wrapped immediately. A bead of sweat trickles down the side of my face as we continue on our way.

A couple more hours following the wide, gravelly path, and an inn appears in the distance. It's a decent size, as if this part of Haythen was once a thriving hub for travelers coming and going from Thenstra. The promise of a hot meal and soft bed make me want to run. But exhaustion and depletion keep me methodically moving one foot in front of the other. Roan also perks up at the sight, giving my aching legs a reprieve from carrying so much of his weight.

The door swings open, slamming against the back wall as I push it with a little too much gusto. It gets the attention of the keeper at least. My muscles are huffing out their last breath as I get Roan safely inside, sitting him on a bench beside the nearest table.

"I need a couple rooms. Preferably in the back and away from the normal traffic. Some clean clothes, clean wrappings for a wound, and whatever food you have that's hot." My words come out so fast I have to mentally make sure I covered all the main points.

The man looks Roan up and down before turning to me and doing the same. Dried mud flecks across his floor as our clothes bend and crack with each change of position, leaving a trail of dirt in our path. "I only have one room open," he says, scowling at the mess we brought in.

Of course. A week ago I would've rolled my eyes and prodded the keeper for something more. The main room's tables are empty, but the smell of cooking food takes away my usual stubbornness, quieting the fire that would demand rooms I know to be available. But today I won't even mind sleeping on the floor. It's an upgrade from the hell we've endured this last week.

"Fine. Point me in the right direction," I say.

The man holds out his hand. "Pay. Up front."

I grimace, but as I take the first assessment of myself since we left this morning, it makes sense. I don't know if I would even recognize myself if I stared at my own, dirty reflection. When the keeper doesn't move I reach down across Roan. His eyes are closed, and it almost looks like he's asleep, his pale face as still as a morning pond.

I don't have time to be fumbling around with money. Infection may have already taken root within his deeper cuts. Doing my best to not disturb the worst of his injuries, I feel around his chest and pockets. Where would the Captain of the Royal Guard stash his money?

Roan winces as I dig around, but tries his best to hide the pain. "Can you at least give me a hint of where I need to be looking?" I whisper to him. He opens an eye long enough to look down.

"Is this how graceful you are with all your marks?" he asks.

I arch a brow. "Maybe you should use what little energy you have left to tell me where it is instead of making me guess."

His attempt at a laugh is pitiful, and I glare at him for trying. When he lifts his good leg, I don't hesitate as I pull off the boot, a few coins rolling onto the floor. I can't help but laugh, mostly from sheer relief that we didn't come this far to be turned out.

The keeper takes a look at the coins on the ground and begins shouting orders. "Shiren! Come take these two to their room." He turns back to us. "Do you want your food up there, or down here?"

"Our room," I say, gathering Roan from the bench. "But we need the washroom first."

"Aye. I can see that. Down the hall and to your right. Leave your clothes outside. They will be clean and dry by morning, and I'll rustle up some temporary clothes for tonight."

Roan seems like he's drifted off to sleep again. "We need to clean up before we rest so I can dress your cuts properly. Do you have the strength to take a bath?" I whisper in his ear. "If you need help—"

"I'm not so far gone that I need you to bathe me, Ari. Although, if you're offering..." He slits one eye open as he talks, a boyish grin crossing his lips. My eyes flit to those lips, the memory of them sending a shiver up my spine.

I snap myself back the minute I realize where my mind has taken me. Being wounded has made him bold, talking like we've known each other much longer than we actually have. I make a mental note to pummel him when he's feeling better. But I can't help the grin that crosses my face.

The warm water eases the last few day's aches and pains. The bath is clean, as if we are the first patrons of the day. I don't complain. If the promise of real food weren't waiting for me upstairs in our room, and Roan didn't need to be stitched up, and if a flurry of madmen weren't trying to kill us, I would stay here all day.

My elbows are burned from the friction of sliding down the mud, and they sting as they dip below the water. I take a deep breath before submerging my head. Once I'm under, I release a scream that resembles more of something you'd hear from an animal than a girl. Bubbles rise through the liquid, the water muffling the sound just as I wished. And when I surface again, my shoulders sag, and the weight of my body floats on the surface.

I let my mind drift away, not allowing thoughts of Reynauld, Silas, Tamen, or Jaren push me back under the surface. I will have to let them back in, eventually. I will have to become the thief again once I leave this water. Strategizing our way into Thenstra. Healing Roan. Finding and saving the princess. Figuring out the wretched plan these men have in store for her and Felshan, and effectively putting an end to it.

But for now, I let myself nestle into the support of the warmth that seeps into me.

Days of dirt and grime rinse from my hair and body, leaving the bath water a murky brown of floating leaves and swirling dirt. My stomach grumbles, and the fragrance of steeped broth and fresh bread makes the hollowness more painful.

I finally rise, drying myself and dressing in the temporary clothes the keeper dredged up for me. Shiren, the keeper's assistant and maid, is waiting for us outside. She helps me get Roan up the stairs and in the bed. I'm so grateful for the extra help I could hug her. When my body tenses to move as if I might, I take a step back instead.

Roan drifts in and out of sleep as I lift his shirt and pant leg to examine his wounds. His clean body takes me back to the first night we met, the moonlight rippling down his dark hair and reflecting off his skin.

"What happened to you two?" Shiren asks, an innocence to her demeanor. I blush as I notice her attention on me, as if she can read every thought that just rolled through my mind. But I hide it well, turning to pull the sheets up and over a now sleeping Roan.

"A lot." All I want to do is lie down and sleep. A simple bed, chair, and table are laid out across the space, as well as clean dressings, two bowls of food, and an extra blanket that are waiting for me atop the table. My mouth waters instantly.

"A lot doesn't even begin to cover it," Roan mumbles, startling me. I thought for sure he'd fallen asleep.

"Do any doctors come around here?" I ask her, curling my leg beneath me as I sit down on the edge of the bed.

"Um. Not really. I've seen one or two pass through, but none live close by. The nearest one would be the outskirts of the capital," the girl says.

"Thenstra?" It's more a statement than a question as I breathe the word.

"Yes. Thenstra. It's about a day's ride from here." We are close, closer than I dared hope before now.

"But the gates are closed," I say, and she easily picks up on my questioning tone.

"Aye. The gates are closed, but—" Shiren looks at me, then down to Roan's stomach, her brows kissing as she again takes in his condition. "—I'm sure we can figure it out," she quietly finishes, looking around as if someone else may have been listening.

My stomach leaps, and Roan coughs to hide his surprise of our rare good luck. She knows something. I busy myself assessing Roan's stomach, moving to his leg to do the same. It takes every ounce of self-control I possess not to demand Shiren tell us everything she knows.

Usually slow and steady is my expertise, getting to revel in each small moment of victory as my mark hands me everything I need— whether it be goods, information, or even people. But I feel a hurriedness, needing to uncover the mystery not just for the princess, but for my friend. Roan needs a doctor's help.

My friend. Yes, I suppose the captain is my friend. Part of me wants to analyze every moment to see when the shift began. To prevent this kind of behavior in the future. And the other part can't help but go back to my realization back in that forsaken pile of mud— Mother would have liked him. A warmth fills me at her memory. And for the first time, pain doesn't accompany it.

I continue my assessment. Roan's wounds do look more aggravated than before, but it's no longer seeping blood or filled with mud. I don't know if we got to them in time, but all I can do now is clean it more thoroughly and close it up. "I need a needle and suture material. Do you have any?"

"Aye. I think we have some down in the kitchen." Shiren's face goes pale as she inches closer, looking at Roan's injuries for a third time.

"Can you also bring a fresh pitcher of water, and maybe a cup of wine or ale?" She nods her head, and returns a few minutes later.

It takes most of the evening, but Shiren and I finish stitching and dressing his wounds. The alcohol knocked Roan out halfway through, easing the panic I felt at every wince and twinge he made in the process.

"Now we just wait and hope it's enough," I whisper, more to myself than to anyone. Shiren wipes her hands on her skirt as she stands up and walks to the door.

"Thank you." I'm not even sure thank you is enough to express how grateful I am for her help. It would have taken me well into the night to finish up by myself, and I realize I have no extra compensation to give her. My words will have to do.

"You're welcome," she replies, dipping her head. My heart inexplicably warms. I think I could be friends with her, if I wanted. A sweet girl on the border of Felshan and Thenstra. If by some wayward chance we happened to grow up in the same place and in different circumstances. She walks out the door, carefully clicking it closed.

I turn back to Roan. His chest rises and falls evenly, and a bit of relief courses through me. Seeing him laying among the mud, unable to move. It was more difficult than I want to admit.

A small moment tugs at my memory—he had called me Evander. I realize he may not have been fully aware of what he was saying, but it was strange.

Evander is the name of the dead prince. He told me he grew up at the palace and was good friends with the boy before he died, so it would make sense. Maybe it was nothing. I make a mental note to ask him about it later. There will be plenty of time as we trek to Thenstra.

I sway on my feet, the heavy weight of exhaustion finally breaking through.

His bowl of stew lies half eaten next to him, and I move it to the floor. I hope more than anything that we cleaned the wounds in time. His face is peaceful as he sleeps, and I pray that the pallor of his skin is simply from the little food we've had these last few days. Sleep does wonders, but I don't know if one night's sleep will be enough for Roan to be able to make it to Thenstra tomorrow.

My heart sinks. We shouldn' risk staying here another day.

I stretch out on the floor, barely covering myself with a blanket before I let my fatigue finally spill over me. Roan's even breathing fills the quiet room. The work is done for now, and my eyelids gently drift closed.

Oddly enough, it's Reynauld's beady eyes, his velvet jacket, slick hair, and bony fingers digging into my arm that cross my thoughts before sleep claims me.

36

ROAN

I WAKE TO A sharp pain in my side, and reality pounds back into me as I orient myself from sleep.

How long have I been out? And why in the Four Kingdoms is it so hot in here? Sweat gathers at my hairline and drips down my face. I move to pull the blankets off of me when a deep burning obscures my vision. Confusion slowly gives way to memory. Mud. Ground. Walking. Blood. Bed. Ari. *Where is Ari?*

Nausea roils through me as more pain shoots across my body. I lean as far over the bed as I can without aggravating the already painful tug, just in case the meager contents of my stomach decide to make a second appearance. *Deep breaths. Deep breaths.*

I lie my head back down on the pillow as more sweat trickles down my face. I turn to the pain in my side, gently lifting my shirt to see how Ari did, remembering her careful concentration as she worked to close the wounds scattering across me. A mostly neat row of stitches runs from just above my hip up to the end of my first rib. A small tremor runs through me at the memory of her hands on my skin.

As I attempt to sit up and check my leg, another wave of dizziness forces me back down. *Lena. Lena. I need to find Lena. And Ari, where's Ari?* I need to get up. I need to get out of this bed. But the more I try, the worse I feel. Heavy exhaustion ripples through me the longer I'm awake. However long I slept it wasn't enough.

I drift in and out of consciousness, the room full of light, and a moment later, darkness. A weight pulls down one side of the bed, but I haven't the strength to look and see what is causing it.

As my eyes drift open again, sunshine bounces off the earthy hues of wood within the space. I try to feel at my stomach, the pain still sharply evident, but slightly less severe.

"Oh good grief Roan, sit still. I leave you for five minutes and come back to you clawing at your stitches." Ari is standing over me. I open my mouth to speak, but no matter how hard I try I just can't form the right sounds together.

A swollen tongue and pounding headache compels me to keep going, determined to make sense of what I need. But she already knows. Slipping an arm behind my neck, Ari tips my head forward until cool liquid touches my lips. The water feels like life in the middle of carnage, soothing my dry throat as I gulp it down as fast as my weakened body will allow.

"You should try to sleep more," she says, laying me back down and pulling her arm from behind me. I groan in protest, not sure if it's because I want more water or because I want to feel her close to me again. Part of me is glad that my body won't form the words my mind wants to say. My lucid state would give life to many private thoughts I swore to keep to myself for now.

"As far as I can tell, you don't have any infection. After two days, the likelihood of your wounds festering drops dramatically. We are in the clear. I need you to rest so we can leave as soon as possible. Not just for the princess, but staying in one place for too long increases our chances of Jaren finding us again," she tells me.

Two days. Two days? I've been asleep for two days?

"I don't want to put these people in danger. Shiren and John have been kind to us, keeping us off the books and in the farthest room. I'm trying to procure a horse so you can ride the rest of the way to Thenstra. It's only about a day's ride from here. With a horse I think we can make it one piece without to much risk of running into trouble."

As she talks I can't help but stare at her. I understand what she's saying, but— the way her mouth moves to form each word, her hair swaying as she takes a step, her features shifting with her thoughts.

She's so beautiful. I don't know why I haven't told her yet.

Before I have a conscious desire to do so, my thumb brushes her jaw, the final yellowing of her bruise there fading away. In the same motion I trace my fingers over a long but superficial cut down the side of her neck. My voice may not work, but it looks as if my hands do. She stops talking when she feels my hand skim across her face, swallowing whatever words were about to come next. I find her hand, threading my fingers through her own.

For the first time in ages, I don't feel burdened with the weight of my fallen friend and all the things he was supposed to be. I don't feel that I have to be all of those things for him anymore. His memory can live on through everyone's joy, living in a way that he would want us to, so we could be happy. That is how we honor him.

Maybe I can finally just be Roan Montgomery. Maybe I can go home and see my family, and help my brother and sisters take over the run and trade of Port Riga, like was planned before Evander died.

My inhibitions seem to have left alongside with my resolve to be Captain Montgomery, betrothed to Princess Adalena, soon-to-be king consort of Felshan. My eyes lock with Ari's, and more than anything in this moment I want to be next to her, touching her, running my fingers through her soft hair, pulling her face to reach my own.

She looks at me, her gaze shifting to my mouth, and back up to meet my eyes. My rogue arm knows exactly what I want it to do before I think it, and I don't try and stop myself as I untangle my fingers from her own, sliding up her arm before gripping her tightly and pulling her down to me.

Up until now, part of me thought that maybe I was simply dreaming. But feeling her underneath my hand, feeling her warm, soft skin, the realness brings my mind into sharp focus.

Half of me is screaming that I will ruin everything, I will hurt people I love if I let myself kiss her again. But I don't care. It feels like I was meant to be here, this single moment in time that was meant to change everything. My body may be weak and in pain, but I've never felt so strong and alive. I don't know what is happening to me, but I like it. I want more of it.

Gone is Captain Montgomery, and in his place is a man who desperately wants to love and to be loved. To live a life of his choosing. To feel the lips of the thief who threw him on his back, the girl who busted his lip at the stables, and the woman who saved his life from the mudslide that was ready to swallow him whole.

My sentiment from a few days ago flows through me again. Lena and I do not love each other. No part of me wants Lena to hurt. But I'm not sure she wants to be tied to me either. I will get her home safely, of that I'm certain. But after that, my future feels unsure, unknown, and unplanned.

Her eyes search earnestly through my own as she comes in closer.

"I don't want to hurt you," she whispers, her breath mingling with my own.

"I would feel any amount of pain if meant being close to you." The words are out before I even realize I've finally put words together. My fingers thread behind her neck and through her hair as she pauses just above me, an arm on either side of my shoulders. We stare at each other, the silence deafening as we both consider the words neither of us has spoken, and the future that has yet to be written.

A knock at the door sounds through the small space. Ari instantly sits back up, her arms in her lap, a pinkness rising to her cheeks.

"Sorry to bother you," Shiren says from behind the door. "May I come in?"

"Yes, of course." Ari stands to open the door, and my shoulders sag against the bed.

"Hello," she greets us. "Dinner is almost ready. Roasted venison, root vegetables, and fresh bread. I wasn't sure if Roan was awake and wanted—" her eyes scan the room before landing on me, her questioned answered. "I will bring some up right away," she finishes, the door closing quietly behind her.

"Help me sit up," I say, holding up my hand.

Ari grasps it with her own and slowly helps me rise as she says, "Take it easy. You've been down for a while. Your body will need some time to adjust." And of course, she was right. My vision swirls, black dots poking around the edges as a brief wave of nausea rolls through me. "Take deep breaths, in and out, in and out." She copies the motion with her breathing, the air swooshing past me with every exhale, and I try to follow her rhythm.

We scarf down our food, unashamed of any ill manners in the process. "I'm going to go find Shiren. She's helping me finalize our plans to leave tomorrow. Get some rest while I'm gone, and stop trying to escape your bed." A coy smile tugs at the corners of her lips. She leans down, placing a unexpected kiss to my cheek.

I can't help but stare after her as she walks away.

37

ARI

"**T**HERE IS A WAY," Shiren tells me.

John, the innkeeper, looks up at her words. "Stop. You're going to get these people killed, girl." A look passes between them, a silent conversation that I'm not privy to. We stand around the center counter in the kitchen as we talk, a few smudges of flour now speckling across my pants, courtesy of leaning in a little too close to the structure.

"You've heard their story, John. At least this will give them a chance," the girl replies. I shared what I could, what truths were mine to share at least. Enough to please Marg's request, and help this maid and innkeeper see the direness of our situation. Anything to prod them to assist us into Thenstra, the last block in our way of the princess.

The last block I *hoped* was in our way at least.

"There's a passage up the mountain. Horses can't make the journey. You'll have to walk the last part on foot," Shiren tells me.

John is visibly uncomfortable, running his hands down the side of his face and through his quite lengthy beard. "If you are caught and you mention this place, Shiren or myself, I will personally be your end." There's no offense in his words, only truth. Shiren isn't his daughter, but there's a love there. A respect. I nod to signal my understanding.

"I will map it out for you." Shiren proceeds to draw the inn and surrounding mountains, including as much detail as she can to help catch familiarity with the area for someone who has never before set foot there. She explains the directions— what to look out for, where to turn, how long each element is expected it to take, and what to do if we run into anyone else.

"Hide if you can. If you're spotted, let them know you're with..." She looks around, taking a deep inhale before continuing, as if what she's about to say will damn her. "Let them know you're with Sutter." John hisses at the name, but she continues as if she doesn't hear the sound. "If they still approach you, or seem hostile, get ready to fight for your life. They won't ask you questions. They will just attack"

"I understand," I tell her. "Thank you." It's a rare thing for me to say, but I can't help but express my gratitude again. "You don't know how much good you've done here." I let out a breath I didn't realize I was holding. Shiren's kindness is more than I could have hoped for.

She smiles gently, her youthfulness showing through it.

I look back to the drawing, trying to make sense of everything she's written. She does her best to explain and reiterates everything on her makeshift map, but I can only pray I remember it all.

"We will be leaving tomorrow," I tell Shiren and John. I fidget with my sleeve a moment, toying with the rolled up corner. Collectively their gazes turn to me.

"That boy can hardly sit up let alone walk," John exclaims, the lines on his forehead deepening.

I meet his eyes, shifting the weight on my feet as I do. "I know. It will be immensely difficult for him. But we've already stayed here too long. And the longer we stay, the longer not only our lives are at risk, but yours as well.

You've helped us more than I could have ever hoped receive. And now we must return the favor."

Of course it's a horrible idea, taking Roan away in his condition. But I know— I know it's what he would choose if I asked him. I could see it in his eyes when I told him how long he'd slept. We've been here two days too long.

They are reluctant, but truth always wins. Neither of them nod their understanding, but they don't press it any further. I don't like it any more than they do, but we are sitting ducks here, waiting for the hunter to bury his arrow in our heart. John marches out of the kitchen. Shiren's eyes droop down as she looks to me, leaving a soft smile before she follows after him.

Thankfully Roan is asleep when I head back to our room. It would be wise to let him rest and recover here for at least another week, maybe even two or three before venturing out. But we just don't have the luxury of time on our side. Jaren and his men could find us at any moment, and Princess Adalena gets further from our grasp with each passing breath.

A headache begins to form, and I do my best to rub it out. Eventually I decide that sleep may be the only cure. A few blankets and a pillow lie at my feet. I prop the pillow against the bed, my head resting against the mattress so I can keep an eye on Roan.

I awake suddenly, startled. My senses spring to life, looking around the room for threats, waiting and listening intently. But I find nothing. It's quiet as night has fully descended upon the inn, the only sound coming from rustling trees and a few creaks from the settling structure.

After sufficiently searching the room, opening the door and assessing the hallway to be empty, I return to the bed, hoping by some miracle to fall back asleep. Maybe I can get a few more hours before the grueling day ahead.

I sit down, leaning back against the bed and the comfortable pillow wait-ing for me. As I adjust my position, two eyes stare at me from a few feet away. Roan is awake, his blue gaze fixed intently on my face.

Worried, I ask, "Are you in pain?"

"A little. But I'll live," he breathes out. His brows are pulled together, his lips a hard line, the painful inhale of each breath obvious in his tense form.

"I can get you something to help if you need it."

I move from my makeshift bed over to the table, my feet nimble as I try not to make the floorboards beneath me quiver and moan. My hand reaches for a small bag, dumping its contents of herbs into a small cup of water. Shiren uses them to ease headaches, from what she told me, harvested from her small garden out back. The girl gave some to me to help Roan recover more easily, easing his pain in whatever way it could.

I hand the cup to Roan, looping my arm behind his neck to elevate him and avoid the medicinal liquid from spilling down his face and neck. He drinks hastily, like he hasn't had water all day, his eyes leaving mine for only a moment as he gulps down the cup's contents.

He finishes, and I gently lay him back down. His eyes find mine again, and suddenly I'm very aware of just how close we are. My body is lying flush next to his on the bed, the natural heat from him mingling with my own. Awkwardness fills me as I see him continue to stare at me, a depth to his gaze that feels foreign and vulnerable.

The lack of confidence I felt earlier staring at Shiren's map created a chasm in my shield, a hole that I wish I could rebuild in this moment to save me from the strangeness I feel at our proximity, and the eyes that are trying to tell me more than I'm ready to hear.

"You don't feel as warm tonight," I mumble, my gaze wandering any-where but to his own.

"I feel much better. Other than the burning in my side that comes every time I breathe, or move." There's a bit of mirth in his reply, and I can't help but feel relieved that his wit is alive. Hopefully, his strength will build quicker than I anticipated.

"We will leave first thing in the morning. I know you won't be nearly well enough as would be ideal for such a journey, but we can't risk being found in the state we are in. I think it's wise we move on as soon as possible."

"I agree." His voice is husky, a mix of tiredness and pain.

"Shiren, the girl who's been helping us, drew me a map. There are some tunnels that naturally carve through the mountains. They will get us into Thenstra undetected." What I don't tell him is that others use those tunnels. And from what Shiren mentioned, they won't be friendly to unfamiliar faces.

Roan's eyes flutter open and closed again, as if it takes great effort to keep them open. "How did you convince her to give us the information?"

I stay silent, again unwilling to meet his gaze. Not because I'm afraid of him, but because I don't know if bringing Shiren and John into the mix was a good idea. They could get hurt, or punished for handing over this information.

His eyes go wide. "You told her of Lena?"

"No, of course not. I'm not that stupid." I plant my feet firmly beneath me, getting ready to push myself off the bed if need be.

We've had plenty of moments where explaining our true purpose could have saved us time and pain. Tess and Liam cross my mind. But still, we kept our intentions close to the vest, just as Marg asked. Does he really think I would blow that now? And even if I did, I wouldn't do it lightly.

I keep my voice firm. "But I did explain that we were searching for someone, that retrieving this person was of the utmost importance, and it was to be kept a secret. That no one was to know, and I may never be able to tell her who we are looking for. I did tell her of Jaren. The danger all of us are in the longer we stay here. She understood, and she wanted to help."

His eyes closed as I spoke. He contemplates what I tell him for so long, I fear he may have fallen back asleep. "Roan?"

A deep exhale escapes his lips, relaxing my stiffened shoulders. "Tell Shiren thank you." He is calm as he says it and my face softens.

"I did." The captain only nods. "Do you think Otto and Aiden are alright?" I ask, the memory of their parting tugging in my mind, while I also try to change the subject.

"Well, if I know them like I think I do, they are fine. If things go in our favor, we should meet up with them soon. Who knows. Maybe they found Lena and are already headed back to Turin." It's a far stretch, and we both know it. But it doesn't hurt to dream I suppose.

He lays his head back against his pillows before I realize my arm is still around him. I'm sure he's exhausted, and tonight more than ever he needs a good night's rest. I move to pull out my arm, but he reaches up to stop me. My eyes focus on his, alert at his touch.

We stare at each other in silence, the ticking moment spent trying to read what the other isn't saying, picking up where we left off before Shiren knocked at our door earlier.

"Don't go," he whispers, his arm reaching around my waist. Roan's other hand releases its grip from my arm, his eyes dropping to my lips as he traces another small cut on my cheek.

He keeps staring at the bruise on my jaw, now almost completely healed. "Does it hurt anymore?" he asks me.

"No." I give a gentle grin, but his brows stay furrowed. I thought I saw guilt pass through his eyes in the previous days when I would catch him staring at the blooming purple and blue on my face. Now, being so close, the look is unmistakable.

"It wasn't your fault, Roan." His eyes move to the superficial cuts dotting my face and neck.

He continues tracing the line of my jaw, back and forth. "If I had gotten there sooner..."

"This isn't the first time I've ever been hit. In fact, it's probably a mild version of things I've endured. Don't blame yourself. I shouldn't have let him pin me down. If anything, it was a good reminder to always be on top." A flush rushes to my cheeks, and I hope he understood my real meaning. On top while in a fight, not... not anything else.

I'm still flustered when he opens his mouth to speak again. "What have you endured, Ari? Will you tell me?" His words are genuine, and their softness gets caught in my chest.

Part of me wants to tell him everything. The other wants to clamp my mouth shut, run out the door, and never return.

He must sense the war in me, because he says, "You don't have to tell me if it's uncomfortable. I just— I can see in your eyes that there is pain you don't talk about. Things from your past that you want to keep hidden. I recognize it because... because so do I. Things I want to forget, things I wish so badly I could change." He adjusts himself in the bed to face me fully, clenching his teeth from the pain of the movement. The smallest flinch is the only indication of the discomfort that is surely burning through him.

Or maybe something else is burning through him, because when his eyes meet mine again, it's not misery that I see. His hand cups my face as he leans forward, resting his forehead against mine.

Every instinct is telling me to move away. But I don't listen. I don't want to leave the warmth of his body against mine, his breath on my face, and the safety of his arm around me. I can't remember the last time I felt so comfortable besides the last time his arms were around me.

I pull away just enough to catch his gaze. "My mother died." Something catches in my throat. I've never told anyone this. Never voiced this out loud to a single person. I told Marg that my mother was gone, but not about her death.

I hesitate a moment, closing my eyes and taking a deep breath. He doesn't push me, doesn't try to force my words, only sits quietly as I try and make up my mind. His finger twirls through my hair before running coolly down my neck. The motion is so soothing that I almost gasp in relief as his other fingers join, kneading down my tense muscles from my neck to my shoulder.

"My mother was a seamstress," I whisper, clearing my throat before I continue. "One of the best in the city. I would help her when I could, and she would teach me. I also did odd jobs here and there to bring in some extra money. Shine shoes, scale fish."

"Shave beards," he adds, and I can't help but smile.

But that smile quickly fades as I go on. "I was twelve when the prince died, and it was like work had dried up overnight. We went from three meals a day with extra money for a small treat or trinket every now and then, even helping those around us who needed it, to starving in less than a week's time. It was like all joy and happiness had been sucked out of Turin. We would do anything we could for a few coins to buy food, but often we found ourselves going to sleep hungry." I rub my stomach, the hollow memory returning as if it were only yesterday.

"My mother was so optimistic, talking about how tomorrow we would have full bellies and find a piece of cake to share. But I knew. I knew what tomorrow would hold." The emotion I thought would rise in me as I relieved these moments is absent, a shell of nothingness greeting me instead. "I walked past a table at market, beautiful apples lining every inch. I just reached out. I reached out and took one, quickly hiding it in my pocket. My heart was beating so fast. I was sure someone had seen, would catch me. But no one did." Roan continues the trailing of his fingers, now twisting down the back of my arm, patiently waiting as my story unfolds.

"I was really good at it, stealing. I came close to getting caught once or twice. But I analyzed what I had done wrong, and righted it the next time. It was like I was a shadow in the sunlight; nobody could see what I was doing.

And when I would come home, Mother would be so upset. She would tell me we would find another way. But we both knew. We both knew there was no other way. We were starving, and short of my mother selling herself on the street, we had no options."

I take a deep breath, closing my eyes as I prepare for what comes next. Roan winds his fingers through my own, gently squeezing my hand. "My luck ran out one day. I don't know how they saw me," I shake my head, still in disbelief, "and within minutes of returning home, there was a knock at the door. There were three guards standing there." Roan stiffens, his eyes dimming as my words sink in.

"They said goods had been stolen from the market, and they saw the thief run into our home. They wanted to search it. My mother knew. She knew it was me, and I had been caught. There was no hesitation as she told them it had been her." I still remember when her wide eyes turned soft, the tiniest smile turned up her lips as she looked at me.

"They asked for payment. But they knew we had none. They dragged her from our home. I screamed that it wasn't her. I told them she had been home all day. That I had been the one to take the food. But it didn't matter. They took her anyway. She didn't kick, she didn't fight, she didn't try to get away. She just went with them. To protect me." My eyes glaze over as I remember her even steps and her lack of struggle.

"They threw her in prison. Telling me it would take a few days time to process her crimes and sentence her. But days turned into weeks, which turned into months. Winter came fast that year, and each time I would visit her, more of her life had seeped away with the oncoming cold."

I shudder, remembering the chill that spread to my bones that winter and the blue tinge to her lips whenever she tried to smile at me. "She was dying, I realized. She had been so young and full of life just a few months before, and here she was— her vitality dwindling right in front of me. They gave her a blanket no thicker than a piece of parchment to keep warm. I was fourteen at this point, just coming in to my body and its... feminine nature." I run my fingers through the air, mimicking the curves of a matured woman.

"The same guards that took her ran the prison, and the desire in their gazes as they looked upon me during my visits wasn't lost on me." Roan says nothing as I continue, his eyes now a shade of the deepest blue I've ever seen.

"I offered anything I could think of. Doing whatever I could to convince them to release her. But what they wanted, I just couldn't give." I pause now, a single tear escaping the corner of my eye. Roan wipes it away, his calloused thumb scraping across my cheek.

"She died two weeks later from exposure. And I hate myself every day that I couldn't bring myself to sell my body for her. If I could go back, I would have given myself every night for the next fifty years if it meant having her in my life." Another tear falls, but he doesn't wipe this one away. The man across from me looks like he might burst into flame if given the smallest bit of kindling.

I don't tell him that for the next couple months, they haunted the roads in search of me, as if my only protection was now buried in the ground. I don't tell him how I hardly ate, fearing that if I stepped one foot in the city they would find me. Luckily, Marg found me first. But by the time I had completed her training, they had disappeared. Not even a whiff of them or where they had gone.

"That's why you hated me, and the Guard," he says. I can't do anything but nod, not even looking him in the eyes. "Ari," his hand clenches into a fist, unclenching again before he continues. "Thank you for telling me."

I try to smile, to make it seem like it's not anything important. That somehow in the last five years I've gotten over it— the fear and grief. But he sees right through my charade.

"Don't. You don't need to pretend you're ok. No one would be ok after something like that, no matter how much time passes. I know it feels more brave to pretend, for the sake of others." He runs his hand through his dark hair. "Trust me. I know," he adds quietly. "But one of the most courageous things we can do is share the truth of our stories."

His face softens, his muscles finally unclenching as he takes a deep breath. A few moments pass as I fidget with a loose thread on the blanket. When I look back up at him he seems hesitant, as if there's more he wishes to say, or perhaps something he knows and isn't telling me.

My numbed mind starts to thaw. "What's wrong?"

His eyes dart to me, then to his lap. "You don't, by chance, know who the guards were who took her?" He asks his question so gently, not wanting to push too me too far. I shake my head. If I knew who they were or where they were, they'd already be dead. But I keep that last part to myself. "Do you remember what they look like?"

Now this I do know. How could I ever forget? The red and gold adorning their coats and swords. Their dark eyes. Their yellow smiles as I screamed. Their hair, different shades of brown— one the color of fresh soil, the other of silt, the other like the browned top of perfectly baked bread. "I do. But I've looked for them. For four long years I've looked for them. After Marg took me in... well... I never saw them after that." A laugh huffs out of me. "No matter how much I tried."

He doesn't push for the description, only nodding his head while he con-templates what I just told him. It didn't dawn on me until now that Roan might know them. He might have seen these men. He's been Captain for three years, and there's a four year training period. He would have been new into the barracks, but he might have seen them.

But I can sense my body has done too much today, just reliving that one moment has drained the last of my energy. Tomorrow. Perhaps tomorrow on the hike up the mountain I will ask him.

Roan looks like he wants to continue the conversation, like every nerve in his body is alert. Instead he lifts his hand, tracing my cheek before tucking a stray strand of hair behind my ear.

His touch feels electrifying, igniting a warmth deep in my stomach. I close my eyes, letting the comfort of that warmth fill the empty holes of my soul. His fingers trail down my arm, grabbing my hand. He turns my hand over, pulling it to his mouth, planting a soft kiss on the underside of my wrist. My breathing deepens as my heart flutters faster and faster.

Gently, he places my hand back on the bed, retreating his own. I don't think as I grab his hand back, rubbing both my hands in and around it before bringing it up to my cheek, leaning my face into its heated hollow. I've been alone for so long that I've forgotten how it feels to be cared for, for someone to want to know me, to want to help me. The dark of night and my raw emotions once again lower my shields. I glide my teeth over my bottom lip. His eyes catch the movement, his own breath deepening at the sight.

His strong arms wrap around my body, a gale swirling amidst his eyes as they focus on me. Roan's desire to be with me is as strong as my own for him. It took me longer to accept, to realize how I felt toward him. But now that it's here, our tether feels too strong to deny in this moment.

I adjust my position, leaning myself forward so he won't have to move, giving him access for more if he wants it. I want this to happen, but admitting it feels too much, even unspoken. I don't move the full distance, stopping just short of his lips. Roan senses my permission immediately. He tangles his hand in my hair as he moves it behind my neck. I follow his lead, scooting myself down on the bed so our eyes are level with each other. Gently, he pulls me in the rest of the way.

His scent fills me— leather, fresh rain, and subtle spice— cloves? I don't have time to finish my pondering before his lips reach my own.

Heat bursts through me. My free hand cups his face, finding its way across his cheek and into his dark hair. A low moan escapes him, reverberating through me as our lips continue to mold to one another's. He clings to me, his hands the only anchor as my soul wants to lift into the sky.

The kiss starts off soft, getting to know the curves and shape of each other once again. But as his hand moves down my arm and across my hip, a surge of desire sparks in me. I deepen the kiss, needing more of him as fast as I can find it. He returns my urgency, his hand pulling behind my thigh, guiding my leg over him until he's underneath me. I don't dare put my weight on him, and I make sure I won't cause him more pain before my mouth finds his again.

I've kissed before, but always random men I found at the local tavern, and nothing that ever meant anything. This feels so different. There's meaning behind our touch. Unspoken desire, longing, and... affection. Could we truly care for one another? The captain and the thief, the most unexpected of pairings. But a uniting that neither of us can deny as we get lost in each other.

We fit together. His lips dance over mine in a lilting, melodic rhythm, like a waltz under a starry sky. It's as if we were always meant to find each other, the missing pieces of a long-forgotten dream. I melt into him as his hands grip my waist, moving up my back and winding into my hair loose about my shoulders.

He breaks our embrace, pulling back to look into my eyes as panting breaths escape between us. "I wanted to kiss you that day I saw you at Reynauld's."

"Why didn't you?" I search his face for any answers he's not brave enough to voice.

"Because I'm a fool."

I can't help but smile at his response. "At least we can both agree on that."

A low growl erupts from him as a grin spreads across his lips. "And because I valued my head, and I'm not sure I would have left with it that night had I tried."

I smile as I shrug my shoulders, and he pulls me back down to pepper me with a few more quick, gentle kisses before I rest my head against his chest.

I move to lie next to him again, being careful of his side, my arms wrapping around his waist but stopping short of his stitches. He plays with my hair, sending a gentle wave of contentment rolling through me.

I trace his hand, drawing circles in his palm before charting lines up his wrist. I can't help the wide smile now covering my face as we lay in each other's arms.

My mind begins to drift off to sleep. But the solid memory of being called Evander once again strokes through my consciousness. I open my eyes, looking toward Roan. His eyes are closed, but his fingers still gently rub through my own. He's not asleep yet. I could easily bring it up. But a bit of unease snakes around my heart, and I falter. I want to ask, but my mouth doesn't seem to want to form the words. *There will be time*, I tell myself.

Why ruin such a perfect moment by bringing up his fallen friend?

38

ROAN

I WAKE, DARKNESS OVERPOWERING the space. A single candle sits on the small table across the room, the wax gathered in large clumps at its bottom.

Ari's arms are still wrapped around me. Her face is nestled in the crook of my neck, our legs entwined together on the bed. I let myself lie there a few more moments, soaking in the memory of a few hours ago as I run my fingers across her arm. There was so much underneath that kiss, and the possibilities both make me smile as wide as my face will allow me while also twisting my stomach into knots.

I won't let myself move into the future until we have found Lena, and returned safely to Turin. Until I've told Ari of my betrothal, one I fully intend to break with Lena's sure blessing. My gut coils tightly as I think of that conversation. I have no doubt that Lena will agree. Our hastiness to apease her parent's wishes trapped us both after all. But it won't make the discussion any less difficult.

Ari stirs next to me, tightening her hold. "How are you feeling?" I ask her.

She carefully tries to adjust her position, steering clear of my injuries. "Better than I have in my entire life." She opens one eye, sleep still clinging to the other.

"Liar," I jest. She moves to look up at me with both eyes this time.

"I don't lie." Her smile is broad, and I can't help but match it.

"Silas might disagree," I say lightheartedly, moving to warm her forehead with a kiss. And somehow, it warms me too.

How can one moment change everything? How can a simple kiss shift everything inside of me? Maybe I am the liar if I'm willing to call it simple—it was anything but. I only wish I had the full function of my body to have made our second kiss one she'd never forget.

It would be wise to attempt to get up, to start readying for the day ahead. It will take me twice as long as Ari to prepare. *Just a little longer*, I tell myself. Just a little longer before I leave the cocoon of her arms. Just a little longer before we have to figure out just what this is between us. Just a little longer before we head toward the unknown of a country that hopefully harbors the most important person to Felshan's future. Just a little longer before the stress and worry for Lena's wellbeing take hold. Just a little longer before the danger of what comes next takes precedence over this perfect moment.

I don't want to move, but I know it's time. Ari knows it too, and I don't try and stop her as she sits up.

"I will go pack the horse. I'll be back soon with a little breakfast. Rest while you can. We should plan to leave by first light."

I nod, watching as she quietly slips out the door.

Something slams, jolting me from my sleepy daze.

"We need to go. Now." Ari rushes to my bedside, slipping her arm underneath my back to help me move. Her face is pinched, her movements precise, effectively driving away any residual drowsiness I felt only moments ago.

"What?" My brows weave together, waiting for her explanation as my feet touch the ground for the first time in days. My hurt leg sings as I put the smallest weight on it, eliciting a sharp gasp I can't contain.

"Silas. Him and his men came late in the night. While we were asleep. They're downstairs." Her voice is clipped, her face blank. A tremor rolls through her hand before she shakes it away. My chest feels heavy enough that my breathing becomes labored, my mind trying desperately to process her words and come up with a plan.

With Ari's help taking some weight from my leg, she leads me to the lone window. How on earth am I going to get down from the window? I can barely walk let alone jump two stories down.

My head snaps from that window to her, my eyes wide. "We can't go out the door. The only way out is down the stairs, and Silas's men are gathered in that main room. We'd never be able to sneak out, especially side by side, especially with you injured." I could walk without her, but not well. Not well enough to sneak past a room full of blood thirsty scoundrels anyway.

I know what will happen should Silas find us, and I'll be nothing more than a prop as I watch his men bring Ari down.

The thief. *My thief.*

I won't let it happen. Refuse to let it happen. "Go," I say just before we reach the window, nodding to the only exit that may keep her alive. She will have a chance without me. If I stay behind she will at least have a chance to slip away.

Her eyes widen for the slightest moment before her focus turns into steely resolve. "I'm not leaving you behind. We both go, or we both stay. And I'm not staying, so move your feet." Her stubbornness makes me want to smile. And I would if Silas wasn't downstairs— once again blocking not only our path to safety, but the path to Lena as well.

I take the last few steps, Ari reaching for the sill of the already opened window, placing my hands there to hold my balance. The breeze hits my face, bringing with it the undeniable smell of fresh rain. Her head moves through the open space, searching for any way down.

The storm has yet to open up its deluge, a mere sprinkle of what is to come landing on the ground below us and dotting Ari's face before she ducks back inside. Somewhere in the distance lightning brightens the sky, followed by the low boom of thunder a breath later.

I put some pressure on my leg, and I'm met with a sickening flare of pain that causes me to tumble back onto my good leg, the suddenness pulling at the stitches in my stomach in a way that makes my vision swirl. Ari's lips sit in a firm line, holding her breath as she witnesses the contorting of my face and the wave of dizziness that almost lands me to the floor.

There's no way I'm making it out of this window.

Her eyes flick to the door, back to the window, then to meet my own. This may be the first time I've seen her speechless. The only chance I have is the stairs, with a shoal of piranhas waiting for me at the bottom.

"You go out the window, and ready our horse. I will make my way down the stairs and meet you," I say firmly. I won't yield on this. If I get caught, she can still get away.

"And if they see you?" If there was worry in her eyes before, now there is true fear. She isn't sure if I can do it. And quite frankly, I'm not sure I can either.

"Then I suppose I'll have to take a page from your book and woo Silas." I mean it as a joke, but I'm the only one whose mouth turns upward.

She raises a single eyebrow, no time for the admonishment I know she wishes to give. "There's a back door, behind the bathing rooms. If you can make it down without being seen, make your way there." I nod, but neither of us moves, silence stretching between us.

She fidgets with her hands, her gaze resting upon my chest and shoulders. "This isn't the end, Ari." I brush my thumb across her lips, pulling her carefully into an embrace as my fingers tangle through her hair.

I don't know if my words are true, but I will it to be so. I just found her, just found myself. For the first time, I feel hope that regret and guilt won't rule my life forever. That somehow by living, I will make right all the wrongs I created seven years ago.

It isn't the end.

She pulls away, her eyes darting to my side where the stitches lay just beneath my shirt. She takes a steadying breath before she speaks. "Use your sword to help you walk— to balance." She puts the weapon in my hand. "And if they see you, stick them with the pointy end." A gleam stirs within her eyes as they finally flit up to mine. "I will be just behind the door, waiting outside. Whatever you do, make sure you get there."

"I will." My eyes never leave her face. I can't help myself as I reach for her, my hand grazing along her cheek one more time. She leans into my touch, her hand moving to cup my own.

And before I know it Ari lets go, swinging her legs up and over the side of the window. She levels one last look at me. "Be careful," she says before gripping the edges, lowering herself down and dropping to the ground with gentle *thud*. A thick pile of hay eases her fall, and I release my held breath as I see her run toward the stable and a thick copse of trees.

Slowly, painstakingly, I make my way through the upper hallway, descending the stairs with a haphazard stride. Sweat drips down my brow as I make my way down, swallowing each whimper and yelp as the slightest movement sends blazing misery extending from both my injuries. I don't let my thoughts stray from Lena and my promise to bring her home. And Ari, waiting for me just outside the door.

The sounds of revelry gets louder as I approach the bottom. I know better than to think they won't fight me and win, even in their apparently drunken state. I slow my movements even more, keeping myself in the shadows as long as possible.

Both Shiren and John are in the room, serving and cleaning up after these men. I doubt this is their usual way of doing things, which prompts a well of gratitude to form deep inside me. They are doing this for us. They agreed to stay and oblige them in order to help us— to get the men drunk in hopes we might make our escape.

Shiren's eyes meet mine. She doesn't react or acknowledge my presence in any form, simply continuing to pour drinks before walking toward the innkeeper and whispering in his ear. He gives no indication of what she spoke, simply nodding his head before moving about his business.

Shiren walks to the front of the room, turning to face them and my precarious perch on the stairs. "Excuse me!" she yells over the boisterous voices of the men, effectively diverting any wayward eyes from spotting me. "Someone tells me you lot are grand singers."

A few holler at her words, joining their voices in agreement. "Alright, alright. Settle down now." She waits for the room to quiet, the clink of glasses finally resting against their tables. I try to hold my position, standing as still as possible despite the searing pain pulling on my leg and stomach, evening out my breaths so I can mold efficiently into the background. "I will start. And if you know it, join me for the second verse," she relays to the group staring voraciously at her young face, waiting for their entertainment.

Shiren opens her mouth, the loveliest voice wafting through the odious crowd. The song is one I recognize, about a boy who sees a maiden as he walks to town, falling in love the moment he sees her. As Shiren moves to start the second verse, where the boy grows older and continues to pine after the maiden, the others join in.

My steps are slow as I walk around the banister, holding my breath to keep any sound from attracting the attention of Silas or his crew. I don't see Jaren sitting amongst the crowd. My teeth grit together as I imagine what hole that snake has slithered into now, waiting to strike his poisonous venom.

The back door is in view, each breath becoming more labored as I make my way. Shiren's song still flows through the inn, getting softer and softer with each step. *Almost there.*

I reach for the handle of the door, gently easing it open like I'm attempting to escape the pen of a sleeping bull and any noise would effectively wake the beast. Ari reaches her hand through, gripping my elbow to alleviate the weight on my injured leg, allowing me enough time to exit without causing further discomfort.

The door begins to close when a clang erupts from behind us, a man exiting the bathing room. Our eyes lock. There's no time to think before Ari slams the door into his face, forcefully ending our silent retreat. The man staggers back, too stunned and in too much pain, from what I'm sure is now a broken nose, to do much else.

"Go!" She screams at me, grabbing my arm and urging me forward.

I feel the stitches pulling free as I run the last few strides to the horse, ready and waiting, clenching my teeth to keep from crying out. She leaps atop the black mare before leaning down to grab my arm, my good leg driving into the stirrup as she pulls with all her strength to land me behind her.

Men barrel out from behind, none of which are Silas. They watch in a stupor as Ari kicks our horse into a gallop. Night still cloaks the land as we turn around the inn, the clouds blocking out any sign of the approaching dawn. We ride swiftly toward the front of the property, moving around the corner of the inn in a smooth stride.

Without notice the horse stops, and I slam forcefully into Ari's back. I gasp as I reach for my side, trying to stop any bleeding from my opened stitches. Our horse tromps the ground as I try to take in the scene before us, my vision blurring from the spasms of pain radiating through me with every movement.

Three men stand there, two of them holding John and Shiren with swords raised, while in between them stands Silas. His smile is cool and collected, but his eyes are vicious daggers as they take in Ari— hardly giving me any thought at all. What I wouldn't give for my body to be healed and whole, so I could take my sword and personally watch the life drain from his body. A snarl escapes me, both from fury and the burning in my side, finally sending Silas's gaze my way.

"Get off the horse, and we'll let them live." His even words don't convey the thirst in his eyes.

Several snorting breaths sends my focus to the horses tied up to the front of the inn, only a few strides from Shiren and John. I don't miss Ari's quick scan of the beasts, obviously searching for the beloved buckskin she had to leave behind. Her shoulders sag almost imperceptibly when none of them are Prue.

"How long did it take you to find them?" I yell, nodding towards the animals, not bothering to hide my smug smile. It was a last minute decision, to scatter their horses at the mail outpost. One that I knew would keep our party ahead and out of reach, giving us time to hopefully reach Lena before they could catch up and stop us.

For the briefest moment Silas's face flickers with rage, his lips curling in raw disgust as he looks upon me, before consciously composing himself back into his serene mask. Another bolt of lightning lights up the sky with its accompanying boom of thunder.

"Time is ticking, little liar," he taunts, his focus returning to Ari. "Your life and Captain Montgomery's, or the innkeeper and his daughter." My body goes rigid, pain still blazing through me. *He knows me.* And if he knows me, he may know my connection to Lena and... and hurt her just to hurt me.

"You've lost Silas. Give it up," Ari declares, as at ease as the day she sat across from him at that table.

He laughs, the sound booming through the patchy yard. The hairs rise on Ari's arms. "You are outnumbered, yet again. And you have no companions to back you up this time."

Otto. Aiden. Did he find them? Hurt them? Are they ok? Ari tenses, her jaw clenching as the realization dawns through her as well. But she plays it off, continuing her ruse yet again.

"Half the Felshan army is on their way. We sent word at Fort Lowsan of you and your men. That you know the whereabouts of Princess Adalena. It's only a matter of time before you're caught and tried for your crimes." The lie flows effortlessly from her lips.

"My little liar," he croons, his words stroking the air as our horse shifts again beneath us.

He takes a step forward. Before he can take another, Ari reaches for the dagger hidden in her boot, throwing it in a single, fluid motion, aiming with absolute precision. It lands in the throat of Shiren's captor, the girl leaping out of his grasp without hesitation. John twists, elbowing the man holding him square in the eye, giving him enough room to land a fist to the man's jaw.

"Run, Shiren!" I hear the innkeeper yell as the girl pulls the dagger from her captor's neck, blood spurting from the wound. Not an ounce of concern crosses her face as she bounds to the tied-up horses and cuts through the tie on the nearest one, leaping atop its white back and turning to blaze a trail to John. Silas releases his sword from its sheath, heading straight for the innkeeper.

Ari jumps down before I can stop her, the men finally barreling from the back of the inn toward the commotion. Luckily, they are as drunk as a sailor on leave, and Ari weaves through them smoothly.

John turns to face Silas, distracting him so Shiren can get away. But the girl, as stubborn as Ari, heads straight for the duo.

"Throw me my dagger!" Ari yells to her.

Shiren flits her gaze around before yelling back, "I... I dropped it!"

But Ari doesn't break stride, still heading straight for Silas. He waits for her, his focus now completely honed on the thief, *my* thief, hurdling toward him. His sword is raised, ready to cut away her life as if it's nothing more than the nuisance of a dangling thread from his shirt.

A few more men run forward, moving to intercept Ari before she can reach him. I would be of no use on the ground, my leg making it impossible to reach her in time. Instead I grab the reins of the horse in one hand, gripping my sword with the only strength I have left as I spur the beast forward. They jump away as I swing. No damage is done, but I buy Ari just enough time to reach Silas.

His eyes boast a readiness to feel his sword slide through her flesh like butter. He moves to strike. Ari ducks, rolling toward him, landing a blow to his stomach so hard he gasps for air. In the same fluid motion she turns her back to him, raising an arm upward as she loops and traps his arm under her own, twisting until a painful crack rings through the air.

Silas yelps in pain, his broken wrist releasing his grip on the sword. Rage warps his face, the hatred centering on a single point— Ari. He reaches his other hand into her hair, yanking back her head against his shoulder, whispering something into her ear.

A faint smile tugs at her lips before she stomps a heel onto his foot, loosening his grip just enough to twist herself away. His sword lies gleaming in her hands, and she doesn't hesitate to slide that sword up and across his chest. Silas falls in a heap, blood soaking through his shirt and pooling quickly underneath him. His cold eyes stare at her as she towers above him, throwing his bloodied sword before turning away without a second thought.

In only a breaths time, I'm to her side. Her features boast neither victory nor regret, satisfaction nor guilt. Rather that she knew what needed to be done, and did it. Her foot finds the stirrup, and she leaps back to her spot in front of me.

Shiren reaches a hand out for John, pulling him onto her horse as he jumps with equal energy. None of us spare a parting glance for our fallen foe, now lifeless on the ground.

Rain begins to fall more steadily now as Ari maneuvers our horse to ride away from the scene, Silas's drunken men still trying to make sense of everything that just happened. But a creaking door grabs my attention, my gaze flicking back toward the inn. An unease burrows deep in my gut as a shadow emerges from inside. The light from within gives a silhouetted glow to the form before that shadow walks through the doorway and his face is illuminated by the lanterns that line the front porch.

The sneering smile of Sir Reynauld levels the final kernal of light in Ari's face.

Our horse skitters around as she decides what to do next, the full weight of his gaze resting on me, and hers on Reynauld.

It was him. He was part of this all along— kidnapping Lena. My jaw tenses, my stomach searing in pain as I lift my sword one last time, pointing it directly at him. His smile only widens.

"Ari, let's go!" Shiren shouts from somewhere in front of us.

The sound of her name triggers his attention to lock onto Ari, the thief who bested him in the market square. His smile fades into something dark, something sinister. He recognizes her.

Her breaths come fast and shallow, the horse continuing to prance anxiously around as she stares at him. "I'm coming for you," Ari says, her voice neither a shout nor a whisper.

"I do look forward to it," Reynauld replies, the corner of his mouth ticking upward ever so slightly.

And with those final words Ari nudges the horse forward, and we ride away underneath the lightening sky of dawn.

39

ARI

"I'M SO SORRY," I say once we slow and guide our horses to the forest edge, the road meeting an incline of land. The storm passed quickly, the smallest sliver of blue sky poking through the clouds as I dismount.

John and Shiren look mostly untouched, though dried blood stains the front of Shiren's dress and down one arm. Not her blood, I realize. But the first man I killed tonight. The one holding her. The second being Silas. No remorse comes for the death of those men at my hand.

The innkeeper says nothing, rummaging through the saddle bags for anything that might be helpful. "We knew what we were doing when we agreed to let you stay," Shiren says, helping John gather whatever supplies they can find.

I help Roan get down, scowling at his bloodied shirt. Shiren follows my gaze, something akin to concern showing through her eyes. "Once we cross into Thenstra I can get more suturing material. It's not ideal to wait, but we don't have much of a choice I'm afraid." Roan will have to go the rest away with a gaping cut across his stomach. I try not to wince as the realization hits me.

"How's your leg?" I ask, looking down to see if blood soaks his pant leg as well. It looks clean, and I want to sigh with relief.

"The stitches mostly held somehow," he says, propped against his sword. I find a sturdy stick close by, just long enough to help him keep his balance. I break off the smaller branches from the fallen limb, handing it to Roan. He leans into it, taking more weight away from his injured leg.

"We need to get going," I say. "If they haven't rallied themselves yet, they will soon. We should thank the Four Kingdoms that most of them were drunk." At least, everyone but Reynauld. His eyes were clear as they bore into mine, all his malevolence shining through with absolute clarity. I try to push his image out of my mind, the way he smiled at me, the way he looked at Roan.

My rain dampened shirt blows against me in the breeze, the cooling mountain air sending a shiver through me.

John eyes me and Roan before turning his attention to Shiren. "You may have to help the captain as we go. Ari won't be able to hold him on her own the whole way." There's no emotion in his voice, only a matter-of-factness that makes me flinch. "We will need to tell," he looks at me again, lowering his voice, "we will need to tell Sutter that the inn is compromised. We won't be able to go back."

Sutter. That was the name Shiren had given me. I was to say he sent us if Roan and I had been caught trying to make our way into Thenstra. John gives me a wary look, but I hold his gaze.

He had warned me, warned her. Told Shiren she was in too deep. Told me he wouldn't risk the girl. And here they are, running for their lives without any context as to why. My stomach twists as I see him regard Shiren with anxiousness in his eyes. Those eyes then move to me. I don't shrink under his scrutiny, but I find myself wanting to beg his forgiveness. I was wrong to ask them for help, to put them directly in the path of Silas and his men. And now Reynauld.

John starts walking up the mountainside, leaving the road and horses behind. As if sensing my confusion, Shiren says, "Here we must leave the horses and travel on foot. The gates are a morning's ride ahead, but they haven't opened for anyone in over twenty years. If you want in, you must go up." She points upward, and I look toward the ascending land.

Her meticulously drawn map dawns through my mind. Up through the mountains, up the rocky cliffs, and through a tunnel inlaid straight through the side of the Prythan Mountains. That's our way into Thenstra. I look to Roan, and I can't keep the pity from my gaze as I stare toward the patch of blood on his shirt and the wound that lay beneath it.

We move up the incline, a steady walk to keep the man next to me as comfortable as possible. As much as is possible in his condition anyway. I look ahead, the foreign land crunching underneath my boots. Who knows what will come as we move toward Thenstra, a country as unfamiliar as my feelings for Roan.

The slope of our journey rises rapidly. Each jolt and sudden move sends Roan's features into a sharp grimace. There's not much that can be done in that regard, unfortunately, besides go back. And going back is not an option. Not with Reynauld behind us now.

Our ragged breaths add to the cadence of our steps, but the silence weaving between us gives me ample time to think. Time to figure out how Reynauld and the princess fit together. He almost has full run of the city of Turin— with only minor set backs from King Cassus. So, what could Reynauld possibly gain from taking the princess that he didn't already have? And what about Silas and the Cranes? What role do they have in all of this?

Again, Evander tugs at the corner of my mind. Roan called me by the prince's name, and for whatever reason that moment continues to nudge at the corners of my consciousness. Until now, I haven't had the time or boldness to bring it up. But seeing Reynauld this morning and feeling his unearthly presence, I disregard any of my previous caution.

"Roan," I say quietly, not wanting to ruffle John and Shiren anymore than we already have today.

"Yes," he huffs back, his pained face the only confirmation I need that every step for him is a struggle.

An uneasiness I don't fully understand brews around me. "Do you— do you remember when I found you the other day, after the mountainside gave way?"

"Yes," he breaths, his eyes darting to me.

My heart is suddenly pounding in my chest. "Do you remember what you called me?"

"I'm hoping... I called you... Ari." He chuckles a little, as much as his injuries will allow.

The unease is shouting at me, telling me to shut my mouth, to turn away and leave this behind. But I don't give in. I don't allow myself to hesitate. "You called me Evander. And then you said, *I'm so sorry. It was all my fault.*" He stiffens beside me. "What did you mean it was all your fault? What was all your fault?"

His voice is stoic and unwaveringly resolute. "Nothing. I was delusional it would appear."

"Are you sure? It seemed very real. And the way you spoke his name—"

"I said it was nothing," he snaps at me.

My forehead wrinkles as my eyes narrow in his direction. I know when I'm being lied to, and my hackles are raised. The ability to deflect is a personal specialty, and I can recognize someone throwing an air of nonchalance to cover up something deeper when I see it.

I focus on my breathing, trying to relax my raised shoulders and soften my gaze. "Roan, you don't have to pretend with me, you know? Your words— they sounded as if you were... are... troubled. Like you've wanted to say them for so long, but they never found their voice." I look forward, a soft mountain breeze rustling my hair.

His body remains tense, taking his arm from around my waist and resting it on his hip, pausing his steps and taking a deep breath. John turns, an eyebrow raised. I wave him onward, wrapping Roan's arm around me once again. We continue forward, the sound of crunching rocks becoming the backdrop to the melody of mountain meadows.

He doesn't want to talk, and I do my best to respect it, keeping my mouth closed. I try to keep my breathing even, taking in the scenery of large grassy cliffs, and jutting peaks poking through the not-so-distant distance. The tallest of the Prythan Mountains I realize. Thenstra lays nestled somewhere between its monstrous summit.

"It was my fault." A whisper from beside me startles me from my trance.

I turn as much as I can to look at him without pulling at his arm around me. "What?" I ask.

"Evander. His death. It was my fault." Roan's face looks completely blank, the only hint of emotion showing through glassy eyes.

"I don't understand. You killed the prince?"

"Yes. And no. Not directly." His eyes shift around the mountainside before he faces forward once again. "We were fifteen. There's something called the First Hunt. It's a big deal. All the loyal families of the Crown come together to mark the beginning of the hunting season." He pauses, as if the memory is too much to bear. I reach for his hand, gripping it hard between my own.

"I wanted to go. I felt it was our right to go. Evander was unsure. He didn't want to say anything if we weren't out-right invited. But I asked him go talk to his father, to the king. I made him get us an invite. Then, when it was time to break for the hunt, his father told us we had to stay back. We were to watch only. But that wasn't good enough. It wasn't good enough for me."

He rakes a hand through his hair, his eyes going distant. "So we went. We broke his father's command. And Evander— he paid the price for my arrogance."

"Roan," I breathe. "Roan, I'm so sorry." I want to ask the details. I want to pry and press until I hear everything. But I bite my tongue. He says nothing else, taking another pained step.

I help him a few more steps forward, letting his words fill in the blank of my question. He feels responsible for the prince's death. It's no wonder he spoke Evander's name when his mind was hazy. He's been holding on to this for seven years. That kind of guilt would eat away at anyone, changing the fabric of their life forever.

It certainly changed mine.

We take another step just as a memory trickles its way back to me. The words from Sir Crane's office as I stood just outside it. *Almost a decade in the making, Phillip. Can you believe we're finally here? And we didn't even have to lure the mouse in with the promise of cheese.*

Then, Tamen's words in the courtyard. *Not the throne of the city. The throne of Turin, the whole of Felshan.* My brows push together as I try to make sense of those few sentences.

And then a wildfire ignites in my mind, spreading hot and fierce. *No. No, no, no, no.* My thoughts are racing, twisting away then coming back together. I turn to Roan, torn between finding answers and saving him from the truth.

"I'm sorry for asking this, but— how did Evander die?" My heart is beating wildly in my chest, my breathing coming heavy and shallow like I'm carrying Roan's full weight on my back.

"He— Evander, he—" Roan takes a deep breath before continuing. "An arrow. We were making our way across the Rashan, meeting up with the king's men on the other side. A deer was coming to drink on the banks, and the man didn't see us. He shot Evander on accident."

"Who? Who was it? Who shot the arrow?" My eyes are pleading, his lips pulling into a frown.

"They weren't sure, a couple men had shot at the same time. They never pinpointed exactly whose arrow took the killing blow."

"Who did they suspect? Who were the men who shot their arrows?" My thoughts are jumbled, racing, but all pointing in the same direction with every word he speaks. He pauses, staring me in the eyes. "Who?" I ask again, my voice rising the longer I wait for my suspicions to be confirmed.

"I believe it was—" his voice lowers, and we stop completely on the path. His breathing quickens, his head tilting back. "There were two. One from the Buchanans, and another from the Davenport family," he all but whispers. His eyes go wide, his head shaking as he tries to swallow. "Robert Buchanan... his wife was Phillip Crane's sister. And Lord Davenport, his wife is Reynauld's cousin. Lena was also betrothed to their son before—" he pauses, his eyes darting to the ground, "before Evander died. The queen ended the betrothal after his death." Roan looks at me like there's something he isn't telling me. But whatever it is, he doesn't speak it. Instead turning toward the looming mountain peaks ahead.

"How did I not see this," he says to himself. A single laugh escapes him. "It was right in front of me the whole time." He rubs a hand down his face, leaning heavily on the walking stick I gave him and away from me.

"Were these men never investigated? Held accountable in some way?" I ask.

"A third family, the Ashcrofts, one not involved in what happened, examined and scrutinized every detail. They deemed it an accident. No further inquiry was made." He lets out a heavy breath, another laugh huffing out of him. "The Ashcrofts. They are tied to the Davenports. His brother married a Davenport a few years earlier."

I've never met the Davenports, but I've heard them mentioned so many times in the last couple weeks that I'm not sure I'll ever forget their name again. "Why did they choose the Davenport's son for the princess?"

His face is devoid of color, as if he will pass out at any moment. "They own and run Fort Kotar, deep in the Kotar Mountains, just west of Turin. They mine a large portion of the ore in Felshan. And that ore accounts for more than half of Felshan's export commodities. It would effectively choke our kingdom if the mines ran dry, or if the Davenports decided they no longer support the king and queen and stopped trade altogether."

The last few pieces finally fit together.

The words from Phillip Crane's office, from Tamen, finally make sense. Almost ten years of scheming, with Prince Evander and Princess Adalena becoming victims to their horrific design. A murder and a kidnapping.

Two fists ball beside me, understanding finally catching up to the truth. "This will be answered, Roan. I promise you." And when our gazes meet, all I see is burning fire. "We will make them pay. Over, and over, and over again," I say, my heartbeat roaring in my ears.

They are the last words I speak before we cross the border into Thenstra.

Acknowledgements

What a journey it has been. First of all, I want to thank my beautiful editor, Arielle Hadfield. If it weren't for you, I would still be writing this book. A huge thank you to Shalese Clements for helping me brainstorm ideas, and reading it when I was too afraid to let anyone else. To all the beta readers and arc readers— you're amazing. It's no small thing to devote time to a novel and an author whose work you don't know. To all my coaches and friends that cheered me on— and there were many— thank you for all your love and support. It means the world to me.

And to my husband Brandon, and my children— London, Charlie, Chandler, and Luke— thank you for helping my dreams come true.

This one is for all of you.

About the Author

Jacqlin Guernsey has loved reading since she was a child, and dreamed of writing her first novel after reading The Chronicles of Narnia series by C.S. Lewis. She currently lives in Washington state with her four young boys and her wonderful husband. Jacqlin loves to take long walks and hikes, watch movies with her family, and dream up possibilities for her next story. Her biggest bucket list items are to see the Northern Lights, and visit the Mediterranean Sea.

www.ingramcontent.com/pod-product-compliance
Lightning Source LLC
Chambersburg PA
CBHW021134260626
47169CB00005B/1598